By the same author

Notting Hell

In a Good Place

RACHEL JOHNSON

A Touchstone Book
Published by Simon & Schuster
New York London Toronto Sydney

Touchstone
A Division of Simon & Schuster, Inc.
1230 Avenue of the Americas
New York, NY 10020

Copyright © 2008 by Rachel Johnson
Originally published in Great Britain in 2008 by Penguin Books

First Touchstone trade paperback edition June 2009

TOUCHSTONE and colophon are registered trademarks of Simon & Schuster, Inc.

For information about special discounts for bulk purchases, please contact Simon & Schuster Special Sales at 1-866-506-1949 or business@simonandschuster.com.

The Simon & Schuster Speakers Bureau can bring authors to your live event. For more information or to book an event contact the Simon & Schuster Speakers Bureau at 866-248-3049 or visit our website at www.simonspeakers.com.

Manufactured in the United States of America

10 9 8 7 6 5 4 3 2 1

ISBN 978-1-4165-3208-8
ISBN 978-1-4169-8713-0 (ebook)

To my father, for everything

Cast of Characters

Mimi Fleming (*née* Malone): curly-haired former Notting Hill journalist, now full-time Dorset farmhouse frau, who fights off continuous hunger with homemade scones, and perpetual cold with one of those green, padded, poppered jerkins called a Husky, which she even wears in bed.

Ralph Fleming: passionate only about dry fly-fishing and wild trout, Ralph (pronounced Rafe) is a consultant in oil and gas and a pro at avoiding anyone who falls into the dread category of "New People."

Mirabel Fleming: thirteen, sulky teen who thinks both her parents are, like, totally skanky and sad.

Casimir Fleming: twelve, lives for cricket and Clarkson.

Posy Fleming: nine, collects free toiletries from hotels and believes in unicorns.

The Flemings live at **Home Farm** with **Ana from Poland**, the au pair girl, and **Calypso**, the dog.

Rose Musgrove: Honeyborne's answer to Martha Stewart, with plans for her own heritage cheese, Rose has impeccable taste in everything *House and Garden*, wears Ralph Lauren tailored tweed, and slips up only when it comes to choosing other people's husbands.

Pierre Musgrove: a sculptor whose glittering future recedes daily, Pierre reserves his artistry for ever-more-fiendish ways of annoying Rose.

Ceci Musgrove: thirteen, their perfect only child.

The Musgroves live at the **Dairy**, which is tended by Rose's much-coveted daily, **Joan**.

Catherine Cobb: California-born superwoman, mother of four, châtelaine of **Court Place**, and owner-manager of the breath-takingly swanky Court Place Farm Shop.

Granville Cobb: the husband and bankroller of the above.

Serena Cobb: the blond daughter with vanity job in magazine PR.

The Cobbs also have three sons, **Hector, Marco,** and **Florian**, and also live in **Gstaad, Tuscany,** and **California**, even though the superrich can only ever be in one superprime property at any one time.

Ned Bryanston: local landowner, living on capital, with an expensive second wife.

Lulu Bryanston: former model-actress-whatever, Lulu now wrangles literary figures for display at her annual writers' shindig, the GodLitFest.

Jesse Marlon Bryanston: Ned's first son by his starter marriage to **Judith** (now called **Jude**, a poet and a lesbian).

Little Ned and Fred Bryanston: eleven; spoiled twins by Ned and out of Lulu, although she annoyingly looks much too young and buff to have had one child, let alone twins.

Celia Bryanston: Ned Bryanston's widowed mother, who takes dowagery spikiness to the next level. All the Bryanstons except Jesse Marlon live at **Godminster Hall**.

Sir Michael Hutton: ancient and crusty baronet, married but without issue to **Lady Elizabeth**.

The Huttons' ancestral seat plus estates measureless to man is at **Hutton Hall, Hutton**.

Virginie Lacoste: stone-cold French superfox and children's culotte magnate who never *regrettes rien*.

Mathieu Lacoste: her colorless walkover of a husband who is big in L'Oréal.

The Lacostes have three children, **Guy, Capucine,** and **Clementine,** who love their nanny, **NouNou,** much more than their parents.

The Lacostes live in **Lonsdale Gardens, London, W11.**

Clare Sturgis: Mimi's former neighbor in Notting Hill, Clare is a garden designer and elderly prima gravida who bought the shabby Fleming house on the communal garden from Ralph, mainly to install her housekeeper and nanny in.

Joe Sturgis: her toddler son, whom Clare and successful architect husband **Gideon** are currently failing to enroll in the impregnable **Ponsonby Prep,** alma mater of Mirabel, Posy, and Cas (as well as the adorable scions of many Notting Hill haves and have-yachts).

The Sturgises live in **Colville Crescent, London, W11.**

Sophy Mills: a hippie herbalist and single mother of

Noah Mills: a teething baby of indeterminate paternity and

Spike Mills: thirteen, a well-adjusted pupil at Acland's who is "friendboy" to Mirabel and Ceci.

The Mills family lives in the eco-village **Spodden's Hatch,** in a pitchy yurt near the handmade house of Jesse Marlon Bryanston, who also dwells there.

Gwenda Melplash: known as Scary Gwenda, and preferring horses to humans, Miss Melplash lives in jodhpurs and cracks the whip at **Honeyborne Stables and Livery Yard.**

Colin Watts: adopted son of the butchers, Colin is a local log supplier who has his own van, ergo is one of the most eligible males for literally miles around.

He lives in **Stable Cottage.**

Henry Pike: the Master of Foxhounds, lunger, toper, shagger, and the only resident of Honeyborne who is allowed to enter the **Stores** on horseback.

Biddy Pike: his Boden-clad wife and stalwart of many Pony Club Summer Camps.

Flavia (Flaves) Pike and **Harry Pike** are their two never knowingly unhorsed children.

The Pikes live at **Lower Foxcombe** with their terriers, **Jiggy** and **Frisky**.

Mr. and Mrs. Hitchens: master and mistress of the village **Post Office and Stores** (aka the gossip interchange).

Garry and **Debbie:** publicans of the **Stag**, in which they serve locals with slopping pints of Badger ale and keep a wolf.

Dr. Ashburton: GP who hunts, grunts, and reluctantly runs **the surgery** in his spare time.

Esmond d'Oplinter: aka the Bonking Baron, a courtly Frenchman married to the defiantly hideous **Jacqueline,** his even more aristocratic wife. They live in Paris but shoot in the West Country twice a year.

Reverend Wyldbore-Smith: vicar of **St. Mary of All Angels** and the go-to man if you want to secure a plot in the graveyard. He lives in **The Rectory**.

PART ONE

Mimi

I'm sitting in the kitchen, the only warm place in the house.

I have a pint of coffee in my Thermos (bought from the Wild Bean Café at service station, price of latte redeemed against price of cup) to my right, and am reading the paper. Calypso is lying pressed against my feet, which are—I'm ashamed to report—inserted into my exciting new fake-fur electric foot warmer with dual-setting massager which I ordered off the Argos Web site during one of my more recent online shopping jags. (I easily justify the regular delivery of squishy parcels addressed to me by telling myself there are no normal shops—i.e., ones selling Swarovski-crystal-encrusted designer jeans, organic hemp baby clothes, Elle MacPherson Intimates—within a hundred-mile radius of Home Farm. Works for me.)

The radio is on, and I am half listening to a report on shea butter made by a women's collective in northern Ghana on *Woman's Hour.*

Inside the foot warmer, I am wearing my favorite cashmere socks from Brora, sadly tiger-striped from having been dried and scorched on the Aga.

I am also "working" some long johns, last year's "boyfriend" jeans (skinny jeans are so over, according to Mirabel, which is a relief), an M&S merino thermal vest, an army surplus jersey, a scarf, and a quilted padded waistcoat in army green with brass popper buttons of the type that used to be seen, in the days, on Lady Diana before she became Princess of Wales.

Yes, I am wearing a Husky.

Like tapestry-patterned hand-knitted cardigans with toggles, crewelwork, English teeth, women in rugby shirts tucked into fractionally too tight high-waisted jeans, the Conservative Party, and Grow the Longest Carrot contests, Huskys have never gone out of fashion outside built-up areas.

I am taking full advantage of this reassuring fact.

The telephone.

"Hello?" I say, powering up my laptop so I can multitask while taking the call.

"Mimi?" comes a tweeting voice I know well. "It's Fenella!" she announces with excitement, as if she has produced her own grandchild.

"*Hiiiii!*" I cry.

Fenella Prigeon is the beauty editor of *Results** magazine. We used to work together on the *Telegraph*, a million years ago. Last glimpsed by me at a tea party in Burlington Arcade for *Tatler* types and their posh pets (I was returning a pair of Vilebrequin swimming trunks that I'd bought for Ralph as a lovely present, which he had spurned without a second glance, reminding me that his old pair, minus elastic, were absolutely fine, and would be for many years, thank you very much).

"So, how *are* you?" I cry, as if I really, really want to know, automatically slipping back into insincere mode. I have never mastered the trick of simply being the same with everyone. With Fenella, therefore, I go all glossy and gushy.

"Oh," comes a faint sigh, an exhalation, as if I simply can't imagine the suffering. "I don't honestly think I've ever been so exhausted. It's been completely utterly frantic. Really manic."

I log on, input my password.

"Why?" I ask, knowing what's to come. Ralph has a theory that, if you listen to Fenella talk, you'd think that in harsh contrast to testing cellulite gels and nasolabial creams for a monthly magazine, slogging it out in the trenches of the Somme was a teddy bears' picnic.

"It's the, the *spa guide,*" says Fenella, with a break in her voice. "I've had to write up no fewer than fifty—that's five zero—spas over the past six months, including some in the Far East and the Caribbean. I'm totally wiped out, before I've even begun on the living nightmare that is the annual teenage skin-care issue."

"You poor thing," I say automatically.

"That's why I'm calling you, actually . . ." Fenella goes on, a wheedling note entering her voice. "There's this new spa, I thought you could go, take Mirabel. You only have to write a hundred fifty words, and you'd get, I'd say, at least two free treatments." Fenella throws this morsel in knowing full well that there's nothing, *nothing,* I like more than a luxury junket.

As she speaks, I am already picturing my eldest daughter and me lounging around in fluffy white robes, having massages to tinkling New Age music—somewhere hot, I'm thinking, Bali, or the Maldives—while demure maidens minister silently and with total concentration to our toenails.

"Gosh, Fenella," I say, playing it cool, wanting her to think I'm still a player, "I have a black diary at the moment, things are sooo busy, I don't know if I could squeeze a minibreak abroad in right now . . . where is it?"

"It's in Somerset," she says, in the reverential tones of one who has dutifully swallowed all the guff about expensive English holidays in the rain being so much nicer than cheap hot hols abroad. "On an organic farm, where they make their own pizza and muesli and bread, with—hold on, let me just grab the bumf—spelt. Spelt. Apparently it's some ancient type of wheat—hold on, it's a grain from the grass family with a fragile gluten content, whatever that means. Anyway, all the therapies in the spa, and treatments, well, they're spelt-based, too, and I just thought, well, you've lost your column on the mag, you're local, aren't you?—you're in Dorset—there's no way I can fit it in with all my other commitments to do with the eco hair products special issue we're planning for the spring, just no conceivable way! Not from London. It takes longer to get to Somerset than it does to Ibiza. I can't pay you, but you could drive over, check it out, file a hundred fifty words . . . I thought it'd be a treat."

I replace the receiver with a sigh, having promised Fenella that I'd get back to her on the spelt spa gig.

Nothing could make it clearer. My friends, my former colleagues, my old neighbors think I'm flying below the radar. I've gone . . . free-range.

It's time to face it.

I'm not in Notting Hill now. I am not obeying an unwritten law that all women approaching forty have to weigh eight stone, wrangle with celebrities, interact with the atrophy wives, take their pedigree pets to the new dog spa and deli off Westbourne Park Road, and pretend to one another they don't suffer from "bonus envy."

I'm not doing the supermodel sweep at the Whole Foods Market on Kensington High Street as they load up on acai berries and seeds from the Food Doctor while bragging about how they, like, never go to the gym, and how they're, like, so busy *running after their kids* they don't need to work out, they're just *naturally this skinny,* and they are *trying and trying* but they can just never *put on weight* even though we know and they know, it's nil by mouth for them for literally *years* at a time.

What a relief, in so many ways.

But.

Because there always is a but.

But, to be brutally honest, though it is a relief, I stand by that, of course—I love the grass, the mud, the fact that I have a view of the rest of Dorset and the sea from my bedroom window (if I stand on tiptoe), and I love drinking in the fresh and clean smell of the countryside, with its wholesome tangy topnote of manure. I love the chill evening airs, the silence, the peace, and I love the fact that I can see all the stars on a clear night, and the Milky Way, and have become best friends with some barn owls, i.e., have allowed myself to be fully penetrated by the beauties of nature—I do still kind of miss it. London. Notting Hill, and all that.

But mainly I miss it because there's no going back. After all, as everyone knows, and does so love repeating to you, once it's too late, as if I have made a brave lifestyle choice to dwell in the seventh circle of hell rather than in an utterly idyllic Dorset model village, "Once you're out of the *London property market,* Mimi, that's it, you know! *You never get back in.*"

All the children are at school, but it's already 10:30 A.M. so it'll be dark in a few hours, and if I don't leave the house soon and walk Calypso I'll be tempted to go back to bed for a snooze, as that's so much more inviting a prospect than finally getting to grips with the vegetable patch. My morning dog-walk circuit takes in the Post Office and Stores, the pub, the Stag, and the village green.

Okay, the Stag: standard-issue Dorset pub, i.e., it's wall-to-wall roaring fireplaces, growling local "characters," smell of old pipe smoke from before smoking ban, nicotine-stained orange ceilings, skull-cracking low beams, Badger ale, famous for . . . not the beer, not the snug, certainly not the food or the friendliness of its regulars—the chain-smoking woodcutter "young" Colin Watts, the butcher's son (young only in comparison to most drinkers); the Melplashes; the farmers; the farriers; and so on—but its annual nettle-eating competition, and the house pet.

I didn't know anything about it until Garry, the landlord, who serves underneath a sign saying GARRY'S BAR, asked me if Calypso was "okay around wolves."

I didn't really take it in and then he said, "Because they smell different than dogs."

And then he brought this rangy, ribby thing with pale eyes and trembling flanks through on a lead, and I quivered, "What sort of wolf is it?" drawing Calypso close, and he said, "A wolf wolf," and that he had gone to Alaska to get it when it was so big, holding his hands apart like an angler describing his catch. Anyway, the animal's name is Cherokee, but the children call it Wolf Wolf.

As for the nettle-eating contest, well, that's a contest during which people eat as many yards of nettles as they can, and if you don't believe me, there're pictures of contestants, gaping mouths stained with green, pinned up next to the postcard advertising the next meeting of the Pudding Club.

You have (2) New Messages

Although I had discovered after doing an online search that there is a riding stable in Honeyborne with "qualified owner on site" and "excellent hacking" that takes children of all ages and abilities, I couldn't resist switching screens and clicking open the new arrivals.

It takes ages to open files on my laptop—so annoying, I must have a virus. It's funny how a delay of just a few seconds can have the power to irritate so much.

"British Gas Launches New Web Site" is the first message.

But the second I stare at for ages before opening. It's from Clare Sturgis. My heart lurches, and then starts hammering, just seeing her name in my in-box.

I'm reading it now.

It's like a digest of all the news and gossip from Lonsdale Gardens in one mouthful. Everything I ever wanted to know about what's going on back in Notting Hill—but was too proud to ask.

Here we go.

I wonder who gave her my new e-mail address.

She hopes I'm well . . . she misses me (yeah, right—she

bought my house, my children's home, from my husband behind my back, but hey, what's a £2 million house on a Notting Hill communal garden between friends) . . . my old cleaner, Fatima (Clare poached her, too), is very well and Fatty would send love but has sciatica and isn't working this week . . . baby Joe is toddling . . . Trish and Jeremy Dodd-Noble have bought a superyacht . . . Anoushka is pregnant with number two (Oof. Hurts. I've only just recovered from the cosh blow of little Darius coming along while Si Kasparian was supposed to be in an exclusive extramarital relationship with ME) . . . stuff about her boring garden design being on hold during Joe's "precious early childhood years" . . . how she's interested in the broader possibilities of smallholding and growing veg and becoming more self-sufficient . . . stuff about London being in the flood zone, and needing to find a bolt hole with food security on higher ground . . . how Gideon is finding the communal garden "too intense" now they're parents . . . what's it like in Dorset . . . how is Ralph . . . da da da . . . and oh, yes, here we are. Here we go.

The point of the e-mail. The "ask," as Ralph puts it, with inverted commas, of course.

I'm going to answer it straightaway while I have the wind in my sails and bit between teeth—which means that the dog walk and the kitchen garden will just have to wait.

From: mimimalone@homefarm.com
To: claresturgis@gmail.com
Dear Clare
Thanks so much for your lovely e-mail. Crikey, it's been a long time. It feels about a hundred years since I was last in Fresh & Wild (which has, apparently, closed) trying to persuade myself that a large slab of vegan tofu banana cheesecake for pudding was, actually, really healthy.

I'm really glad, tho', you got in touch, and don't remotely mind that the main object of your contact (reading between the lines) was how to get baby Joe into nursery at Ponsonby

Prep. Isn't he getting on for two now? I presume you put him down in utero. And that he is completely proficient in the basics—sackbut, Albanian nose flute, Sanskrit, etc.

Well . . . I have to warn you.

One Notting Hill mother—Helene, you must remember her, that power-wife married to Goldman Sachs banker on £5m a year—virtually went down on her knees and begged all the other mothers inc. me to compose handwritten letters of personal recommendation to Doc H on behalf of her daughter Camille. This would have been fine but 1. I'd never met Camille and 2. Camille was all of five months, and I couldn't really vouch for her precocity in key skills like napping and smearing pureed sweet potato on her high chair, but that didn't matter to Helene, of course.

Helene in addition sent the admissions secretary a bunch of flowers every week for a whole school year before even getting on the waiting list, so watch out. Doc H reminded Helene that Ponsonby (where it is, I remind you, harder to get a place than a table at the Ivy) allocates only five places per month, on a first come, first served basis. He said it was better not to leave it until five months after delivery but to "schedule a caesarean" for the 30th or the 31st (as if real due date and Mother Nature, etc., a complete irrelevance) so that "in an ideal world" she would have been first in the queue with a filled-in registration form on the first of the month.

When I told Ralph he listened in silence and then commented, "It after all wasn't easier for a Camille to pass through the doors of Ponsonby Prep ho ho ho than a rich man to enter the kingdom of God ha ha ha," and laughed out loud at his own not very good joke.

God, Clare, I thought I would feel all cross and hoity when I saw the e-mail was from you, but I didn't. I felt pleased. I now realize, and I hope you believe me, that I'm glad YOU bought the house from Ralph and no one else. I was knocked sideways at the time, and now I really am okay about it.

The way things are going in Notting Hill, from what I hear, is that the Russians are block-buying whole London squares without even asking the price, so it's nice to think of someone reasonably normal like you and Gideon and of course baby Joe and Fatima in the old wreck rather than some flashy private equity magnate or hedge funder. I miss you all, and I miss the garden, now that I'm Country Barbie down here. I miss Fatima's help—I never realized how much she did.

Anyway, must stop now, and go and stare at green fields through the kitchen window. It's pouring again. I should really go upstairs, and tidy the linen cupboard, and make my bed.

I can't get away from the fact that I'm bored, I admit it, and Ralph is always away. It was really good to hear from you. I feel so left out. Okay, Marguerite calls occasionally, and I do get news of Si from the Sunday Times Rich List and so on, but I totally got the feeling that you think I've moved the show off Broadway.

I do know I can't offer any of the deluxe country-house-hotel comforts that townies now expect, having their rooms tidied and suitcases unpacked, masses to eat, hot towel rails, goose down mattress toppers, ever-changing cast of amusing guests. Plus, we live in an ancient stone farmhouse in a remote river valley that comes into its own in the summer months without, as one cannot emphasize enough, central heating.

I can—just—survive without being surrounded by cafés, shops, girly boutiques, spas, chi-chi delis, world-class restaurants, cinemas, clubs, vintage markets, and all the delights that Notting Hill had to offer.

But going without my lovely, rich, fair-weather London FRIENDS (especially you, of course!) is almost too much.

Love, Mimi

P.S. Can't resist saying can't believe this e-mail is so long and boring—more like a LibDem manifesto than a quick reply so sorry . . . I do hope it's all right—now you've had Joe—I think I'm pregnant again. Must be Ralph's world-beating potency. Am sitting here with boobs like Zeppelins, hot flushing, with metallic taste in mouth and, even more telling, could only drink one glass of white wine last night rather than entire bottle on my own before the end of the six o'clock news, and haven't even missed a period yet. It tasted like vinegar and went down like paint stripper rather than promised fleshy, flirty, vanilla notes on the palate with a long, buttery finish. Also found myself listening quite happily to Wogan show on Radio 2 and sobbing to "Just When I Needed You Most" by Randy VanWarmer.

When I just hinted, very offhand, not giving anything away, Ralph only flinched very slightly at the mere topic of pregnancy, rather than blenching, so felt encouraged, but then he said that in his experience women always thought they were in pig but never were.

I press send. I know that telling Clare I might be pregnant is perhaps inadvisable, given her ten-year struggle to conceive, but I simply—given all that's gone on—can't resist it.

Rose

"Pierre has started carrying a log around the house," I say, getting straight to the point as I take off my YSL jacket and hang it up, so Mimi, who is rather accident-prone and doesn't notice stains on her own clothes so won't worry about soiling mine, won't spill anything on it.

"Mmm," says Mimi.

"When I ask him why he's carrying a log under his arm, like Paris Hilton carrying Tinkerbell, he just says, 'For goodness' sake, Rose, why do you think I'm carrying a log?' Then I start noticing that it's always the same log, with silvery bark, sort of peeling off. I'd recognize that log anywhere. I'm beginning to see more of the log than I do of my own daughter."

Instead of joining in and validating me about how irritating Pierre is at the moment, she howls with laughter.

We are splitting a raspberry flapjack over coffee at our crisis meeting at That New Place, the only café within a radius of about ten miles that serves fluffy coffee, still called That New Place even though it opened we think some time in the eighties, when morning coffee meant Nescafé, if you were lucky, and a digestive, rather than a freshly ground Fair Trade cappuccino accompanied by a Honeybuns gluten-free polenta cranberry shortbread slice.

I'd taken Ceci to Acland's, the secondary school in Godminster, which is co-ed, progressive, well run, and beacon-status but, most important, if you are the sole breadwinner with a home business to run and an artist husband to support, completely free. Mimi had taken Mirabel, Cas, and Spike, whose mother is Sophy Mills, a hippie herbalist. Sophy doesn't drive, fly, indeed do anything that depletes the fragile earth's finite resources. Sophy makes her own clothes, forages, and lives in a yurt.

Not that we would ever admit this to Sophy, but we came in two cars. We could, we both know, share the school run; but we also both know that school runs can end female friendships faster than running off with your best friend's husband or poaching a friend's nanny—so we are not rushing into anything, yet.

Mimi rang after school yesterday to see if we could meet. I was sterilizing a huge batch of Le Parfait jars in the dishwasher for the next batch of my legendary Plum and Rhubarb Compote, so I had to run to catch it.

"We have a crisis on our hands," she said, not asking if it was a good time, or if I was busy, or why I was panting. "Are you alone?"

"Yes," I said, as Ceci was upstairs doing homework, I hoped, in her bedroom, and Pierre was out in the fields, looking for flints. Useless.

"What is it?"

"Well," Mimi said slowly, "I'm afraid I found the girls with some magazines. It's terribly worrying."

"Oh Lord," I said. "Don't tell me. Oral sex! Oral sex with animals!! What?"

"No," said Mimi. "Worse. Meet me in That New Place at nine-fifteen."

To begin with, though, I say to Mimi, getting it off my chest straightaway, how sad it is that we've turned out like every other married couple, with our strengths having become our weaknesses, and the exact things we previously used to find charming and attractive, we now find irritating.

Mimi isn't interested in the fact that our marriage is as awful as everyone else's, but she does perk up at the mention of the log.

"Oh, that! That's an old country-house trick," she tells me. She speaks as if I had never stayed at a country-house weekend, as if I had never experienced the joys of forty-eight hours in which everyone tucks into huge fried breakfasts before going out to kill things, or plays vicious games of croquet, gossips about their mutual friends, name-drops so loudly you can hear it in the next county, and then passes out in freezing bedrooms after late-night drinking jags of whiskey and playing Freda, a lethal but much loved upper-class icebreaker of a game that demands all age groups run at high speed round and round the full-size billiards table instead of talking to one another. The whiskey and the Freda are essential tools of survival in country houses, being the only two things that stop guests freezing to death, of course.

One of the nice things about having our own lovely place in the country, lovely enough to have featured in *Dorset Living*, *House and Garden*, and, I hope, eventually, *Gardens Illustrated*, is that it completely kills the desire to stay in anyone else's lovely place in the country. I can't stand the fact that guests, even sensitive ones, are expected to play ghastly after-dinner games, requiring me to go and hide somewhere remote, like the icehouse or the pets' graveyard, until it's safely over, which is usually not for hours.

"If you're staying in someone's house, a big one, and they don't have much help, the key thing is to avoid being given tasks to do by your hostess," Mimi confides, "so you carry a log purposefully from room to room, as if you are in the middle of nobly building a roaring blaze for everyone. See, if a hostess has a big house, lots of friends, she'll never, generally speaking, have enough help, she quite understandably wants guests to earn their keep, and will treat them as unpaid *Gastarbeiter*."

Mimi then tells me all about various friend-rich, staff-poor friends of hers who wait till they have huge house parties be-fore deciding to move all the furniture around, assemble four-posters, clear out attics, or suddenly bray that the "team" must earn their keep by removing rocks from some field on the estate, so the hosts can erect a marquee or something.

"But Pierre isn't ligging in some remote Scottish pile like some awful castle climber," I point out to Mimi when she's finished. "He's in his own home, where he should be pitching in without complaint, and pulling his weight. Far from pitch-ing in, he creates more work. Did I ever tell you about the rivers-of-jam episode, when I was making jam, and he insisted I help him find something he accused me of moving, so I left him in the kitchen for a second and when I came back the whole saucepan of boiling jam where I was bubbling off the scum—"

"But Pierre *is* in his own home, Rose," Mimi interrupts, taking something out of her bag. Oh my God—she lays them facedown on the table, so all I can see is a picture of an oiled torso and a pair of white swimming trunks containing a bulging crotch thrusting forwards out of the picture that is the latest Dolce & Gabbana aftershave ad. My heart sinks.

But I don't ask yet. I can't exactly say this to Mimi—even though we are past the stage of pretending to each other that we have perfect lives and are still deeply in love with our hus-bands, we haven't properly begun to share yet—but everything about Pierre is beginning to grate.

Everything I used to love. His fisherman's smock. His hands grimed with clay; his being "artistic"; even his name, which I used to find terribly attractive, even hip.

Now all these things make me feel cross. Why didn't his pretentious parents from Biggleswade call him Peter? It's not as if he's French.

Some of this spills out to Mimi.

"He is in his home, but I'm the only one at the Dairy who works," I point out when our coffees finally arrive, after much hissing and jetting of milk and steam, slopping over the sides of the cups. I mop the table and set the cup on the napkin, while Mimi brings hers straight to her lips and sips without noticing that foamy brown liquid is coursing down the side and onto the table. I go up to the counter, looking bleakly at the cakes and things underneath glass at the front, wish for a second that I was tempted, and take a few napkins from the pile.

Apart from a man with a collie and a woman in a head scarf with a Labrador and a terrier, both reading the *Daily Telegraph*, we are That New Place's only customers.

"Not him. I'm the main breadwinner, and I do all the gardening, the cooking, the shopping, the child care," I say, rejoining Mimi. "You know, my jams and chutneys are doing really well, so are my hampers—*Waitrose Food Illustrated* has just done a thing on them, so has the *Observer Food Monthly*, which is great. I don't know if you know this, but I do the labels, the khaki-and-plum ones, handwritten, for those tall, thin, flavored vodkas, beetroot, horseradish, and what have you. And then I'm doing the air-dried slices of apples and pears idea I mentioned as an alternative to crisps. I may even be bringing out my own cheese next year."

I don't know why it all gushed out, not all of it is even strictly true—the bit about the cheese is definitely somewhat premature. I do want to produce my own cheese, as cheese is not only milk's leap to immortality, it's a lovely way of showing how connected to the *terroir* one is, and one of my biggest worries at the moment is that Cath will unveil her Honeyborne Blue or her Court Place Cheddar before I do.

"Golly, you're Dorset's answer to Martha Stewart," Mimi says as she breaks the flapjack in two and takes the nice crunchy half for herself, leaving me the flabby bit. "You're a one-woman cottage industry. Remind me not to tell Ralph. He's been muttering about me retraining as a country solicitor and us getting an au pair so I can pull my weight again."

She munches away.

"Did I tell you, I went into the Stores to see if Mrs. Hitchens could help, about my cleaner crisis?"

I shake my head, enjoying the fact that, with Mimi, everything is a drama and a crisis.

"She merely sighed and opened a drawer under the till. It was like this, you know, dog-eared piece of A4, absolutely covered with scribble, she's obviously had going for ages. So she added my name to the list of those in the area who have needed cleaners for much longer than me, i.e., not just for months, but decades."

I keep quiet, obviously, because I have a cleaner, Joan, and Mimi knows I have a cleaner, but our relationship has not and may, to be honest, never reach the point where I will make the ultimate sacrifice and allow my cleaner to work for her. After all, I barely dare ask Joan to work for *me*, and I've been paying her ten years. And even Mimi knows that even so much as humbly and nervously suggesting I provide her with Joan's number would be too much to ask. So she doesn't.

"So I just say, 'What a good idea, darling,' every time the au pair idea comes up," Mimi continues, "like I do when he talks about renting a cottage on Dartmoor for half term, because I know that if I don't do it, it won't actually happen. But I don't want to, you know, sound totally neg every time he suggests we actually *do* anything."

"But why would you want to rent a cottage on Dartmoor when you've just bought a gorgeous old farmhouse in the wilds of West Dorset?" I ask, pleased that we have swept on past the cleaner issue. "I mean, you're surrounded by beautiful landscape here, and, er, friends. Why would you leave all that to pay a lot of money to go to some cottage in the rain with poly-cotton sheets and nasty thin pillows with no dishwasher? Anyway, don't you want to do the house up a bit first, concentrate on getting it, er, right, rather than spend the money on renting somewhere else?" I don't want to say that Home Farm is a complete wreck, obviously, but it does need some poshing up; I mean, the truth is that Honeyborne is absolutely full of photoshoot-ready country spreads, with trugs and hide gloves artfully arrayed on oak ledges in greenhouses, cutting gardens full of color and bloom, manicured lawns, wildflower meadows, ancient wisteria-clad period dwellings awash with stone floors, sumptuous bathrooms, and sprawling flagstone-floored country kitchens replete with *batterie de cuisine,* working fireplaces, and bread ovens. While Home Farm is still defiantly unmodernized—I don't think they've even got central heating, let alone more than one bathroom, which the Flemings appear content to regard as part of its charm.

"Well, that is my response entirely," says Mimi. "I can't stand the idea of renting, anywhere! Especially one of those places where the owner says, 'It takes *very special people* to appreciate Little Maltings,' and then it turns out that the reason why is because Little Maltings is a hovel in a bog with no running water that the family loves dearly for historic and sentimental reasons but is everyone else's idea of the holiday house from hell. The problem is, though," she says, looking down into her coffee, "well, there's no budget for doing anything at Home Farm at the moment. I thought when we sold our house—well, Ralph's family house, in Notting Hill—that we would be rolling, but then the trustees all waded in, and said though we could sell it, and of course buy Home Farm with cash, we had to leave the remainder in trust, for the children's education. So selling up in London hasn't been the financial lifeboat I thought it might be. The rising property market doesn't, turns out, float all boats. Not ours, anyway. Nice for the children, though. Heigh-ho. So—shall we trickle on home, or shall we go completely wild and get another late?" Mimi giggles when she says "late" rather than "latte." The couple who run the New Place can't spell, a fact that gives her endless pleasure.

"I'm loath to leave the warmth of here and go back to Home Farm. It's like a freezer cabinet." She gets up, with her purse in her hand.

"Mimi," I say, putting my hand on the magazines. "Put me out of my misery. What is all this?"

Mimi subsides back into her chair and flips them over.

We both scream in unison, and the Labrador staggers to his feet and comes over, wagging his tail.

For the magazines our thirteen-year-old girls have been buying, in secret, and poring over while we thought they were safely adding to their Facebook and MySpace pages are . . . *Brides, Modern Brides,* and *Wedding.* And, last but not least, *Martha Stewart Weddings.*

All the covers feature dainty, wasp-waisted damsels in white holding bouquets and have cover lines such as "Perfect Day" and "The Day You Always Dreamed Of," alongside elaborately tiered and stepped cakes adorned with ribbons and crenellated icing or a spun-sugar-laced croquembouche pyramid of choux buns.

We look at each other in horror.

"What did they say?" I breathe. "And how on earth did they get *Martha Stewart Weddings?* The only person around here I can imagine might want it is Serena or Cath Cobb."

"I don't know where they got them, but as for why they got them," Mimi says, "well, according to Ceci and Mirabel, who as you imagine I have interrogated under Gestapo conditions about this worrying development, what they say is—"

"Yes?"

"That all they want when they grow up is for their wedding days to be perfect."

"So what's Pierre doing all day?" Mimi asks, in a leading way, when she returns, balancing our brimming cups, and another flapjack on a saucer, which we have decided we need in the wake of the discovery that our daughters are living and breathing place settings, rose-petal confetti, and trousseaux rather than something healthy, like older boys, skunk, and gangsta rap. "Is he working on some mega-commission?"

"Ha!" I bark.

I think she's getting back at me for suggesting that Home Farm was not just in need of refreshment but in need of being dragged into the twenty-first century.

I explain that Pierre ferries Ceci to and from school once a week, while I'm busy in Godminster with the vodka and my other range of the Dairy-label products. He does a bit of shopping.

"Don't forget the log—he carries his log," adds Mimi. Mimi annoyingly finds the log thing very funny, and I am beginning to wish I had never brought it up.

I explain that though Pierre was—I mean, is—a sculptor of great gifts, Pierre's main occupations, currently, are time-wasting and medical self-diagnosis. "He spends most of his time in that huge shed in the garden, the studio. He makes cups of tea, listens to the radio, bird-watches, reads the *Independent* and the *Art Newspaper* and all his boring magazines, checks his latest symptoms in his massive *Dictionary of Medical Symptoms*. But what he doesn't do, Mimi, is earn money."

I spare her the fact that he uses a sort of outdoor privy, over a trench, on occasion, in order to avoid coming into the house and risk being given a chore by me. He claims "it" disperses into a reed bed, a claim that no one, let alone me, has ever sought to disprove.

"Oh, God, I'm sure that's what Ralph thinks about me," Mimi replies. "I haven't really got my act together yet. Everything takes so long. Just having three meals a day and keeping warm and reasonably clean—me, that is, not the house—is a full-time job. There literally isn't any time at all!"

"Well, it does take a while to find one's feet, I agree," I admit. "It's taken me ten years, and you've only been here, what, a year and a bit."

"Anyway, I think Pierre is charm itself," Mimi tells me. "He's soooo good-looking! Sort of teddy-bearish, all rumply, and he's still got masses of lovely tufty hair. I love brown hair. It's terribly underrated, don't you think? Thank God Ralph hasn't lost his, either! And I like the way he does that funny walk in his slippers to make the girls laugh, with his feet turned out, like a penguin . . ."

I am a bit sharp with Mimi at this point.

"I'd be very good-looking, too, if I had never had any stress of any kind in my entire adult life," I snap. "I'd look ten years younger than I do if I was being kept by someone else, without working or exerting myself in any way. And, anyway, that's not a funny walk, it's how Pierre walks."

At this point I am sorely tempted to tell Mimi about Jesse Marlon. I'm longing to tell someone.

Jesse Marlon Bryanston—the son of Ned, but not the son of Lulu—he's started coming up to the Dairy to help out. It's become our little routine. But I don't tell her. After he's done his chores at Spodden's Hatch—he is a little vague about them, but slug clearance seems to feature quite a lot—he's up to the Dairy quite often, if it's not a "communal work day," when they all do horrible jobs like moving compost heaps or stripping down the steam engine that cuts all the trees into planks and oiling all the moving parts.

But I do clue Mimi in about the Bryanstons and Godminster Hall, just to give her the headlines, because she asks who the "village rock star" is and describes Jesse Marlon to a tee, having spotted him in Horse Supplies a couple of days ago.

"Tall, with dark hair, jeans," she asks. "Er, T-shirt with aggressive slogan?"

So I rather formally explain that the raven-haired youth in jeans and Every Little Hurts Fuck Tesco T-shirt is without any doubt Jesse Marlon, Ned Bryanston's oldest son and heir by his starter marriage to Jude, a poet. I feel my stomach do a little flip when I say his name, which is how I know.

I have started on that road again.

"She could afford to be a poet," I explain, thinking, Oh, Lord, here we go. "Not because Ned is loaded, though. He did come into some capital, but inherited wealth doesn't get you very far these days. No, Jude's father made a fortune in something"—I pause, trying to remember—"spackle. It's like Polyfilla, I think."

Then I give her the bare bones of the Bryanston backstory. It's only fair, as Mimi is new to the village.

"Anyway, the marriage broke down shortly after Jesse Marlon was born, when Big Ned ran off with, among several others, Lulu Fitch, now Bryanston, a model-actress-whatever with whom he has the twins, Little Ned and Fred. And Judith, I mean Jude, disappeared back to the East Coast, where she now runs an exclusive writers' retreat in the Catskills with her new partner, Kit, and they have a child."

"So Lulu toppled Jude, and now Jude lives in America, and Lulu and Ned are married, and produced twins. Does she ever come over and see Jesse Marlon with him, with, erm, Kit, I mean?" Mimi asks.

"With her," I say. "She does indeed. She came over with Kit one summer, to see her son—we were all agog. Turned out that her partner, Kit, was a lesbian, as is Jude, and their child, called Jeremy, was a golden-haired Rapunzel. A girl. Anyway, Ned's father, Gerard, died about five years ago, and Ned and Lulu moved from the cottage *ornée* into the big house—"

"The cottage what?" Mimi asks, slightly imitating my French pronunciation.

"*Ornée*," I say. "And anyway, Ned's mother, Celia, has been living with them ever since, which only partly explains, we think, why Lulu is always in such a vile mood.

"Celia is rather marvelous in a Lady Bracknell way, but Lulu calls her 'the monster' behind her back, which isn't surprising, I suppose.

"Lulu complains that living with Celia is worse than a State Visit from the Queen, because at least the Royals are trained to make an effort. Celia has capably swatted away all attempts to park her in the Gatehouse, or the Ciderhouse, or a cottage, with the promise that 'she will never live in some Dower House,' and that if they want her to leave Godminster Hall, against her will and against Gerard's express wishes, it will be 'feetfirst.' "

Anyway, Mimi doesn't bat an eyelid at any of this mass of pointless personal data, as I knew she wouldn't, as she adores trivia and claims to remember everything she's ever read in *Heat* or *Grazia* but not a single fact from her four-year university degree course in Edinburgh, where she met Ralph.

"At the time this caused a frisson in the village, but only a mild frisson," I tell Mimi. "Everyone's glued to *The Archers,* so nothing—gay marriage, incest, poaching, blended families— surprises them any longer, let alone a little light lesbianism."

"Mild frisson . . . maybe I'm in cold turkey cos there're so few expensive shops in Dorset, but that does sound lovely, don't you think?" Mimi says with a dreamy sigh. "Like a French shoe de- signer . . ." Then she pauses. "By the way, I wasn't worried about the wedding magazines, actually," she admits, stuffing them back into her bag. Then she covers her face with her hands. "I haven't told anyone yet. Not even Ralph, and I haven't found out for sure yet, but I think I'm . . ."

I raise my eyebrows, and Mimi nods.

I like to be in the kitchen when Jesse Marlon arrives; it looks more inviting. This morning I'm holding on to the kettle's black Bakelite handle as if for strength, thinking, rather Mimi than me.

There are some women who just love being pregnant, relish the attention and the power, and revel in the role of mother hen with all their pretty chicks, and are quite happy at the sandpit or the swings, and enjoy the company of other mums at playgroup and one o'clock club, or under-fives drop-ins in dark churches, making homemade chicken nuggets and Play-Doh and clever things with felt and pipe cleaners.

Not me. The nursery world is too dreary for words. I fall into the category of women for whom "Mummmeeee! Can we do fingerpainting?" are among the most terrifying words in the English language, and feel endlessly grateful that I was blessed with Ceci, who was a bookish, easygoing pre-Raphaelite little girlchild I could dress like a dolly in smocks by Valerie Goad. I could have so easily had a little Action Man–type boy who wanted a skinhead haircut and to dress in camouflage and combat gear. You just never know what you're going to get, it seems, with children, and I don't really like surprises. As for the thought of having a baby now, just as I am putting the Dairy products on the Dorset food map . . . makes my blood run cold.

As I think about Mimi, and wonder whether she's going to want me to be *involved* in any way, I'm clearing the bowls that have held mine and Ceci's breakfast of Dorset Cereals Cherry, Cranberry, and Almond muesli topped with nonfat yogurt and milled linseed and blueberries before they get to the point when I have to pick the flakes with my fingernails before popping them into the Miele.

I'm arranging the scene just so, with the sparkling cafetière sitting in a patch of weak sunlight on the beech worktop next to two glazed French earthenware mugs and some homemade shortbread in a battered enamel tin, with all the auteurish eye of Sofia Coppola styling a film set. The kitchen is warm, peaceful, filled with a glow from the light coming through the windows and bouncing off the walls painted a Provençal yellow I mixed myself. What I think of as the color of sunshine.

I can't help it. Unlike Pierre, I cannot regard houses as machines for living in. It's as if I suffer from a higher aesthetic sensibility, and I cannot help but arrange each room, down to the way the linen glass cloths hang just so over the Aga rail and the flowers bloom in their lusterware vases, as if they are being seen for the first time by someone else, someone very smart whom I want to impress with my own impeccable, yet effortless, taste. All the bedrooms upstairs are made up with crisp linen and plump duvets and plenty of pillows, ready for guests, with clean snowy towels lying on heated rails in the bathrooms and boxes of unopened Roger & Gallet lily of the valley soap in cupboards. I don't believe in God, but I do believe in comfort and style. And I mind—terribly—about how things look. For instance, I do not want any coffee, not after two cups in God-minster, but I do like the sight of the glass sides of the cafetière, not to mention the roasty aroma that fills the warm kitchen when the boiling water hits the freshly ground beans.

Just as I am expecting Jesse Marlon, Pierre comes into the kitchen, carrying his log. Damn!

Pierre's kilim leather-soled slippers make a shuffling noise on the wonderful slate-flagged floor, found in Brittany, as he wanders over. Then he places the log carefully on the wine rack underneath the butcher's block, as if that is where it lives.

I look on in horror, but Pierre doesn't seem to notice. He is completely, 100 percent wrapped up in himself, as usual. It is as if Ceci and I do not exist. As if food appears on plates, ironed shirts in cupboards, petrol in cars, rubbish sacks in the wheelie bins—*as if by magic*.

He goes into the larder—slop, slop, his slippers go over the floor—and takes out eggs from the marble, then bacon from the fridge. It's so annoying the way he always eats a full English of porridge and a fried breakfast in the morning. He's one of those men who takes all the PR about breakfast to heart, as if not to eat a plateful of fried food, even for one morning, could possibly result in what he calls "muesli-belt malnutrition."

"What've you done with my spurtle?" he then asks accusingly, having peered into the earthenware jar by the Aga where I keep wooden spoons, rolling pins, and spatulas, and indeed the special wooden spurtle he uses to stir his porridge. Pierre even looks into the dishwasher in the kitchen, which I intend to run later, on the intensive 75 degree program, after Jesse Marlon's and my coffee cups have gone in (I could wait till after supper, but it's more than two-thirds full now).

"It's in the sink," I reply in a sharp voice, thinking Pierre should know by now not to look there; wood should never go in the dishwasher.

And that's it—"Where's my spurtle?" "In the sink"—that's the extent of our communication for the day, until Pierre will wander into the kitchen and find me listening to *The Archers* and making supper, still *doing*.

Pierre doesn't say anything but runs the spurtle under the tap.

I don't say anything as, according to Pierre, I am not more efficient and productive than he is, only more bossy. He also says that his slobbishness is his way of challenging my "female domestic domination," and the only way he can leave his mark on the house is by making it untidy and dirty and leaving his spoor on my wiped surfaces.

I merely bear silent witness, with the same expression as a female war reporter in a conflict zone, as he hacks at the loaf of brown bread that sits on a board on the beech worktop and note that he is efficiently spraying crumbs in a radius of about two feet.

And then, as I'm wondering whether a controlled explosion would have done a better job of distributing crumbs around the kitchen, he toasts the bread, and then butters it without using a side plate, then takes huge bites standing up while trailing around, something comes unbidden into my mind, these awful words:

My marriage is over.

I force myself to swallow the words down again, but I do decide . . . something.

Thank God Jesse Marlon comes, shortly after Pierre has sloped back to the shed with a copy of today's *Independent*.

He'll be gone for hours, because he said he was heading for the studio, but before that he has to call in at the privy. Pierre is inordinately proud of his privy, and I'm all in favor, too, though not because it's green, but because it helps to keep Pierre out of the house, where his main occupation is creating mess, disturbing my tableaux, and demanding to know where he's left critical items such as some special fossil, or a bird's egg, just when I am in the middle of making my special summer spiced chutney for the fête.

All my friends adore him, of course, but he has the management skills of a border terrier puppy, has lost all his drive or ambition, and once asked whether "work–life balance" was a sort of low-calorie yogurt. He put up a pretense of working while Ceci was a baby, largely in order not to be saddled with child-care duties best left to Mother, but, as soon as I was back at work, he put his feet up again.

When I look at Pierre, the awful thing is I no longer see his weatherbeaten brown face, glowing and healthy and tanned from tramping the hills, the crinkles around his blue eyes, the well-shaped bow of his wide upper lip. I no longer notice the attributes that Mimi, with fresh eyes, declared she found handsome.

My heart no longer skips a beat when I see his big, beautiful sculptor's hands, or his bum in old jeans, as it always used to. I just think, *Why was I moronic enough to marry an artist?*

And now Jesse Marlon has come into my kitchen, and my heart hammers. Navy jersey, jeans, and battered brown rigger boots.

I wouldn't necessarily call him "rock star," which was Mimi's description, but he is athletic from all the hewing of wood and drawing of water he has to do at Spodden's Hatch, with thick eyebrows, and curly black hair springing away from a high, patrician forehead.

He always smells deliciously smoky because of the wood burner in his house, and roll-up cigarettes. He strolls in as if he, not Pierre, has the freedom of my kitchen, and comes over to warm his narrow hips on the Aga.

Doors are always left unlocked around here, and keys in ignitions as a sign of trust.

Jesse Marlon leans against the rail, removes a pouch of tobacco from a pocket, and starts rolling. But what makes me catch my breath is that as he does this, his eyes are not on the little white tube in his fingers, but on me, as I reboil the kettle, remove it from the hot plate, and then concentrate as I pour the water over the Arabica ground beans (from the Court Place Farm Shop—I like to buy Cath Cobb's stuff to show I don't mind how successful she is). I am facing into the Aga, he's facing out, with his jeaned hip touching my Ralph Lauren patchwork cowgirl skirt.

"So . . . you on your own?" He checks. My heart now backflips. Why does he want to know? What does it matter?

I nod casually. "Yes. Pierre's out."

And I can't help but feel his hip burn into me, as if we're soldered together. I definitely hold the pose for a beat longer than is strictly necessary (the steam is merrily spigoting out of the Aga kettle and making a very apposite whistling sound).

I suddenly have that faraway, long-lost sensation, that wonderful warm itch, that feeling of rats swarming through the dark sewers of my own entrails.

I allow the fierce heat of the boiling plate to scorch my face, a move that I hope will save me from grabbing him and making an utter fool of myself. He stays close by. Very close, in fact. We are almost on top of each other.

Well, I suppose I am fairly appealing compared to the hairy women in the eco-village, who all seem to have children at least four years old perma-clamped to the breast and wear jumpers that look as if they have been knitted out of reeds.

But Jesse Marlon . . . he is probably thinking, *Steady on, Grandma*, even though I'm only just forty. But still, I am almost twice his age and could easily be his mother. Oh, I don't know. All I can safely say is that the whole episode, although nothing, of course, actually happens, ignites something inside.

I think I must have started sniffing the air around him, as if I were trying to inhale him, because he suddenly asks me if I have an allergy and starts asking whether the Aga runs on oil or gas or some other renewable energy source.

Trying to look environmentally concerned, I say it's oil, but that we are, actually, thinking of converting it to a biofuel in the near future. Which is a white lie, of course.

"I'm glad to hear it," he says and holds up his palm to me. "You know, it really matters that where I work as well as where I live people are at least trying to do the right thing." His palm is still aloft, and I finally get it.

"High five!" I say, sounding silly, and place my hand against his, where it looks pleasingly small and girlish. I'm not sure what "high five" is or whether this is what I should be saying at this point, but it doesn't matter.

As our palms touch, I feel a crackling tingle of electricity pass between us and—I know this sounds odd—but I sort of lose consciousness for a second. I find myself just staring at him, but after that he just drinks his coffee quite quickly, grabs a handful of shortbread from the enamel tin, an apple and a banana from the fruit bowl, and says he's going off to the barns to see how many hampers we have left in storage.

I wave and then sort of collapse at the kitchen table, holding my mug with its untouched coffee.

After a while I wander into the study. I can't concentrate. I have to stop myself from rushing out to the barns, and seeing . . . if Jesse Marlon felt it, too, whether such a current of electricity, apparently passing between two people, can be experienced by only one . . . I force myself to do some paperwork, and open my e-mails instead.

They are all boring apart from a strange one, from a woman who'd found my name on the Internet on the EatDorset site after reading the piece in *Country Living*. I say "a woman," as if I don't know her, but I do, only when I knew Clare, she was called something else, she wasn't called Clare Sturgis but Clare Lowell, and we were at Cambridge together, on the same staircase in our first year, when I was reading Modern Languages and, I think, she was reading English.

In her e-mail, she apologizes for coming over all Friends Reunited but says she is keen to see me again and catch up, because our life journeys seem to be following similar paths. Now she's a garden designer, but taking a break from her clients, and looking to explore lots of options. She wants to come and see me at the Dairy, and says she is really interested in the potential cross-marketing opportunities of smallholdings, stuff like physic gardens and homeopathy as well as consumables.

She mentions en passant she is also going to see Sarah Raven at Perch Hill, so, of course, I feel very flattered to be mentioned in the same breath as the Queen of Cutting Gardens, and tell her in a long, welcoming e-mail back that I'd love to see her any time. And I tell Clare Sturgis/Lowell to bring her little baby—Joe—with her, if she likes.

Mimi

To: claresturgis@gmail.com
From: mimimalone@homefarm.com
Dear Clare

I'm really sorry that the school secretary wasn't more helpful. My advice is, persevere. Write a letter addressed to Doc H and copied to the sec saying you only bought the house on the communal garden because you wanted to send a child to Ponsonby, and your life won't be worth living unless you can at least look round. Which may not work, but has the small merit of being true (and therefore marginally more persuasive than most of the intergalactic bollocks desperate, pushy parents come up with when they are trying to get their children in).

I can't believe she wouldn't put you down even on the waiting list, though. My instinct is to keep going. Eve is doubtless told by Doc H to say the waiting list is closed till Kingdom Come to all the parents. Then the usual procedure is, he looks at the names and cherry-picks out the ones he's heard of and wants to pal up with.

It's astonishing how heads who say that their school is completely chocker, lists closed, can always find a place for the child of a supermodel/Gazprom oligarch/international celebrity, so never take no as an answer. Write. Ring. Doorstep. Get Gideon involved. All heads love nothing more than to see alpha fathers begging and pleading on behalf of a blastocyte. It's one of the things that gives their life most meaning.

I am ready to step in—not that I carry much clout. Just let me know.

As you asked, well . . . moving to the country and leaving London is just as havoc-making as moving to, say, Kandahar, with the only real difference being that if you only move to the shires rather than to Afghanistan, you get no offers of sympathy or help and no armed protection when you leave the house.

Plus you only exchange one set of tribes/cliques for another. In Notting Hill, it was bankers, killer mummies, Americans, high-rolling creatives. Whereas here there are three distinct groups:

1. The ur-villagers, who have lived and worked in Dorset all their life, who can't afford to shop or eat organic, who drive old bangers that still run on petrol, rather than electricity or corn oil, and whose children burn stuff/torture hedgehogs/sniff glue in the absence of anything else to do.

2. The green nomads/eco Nazis in Spodden's Hatch, whose penitential, low-impact lifestyle off the grid is a full-time job and whose lives represent a permanent rebuke to . . .

3. The "agrivistes": you know, the superrich noovs who've been mopping up their bonuses with everything that's come on the market for years, sight unseen, who use their country estates, with their gamekeeper's cottages and lodges and so on, as vast playpens, and put their own staff into the cottages that locals can't begin to afford to buy, and helipads and gyms and pools into the extensive grounds. If you look closely, all their Humvees, Range Rovers, and so on have Kensington and Chelsea residents' parking permits stuck to their windscreens, so in fact, this £5 million spread is only

somewhere they can "split" to, to "decompress," and only if they feel like it, on weekends.

Get the picture?

BTW, I have to say, I'm v impressed by how Gideon's career has moved from the architectural monthlies to the house and garden magazines to the news sections of the broadsheets, I really am, and I'm glad he's leading the campaign against all these basement ozone pools everyone is putting in around us or, shd I say, you.

Anyway, must dash. Ralph has found an au pair, and put her on the train from Waterloo. I've got to pick her up from Godminster. All I know, she's called Ana. Full name, "Ana from Poland."

Obviously, I can't wait to meet her.

Love,
Mimi x

I press send and hurtle into the Subaru.

Now I'm back from G'minster. With Ana.

I'm sitting in the kitchen with the *Telegraph* open on the table to the Court and Social page, with that sinking feeling, which I know is to do with the fact that Ana is here, and already, I can tell . . . I don't think it's going to work.

Why did I ever think it would? Having decided that Ralph was right, and that I really did need an extra pair of hands, especially with the driving, I now think he was barking even to suggest it. Two pubescents and one preteen . . . one generally grumpy and absent old sod of an Old Etonian husband . . . one bored, not to mention hormonal, housewife . . . In fact, I feel even sorrier for her than I do for me.

She's away from home living with a family that I described in the Gumtree ad as "chilled, laid-back, and welcoming" and now she, like me, is facing grim reality.

So Ana is unpacking her stuff into the spare bedroom (she called it "her accommodations"), and I am trying to put a brave face on it, despite the obvious fact that we are never going to have anything in common. If Ana and I had been speed-dating, we would have given each other three seconds. Now, we have—in theory at least—a year under the same roof to get through. As we drive through the village, I say, there's the pub! and there's the shop! and there's the church! The war memorial! And here's the village green, if you're into maypoles and Morris dancing (I'll explain later), and this is important, this is the recycling place, where I bring all our bottles, ha-ha, and, oh yes, there's the bus stop, where you can get the bus to Godminster and Bridport, there's a cinema there now, it's repertory and arthousey and rather good, and now, here we are, this is us, the turning past the church by this old milestone.

I dart her a quick look, and she's not looking out of the window, drinking in the sublime English scenery, a vista of woods and fields and grazing sheep so beautiful it brings tears to my own eyes, every day, and one that Ana is unlikely ever to have seen before in her entire life. She is checking her mobile. Then she says, what is this thing, a ducks crossing? I almost hug her, as she has found the sign between the duck pond and green in friendly lower-case writing (rather than hectoring shouty capitals) that is supposed to charm drivers into slowing down for ducks at least worthy of notice.

Honeyborne is sparkling in the weak sunlight, even the bilious sign offering Morning Coffee, Light Bites, and Sunday Roasts—as if Starbucks, wheat intolerance, and the revulsion against methane and red meat belonged to another era—outside the crazily timbered Lamb Inn. The thatch-fringed cottages set in the plunging declivity of a plump green valley gleam, as if freshly painted for Ana's arrival. Today, even the tarmac on the roads through the village that segue Honeyborne to Larcombe and Chesilborne and thence to Godminster is glossy, as if recently bootblacked by a SWAT team of shoeshine boys. I turn into the drive and see our own Home Farm, set on the green hill, through her eyes, looking sweet-faced and chocolate-boxy.

I glance at her again. She is very skinny, with long straight brown hair, and wearing tight jeans and high heels and a white anorak with fake fur around the hood.

I can't help saying something about the shoes. "Didn't my husband explain that there aren't pavements, Ana?" I say. "Apart from in towns? It's not really a high heels kind of place; you might fall over."

"Yes?" Ana says, with a rising inflection, as if she's been watching too much cable TV, as she edges away from Calypso, who was trying to make friends.

But she doesn't seem to understand. Though she is quite self-possessed. She doesn't seem to be appalled when we reach Home Farm, which is a relief, and actually smiles when she presents me with a house present of a three-foot-long skinny salami that looks exactly like the bull's pizzles they sell in Horse Supplies. I exclaim with delight and hide it on a high shelf in the larder in case the children find it and get scared, or Mirabel brings it out and tries to frighten Posy with it.

I offer her tea, then coffee, but she says she doesn't drink either tea or coffee. I feel this is a somewhat lowering development. I've never been friends with anyone (1) who doesn't need industrial-strength jags of coffee before they can face the day or (2) doesn't like dogs.

"So, are you hungry?" I try next, in a bright voice. "I'm going to have to get the children from school in an hour or so. Did you have anything on the train, or did you get something at the station? I always have the cinnamon bagel with cream cheese at the Bagel Buffet, and a double-shot large latte, and take it with me on the train, as a treat," I babble. Ana looks at me without understanding.

"Yes?" she says.

"I know," I say, desperately, deciding in that moment that

she is not a candidate for nightly candlelit dinner à trois with Ralph and me. "The children eat at six-thirty P.M., you might want something by then, I think I'll give them peas and lasagna tonight. Why don't you settle in and unpack?"

Which is where she is now. Upstairs, tramping about. I remove the lasagna from the freezer and put it by the Aga to defrost, and try to decide what I'm feeling about this latest development.

So now I've got an au pair, even if she does only say, intermittently, "Yes?"

Who on earth is she going to hang out with in Honeyborne? I am wondering, mainly so that I am not her only friend, and then I remember—Colin Watts! The wood guy. The tall son of Thomas Watts the butcher, adopted I think, who drives around in that white van that says COLIN WATTS, LOGS, KINDLING, AND BARK on the side, which the children think is so funny. He's young, he's tall, and he's got longish legs; he's always in the pub. He's single. He's got a pulse. In other words, he will most certainly do.

I am so excited at matchmaking Ana with Colin Watts that I almost celebrate by making an impulse purchase of a "pack-away TV blanket," which folds into a cushion with a handy pocket. It costs a bargain price of only £19.95. To use during all the downtime I am clearly not going to have now that I have help.

I am staring hard at the picture in the newspaper of the woman in the ad, waiting for the endorphin rush that will make me pick up the telephone and order it. She is sitting on a spotless cream sofa next to a cheese plant, entirely swaddled head to toe in blue microfiber. Her feet are, we are invited to imagine, tucked into the sort of flap at the bottom and there are TV guides, spectacles, and remote controls sticking out from pockets around her waist, so she looks like a bit like a Home Counties suicide bomber in a burqa. I am trying to imagine me in the pack-away TV blanket while Ana gets on with the laundry or picks apples with Posy, or me out and about doing something for myself—and am failing somehow. Now I have Ana to take charge of what she calls "the houseworks," I could, in theory, get out more, and do something.

But what, and where?

If you don't ride and aren't a keen gardener, there's less to do in Honeyborne than in Open Prison. In prison, at least inmates never have a minute free, inundated as they are with pleasant "intramural" activities: craft classes, salsa lessons, computer courses, help with CVs, professional-level theatre workshops run by concerned, compassionate actors, and so on, not to mention Italian cultural days where they eat gnocchi and tiramisu prepared by gorgeous Giorgio Locatelli or someone while being serenaded by tenors.

For a start, the only shop here for miles around, apart from the Post Office, is the aforementioned one called Horse Supplies.

Horse Supplies and Saddlery—to give it its full name—provides us with the only retail opportunity for miles around. It has a concrete floor, hard-core notice board pinned up with job ads for poultry sexers, pignuts, chain links—that sort of thing— and possibly ranks as the least glamorous outlet in the Western world, but I rather love it.

Even when I allow myself to dwell on what "shopping" used to be like.

I'd go out to Westbourne Grove, or Kensington Park Road, just to see if there was anything I "needed," i.e., a new pair of Sass & Bide jeans from Coco Ribbon, to showcase my Inner Me, or one of those signature zipped shirt dresses from West Village—in other words, self-indulgent designer pieces I would hide in a bag from Ralph and draw out when the coast was clear. I'd put it on and say, if Mirabel or Ralph narrowly asked, "Oh! What? This old thing?" and give a brittle, tinkling laugh as I looked down in surprise at the garment, as if seeing it anew after a long absence. "I've had it for ages!" or even, to puzzle him further, as he hasn't a clue what it means, "It's vintage!"

Now I buy only the things I really do need. Like kibble for Calypso and yet more fire lighters. Which reminds me: I need some baling twine for the gates at Home Farm.

Not that the gates aren't perfectly good. They are. But I have to get my gates right. For example, if you are a yeoman farmer, or proper local, your gates must be greenish, sick-looking structures, made of warped planks that can be secured against the steaming ingress of barnyard animals only by knotted bright blue twine and rusting, twisty wire. This is to discourage trespassers on your land. Walking across a farmer's land in the country, unless you are on a footpath or bridle path, of course, is considered more intrusive than breaking into someone's house in London and helping yourself to their family heirlooms.

And if you live in the country all the time and want to fit in, you have to observe the Ten Rules, which are, I have worked out after exactly one and a half year's residence, as follows:

The Ten Rules of Country Living

1. Never lock your back or front door in the country. Your house must be open at all times in case someone has fallen from their horse during the chase and needs a large drink, which they will expect to be offered before medical assistance or the use of your telephone.

2. Always buy the vegetables at the village shop, even if this means you will exist on a diet of curly carrots and swedes like cannonballs and your children develop rickets. In fact, you must claim to buy everything at the village shop, including all Christmas presents, even if the choice is restricted to a box of fudge with the picture of the Cobb at Lyme Regis on it and something called Local Honey. Actually, as everyone knows, you use the shop only for papers, milk, and emergency supplies of whiskey, bread, and loo paper, but you must never, ever admit this.

3. You must drink at the village pub and buy the barman a drink, even if the pub changes hands every five minutes and serves horrible, pretentious food at London prices, and even if the barman has never acknowledged your existence and looks like (and probably is) a serial killer and/or sheep shagger.

4. You must never venture outside unless you are accompanied by a dog or astride a horse. If you do, you will be taken for a poacher or, even worse, a rambler, and probably shot, and your body will be hung from the gibbet as a public warning to others.

5. You must drive a battered green Land Rover at warp speed in steep-sided, narrow lanes with blind corners, howling drunk. Your dog, preferably a collie, must be in the passenger's seat with its head hanging out of the window and tongue whipping in the tailwind. In the back you must keep an assortment of leads, tools, and bales of hay, and you must affix a Countryside Alliance sticker by the license plate.

6. You must welcome all dogs into your house, wet or dry, and make endless allowances when other people's dogs, whom they love infinitely more than their spouses or children, pee on sofas or maul babies. Remember, dogs come first, and it is never, ever the dog's fault.

7. If engaged in conversation, you must avoid topics, such as work or Westminster or culture, which mark you out as a townie, and focus entirely on television, hunting, the weather, holidays, the harvest, and the decline in rural bus services. You must join in with gusto when a farmer brings up scab/scrapie/staggers/spangles or other veterinary conditions at village dos. When someone says "the other day," you must not look surprised when it turns out he is referring to a famous incident, often involving ferrets, that happened in

the middle of the last century, and must nod knowledgeably when your interlocutor talks about farrowing or whelping.

8. Even though you have moved to the country to escape built-up areas, and for the views, you must support publicly those who want to carpet National Parks and the nation's few remaining areas of outstanding natural beauty with hideous, low-cost housing for locals, with satellite dishes invariably affixed. You must join in the loud complaints about how second homers have driven up rural house prices, making country living completely unaffordable unless you work in town.

9. When the hunt churns up your meadows and breaks your gates down, you must rush out with a beaming smile bearing stirrup cup and sweetly offer doubles all round.

10. So, unless you want to be taken for an incomer, a rich townie, whose gates are made of clean-limbed new pine and clip shut thanks to oiled latches, metal spigots, and hinges, which of course I don't, you must follow all of the above, and have wonky gates.

See, I'd hate it if anyone stood in our yard at Home Farm thinking the worst. That a second homer lived here. Everything bad that happens is blamed on second homers, just as we used to blame City bankers for everything we pretended not to like about Notting Hill.

Plus, the action, such as it is, is in Godminster, seven miles away, where there is a Waitrose (*Allahu Akbar!*), a pannier market with wet fish stand on Thursday and Saturday, a saddlery, two hairdressers, three pet shops, a Spar, a tea shop, a takeout place, a derelict and mysterious Men's Institute, That New Place, Scrimpers the secondhand shop, two delis, six gift shops all selling identical Linum linen tablecloths in restrained Swedish neutrals, splashy Cath Kidston aprons and ironing-board covers in spriggy florals, Dr. Hauschka products, Damask nighties, etc.—in other words, a fairly typical, slow-food, West Country town of the type that almost makes me long for take-over by brand retailers like Gap and Starbucks, but not quite.

I can hear Ana moving around upstairs, in the guest room. Creak, thump, creak, and crunkle (the loose floorboard by the cupboard). For someone who looks like a size-double-zero Polish sex worker trying to break into glamour modeling, she's jolly heavy on her feet, I must say.

Whoa.

I just checked my in-box—and guess what? As well as one from Hugh Fearnley-Whittingstall at River Cottage, and one from Sarah Raven and one from Johnnie Boden (I feel as if they are not superbrands but close personal friends), there is one in my bulk folder that I happened to check rather than delete.

It was from an address I didn't recognize, maman@lacoste .com, which I thought must be a sneaky one alerting me to the new fitted polo shirts in this spring's "irresistible" boiled-sweet colors at the Lacoste store, where I once shopped while doing Covent Garden with Mirabel.

But it is not.

It's from Virginie Lacoste. Virginie Lacoste. The slippery blond Frenchwoman who ran circles around us all. Who we thought was having it off with the gingery Bob, the Bostonian banker, but wasn't. But only because she was fully occupied having it off with Sally, his slender, crop-headed, kickboxing Yankee wife, if not both of them, at the same time.

I've always wondered about that.

> To: mimimalone@homefarm.com
> From: maman@lacoste.com
>
> Hi Mimi, cherie, long time no speaks! How is the country-side?

At this point, one line into her missive, I go into a brief but intense reverie.

Why on God's earth do those who live in cities think that the country is one identikit location, like Center Parcs, or Disneyworld?

I happen to know Ralph has to put up with this sort of thing a lot on the train.

He has to be in London for meetings almost all week. Now, his worst fear is not something bad and nameless happening to me or the children or, even worse, Calypso. It's unheralded engineering works on the Waterloo-to-Godminster line. Or meeting auld acquaintance en route to the Brambletye (the funky, deluxe boutique hotel outside Godminster, modeled on Babington House).

"Ralph? Ralph Fleming?" one half of the eager couple will cry, on the train, moments after he has hidden himself behind some self-published memoir of the chalk streams of Hampshire.

"Oh, hi," Ralph will answer, trying to conceal his panic.

The iron rule on these occasions is: the more faintly Ralph recalls the people hailing him, the more ruthlessly they will lovebomb him. Like cats always cleaving to those who hate cats, Ralph, who hasn't made a new friend since he was in short trousers, is condemned to receive the near ecstatic attentions of almost perfect strangers who met him once at a PTA meeting in year five—a meeting he attended only under the utmost duress, in case he met anyone in the dread category known only as "New People."

"How's Mimi? And the kids? How're they enjoying the move, new schools, and all that? Bit of a change, eh, Dorset? You were in Notting Hill, weren't you? Downshift, did you?"

Ralph, during all this, will be nodding and assenting, hoping in vain that they might let slip one clue, just one clue that will make the penny drop. They might mention a street, a mutual friend, a company, even a school or a child's name might help . . . if not, he is reduced to asking:

"So, why are you two on the Godminster train, then?" spoken in a hearty way, as if he is, if only up to a point, interested in the answer.

"We're going to The Country!" the generic couple in their Barbours or tailored tweeds will reply smugly, with a nod towards an Aspinal holdall (his) and Lulu Guinness weekend bag (hers).

"We're leaving Blank (fill in name of privately educated, whey-faced London child) and Blank (fill in name of the younger sibling) with Blank (fill in name of nanny whom couple smugly brag has become part of the family) until Sunday night, for our sins—and spending the weekend à deux at Brambletye House! A sort of second honeymoon, eh, Blank!" (fill in nickname, such as Wiggle, of former Sloane, now Fulham mummy, in chocolate moleskin coat, bought specially for this outing to the wild and woolly environs of a boutique hotel).

Then the husband will turn to Wiggle/Podge/Trinny with a horrible leer, leaving poor Ralph in no doubt that rekindling the flames of passion long extinguished by the harrowing demands of young children is very much "on the agenda" and "in the diary."

When Ralph tells me about these couples, having finally remembered who the pair are, or were, as I stand in the kitchen on the flagstones, by the Aga, in my Hunter wellies and green army jersey with suede patches at elbows and shoulders, making kedgeree, he does so with grim relish.

And we both hoot with scorn at the idea that Brambletye—with its cinemas and playrooms, its heated ozone pools, its highly variegated clientele (oh yes, Brambletye's owner likes to mix it up a little: he has the Primrose Hill set, the Notting Hill set, and the international jet set, all under one roof) and so forth—is The Country, as if it were quite normal to stay in houses with their own pillow menus and water menus and even their own "fire" menus, where guests are encouraged to select their own logs or coal from the house cellars.

Just as we honked with amusement when a Notting Hill friend who had just bought a pile in Oxfordshire as a second home announced he had "moved to the country."

He wrote a long, dewy piece that stretched to four thousand words, so lyrical it almost brought tears to the eyes, all about wanting to give his children an opportunity to dam streams and follow the hunt and breathe fresh, unpolluted clean air, never letting on to the readers of the *Telegraph* that he and his wife were spending the inside of the week in their trendy town house in W11 so that he could continue to run his publishing empire and the children could continue to attend their top London day schools.

Gah!

Anyway, back to Virginie's e-mail:

We miss you here on the garden, Lonsdale Gardens seem very quiet and tidy and peaceful *sans la famille* Fleming. And Clare is so absorb in her new baby, honestly, it is like *histoire* repeating, she in your house with baby Joe remind me so much of when you had Casimir, just the same curly hair, like the little Lord Fauntleroy! And Capucine and Clementine, they always are asking me, how are Casimir, Mirabel, and *la petite* Posy?

Now—I have a question!

Mathieu and I are very interested in a beautiful house our buying agent Catherine Faulks has seen, not too grand, only seven bedrooms, no more than 60 acres, somewhere outside Godminster. Is that near you guys?

Now the girls are starting at the Lycée, and I have sold BCBG to Bonpoint, though I am still consultant, we cannot travel to Soissons or Île de Rey so easily, and we are asking ourselves, maybe we buy a country house here instead or, even, as well! So, *dis-moi*—the "inside track" I beg of you. What is Godminster like? I have great friends there, *en fait,* but I would like to know from you, *comme* newcomers!

Bisous, Mimi, and a big embrace to Ralph and *les enfants*—I have a conference call with Louis Vuitton Moët-Hennessy scheduled, so I must run. But e-mail me quick—promise?

xxx

Ana has entered the kitchen.

She came in, saw me at the laptop, and without asking me if there was anything she could do, sat down at the table opposite me, opened a diary with a furry cover and padlock, and started writing in it with an extralong biro that ends in a fluffy yellow chick. And instead of leaping to my feet, briskly, to say, "Now, Ana," in a cozy-but-firm way, "shall we go over what your duties are now?" and then handing her a list and a schedule, like any other normal woman would, I sit there fuming. Which is utterly pathetic of me, I know.

Ana doesn't know there's no bread in the house, the milk is running out (Cas, aged twelve, is now called the "human bin" and shovels his food à la Shrek). She doesn't know where the larder is or when the children have supper. I've got to tell her.

Of course she hasn't come here so I can wait on her hand and foot. Of course she doesn't think she's come to Home Farm for a holiday.

At least I hope she doesn't.

So I smile at her, and say, "How nice that you write a diary! Most girls your age are writing explicit blogs about their colorful sex lives and posting them online."

"Yes?" says Ana, her biro with its furry chick motionless.

"Never mind," I say, still smiling, and realizing that if Ana had color in her cheeks, clean hair, and any expression whatsoever, she could be very pretty. "Can you make supper for the children? I'll show you round the kitchen and everything later, but there's a lasagna defrosting, and some peas in the freezer, and you could do some carrots. Why don't you pop the lasagna into the Aga now and lay the table?"

Ana looks blank at the word "Aga," but I am looking down at the e-mail from Virginie Lacoste with renewed concern, having taken in what the stone-cold French superfox is actually on about.

Why, of all the small market towns in the world in which to purchase a modest, four-million-pound country pile, does the "French lezzer," as I am afraid Mirabel calls Virginie, have to choose mine?

> To: maman@lacoste.com
> From: mimimalone@homefarm.com
> Lovely to hear from you, and great news about Bonpoint!
> As to your question—let me think . . . Godminster is just a little bit dull. For us, the big draw was Acland's, which is great, much better than the sink comp in Larmouth, but you'll be living mainly in London and using the Lycée, I presume, for the twins and Guy; schools won't be such an issue for you. You French have NO idea how lucky you are, with your education system. So it depends whether the West Country is your thing or not. Godminster's got a nice market on Saturdays, but the other shops are bog-standard and the Farmers' Market in Notting Hill Gate on Saturday morning has just as good suppliers, with the added bonus that it's in London, not two and half hours away from anywhere.
>
> The houses, especially the manor houses and small country estates, are jolly pricey, because it's near the Heritage or Jurassic Coast, etc., totally romantic and unspoiled. Dorset is the new Gloucestershire, not that price will put you off.
>
> To be honest, lovely though it would be of course to have you and Mathieu and the children so close, I'm not convinced that Godminster's really what you're looking for. But you should come and have a look and see for yourself.
>
> Do let me know if there's any more I can do, and send my love to Capucine, Clementine, Guy, and of course Mathieu.
>
> Mimi

Amusing to see that Virginie's radar for chic hasn't deserted her, I think as I press send on this highly misleading review of our local town. You wouldn't know it from my e-mail, but Godminster is, in fact, a haven for all sorts of successful creatives who seem determined to reinvent English country-house living for the modern, wireless, organic, anti-supermarket age—think the *Vogue* shoot of Madonna in Cecil Beaton's old house, all directional tweeds, ironic pearls, ponies, peonies, croquet, and cream tea served on the lawn in bone-china cups.

Also, why would I convey to Virginie the deep, bone-marrow joy of performing small physical tasks, like shelling peas or pegging out washing or kneading dough, joys I had no knowledge of before I fetched up in Home Farm?

When I make scones, or chop, or flap out sheets in the sweet, salt-washed breeze, it's as if I am recalling the collective muscle memory of all the housewives before me, for hundreds of years, who have done the same in this dear and ancient spot.

And I don't want *la* Virginie here, in her capri pants and little cardigans and silky swinging curtain of blond hair ruining it all. Do I?

Before picking up the children I sneak into the chemist, not the one I use on the main street, where the market is (too embarrassing—"Face it, Mum," as Mirabel said when she got her period for the first time, "you're now officially old enough to have grandchildren"). I pay cash for a First Response economy pack of two.

Belt home. Ana is there, as I had warned the children.

She smiles really sweetly at them when they all pop in like Champagne corks. Mirabel has her iPod on, and is clearly listening to one of her old favorites, by the laureates of lyrics called the Black-Eyed Peas.

"Mirabel," I call in a loud but pleasant voice. "Can you turn that off and say hello to Ana, darling! She's our new au pair girl."

"Hello, I am Ana," Ana says, coming forward to kiss them on both cheeks in a formal, somewhat East European way, making me think it's lucky they've all seen *Borat* and do not recoil in horror.

"Wow! Are you really, like, Ana?" says Mirabel, who has removed one earphone from her Nano as a concession. She sounds impressed, and looks Ana up and down.

There is something not quite right about this exchange, but then, I am so used to not understanding what Mirabel says or is cross about, I tend to let most of it pass. Mirabel sinks down at the kitchen table and replaces her earphone. "In the back and in the front! Check it out!"

Rush upstairs, rip open package with teeth, almost losing incisor in process, then read leaflet saying it can detect something called hCG in my urine up to four days before my period is due. At this point I pause.

I never know when it's due.

Does anyone who isn't trying to get pregnant as a vocation ever, actually, bother to keep track? It's been at least eight years since I even thought about all this.

In London, I was kept so busy monitoring Clare's ovulation schedule, I completely ignored mine.

The only way I can tell my period is due is because I start muttering out loud and flinging pans into the sink, while Ralph carries on reading *Country Life*. Then Ralph says something out loud to no one in particular about "that time of the month," before remarking that the Girl in Pearls in this week's edition is doing a thesis on renewable energy solutions including bioenergy yet again, and what on earth was wrong with a nice degree in Art History at Bristol, or working in the watercolor department at Sotheby's, he wants to know.

Then he says, "It's global warming," all of which cumulatively makes me scream, "Of course it's not that time of the month, I am merely sick to death of ALWAYS clearing up

EVERY MEAL on MY OWN and why shouldn't a SLOANE have a WORTHWHILE career in environmental technology if THAT'S WHAT SHE WANTS???"

Then, sure as night follows day, I have my period the next day.

I go ahead anyway and waste one of the two sticks, but, predictably, all I can detect in the results panel is a thick red line telling me I am NOT pregnant instead of two thick red lines.

I feel a flicker of disappointment, then I think—it's just as well, because I know for a certain fact that Ralph's world would crumble to dust if it were otherwise.

But then, just as I am wrapping the plastic stick in a paper towel in order to secrete it in a clotted-cream carton Calypso had been licking, before putting it in the black bag I've already bagged up, I notice this other, fainter line in the results window, which I peer at, hard, before stuffing it down in the rubbish.

I don't breathe a word of this to anyone—least of all Ralph. Though when we were clearing up supper and Ana was having a bath and the children were watching TV, I did say, "Er, Ralph, can I ask you something?" in a small, wondering voice.

But he snapped, "If it's something silly, no. I don't think I could take it. Especially if it's some New Age green is the new black bollocks."

It's a bore, but Ralph is in the middle of doing something utterly incomprehensible and dull to do with work, um, brokering the gas price between the Russians and the Ukrainians, I think, to maintain supplies to Western Europe.

All I know is that it means he's in a very bad mood and not a little ray of sunshine at all.

So I am keeping my trap shut for the mo, apart from having bravely steeled myself to call the surgery and make an appointment with Dr. Ashburton (hunts, v hairy ears), and doubtless all will become clear.

(1) I have to accept that Ralph has maintained absolute
consistency in his desire not to have further issue, and
(2) I feel very silly that I appear to have achieved, despite
this, the physical impossibility of being slightly pregnant.

I must call Rose.

Rose

Mimi calls and asks if I'll accompany her to the stables to see Gwenda Melplash to sort out riding for the children.

"Lovely though it always is to see you, but why?" I ask. "Are the stables that dangerous? Can't you go alone? Does it really require an escort?"

"I'm desperate to get out of the house," Mimi replies in a stage whisper. "Ana, the new au pair, Ana from Poland, has a pair of big pink slippers which make her legs look as if they end in a pair of piglets, and she wears them *all the time*."

"I see," I say.

"I know I sound horrible and critical but the slippers have an actual snout face with a smiley on each toe," Mimi continues. "I'm okay with Ana wearing high heels outside in the mud, but I don't know if I can take the novelty slippers. Not inside my own house."

Then she goes on to worry out loud over the phone that Ana has some sort of allergy to something in the house, which means she sniffs constantly and blows her nose. "And Mirabel thought that when Ana said, 'I am Ana,' the girl was announcing she was anorexic," Mimi continues, "so now Mirabel is in a huff because I laughed at her and is refusing to speak to Ana, who she says is a neek."

There is a pause. "What's a neek?"

"I don't know," I say. "I could always ask Ceci."

Mimi is telephoning from her bedroom, out of earshot. "So then I told Mirabel that any young girl who was prepared to give up the best years of her life living with us in the back of beyond's bound to be a little bit strange, and she should try to be nice to her, and Mirabel says, like a shot, 'Well, you're not nice to her and I heard you say horrid things about her behind her back to Dad when he came home, so why should I?'"

"Did you?" I ask, smoothing the embroidered linen runner on my dressing table and aligning my collection of cut-glass antique Guerlain scent bottles around a blowsy vase of peonies. "Thank God I only have Ceci," I say. I take the telephone and walk over to the windows and retie the swags on the bedroom curtains; they're so pretty, with toile de Jouy on one side and lined with cashmere on the other. "Even though having Pierre is like having a two-year-old in the house all the time, I've never needed help," I say, as if I do all my cleaning and child care myself, which I don't, because I have Joan, of course. "I could never bear to share my house with anyone who wasn't family and go through all that palaver. Nannies' egos and au pairs' period pains and homesickness, all of that. So exhausting."

"Please come with me," begs Mimi, "to the stables! Everyone here's either on horseback or in huge off-roaders; it's as if everyone's looking down on me . . . it makes me worry that the real reason everyone rides is so they can literally feel superior to the little people who don't. And, by the way, you know what I said in That New Place?"

"Yes," I say, alertly.

"Well, I think I am," she says, then lowers her voice, "pregnant," she whispers. "I did a test."

So of course I say yes. Not only is Mimi in need, she is also having entry problems to our closed rural community, and, as her only friend, I feel I should help.

We were in the village shop only yesterday, and Mrs. Hitchens was telling me in her happy voice, the one she reserves to impart bad news, that the horrible supermarket in Godminster was to close after thirty years of supplying locals with addictive substances and processed food past its sell-by date.

"But I didn't even realize there *was* a spa in Godminster," Mimi had exclaimed, loudly, excitedly. "I've been looking for somewhere to take care of my, you know, female admin for ages! I used to go to the Cowshed in Clarendon Cross, you know, next to Julie's" (this last bit was directed at me, rather than the red-faced rep from the feedstock supplier) "and now it's closed before I can even get a wax or a peel. Damn! Bang go my plans for Botox and nonsurgical liposuction. What a shame. Maybe I will go to that spelt spa after all."

You can imagine the looks on everyone's faces—Mrs. Hitchens and so on—while Mimi described the spelt spa in Somerset that she and Mirabel might be going to visit for some glossy magazine. Locals love nothing more than putting incomers— and since I've been here only ten years, I am still classed as one, and will be until my descendants have tilled the same soil for at least three centuries—back in their boxes.

But Mimi was oblivious. To her, coming from Lonsdale Gardens in the heart of Notting Hill, it was only to be expected that, in Godminster, darling emporia selling little earthenware dishes of wheat-free plum crumble with nutty all-butter topping and champ would outnumber even charity shops and pet suppliers. To her, coming from the chi-chi environs of Notting Hill, where you need to take out a small mortgage just to buy lunch and a new coat costs the same as an IKEA kitchen, it was to be expected that the local town could supply her with somewhere she could repose in peace, listening to Enya or Clannad while some young woman in a white coat whipped her winter coat from her legs, rather than a neon-lit shop selling Rizlas and Tennent's lager.

"Have you noticed, Rose," Mimi continued, unaware of the audience in the Stores, "that when you have anything done now at a spa, they don't call it a treatment anymore? They're called rituals, or journeys, as if after you've done your eyebrow tweezing, you'll be *somewhere else entirely*," she shrieked. "Isn't it utterly ridiculous?"

At this point Celia Bryanston, Ned's widowed mother, the Dowager of Godminster Hall, who had been studying a jumbo box of Baker's Complete Meaty Meals intently during all this, grabbed Mimi with a clawlike arm.

"And who are you?" Celia B asked Mimi.

Mimi preened, as if she had been recognized by a fan. "I'm Mimi Fleming, though I did use to have a column in the *Telegraph*, under my maiden name, er, which is Mimi Malone," Mimi answered.

"Mimi Malone?" Celia roared, in a voice much bigger than her wizened frame suggested was possible. "Or Mimi Fleming? Do make your mind up, gel!"

Celia went to open the freezer section, removed a Cottage Catering frozen sticky toffee pudding for one, and dropped it into her basket. "Never heard of you. Either of you." Then Celia left the shop, still carrying the basket, and Mrs. Hitchens rolled her eyes and shouted, "You've left without paying again, Mrs. Bryanston."

So, after I hang up, I leave the bedroom and duck into my dressing room to change out of my Spanish riding boots, and out of my specially selected vintage tweed pencil skirt edged with suede piping, and a cashmere cardie. (All men absolutely love the new Duchess of Windsor prim, even proto-eco-hippies like Jesse Marlon; it's a banker of a look, but it wouldn't do at the stables.)

I walk downstairs now wearing a herringbone-tweed skirt and a blue poplin pin-tucked blouse from Toast, and, as luck would have it, Jesse Marlon is standing in the hall. I saunter down, holding his gaze, without even, in fact, trying to hide the fact that I am staring at him.

We are doing quite a lot of staring moodily at each other at the moment, in the barns, or in the kitchen, while Pierre, of course, notices nothing, being completely wrapped up in himself, and even seems to think Jesse Marlon might welcome news of some minor digestive complaint, or the fact that a new delivery of stone has arrived, and that Pierre is exploring in his work the possibilities of "making body into sky."

We'd been shifting some boxes earlier, before Mimi called.

JM mentioned he'd seen *Prime*, this movie about how Uma Thurman starts dating a man in his twenties.

"Oh, is that on in Godminster?" I'd asked, my antennae twitching. "But I thought that came out a while ago."

"No, saw the DVD," he replied. I was on my knees, pinning up my thick skeins of brown hair, which was falling into my eyes as we crouched over the fruit laid out on the barn floor for the chutney, chucking out bad apples into a crate. My tweed pencil skirt had ridden quite far up my thighs, as I thought it might. "I didn't quite get it, the concept, the pitch, or whatever," said Jesse Marlon. "It was supposed to be, like, transgressive because the guy's in his twenties. But she's a total hottie in her thirties. That's not what I call transgressive." He gave me a lazy look, which left me slightly flustered. "Young guy. Uma Thurman. What's not to like?"

Then he did a very poor imitation of Uma Thurman: "But I've got T-shirts older than you!" he squeaked, chucking a rotten russet into the bad-apple bucket with a flick of his wrist.

"I didn't think you had electricity at Spodden's Hatch," I'd said. "Let alone a DVD player or home cinema or whatever."

Jesse Marlon has often described the eco-village's alternative, low-impact lifestyle to me in detail, and, from what I gather, it's all very extreme and Amish. No fossil fuels or internal combustion engines are used, so they scythe rather than strim, the self-built houses on the site are thatched with self-grown wheat, and they eat only what they grow themselves, apart from grains and nuts, which come from a bulk organic distributor; even the milk and yogurt come from Lazy and Daisy, Spodden's milkers. There's even talk of a biomass boiler.

"We don't," he replied shortly. "Watched it at Court Place. In the media room."

I tried not to feel slighted, but I did, just at the mention of Court Place. Apart from Hutton and Godminster Hall, Court Place is the other big spread around here, probably a thousand acres, and it's owned by Cath and Granville Cobb. It's exactly down to the last particular how you would imagine a spread owned and run by an American dynamo married to a British hedge funder to be; it has wonderful plumbing, clockwork catering, manicured grounds, and yet no mud or pee stains on the carpets. As Pierre noted, after one of Cath's Lawn Meets, Court Place is a perfect Anglo American country house in that it fuses the best aspects of both cultures. It's half a mile outside the village, the Lar runs through the place, and it's lapped in luxury, but not in an offensively plutocratic way.

Annoyingly, I muse on my way to the stables, I didn't even know there *was* a media room at Court Place. Cath is always doing things, changing things round, converting barns and installing libraries, and it's also so bloody big that if you want to ask someone something, it's quicker to call them on their mobile. In Cath's case, as her family and friends are often over from Marin County, this often means placing an international call from the Court Place kitchen to a Californian mobile in order to tell someone in the orangery that it's lunchtime. Also, the very fact that they have a media room is, though I hate to say it, rather vulgar. We're in West Dorset. Not the West Coast.

So my hackles rather rise, even though I know that, in fact, Granville would only penetrate the media room in the old granary to watch *Chariots of Fire*, which he says is so good that he prefers to watch it over and over again, tears welling in time to the stirring thumps of the Vangelis sound track, rather than to watch a wintry, Turkish film with subtitles about a couple's disintegrating marriage that's not even set in Istanbul.

And it also annoys me how Cath had nabbed Jesse Marlon.

No doubt her plan is to get him together with that daughter of hers, who's just left Exeter university. Serena. Blond, skinny, glossy, now works in magazine PR.

I bet they watched *Prime* together in the media room on huge suede bean bags that Cath designs herself or on sofas covered with enormous furry throws, with that reindeer-skin floor covering from the Rug Company, but I do not trust myself, not now I have feelings for Jesse Marlon, to ask.

At the yard, girls in jodhpurs the color and patina of field mushrooms, black boots, and navy fleeces circle about with saddles and hats. Mimi and I stand uncertainly as stable girls and grooms lead bulgy ponies and nostrilly horses in and out of a ring, saddles and sweaty numnahs tucked under capable arms. No one takes any notice of us. "Does Gwenda know you're coming?" I ask, suddenly nervous myself.

"No," says Mimi. "Does that matter? Does one need to make an appointment, months in advance, through her PA?"

I can see her point. The Honeyborne Stables and Livery Yard doesn't look very organized. It consists of a farmhouse, where Gwenda lives (no garden—gardening is uninteresting to most people who farm and ride), a large barn, empty save for the obligatory carcasses of several dead cars resting on bricks, and the stables. Empty oil cans litter the dirt floor, along with sacks, cans and bottles, old newspapers, car entrails, and the grot and grime of a hundred years.

"Why do people in the country never throw anything away?" I say to Mimi as we both take in the usual barnyard scene, and I feel like averting my eyes. "Have they no visual sense whatsoever?"

Over by the stables, though, it is a different story, and I mentally withdraw my comment. Here it is quiet professionalism.

Girls are hosing and mucking out and swabbing docks and grooming while murmuring endearments to the animals.

"They look much glossier and healthier than the rural poor, don't they?" muses Mimi.

"Of course they do," I answer. "They have a perfectly bal-
anced diet of oats and hot bran and plenty of exercise, whereas
the poor have to get by on a diet of rusk and lard and sugar and
offcuts, which are then shaped into disgusting and unnourish-
ing economy meals. Speaking of diet, are you feeling okay? Any
strange cravings?"

"Just even hungrier and tireder than usual." Mimi sighs as
we approach the front door to the farmhouse.

Dogs rush out at our approach, barking, and then swarm up
to press damp noses in our crotches—a black Labrador, a Jack
Russell, and a border terrier. We are by now at the porch of
Gwenda's house, a white, two-story farmhouse with horrid new
windows with metal panes, a look that Ceci, who is, like me,
very visually aware, calls "homesick windows."

We navigate the usual muddy clutter of wellies, soiled trainers, slippers, and chaps on the porch, tangled up with old Barbours and hacking jackets, and I wonder why Gwenda doesn't
invest in a boot rack—the Holding Company does a nice one.
So does RH Allison.

RING BELL it commands above a sign that details the nature
of the rides all ages and all levels can safely undertake, hard hats
provided: coastal, in the manège, at hunts, and on the moor.
PLEASE PAY BEFORE LESSON.

I nudge Mimi, to alert her to this edict, which seems to suggest that riding lessons are either so dull or so frightening that
many will be tempted to ditch and do a runner halfway through.
She pulls a pantomime face.

She rings the bell, and I lurk behind her. Gwenda is a woman
who relates well to animals but, like many countrywomen who
prefer the company of dumb beasts to humans, calls a spade a
spade and is thus known with both accuracy and some affection
as "Scary Gwenda."

There is an interval, and then I hear footsteps coming down
the stairs.

"What do you want?" demands Gwenda, scarily, her black

hair tied back, a tattersall checked shirt loosely tucked into filthy jodhpurs. She is in socked feet. At the sight of her, all dogs come whining, and she caresses their heads, and I see them nibble little treats from pockets, out of her brown hand.

And what I also see: a flash of male legs in jeans go past on the landing, a flash that Gwenda sees that I see, but she gives no sign to show us she is aware there is a Man Upstairs in Her House in the Middle of the Day. My eyes flicker back to her face. Her eyes are very blue, and her face has that all-weather skin of the real countrywoman who spends all day every day outside, working in the wind and the sun and the rain, with no thought for the dermatological consequences nor supporting the antiaging industry whatsoever. She presents herself to the world without artifice or apology.

Mimi explains the reason for her visit, and Gwenda gives her an appraising blue stare that starts at Mimi's curly hair, travels past her Husky and V-neck M&S sweater, down to the baggy-fit jeans and clean green Hunter wellies (hardly anyone wears green wellies, but since Mimi arrived in Dorset, hers have barely left her feet. I don't have the heart to tell her they mark her out as a townie).

Then Gwenda says, "Have the children ridden much before? Hunted?"

"Well, Posy has had a few months puttering about on a pony," says Mimi, relieved that negotiations appear to have started. "The Bodens handed him down to us when we arrived." She looks at Gwenda narrowly to see whether the name-drop has blipped on Gwenda's sonar, but, if it has, Gwenda gives no sign. "But now Posy's shot up, we're wondering whether she should have some proper lessons, and maybe keep on Trumpet . . ."

At the mention of the name Trumpet, Gwenda's eyes narrow into slits. It's as if she has Mimi in her sights.

"Pony? Gray Shetland?" She rattles out the question like gunshot.

"Well, I thought he was a white Exmoor," says Mimi.

"Mm," says Gwenda. A vulpine look has come across her face, as if she is on the scent of a quarry. "It's the rufty-tufty ponies that make the best hunters, not the smartly bred ones. Tell you what, Mrs. Fleming, I could use him for the hunt, for the youngsters, to start off their hunting careers."

Then she goes on to talk about Trumpet for some time: "The first time he saw hounds he was on his tiptoes . . . as soon as we moved off he was fine . . . good little jumper . . . bit small but goes like the clappers . . . really used his head," and so on. Then she finishes, "Some ponies, they've been passed from so many hunting families that it's a job remembering who are the actual owners . . . they become the hunt's unofficial property."

She gives Mimi a look designed to ascertain whether Mimi has understood her point, which is that the fact that Trumpet is the much-loved Fleming-slash-Boden family pony, indeed, a member of their family and beloved pet, is mere detail. As a perfect hunting pony, he by rights belongs to her . . . to the hunt.

Even Mimi knows where this is heading. "No problem," she says. "Trumpet's not seeing a lot of action at the moment, Mrs. Melplash."

"Gwenda," said Gwenda. "And it's not Mrs."

"I'm sure it would be okay for you to borrow Trumpet for the hunt, erm, Gwenda," says Mimi. "I'll just check it with Posy, but I don't think she'll mind."

Gwenda looks privately triumphant, and there is a steely glint in her eye as she sees us off the premises.

"I'm beginning to think I've got this whole country thing down," Mimi says, in a satisfied voice, as we walk back, on the road, in a slight drizzle. I am wondering whether Jesse Marlon will still be in the house, or whether he will have gone back to Spodden's Hatch. "I've definitely swung a major discount on riding lessons for the children now, don't you think?"

"I don't think so at all," I reply. "I think you'll be paying twenty-five pounds an hour along with all the other suckers in the bed-and-breakfasts along the Jurassic Coast, and I also think you've just been pony-napped in broad daylight. As soon as Gwenda gets her hands on Trumpet, Posy will never see him again. Gwenda is a force of nature. She is not to be underestimated. She gets what she wants, and she wants what she gets." What I don't say to Mimi is that when Gwenda was less scary and more pretty, in her thirties, she went through most of the able-bodied men in the village like a dose of salts. So Gwenda and I have more in common than might at first appear. We have Henry Pike, for a start. And I've always wondered about her and Sir Michael . . .

"Oh God, I hope you're wrong," Mimi says. "Posy adores Trumpet! Oh yes, did you see who was upstairs at Gwenda Towers while I was being pony-napped?"

"Yes," I say. And then, even though I'm not sure the village tom-tom has filled Mimi in yet as to my terrible reputation as scarlet woman, I say, "Even though, like most men around here, I only recognized him from the waist down."

Mimi

Back from the stables. It's pouring with rain, I'm in the kitchen again, and I've just noticed that, even though it's noon, it's still dark. In fact, I don't think I've seen sunlight for days and I've got SAD. Now I understand why everyone seems to rush to the pub at lunchtime for a quick one and even Rose starts wondering whether it's time for the early evening "vodcast" even before *PM* has finished, as early as around 5:30 P.M. on really dark days . . . although she claims she holds off till *The Archers* . . . and these are, face it, dark days.

What I've realized since moving to Dorset is . . . this, I suppose.

The past isn't a foreign country. The country is a foreign country. In London, you have much more in common with residents of Manhattan, or L.A., or Tokyo, or Hong Kong, than you do with English people who live two miles from a metaled road and kill their own pigs.

A while ago, I was in the car—it was a rare sunny day, so I had my shades on—with all the children and even, I think, Spike, Sophy's son, from the eco-village, Spodden's Hatch, on the way to school. I was singing along to Mika on the CD changer, just past the signs that said, PLEASE DRIVE CAREFULLY THROUGH OUR VILLAGE and ENGLISH CHEDDAR 2 MILES NEW ZEALAND CHEDDAR 11,680 MILES, and this woman on horseback *overtook* me.

She was in Harry Hall jodhpurs with two children behind her, Indian file, in hacking jackets and hard hats, on glossy, high-stepping, chestnut ponies.

I was driving at a crawl through Chesilborne in a muddy Subaru, not hurtling past in a gleaming Land Cruiser, so I thought I was safe from abuse.

But she leaned over, through the open window of the Forester. "Don't any of them ride?" she blared, as if she was inviting me to join some strange cult (which I suppose she was). Then she said something like, "You should join gug," chirruped, "Trot on, trot on!" and I watched her neat rear end bob up and down as she went off in a rising trot with her brood.

In London, parenting is a competitive sport—but here, competitive sports are a competitive sport, and there is nothing more highly prized than physical stamina, guts, and strength, and a mother who jumps eight hedges before breakfast out hunting has a lot more street cred than one who jumps through all the hoops to make sure Poppy gets into Ponsonby Prep. (Found out later who Trot On was: Biddy Pike, district commissioner of Pony Club, mainstay of Pony Camp, married to Henry, referred to as "the master"; she was doing the school run to Chesilborne First School, which gives days off for meets, *on horseback*. I was also told, in tones of amazement that I wasn't a founder member myself, that "gug" is Biddy's own one-woman campaign to get Dorset in the saddle, and is short for Giddy Up Godminster.)

Then I felt my mobile vibrate as I was pulling up at the school. A text. It was from Mirabel. "I h8t u pls take off the puffy thing."

I first looked down to see whether I had my Husky on. I didn't think I was wearing it. But I was. It's become a second skin. I took my glasses off and sought Mirabel's eyes in the rearview mirror to signal apology, but my eldest daughter was staring flintily out of the window, refusing to meet my gaze.

So. "Don't any of them ride?" Well, I suppose that question

sums up why I've been to the stables with Rose all morning instead of working on my new idea.

My new idea is to write a total holistic handbook—i.e., it'll cover everything from exercise to household tips to menus—to help weedy and wet townie women like me survive the bracing transition to rural bliss. It'll be a brilliant mix of the Low Carbon Diet, all those recycle-your-own-compost, hip-to-be-squire books, combined with Scheherazade Goldsmith's slice-of-organic-life handbook, plus recipes and many lush color photos of gorgeous slinky Lulu Bryanston (the only babe in the village) in a bikini and wellies, i.e., a guaranteed mega-seller in this market, for the zillions of people who don't just want the Good Life, they want it to be cutting edge, too.

I'm keeping it under wraps for the moment, just working out themes, but, mainly, I'm thinking about riding.

And, actually, I don't think that I'm up for it. Horses frighten me, with their rolling eyeballs and flaring nostrils and lashing hooves and that alarming sense they convey—with a twitch of a hindquarter, of extreme violence held in check—that twelve hours of neurosurgery and months in rehab are a mere flick away.

(1) There's my possible condition but, (2) I can't help thinking of all the mothers sitting in care homes dribbling for the rest of their lives after their horses pitched them headfirst on to concrete aged just forty.

I have to weigh those factors against the brute reality that not riding is a crushing disability in itself, and not having children who ride in Dorset is almost worse than not being able to drive in L.A., i.e., it's total social exclusion.

Last year, I swanked to Marguerite back in Lonsdale Gardens—I suppose I wanted it to get back to everyone on the communal garden—that we were in clover and it was all peachy and that all the children were hunting all the time with the Bodens (of lamby, funnel-necked-fleeces fame) and it was all a tremendous, rip-roaring success.

Well, I lied!

The truth is, Trumpet, Posy's pony (well, to be strictly honest, he was handed down to us by the Bodens, but we consider him ours now) just wanders about the paddock and the orchard eating windfalls and getting fat, just like me, really. Then, last Sunday I met this woman after church—Ralph says church is nonnegotiable—when I was in the graveyard having a lovely time deciding where I wanted to be buried (graveyard plots in select churchyards are a bit like pushy London private schools; you have to secure your place ages before you actually need it). She looked me up and down, the way country people do when they meet you for the first time, as if you are a hill-bred suckled calf at a livestock sale.

"If you move to Dorset," she said, moving out of earshot of the vicar, the Reverend Wyldbore-Smith, who was merrily gurning at parishioners and pumping their hands, "it's shag, drink, or ride," at which my heart naturally sank, and then she whinnied, "or in my case, all three! Hee-hee!"

I have to admit, on mornings like this, in the rain, I'm finding this whole transition to becoming fully pastoralized . . . a lot harder than I thought. And lonely. So another thing I miss, lots and lots is . . . my old social life, and, as for spontaneity, it's gone out of the window.

Leaving the house for anything is like a Territorial Army expedition, and I always have those little news stories at the back of my mind about climbers on Snowdonia, or wherever, who, the papers sniff, never had the "appropriate equipment" and who set out for the summit "in trainers" in "worsening weather conditions" and without sat nav, compasses, or supplies, as if leaving home without Kendal mint cake were an indictable offense and it was all their fault, as if they were determined to waste taxpayers' money and bother the air ambulance service rather than have a healthful hike in the open air. So any venturing forth requires a minimum of three pairs of shoes and five cagoules, and, if you're going to someone else's house, it's quite normal to come in wellies and then change into slippers, even for a dinner party—and the very few we've been to of those are a sort of three-day event.

We drive for hours in rain like stair rods, and then drink like fish to get through it, and plow our way through soggy quiche followed by damp apple tart with cries of "You are clever, what wonderful pastry" (no way of staying carb—let alone carbon—neutral in the countryside), and stay at least four hours, three of which are consumed with conversation about hunting or who's not speaking to whom or the reclassification of roads used as public paths. Then I have a row with Ralph about which one of us is going to lose our license in order to drive home blind drunk in the pitchy blackness. So, a dinner party basically means driving for two hours to meet exactly the same people, and talk about exactly the same things (you always meet the same people because if anyone gives a dinner party, word quickly gets around and everyone feels mortally insulted if they are not invited, with the result that the same cast of characters convenes monthly, only in different houses, which are all alike in one respect—they are at least half an hour's drive away and cold as tombs). And then, at our age, it takes at least one whole day to recover from the alcoholic overload. It's got to the stage—I put it down to the grueling commute to London, the fact that his new job is really pressurized with the Russian situation re oil and gas and something called the interconnector, whatever that is—where Ralph's only truly happy when the Met issues one of its extreme-weather warnings telling people not to make journeys unless they are strictly necessary. He doesn't seem to get it when I tell him I'll drive any distance, walk over coals, wade through raging torrents, simply to avail the Fleming family of a hot meal I haven't had to cook and clear up after myself. Especially now I'm not within spitting distance of seven world-class delis and have to cook every meal from scratch using challenging nose-to-tail ingredients from the village shop, like turnips and marrowbone.

It was tough enough getting Ralph out of the house in London. If something required any effort on his part, i.e., if during an evening he was obliged to have some sort of exchange with a mummy about her child's special needs or a daddy about his funds under management, he would complain for hours after. It was only if he surprised himself by actually enjoying it—mainly because he had found some soul mate to talk about fly-fishing with—would Ralph warm up. "Painless," he might say or, if he'd really enjoyed himself, "entirely painless."

Now, when I moan about anything, such as mess or the cleaning or the driving, Ralph just says, in that way men do when they think there's a slight risk of having to do something on the home front themselves, "Well, get someone to do the cleaning for you," or "Just buy it all from M&S," as if, ta-da! the dreaded dinner party was sorted, and as if no one had ever had the idea to get a cleaner or buy a prepared meal ever before in the history of mankind. But the problem is, though I'd love to believe in cleaners, I suspect they don't exist here for people like me (i.e., those whose houses actually need cleaning), and now I have Ana, I am probably going to be banned from complaining entirely.

When London friends ring—which is admittedly fairly infrequently—they drawl, "So . . . where exactly are you in Dorset?" in bored voices, as if they know this terrain like the back of their hand. I don't bother to explain. I just say, we're about forty years west of London, which is about right.

Nor do I have anyone to VENT to. There's no book group, there's no yoga group, there's only the pudding club, the pub, and the Women's Institute, which I haven't joined.

It was funny; Clare's next e-mail in reply to my LibDem manifesto one asked me to describe what it's "really like" in Honeyborne, as if I'd been glossing over reality. This is a bit like when friends ask, "But how are you REALLY?" as if they will feel personally, deeply let down unless you can produce, exclusively for them, some report of a recent emotional disaster. Well. Whinge over. Better now. The truth is, wild horses wouldn't drag me back to London, and Ralph knows it.

Rose

Next day, Mimi and I are walking Calypso, after the school run, before the magic hour when Jesse Marlon appears at the Dairy. There's a small crowd outside the Stores. We draw near, as if being pulled by magnetic force. It looks as if something might—for once—be actually happening.

"Two and a half hours, in the cells," Biddy Pike is saying, flushed with all the attention. She does not glance at me as I approach, but I am not deterred.

Mimi has Calypso on a lead. Calypso is greeted with obvious pleasure by all the other dogs, but hardly anyone else even nods when we join the group. There is a somber mood. Mimi and I exchange a glance. Biddy Pike's reputation, like mine, precedes her in this village, only in a different way.

"Have you noticed—the rare moments that she's not on a horse, that is—that she walks leaning forward, as if into the teeth of a gale?" asked Mimi, after she had inspected her the first couple of times. "I am beginning to think she doesn't have feet. I think she might have *hooves*."

When Ceci fell off her pony on her first day out with Gwenda and Biddy, it was Biddy who rang me to say that she would be fine and back in the saddle in no time, as it was "just a scratch." When I rushed to Godminster General, heart thudding, I found Ceci—my *baby*—sitting in Casualty with a bone sticking out of her wrist, with Biddy, as if butter wouldn't melt in her mouth, who just gave me a stare as if to say, "So?" And I couldn't scream and run at her.

Anyway, be that as it may, I now tug at the sleeve of Colin Watts, the leggy, mostly silent mainstay of the Honeyborne cricket team, who is eating a Crunchie in that male, nonchalant way that men do, as if they eat chocolate bars all the time, whereas women do these things as if they are a private, secret indulgence, like reading the *Daily Mail* or masturbating. Colin Watts is one of those people one sees everywhere. He always wears jeans and a heavy leather jacket and work boots, and he usually has a cigarette in his hand. I've even seen him around with the now-adult Cobb sons, Florian and Marco and Hector (Cath must have had a Venice theme going on in her child-bearing years).

"What's going on? Who's in the cells? Everyone seems very up in arms," I say, deliberately not directing my question at Biddy, so Colin Watts answers me.

"Police came at sparrow's fart," he explains, "and arrested Pike, that's what. Took him all the way into Dorchester, loike." At this point Colin Watts pauses for effect. To him, a trip to Dorchester (eighteen miles away) is never an expedition to be undertaken lightly, and the great distance to the destination underlined the high seriousness of the charges. "For questioning." He suddenly makes a circling, whirling movement with his right arm, and I realize—he's practicing his bowling. He is a keen cricketer. In fact, I think he opens the bowling for the village side, and is quite a useful bat, too.

Mrs. Hitchens has a tremendous glint in her eye. There's nothing she likes more than a crisis. Biddy looks as if she might explode, it's all so exciting.

Even Mr. Hitchens, who never likes being parted from his hairy courgettes for long, has left his kitchen garden to join the throng by the growbags in the little cobbled yard just outside the shop.

So after about twenty minutes' gabbling, we gather that

Henry Pike, the master of foxhounds of ten distinguished years' standing, husband of Biddy, pillar of the community, father of two constantly referenced border terriers, Jiggy and Frisky, otherwise known as the "borderline terrorists," and two children, Flavia and Harry (rarely mentioned), and, last but not least, a member of the Independent Working Group on Snares and Traps—in other words, on paper at any rate, no more up-standing citizen in the whole of Dorset—was woken at 6 A.M. and arrested. Handcuffed, he was read his rights and taken to Dorchester Police Station to be interviewed by Dorset CID.

Separately, his whipper-in, Martin Thomas, was also interviewed, and the two were placed in locked cells for three hours before being released on bail.

"As the law stands," Biddy finishes, sweeping the whole audience with a steely gaze, "a fox has more legal rights than my own law-abiding, tax-paying husband."

There follows a general murmur of contempt for the administration that has spent seven hundred hours debating hunting with hounds while farmers went to the wall . . . taken us to war with Iraq . . . put speed cameras on all our roads . . . banned smoking in pubs . . . taxed flying . . . allowed the supermarkets to fleece English producers . . . failed to abolish inheritance tax . . . allowed foreign workers to take our jobs and immigrants our houses . . . and generally set this once great nation on the fast track to hell in a handcart.

"But I still don't understand! What've they been arrested *for?*" Mimi asks, revealing her almost fathomless ignorance of country ways and concerns.

"Breaches of the Hunting Act," Colin replies shortly.

"Ooh, don't say 'breaches' like that," says Clive Maddocks, the Court Place butler, who is openly gay, and everyone groans.

"It's Section One, innit?" Colin carries on, trying not to sound intelligent, in case he is teased, a legacy from having attended Honeyborne First School and the chavvy secondary in

Larmouth and not Acland's, which is seemingly reserved for nice middle-class children like Ceci and Mirabel and Cas and Posy. "A person commits an offense if he hunts a wild mammal with a dog."

At which point Biddy looks, if possible, even fiercer than usual. Her eyes are gleaming, and her blood is up. I see—though I hate to admit it—that she is a fine-looking woman. She never misses a day out with either the foxhounds or the staghounds, which means she is on horseback or behind a trailer pretty much continuously, what with Pony Club and having two children who ride, and all the hacking and cubbing and hunting and point-to-points on a daily basis.

"Joddies off!" I can hear her cry now at the gates of Honeyborne First School. She used to clatter up with a muddy-looking Flavia and little Harry—barely out of nappies—in the car. "Unies on! Come on, Flaves! Hurry up, Harry! Spit spot!" Biddy was, of course, turned out in hunting rig, right down to a white stock and mud-spattered haunches, having already taken her five- and seven-year-old cubbing for a couple of hours, whereas the rest of us had barely crawled out from our bedclothes. Henry is also almost continuously on horseback, apart from when he is taking outside rides, which I used to find terribly attractive. It was something about the straddling and the sweating, not to mention the gleaming cavalry-officer boots and his buttocks in jodhpurs. Anyway, I just had to have him. And I did.

He came round, one morning, when Pierre was in the studio.

I opened the door and he was just showered, just shaved, and wearing a blazer, and he looked like a prep-school boy ready to read the lesson on Sunday. I almost shut the door. I realized—but too late—that I found him attractive only when he was mounted, with a sheen up. Henry had the bit between his teeth, though, and said I had been asking for it, and now it was time for my "daily service," and he hoped I was ready, and that he didn't see why that slacker Pierre should enjoy "sole grazing rights" over me, whatever that meant. So I went through with it, with eyes closed, trying to pretend we were lying on bracken in a cleeve, while the hounds scurried and yapped about us, and our horses munched on sweet Dorset grass, rather than in my cloudy white bed . . . and then, to my surprise and Henry's satisfaction, I came like the proverbial train.

"Yes, Colin, thank you for your expertise," Biddy broke in crisply, interrupting my reverie. I had just got to the bit in my recollection of that inglorious episode where Biddy realized where Henry was. His Fourtrak was at the Dairy, parked round the back, keys in the ignition.

Instead of coming upstairs and catching us in flagrante, she simply removed the keys from the ignition and threw them in the Lar. So when Henry came down he was forced to telephone Biddy from my house and beg her to bring the spare set from the dresser at Lower Foxcombe, so his humiliation was complete.

"But you've forgotten the most important five words of the entire act," Biddy now continues. "A person commits an offense if he hunts a wild mammal with a dog. Unless. His. Hunting. Is. Exempt."

Mimi is fascinated.

"It really is amazing, all this, Rose," she says, pulling at my sleeve. "What I now see is that the Hunting Act has given a tremendous fillip to the countryside simply by making it illegal." She observes this as if no one has ever noticed this paradox before. "In just one muddle-headed act of Parliament, the Labour Party has contrived to make the ancestral pastimes of hunting and shooting and fishing cool, something the Royal Family has seemingly made impossible for hundreds of years."

I start remembering something else about Henry Pike, and tune out, while Mimi warms to her theme.

"Everyone from Kate Moss downwards is doing rock star rural now . . . Alex James . . . Daylesford Organics . . . Damien Hirst . . . Eric Clapton and fly-fishing . . . Guy Ritchie and Madonna . . ." (I'm just giving the main points and name checks) "and Ralph told me that there's a company called Deerstalking .com that has its Land Rovers all parked in Lansdowne Road! I really think there might be a feature in how celebrities are *going back to the land,* or think they are. I'm going to ring the *Telegraph* and offer them an exclusive"—her eyes shine—"from the horse's mouth. When I get back to Home Farm," she announces generally, "I'll ring up and offer them a Mimi Malone special on the trend of Rock Star Rural. I'll try Will, that's Will Lewis, the editor. Or darling Sue Crewe at *House and Garden.* I know her, quite well actually. And I could use some pin money. And Sue's utter bliss. You should meet her, Rose, what with your hampers and apple crisps and the Dairy—it's a Condé Nast wet dream!"

Watts takes a packet of Rothmans from his pocket during Mimi's luvvie outburst. He has rather elegant hands, even if his forefinger is nicotine-stained. I notice Gwenda watching him, rather than Mimi, like a hawk. I haven't seen anyone smoking Rothmans for years. I thought the land's few remaining smokers all smoked Marlboro Lights or Silk Cut.

But then, as I know, products you haven't seen for years, like condensed milk, Camp coffee essence, tinned mandarin segments, butterscotch Angel Delight, Fray Bentos pies— things one assumed died a retail death some time in the reign of George V—are among the only items available for purchase in the remote parts of Dorset.

"Sorry, but did Henry and Martin Thomas actually, um, break the Hunting Act, or are they just being made examples of?" Mimi asks, while I move out of the way as Watts lights up and puffs at me, in case I die of passive smoking and smell like a pub used to . . . for Jesse Marlon.

"It doesn't seem fair if they were hunting within the law . . . and with all these exemptions . . . I don't see how the police had the right to arrest them. I didn't think that hunting was a crime even if it did breach the Hunting Act, I thought it was, you know—"

"Nonrecordable," finishes Biddy. "It is. It means you don't get a criminal record; it's like a traffic offense."

"So why were they arrested then?" Mimi asks desperately. "I still don't understand."

"Put it this way," Colin Watts pronounces, throwing his Rothman into a busy lizzie, from where it is instantly fished out by Greg Hitchens (inordinately proud of Honeyborne's Best Kept Village citation, won a few years ago, an honor for which he took full credit).

"Mrs. . . . ?"

"Er, Fleming."

"Put it this way, Missus Fleming. Say you saw a puppy in the parlor. And a great steaming pile of puppy shit right next to it. Would you think the puppy was responsible, like, for the shit, or would you think the puppy had nothing to do with it?"

"Oh, do shut your trap, Colin Watts," says Gwenda fiercely. But I notice her eyes are glittering and she still stares at him, as I used to stare at Henry Pike, in the buildup to the daily service, that is, when he used to ride his stallion into the Stores to pick up his copy of *Horse and Hound*.

Clutching a cold pint of Court Place milk in a wide-mouthed glass bottle, I say good-bye to Mimi and walk slowly back up the hill to the Dairy. Everyone has dispersed, back to the stables and the feed store and Horse Supplies, and retreated for tea and HobNobs, or for morning coffee at the pub.

Several pickups and Land Rovers hurtle past me, and then one car slows.

It is Garry, the publican, in his Honda Civic. He stops the car and winds down his passenger's-side window by hand.

"Mrs. Musgrove," he says.

"Garry?"

"Well, oi don't know what to say 'n' all, but I think I should say . . ." Garry looks at the dashboard, suddenly shy.

"What, Garry? Say what?" I say crisply. I am long used to

village gossip, advice, kindly warnings, and so on, all of which is, I feel, a form of jealousy for my being prepared to take what I want—behave like a man, in other words.

"Well, I wouldn't if I was you," he said darkly.

"Wouldn't what?"

And then Garry tells me, in brutal language, this awful story.

It was about what sounded like a particularly nasty rape. " 'E 'ad her both ways, if you gets moy meaning," Garry says.

As he speaks, his eyes watch my face very closely and, at its conclusion, he runs a tongue hungrily over his lips, as if he's just eaten a sugar-covered doughnut. I want to run away, very fast up the hill to the Dairy, but that isn't the worst of it.

"Look, Mrs. Musgrove," he goes on. "Don't get me wrong. Like yous, I've never bin one to say no to a spot of malarkey misself, her-her." He sniggers and gives me a filthy, suggestive look. I wonder what on earth the village gossip about me currently is, given that nothing—yet—has happened with Jesse Marlon. "But you've got a young 'un at home, if I've understood correctly. A young, teenage girl." That tongue comes out again. "I'm not saying nothing about nobody, but if I was you, I wouldn't have that Colin Watts anywhere near moy house, if you get moy drift."

Feeling a bit dazed, I press on. I can't think what Garry from the pub is on about, or why he has told me this revolting story about Colin Watts. Why me? It doesn't make any sense. Colin Watts doesn't seem the type, and I'm a pretty good judge. I decide that Garry from the pub has made an early start at the Badger ale, in order to be ahead of his regulars when they arrive at lunchtime.

When I get home, I spend some time in the barns. Then I go through the front door, as I have been checking the beds in the front garden, using my key, rather than going through the back door, which is always left open, unless we're away.

The black-and-white-tiled hall is tidy, and just warm enough to linger in without going straight through to the kitchen. The bunch of flowers above the fireplace is still bouncy and fresh. The room accepts my gaze as if it knows all is in order. Everything is as I have left it, only the long-case clock, I notice, has stopped ticking.

It is one of Pierre's few daily tasks to wind it. Like many men, he can do things only one at a time, and never completes any task without verbal signage. So he will announce he is going to wind the clock, wind the clock, and report back that he has wound the clock, as if he is participating in a television program for preschoolers.

The leather riding boots are arranged in neat pairs in the open-fronted cupboard. Whips, umbrellas, walking sticks, Nordic track poles, and shooting sticks are in the elephant's foot. I go from the cool tiled hall to the warm fug of the Aga kitchen, to put the milk into the fridge.

There is no sign of Pierre, whose inactivity has become even more industrious of late. Nor of Jesse Marlon, for that matter.

I leave the kitchen for the back door, where I'd left my Spanish boots, the ones with a darling little fringed tassel at the zip, to go to the apple store out the back and to pick some kale for tonight's kale, bacon, and chestnut soup.

I bend over, zip one leg of one boot, then the other, and when I come upright again, slightly out of breath, slightly dizzy, I see the shape of a man standing against the etched glass of the back door.

I scream. Not because a man is at my back door, but because I know who it is.

Colin Watts.

It is the same scream I let loose when I suddenly see a mouse looking at me beadily from the larder floor, a scream of sheer female shock.

At the noise, the man moves towards me. Through my open back door. I flatten myself against the wall and hold up my arms, screening my face, as if I expect blows to rain down on me.

Suddenly, Jesse Marlon appears from nowhere, running down the hall with his leather Blundstone boots thudding against the flagstones. He shouts, "Get away from her, get your hands off her!" He flings himself so violently on Colin Watts that I scream again, this time in horror. What on earth has got into them?

The two men topple to the floor, where they begin to struggle and writhe. Awful grunting noises fill my quiet house.

Watts starts saying, "Gerroff me, yer poof," and "Fooking hippie," and shouting other things about Jesse Marlon, awful things.

Meanwhile, I stand by and scream in a reedy voice that sounds ridiculous—posh and flutey—even to my own ears: "Jesse Marlon, will you please, please stop!" Another part of my brain registers the grappling youths and thinks of marbled loins and that ridiculous naked wrestling scene in *Women in Love*. I also think how evenly matched, physically, and even alike, the two young men are, before dismissing the thought, because I do not want even to compare Colin—the lowlife . . . rapist!—with the godlike Jesse Marlon.

Eventually, having held Colin Watts down for a count of ten, Jesse Marlon climbs off.

Colin Watts has a nosebleed. "Well, thank heavens for that!" I exclaim. "Why do you men all think that violence is the answer to everything!"

I go into the kitchen, put the kettle on, fetch a tea towel and come back quickly, in case they start hitting each other again.

The men aren't looking at each other.

"Well, now, Swampy here" (pointing at Jesse Marlon) "has stopped assaulting me, I can ask you, do you wannit in the barn, or the woodshed?" Colin says, mopping his nose.

"Want what?" ask Jesse Marlon and I simultaneously.

"The wood," Colin answers, as if we are both simple. He hands me back the red-stained tea towel. Even though it's one of my favorite soft Irish linen ones, which are brilliant for polishing glasses, I say, "No, no, keep it." He lights another Rothman.

"Mrs. Musgrove, oy would've mentioned it down the shop, but what with the arrests this morning . . . Your old man left a message on moy mobile. Ordered two loads of wood. Oy only toike cash, and unless you want me to make trouble for your toy boy here, oy think you better pay me for three loads 'stead of two."

He draws on his cigarette, and he says something under his breath about how JM has "got wood, too," at which Jesse Marlon hisses, for some reason cross, "Just shut up, will you, you fucking nonce, or I'll deck you."

And then Colin Watts says, "If you ever so much as touch me again, sonny boy, you'll end up in prison, and oy don't need to tell you why," and Jesse Marlon scowls at him.

Obviously, Pierre had called Colin Watts and ordered some wood. I can't think why, as we usually have it delivered from our regular supplier, who can be relied on to sell us bone-dry tinder that goes up like Buncefield Oil depot rather than the saturated new pine he saves for Londoners like the Flemings and the Kinmonths.

I tell Colin we (as in Pierre and me, not Jesse Marlon and me) don't actually need it—we were long on wood as it happened—but as he was here, could he put it as neatly as possible please in the barn?

When Colin Watts has sloped off, after grinding a Rothman butt carefully in the middle of my back steps, I ask Jesse Marlon why Colin had called him a "rancid."

"Because that's what the village calls us," he answers. "Rancids."

I see exactly why the eco-villagers might be called this, having seen them trail glumly around the village in their knitted woolen weeds and having stood a little too close to them as they stocked up on Rizlas in the Stores, but said of course that they weren't rancid at all, what a silly thing to say, and offered to make a fresh pot of coffee for us both. I certainly needed it.

It's not every day, after all, that the village rapist (though I have only Garry-from-the-pub's word on that) comes to call.

And it's certainly not every day that Jesse Marlon comes up behind me while I am fussing over the Aga (I was wiping a spill—if you don't remove them straightaway they burn themselves, like branding scars, onto the enamel) and slowly turns me round so I'm facing him.

He puts down his cup on the side, and then decides it should properly go in the sink, and carefully places it in the wide butler's one, an action that—for someone used to Pierre's slovenly ways—almost makes me come on the spot.

And then. That first touch. It's the touch that—such a cliché, but so true—says it all. I stare at his mouth, which is wide and full, as if willing him to kiss me, and a roaring starts up in my head, as if someone is gunning an engine in a part of my brain, and it suddenly fires into life after years of sitting in an outhouse, under a mildewed tarpaulin shroud.

I don't dare look into his eyes in case he recoils when he sees how much I want him, his youth, his adorable, poreless fresh boy skin, how much I want to graze my lips over the faint stubble peeking through the downy baby fluff on his cleft chin and run my hands over his lean torso unmarked by the passage of time, of boredom, of marriage and disappointment, and slip them under the frayed waistband of his battered Levi's and feel his hardness.

I also don't want him to see, too close up, the laughter lines around my eyes, my deepening crinkle that almost joins my nose to my mouth, like a runnel on the surface of the moon. Facing Jesse Marlon's own unconcerned, magnificent perfection, his own assumption of his own beauty and place in my kitchen and the universe, I feel . . . shy. And bloody old.

But I soon get over it.

He tips my chin, forcing me to look up at him. "I thought

he was going to hurt you," he says. "I thought he was going to . . ." Then he stops, in midflow, as if he'd thought better of what he was going to say, and shakes his curly dark head. My hand reaches up, and without thinking I start twiddling the curls about his ears, as if I own him already.

And then he kisses me, very slowly, and intimately, and with patience, and skill, and infinite variety, for what seems ages, while I completely lose myself in him.

Mimi

After the mandatory hour reading my way through a dog-eared stack of *Dorset Lifes* in the waiting room at the surgery my name is called, just as I've found the new *Vanity Fair* with an exposé of a Hollywood murder in it that looks enjoyably juicy. I lay it down, gather up my things, and go.

"Ah, Mrs. Fleming, a very good morning," Dr. Ashburton says, not looking at me but at the morning appointments on his screen. He has the glum air of the country doctor for whom attending to patients is an unwelcome distraction from the important main business of the day, which is hunting to hounds. "What can I do for you?" he asks, looking at his watch.

Explain I'm feeling, you know . . . slight temperature, chest now so big could eat breakfast off my own boobs, metallic taste in mouth, period late. I pause, as if there was no need to go on.

"Have you been in contact with animals?" is his incisive first question, as he makes tiny marks with his biro on my notes.

"Well, we do have a dog and a pony," I answer. I don't say "Trumpet" because I am now all too aware that everyone in the village is stalking me to steal away Trumpet for the nippers to use on first days "out," which is how the hearty refer to the sacred sport.

"Children ill? Any viruses going round at home?" is his next line of inquiry.

"Not that I know of," I answer. At this, Dr. Ashburton seems well and truly stumped. He takes my temperature, giving me a two-minute opportunity to study the lush thicket of black hair sprouting vigorously from his ear. The thermometer reads 99 degrees. "Is that high?" I ask hopefully.

"No," he answers, putting it back on the desk and looking at me over his spectacles, which I can't help notice have a drab frosting of flakes and smears on the lenses.

"Do you think there's any possible chance I might be, um . . ." I trail off. I want Ashburton to join the dots for me.

"Contagious?" he queries.

"No, I just thought, all my symptoms . . ." I give a light laugh. "To tell you the truth, the last time I felt like this, I was pregnant with Posy."

Dr. Ashburton raises his luxuriant eyebrows, which have long, bristly hairs extruding, and I see him glance at my date of birth on-screen.

I want to shout at him. After all, he has two children, is miles older than me, and I don't hear anyone accusing him of being a medical miracle or a senior father.

Men get away with everything when it comes to parenthood.

Dr. Ashburton sighs heavily. He opens a drawer. Then another. Then he rather reluctantly gets up and leaves the room without explanation. He leaves the door open. He is gone some time. I hear doors open and close in the corridor.

"Have you got a sample?" he says when he comes back with a thin white package. I shake my head. He opens another drawer, takes out a specimen bottle, hands it to me, and points to the door. I meekly exit.

On my return I hand him the warm bottle with a downcast, maidenly look. He unscrews it and jabs in the stick. Then he leaves the stick on the side of the sink.

My heart starts to beat quite loudly. At thirty-eight and a half, I feel myself willing the thin blue line to appear, just to show him that despite advanced age—after all, if this was the Middle Ages I would have been dead years ago—my body is still capable of fruiting in the twilight of its fertility, just as some ancient gnarled *poirier* can suddenly produce one perfect, round, juicy pear in the autumn of its years.

Then, suddenly all cheerful, he smacks his thighs, as if he remembers something, and is making a heroically gentlemanly effort to fill the uncomfortable interlude before we have a result.

"Now then, I've been meaning to ask . . . how's Trumpet?" he asks, rubbing his big hairy hands together before using one spongy forefinger to probe an ear.

"I don't know," I say honestly. Not being at one with the equine kingdom, it's quite hard for me to tell what Trumpet, although a docile enough little beast, enjoys and doesn't enjoy.

Dr. Ashburton in reply starts to do that violent waggling thing men do with their forefinger in their ear, as if trying to dislodge a marble stuck inside their brains. I get the distinct feeling that for Dr. Ashburton, who has small children of Trumpet-appropriate ages, the subject of my pony is not closed. He gets up hurriedly and goes over to peer at the stick.

"Mmm," he says. "Any idea how it happened?"

I look at him, mouth agape. I suddenly find it hard to breathe. It's not clear whether the doctor has led a spectacularly sheltered life, or wants gory details of the actual act itself.

"I presume you have a coil," he goes on. "Most women in their, um, of your age find they get on with them, especially the Mirena, reasonably well."

"No, I don't," I say.

"So what are you going to do?" he asks, his pen hovering.

"That's my business, Dr. Ashburton," I reply, putting on my Husky, in a tone of voice designed to remind him firmly of his Hippocratic oath and that I would be most displeased if my happy news was all around the village by nightfall. "Thank you very much."

When I get home, hugging my secret, the phone's ringing. Ana is sitting at the computer, her diary open, taking down stuff from the Web. I rush to the phone before it stops, shouting, "Ana! Quick! Answer the phone! Quick!"

"Yes?" says Ana, looking up.

"The telephone!" I screech.

As I lift the receiver I make a mental note to check her history directory to see which Web sites she's been visiting. I have a funny feeling. Just to check.

"Mimi?" come crisp, American, can-do tones. "It's Catherine Cobb. Is this a good time?"

"Yeesss!!!" I say as I replace the receiver, punching the air like Andy Murray, and doing a little war dance in the kitchen in front of Ana, who has the grace not to laugh. If she wasn't so thin—so Ana, in fact—I would have hugged her.

Cath invited us to dinner at Court Place! This Friday evening! So what if some other guests have dropped out at the last minute. I haven't felt so happy for ages . . . not since I found out that Ocado was going henceforth to deliver groceries to my postcode.

"Just a bunch of locals," she said, "and my houseguests. It's kind of last minute, I hope you don't mind . . . but I thought I'd try you and Ralph, as it's so awful, you've been here for months and we haven't welcomed you properly. I'm so ashamed! It'll be very honky-tonk, very casual," she added, to my joy. If it really was casual, I could probably deliver Ralph up to Court Place without too much duplicity.

I wouldn't have cared if she was inviting us with Garry and Debbie from the pub and the local knacker. I'd been longing to snoop around Court Place for ages, though it has to be said that Ralph hasn't shown any interest, as (1) he doesn't want to meet New People and (2) Court Place isn't an ancestral seat. Ralph regards inhabiting the same house since the Domesday Book to be the supreme human accomplishment, and Court Place was bought only about seven years, i.e., a nanosecond, ago, by Granville Cobb, who is apparently superrich, according to Rose, who knows these things.

For a second, it almost seems worth having Ana from Poland, just so we can waltz off, but not quite.

So now I have lots to think about, like applying makeup for the first time in three months and also trying out two of my newer online purchases, a pair of Spanx knickers to flatten my tummy, and then, on top, another pair of knickers with a padded panel on the seat to endow me with "booty boost," i.e., a sticky-out bottom, without having to resort to surgery or, even worse, the gym. As a woman with a largeish nose and a flattish bum, who avoids three-way mirrors, it took me years and years to work out that only others know how things on these two key fronts really are, a period of ignorance for which I shall always remain profoundly grateful.

As the countdown to Court Place is under way on Friday, I'm in my bedroom, staring into my hanging cupboard.

I have to wear something tonight, but what? I don't want to look as if I've tried too hard. I don't want to look as if I haven't tried at all. At least, at Court Place, I won't be *cold*. I stare at my clothes for ages. Daywear is no problem, obviously.

For someone as dramatically indecisive as me about clothes, layering has been a godsend, especially as it's warmer outside than in and I have put on a whole stone since moving west. I am for the moment putting all the blame for my weight gain (not that anyone's yet noticed) on scones, to which I have become addicted. They're totally worth the wheat, even when I make them. I also blame everyone else. Everything one is given to eat, in people's houses or in pubs, is either encased in suet and BSE-enriched pastry or covered with a topping of buttery mashed potato peaked into waves, and often both. In fact, so far as the shires are concerned, cuisine minceur is probably just bad French for "100 Ways with Mince."

So, until the blissful time I can download my winter clothes straight from NASA, I just put everything I find on the floor in my room on top of one another, often in the dark, and never take them off, and while I can't boast that wearing thermals in bed does wonders for the sex life, it sort of works for me, if not Ralph, who is starting to wonder out loud if he's ever going to see me nude again . . .

But evening wear in the country? Tricky. One doesn't want to be one of those women from the shires who dresses herself to the nines in designer separates, heels, and full stage makeup for those rare gala nights out; it just looks so scary and desperate.

I become aware of a stormy, disapproving presence hovering in the doorway. It is Mirabel, home from school, a coltish shape wearing opaque black tights, Converse trainers she has customized with Tipp-Ex, a denim miniskirt, and a crop top that skims her navel. Just looking at her dewy, peachy freshness, at a time when I'm rubbing foundation onto the black shadows under my eyes with a piece of kitchen towel, makes me feel my age.

"Mum!" she says in a shocked voice. "You're not. Seriously. Going out like THAT, are you?"

Mirabel and I have reached a new "phase" in our relationship. Basically, she ignores me unless I do something so deliberately annoying—such as dancing/singing along to the radio/ borrowing her special DuWop Lip Venom and managing to "mank it up," i.e., get one single speck of dirt on the lid. Then she will threaten to get a gun and shoot me. At least, that's what she said when I started grooving on down to Lily Allen in front of Aspen from the stable cottages and Spike, Sophy's son, who was also here, from the eco-village. "Nooo!" she started wailing. "Noooooo!" and mimed blasting my head off.

"Why shouldn't I?" I say. I think my grooming is—in comparison with recent sorties, anyway—of a reasonably high standard, if not dressage at International Horse Show Olympia-level.

"What I mean is," says Mirabel in a softer voice, "I'm kidding. Actually, you look sick." She removes her copy of a book called *Bratfest at Tiffany's*, the sequel to *Sealed with a Diss*, from the floor, and makes as if to leave.

"Sick! But you like this dress," I protest, before she exits. "It's not the black one, the one you told me you didn't want even after I was dead! It's a different one, from the Joseph sale."

"Oh Mum, you're, like, so out of date. Sick means good. You're *rocking* that dress. You *own* that dress. You look quite hot—for you, that is," my daughter continues. "Even if you have put on, like, a tiny bit of weight recently, it still looks nice." And I glow with pride. From Mirabel, this is highest praise, even if her compliment contained, as compliments often do, an implied criticism or insult.

It is enough for me, for now, that I look nice in this dress, even if I look nice only compared to how I look the rest of the time.

Ralph points the Subaru in the direction of Court Place, and I look at my makeup in the mirror and perform a swift teeth and nostril check. As Mirabel points out, my teeth act as a sort of trap or net, efficiently snagging food before it passes down my throat, and as for the nostrils—why does no one ever tell you (1) about the sudden efflorescence of nostril hair in one's late thirties and (2) how to remove it?

So, Court Place. At last.

There's a huge house and outbuildings, a shoot and a farm shop with fourteen different sorts of sausage, she's got four children, like all alpha mothers, and he's something in hedge funds or private equity, like all alpha fathers.

While most women with four or more children will never, ever leave this fact alone, Cath does. Four children is just another thing she does along with everything else.

While men with loads of money would never dream of ramming it down your throat, most women with lots of children are always saying things like, "We're taking the four children to Klosters!" to me; or "He's easily the brightest of my five—his IQ is off the charts!" as if I don't know how many children they have, and need reminding; or they piously explain to women who work because they have to, or because they would go mad if they didn't, "With four children and two dogs and three houses to look after, there just isn't much time for work," as if not having a job is the noble price they pay for their high-maintenance show life, and that mothers with the privilege of having to earn a living—the only privilege these poor, unfortunate women lack—should feel *sorry* for *them.*

I can't count the number of times a mother of four has told me that she has "four children in four different schools" and left me in no doubt that she has attended four carol services in one week in December and four sports days in late June, as if there should be some special medal struck in her honor. I don't think I've ever once said, "I'm taking the three children to the dentist or Butlins," for example. Or, "I'm taking all three children to Tesco." I'd sound even dafter than I do already.

As Ralph points out, "Mimi, darling, no man ever gives a moment's thought to how many children a woman has. We can barely remember whether she's married, her husband's name, and what either of them are FOR, let alone the number of babies they have somehow managed to produce, against what look like the heaviest of genetic odds. I just can't think why it matters so much to you women."

But Cath doesn't ram the four-children thing down one's throat at all. No, what she does is even worse. She does everything effortlessly and really seems to enjoy running a business, her four children, umpteen homes, and A-list social life. When I first went round, I sneakily checked out the Court Place visitor's book—talk about *livre d'or*: David Cameron and Samantha, Otis and Bryan, Charles and Camilla—all within about two pages!

I know it's uncool to be impressed, but I was.

Anyway, when we betas (three children, one house, no money) nudged the Subaru at the wrought-iron gates, they swung silently open, and we drove up in silence, drinking it all in: the finely graded, evenly distributed gravel, the beech trees that line the drive all lit up and, dotted around between the trees, a sort of sculpture garden, not just BritArt and Damien Hirst ironic stuff with cows and naked women squatting to pee but wonderful old stuff, too, like Frink and Hepworth and Moore, that must be worth millions . . .

We worry—or rather, I worry—about leaving the Subaru in front of the honey-stoned, colonnaded facade because it really lowers the tone, and wonder whether more frequent, i.e., richer and smarter, guests know to park round the back, at the stables, but then the butler, Maddocks, shimmies out to greet us.

"What ho," says Ralph, predictably, when this man in a dark suit and tie who isn't Granville and who is all too obviously a butler opens the door.

I try to execute a finishing-school exit from the Subaru, a maneuver made more complicated by the fact that I am carrying a bag and my precautionary pashmina, which remains acceptable—just—at evening events, especially ones held in the open air in April.

I am also grasping a precious and pretentiously expensive bottle of Peace Oil to my bosom, produced by Palestinian, Israeli, and Druze farmers working in peace together, and soon to be gifted to Cath (though I'm wondering whether to leave it in the car as it's coals to Newcastle taking a smart present to the rich, who all benefit from the to-those-that-have-shall-even-more-be-given rule, which is all wrong, as is the practice of taking humble scraplike offerings to one's poorest friends).

As soon as we arrive, Ralph's clearly ready to give the house the once-over, to check out proportions, cornices, pictures, and antiques, and especially the Flemish tapestries and modern art, but we are shooed through an enfilade of rooms into this double-length drawing room, which is heated, and when I say "heated" . . . it's hammam temperature.

Two fires blaze in baronial fireplaces. Vast bunches of lilies perfume the air. Cath throws out her arms and gives a cry of pleasure at the sight of us, so I come forward shyly and hand her the Peace Oil.

She thanks me profusely, crooks a finger to Maddocks, and I just hear her say the words "raffle cupboard" as a command as she hands over the precious greeny-gold vial. Then Maddocks returns with a tray of Champagne, and then Cath darts out.

Homemade parsnip and beetroot crisps, perfect cubes of polenta, melted mozzarella adorned with one deep-fried dark-green sage leaf, and minuscule pork pies with crunchy pastry made with real suet are borne on two platters into the drawing room by Cath herself on her return, and handed round as casually as if they were Cheesy Wotsits.

Maddocks scurries around shifting glossy piles of this month's key nonfiction hardbacks written by close friends of the Cobbs to make room for the platters, which are placed on a large footstool in front of the fire, within easy reaching distance, just how I like it.

A deep sense of well-being and comfort is stealing over me, and I try not to think about the fact that we still haven't "done anything" to Home Farm.

Ralph immediately rushes over to inspect the fire and bends over the log basket. He picks up a section of ash, sniffs it, and sighs with self-pity. He still hasn't recovered from the blow of discovering, when he took his log shifter on wheels out to the woodshed, that Colin Watts, the log man (and possibly the rumored village rapist, according to Rose, which slightly puts paid to my plans for him and Ana) had come while we were out.

Watts had filled the barn to the rafters with soaking-wet new pine, full of water and sap. Ralph tried burning some on the fire in the sitting room, but even the drier ones just sat there, mutinously hissing and steaming. Furious, he had called Watts on his mobile.

"I know perfectly well how to make a fire, thank you, otherwise we would have frozen to death this winter, as we don't have central heating," I heard him saying. "My question is, what possessed you to sell us two loads of new wet wood when you could have sold us two loads of dry, seasoned wood?"

Pause.

"No, Colin, it DOES NOT burn if you lay the fire properly, as you suggest. I would go so far as to say that you have sold us two loads of flame-retardant logs. Your logs are so completely fire-resistant I'm surprised they haven't tried to make cheap soft furnishings and children's nightclothes out of them."

Pause.

"Colin, let me say this. There's something nasty in the woodshed and do you know what? I know exactly what it is. It's YOUR WOOD! Do you understand? So unless you bring us some nice dry wood, and take away the nasty wet, I will have no choice but to turn elsewhere for my . . ." But then he stopped.

Longer pause.

He couldn't threaten Watts, or cancel the check—this is Honeyborne, not Highbury and Islington—because if he did, sure as eggs, Ralph would find himself seated next to Colin at the Harvest Supper. In the end, Ralph ended up buying a whole lot more dry wood and agreed to keep all the wet wood as well, which was a result. For Colin Watts.

Seeing Ralph's interest—indeed, as if to draw attention to the lofty proportions of his own heraldic chimneypiece—Granville takes up a seigneurial position with his back to the fire, legs apart. So far, we are the only guests, and I am wondering whether Cath is expecting us to eat all the canapés on our own.

Granville is chatting amiably to Ralph, and I hear him say that crude futures are at over $100 a barrel and something about the price in pounds per therm, and then I hear Ralph talk about the closure of some random pipeline between Belarus and Moscow, and I think, Bo-ring! Who cares if West Germany can't get enough oil?

Meanwhile, Cath is rapidly establishing my credentials and

downloading all my key data as concerns the crucial female subject areas of children's schools, where we lived in London, on
which communal garden, on which side of which garden, down
to what exact house number in Colville Crescent we used to
occupy.

As we both know, these questions are designed to establish
in a short time whether I am important or worth cultivating,
and have to be asked in order for us to progress to the next stage
of our association, which is friendship.

I simply let her get on with it, quite chuffed that Cath seems
to think that my contacts book is worth copying, taking it as a
compliment rather than an inquisition.

"And do you shoot?" Granville asks Ralph during a pause in a
debate over Gazprom and oil levies that remains impregnable
to Cath or me.

Ralph quivers like a gundog at his peg. He loves shooting,
and Cobb's inquiry seems to hint that many fine days out on hill
and heather await him, all fully comped, of course, by Granville
Cobb, Esq.

And so then the men plunge into an animated discussion
about beaters and pegs and the height of birds over coverts. I
haven't heard Ralph so chirpy for ages, and Cath and I relax
that our husbands are getting on so famously, but then I hear
Granville say something.

I find I can no longer focus on Cath's blue gaze and her advanced plans to site her farm shop (Rose is one of many local
suppliers) in the Tithe Barn, and add on an organic café. Could
he—Granville—possibly have said what I heard him saying?

"I'm sorry, Granville," says Ralph. "I must be going deaf. I
don't think I quite caught what you just said."

Granville raises an eyebrow, at which Maddocks bounds
over with a fresh, chilled bottle of Champagne, an ironed white
napkin wrapped around its neck like a scarf on a sickly child.

"It's okay, Ralph, I'm allowed to say it, loud as I like," Granville says. "Eh, Cath? It's the Jackie Mason defense. More Champagne for anyone? Er, Maddocks—" He waves an arm and Maddocks goes around charging our lead-crystal flutes.

Then I begin to get my National Theatre feeling, the one that comes over me at a certain point in the first act, when someone says something, just one thing, and that's the cue for all the cast to start tearing one another to shreds, and the whole thing remains unremittingly nasty till the curtain comes down, and everyone applauds out of sheer, bladder-racked relief.

Cath smiles without opening her mouth to show her very white teeth, and raises her eyebrows at me, as if we are both in this together. I get this very strong feeling that there is some primitive initiation ritual under way, and fight this compulsion to give Ralph the tiniest of glances.

I don't, though; it would have been fatal to semaphore anything at this point. I want to play this one carefully. Cath and Granville are the new king and queen of Honeyborne, so much richer than the old king and queen, the Bryanstons. Money is status now, and it's not about blood, or birth, but billions.

And on that score we Flemings are bottom of the food chain—(1) new arrivals, (2) who don't even hunt, or (3) have a helipad, let alone a farm shop, a shoot, a heated pool, a country-house opera company in the summer months, several thousand rolling acres of prime farmland, four children, a home abroad, or even a London house.

And the Cobbs are at the top.

There seems no option, given his declaration, but to allow Granville the honor of filling the silence he has created.

"If it weren't for me and the other Jewray Henrys," Granville continues, "pumping new life and money into the shires, keeping field sports going, buying up crumbling piles from the aristocracy, a lot more of the English countryside would be carpeted with Tescos and low-cost housing. We're the Consuelo Vanderbilts of the age."

"I think it's a brilliant pun," I say, quite wanting to hear who the other Jewray Henrys are but not daring to ask, "on the term Hooray Henrys! Brilliant! Wish I'd thought of it! All the best puns are economical like that." But I am thinking how different the composition of the English countryside is now compared to ten years ago, before we had million-pound bonuses and hedge funds and private equity. Sitting here in Granville and Cath's sumptuous drawing room, I feel as if the wall of money, a tsunami of dollars that starts to crest in Wall Street, New York, then breaks in sterling over Holland Park and Notting Hill and the City, with backwashes that course out from West London and sluice through Berkshire, Wiltshire, Gloucestershire, and Oxfordshire, is now pressing on in a westerly direction to drench Dorset and Somerset and Devon in a golden tide of wealth.

Then Granville says that, as it happens, he is "auto-Semitic," in that he is trying to make himself more Jewish than he really is, as his Jewishness comes through his mother's father, not his mother's mother. "My father, also called Granville, made his money in gravel. You wouldn't necessarily guess it, I know." Granville gazes around the luxuriously appointed, flower-filled, Nicky Haslam—ed space, which has recently been rehung at the cost of £40,000, I should imagine, with ornate Suzy Hoodless floral wallpaper of poppies and hummingbirds and butterflies, with a generous repeat on a chalky-white background. Huge floral displays sit on mantelpieces and round tables covered with fringed cloths, and picture lights gently illuminate the Cobbs' collection of paintings by the St. Ives school.

I am gazing faithfully at Granville like a smitten puppy, a gaze I perfected in the salons of Notting Hill while trying to secure lucrative columns off important newspaper editors.

"So, in fact, while I'm third-generation Lithuanian Jew, I'm only second-generation Coutts."

"If you don't mind my asking," I ask, "is that why both you and your father are called Granville? As a sort of pun on gravel?"

Ralph puts his head in his hands and makes a slight moaning sound.

"No," says Granville. "But don't worry in the slightest, Mimi. It's a question that my old man was often asked, especially by his grandchildren."

Luckily, the others then burst in, as if they had all been pressed together against the door listening in a pack, which I pray they haven't.

The Reverend Simon Wyldbore-Smith; the Pikes, Henry and Biddy; Ned and Lulu Bryanston; and the Cobb daughter, Serena, all sleek and bronzed and slimline, whose date appears to be Jesse Marlon Bryanston, son and heir to Ned, both of them very similar looking, with thick dark hair, even features, long, upper-class legs, nonchalant mien of the entitled, that sort of thing. I notice that Ralph said Jesse Marlin rather than Marlon, as if he's a sort of fish, but there wasn't a moment to take him aside and, anyway, I was still cross about how he reacted when I asked Granville about gravel—so unsupportive.

"What would you all like to drink?" Cath cries. "Something soft, I think," says Henry. "Red wine?" I hear Biddy announcing proudly to Lulu that Jiggy's having Frisky's puppies. "But aren't they mother and son?" Lulu asks faintly. "Yes!" roars Biddy. "Isn't it lovely?"

Last to arrive is a young goldeny couple whose names I never caught, he = aspiring Tory MP/partner in City law firm, she = utterly adorable pregnant young bride with that glow . . . not to mention dowry of many millions.

When they appear in a sort of vision of youth and beauty in the doorway, Henry Pike glances up and shouts, *"Raus!"* in a Teutonic accent, like a German storm trooper. Biddy is in the middle of saying, "Being master of horse to two dozen juniors was the highlight of last summer" to the assembled company. "I know I was sleeping in the trailer on straw, but, after Pony Camp, can life get any better?"

Naturally, at the bellow of *"Raus!"* after the previous conversation, Ralph and I start anxiously, but Granville rushes over to meet our guests who, it turns out, are Jeremy and Suki Rous, which leads me to conclude that Henry Pike's delightful bark of a command is a famous joke among the gratin of Honeyborne, a joke that in due course I expect to find as funny as my new neighbors do.

And then, of course, there is the surprise.

The houseguests. Virginie and Mathieu Lacoste. We fall on each other with cries of unfeigned joy but I hear a small voice whisper, " '*Ere come trobble.*"

We ooze through to the paneled, medieval dining room, where yet another blazing fire is warming the biosphere.

"Is the paneling old, do you think?" I ask Ralph, who is very attentive to these things, and prefers houses to people.

"No," he replies after a brief glance, taking in the scrolled paneling and the little painted heraldic flags that form a frieze around the cuboid room. "It's Victorian."

Granville seats everyone with fluid competence, placing me on his right, and the reverend on my other side.

"I'm thrilled to have you captive," I say, buttering some crusty brown bread, dense with seeds and grains and Omega goodness. I am feeling very sleepy, suddenly. "By the time the evening's over, I expect to have secured my plot for perpetuity in the graveyard at St. Mary of All Angels." We unfurl our napkins, and, after a very short time, Cath sails in carrying what I think at first is a large yellow pumpkin, which exactly matches the sunny cotton fabric of her ironed Williams-Sonoma apron.

"Or else I want a family vault," I continue, before clapping my hands and making an admiring noise to make Cath feel that someone around her table—another wife and mother—appreciates the effort put into the occasion, which is only right, given that all the men around the table, as usual, think they've put on a jolly good show simply by turning up.

Cath places the pumpkin center table, and I can just make

out the pleasing words PARMIGIANO-REGGIANO stamped into the wax in a repeat pattern, and the words MAGGIORE 97 and a huge Kitemark. She lifts the top half off the cheese, which is, I take a few moments to work out, older than Posy, and a column of steam rises up, making my tummy tighten in delicious expectation of piping-hot food, home-cooked by a hand-picked chef in this home.

"Soul food tonight," Cath announces, digging her spoon into the creamy depths of the cavity and eviscerating generous dollops onto blue and white porcelain dinner plates. "I do hope everyone likes risotto," she adds as the plates are passed around. "Any allergies? The meal is wheat- and fish- and nut-free, but this," she says, looking into the steaming depths, "has cream in it, I'm afraid." And then she whispers in my direction, as if we are sharing a private joke, "And my secret ingredient— Velveeta!"

Everyone cries how lovely, and I hear Ralph politely ask the woman on his right if she has any interesting allergies, as they seem to be in fashion.

"There's green salad in the middle of the table, ready to go, I didn't hold the dressing—I do hope that's okay." And there is a vast green salad of freshly plucked, hand-torn mustard and mizuna leaves and tender baby spinach, plucked herbs fresh from the Cobb kitchen garden polytunnel and greenhouses, lightly dressed with walnut oil and cask-aged red-wine vinegar. "It's *fah*-bu-lous to have these early salads, from the greenhouse, but don't they make you just *long* for summer?" Cath says to no one in particular as she dollops away generously onto plates. "The cutting garden and the kitchen garden, the parterre, the sequoia . . . sometimes I don't think I married Granville. I married the garden. Oh, I should warn you—it's very heavy on garlic. Can you imagine life without garlic?" Cath asks the assembled company.

Ralph looks blank, but the rest of us cry, "Lord no!" and "Perish the thought!"

"Or cilantro? Or zucchini? Or bell peppers? Or even"—Cath shudders at such a grisly thought—"without *tomaytoes*?"

"Life without tomatoes is beyond contemplation," I say. "I do hope there's nothing for mains—" I go on, to annoy Ralph, whom I am still cross with. He hates the word "mains" which he says is a "bastard plural noun made from an adjective." Other banned words and phrases—relating to restaurants and pubs alone, that is—are "Carvery," "Sunday Roasts," and "Sweet Trolley"—which makes eating out in most rural hostelries— another noun unprotected by the First Amendment—a hazardous and rage-flecked enterprise. He once almost left a place when he read the menu and it said, "Herb-crusted rack of lamb sat on a bed of crushed new pots," for all the reasons you might imagine. I gaze at Ralph fondly as I continue, "because risotto's my favorite food in the whole world, followed by Ambrosia creamed rice, which is the next best thing. And I intend to eat a whole lot of it."

"Oh God, me, too," says Granville, as he digs in. "At Harrow, I'd beg Mummy to bring Ambrosia creamed rice as tuck. I could eat a whole tin, cold, with a spoon. Father Christmas used to put a tin opener in my stocking."

"In answer to your question, Mimi," says Cath, "the risotto is the entrée. Grindy pepper, Maddocks?" Maddocks disappears in search of peppermills. "There are several more courses after this, with all the fixin's, sweet honey chile!" She speaks in the warm gravy-and-grits tone of a southern mammy.

After the laughter has died down, we all address our plates, and I begin to worry there'll be a silence. When there was a silence at the last dinner thing we went to, at the Huttons', Celia Bryanston filled it with the words, "Well, it does appear that Rose Musgrove has finally lost her looks," which was so rude and also, for that matter, inaccurate, that I almost fell off my chair. But everyone else just kept on masticating their lamb shanks implacably, as if Celia said this sort of thing all the time.

Ned Bryanston looks over at his current wife, Lulu, and it's as if she's been waiting for this signal. I decide Ned's attractive in an obvious, James Bond kind of way, while Lulu's attractive in an obvious, Bond girl kind of way. I also notice that Ralph is picking out the dried blueberries—which Cath scattered over the leaves at the last minute, "for crunch," as she put it—and leaving them on the side, just as he does with (1) raisins, (2) peppercorns, and (3) bay leaves.

Both Lulu and Cath are blond. But Cath is blond in a creamy way that speaks of generations of inherited wealth on both coasts of the United States; Lulu is blond in an elegant, nervy, desert-bred way, like a saluki. Lulu can get away with almost anything, as she proved when she teamed pink *Nanook of the North* boots dripping with pointless pom-poms with nothing but a Melissa Odabash chambray bikini and a Texan cowboy hat (to the general annoyance of all who carried the X chromosome) when après-skiing last April in Courchevel. Lulu keeps hens, called things like Biker Chick, Rock Chick, and Dixie Chick, to prove she is much younger and hipper and, above all, much thinner than most of the other Dorset wives.

I'm just comforting myself with the thought that Lulu'll find her forties and fifties *even harder* than me, because her face has been her fortune, when Ned holds up a hand to silence Henry Pike.

Henry, though, has started in on one of his favorite topics, which is the impossibility of sex after marriage. This, along with horseflesh and hunting, is a topic that he likes to cover from every angle, especially if everyone in the room has already heard the famous Henry Pike anecdote, which is as follows:

"I was in this bar, in Tokyo, and I saw this girl. The eyes met across a crowded room," the master's story goes, "and I honestly felt the knees go weak. I hadn't had a woman in months. So I pushed through the crowd. Bought her a drink, which was damnably expensive. But my Lord, she was a fine-lookin' piece, long brown hair, bosoms, the whole lot. And then she said, 'You want come back my prace?' And I thought I did, rather. So we left the club, and then we went on foot for hours through sub-urban bloody Tokyo, till we came to this hovel. And then, well, we got down to it. And, erm, well, it was really rather spectacu-lar, as these things go. I'd never had a rogering like it. It was completely thunderous."

Henry will always pause mistily at this point, relishing every detail, as if he were back in the hovel with the Japanese girl, which only goes to heighten expectation.

"So then she said, getting up, 'You want a beer?' And a warning bell started, you know, *tinkling distantly,* and I thought, 'Beer? *Beer?*' "

At this point all the audience will be also crying out, "Beer? *Beer?*" and wiping the tears of merriment from their eyes.

"But I said, 'Sure,' and she went to this mini-fridge in the corner of the room and got out two cans and went back to bed. And then I noticed. As she drank, she had this huge Adam's apple, bobbing up and down, and up and down. Then I looked at her hands. So I pulled on my clothes, and raced for the door, and all I could think was"—and then Henry pauses, so we can all roar the punchline, together—"I'd FUCKED a BLOKE."

After this, Henry will reveal to anyone listening who hasn't heard this most amusing story many times before that yes, she had asked for money at an earlier point in the evening, and that yes, she had a "perfectly tidy front bottom," and until the Adam's apple, he hadn't the faintest.

"Cath, Granville . . . Henry . . ." It is Ned Bryanston, trying to make a speech—or possibly a toast to his hosts—and trying to call pray silence. He nods in a courtly way to the guests. "If I may just say something that concerns us all—or most of us, anyway."

But Henry, or should I say the master, is still in midflow on the subject of mating in captivity at one end of the table. "Prob-lem is, one doesn't want to have sex with one's wife," Henry is saying, as Biddy sits illuminated by candles, looking rather pretty in her Spotty Ruffle Blouse from Boden and completely resigned to his disloyalty. "It's not because you've been in at the kill, that would never put a real man off," he continues. "Christ, no! Specially not one born on a farm as I was. No, it's the bloody boredom of it. The sheer, ruddy tedium. After a while, one can contemplate shagging almost anyone with enthusiasm so long as it's not the lady wife. Frankly, I even find some of my own ewes damned attractive, and I don't mind admitting it."

"Er, Master," says Ned, again trying to have the attention and silence of the room. "Much as we always enjoy hearing about your, erm, lusty, erm, animal urges, might I just . . . erm . . ."

And then Ned says that he has been approached by (which everyone takes to mean he has approached) the local council with a view to placing an industrial-strength wind turbine. On Hamble Hill.

There is a long silence. And then the long silence lengthens.

"But that's where the Clump is!" cries out Granville, finally. The surprise houseguests look alarmed. Maddocks is seamlessly clearing plates. A rather delicious-looking Italianate man who appears as if he has walked out of a Versace ad, wearing a chef's hat and apron, enters bearing a fillet of charred beef surrounded by baby vegetables—leeks, courgettes, carrots—and tiny weeny little baby cauliflowers, so small and tender it seems almost cruel to eat them.

"On the side, please, Giancarlo," says Cath, and gestures to the sideboard, where the vast oval dish is placed.

"Thank you, Granville, I do know that," says Ned. As most around the table know—even me—the Clump, official name Pen's Clump, is this numinous circle of trees on a hilltop. It is said of the Clump that if you run around the circle of trees naked seven times anticlockwise, the devil appears (i.e., the sort of place that is two a penny in this part of Wessex). "Both Pen's Clump and Hamble Hill have been in my family for four hundred years." He glances slyly around to see if anyone is remotely impressed, and is rewarded with a shining gaze from Virginie Lacoste, whose presence confirms that she is, to my only mild surprise, very thick with the Cobbs.

"And so's Clench Common," adds Lulu, which is annoying, as everyone knows that, apart from the Court Place lands, and the Hutton estate, almost everything around Honeyborne, from Spodden's Hatch to the surrounding hills, is owned by Ned.

"But we're in an AONB!" exclaims Granville. Then he stops himself, and adds, for the benefit of the two nonlocals, Virginie and Mathieu, "That's an area of outstanding natural beauty. And isn't Hamble Hill a local landmark? Ancient woodland? SSSI? I mean, site of special scientific interest? Surely there's no way you would swing planning permission? Not there. Not even you, Ned," he says, looking at Lulu, as if it is Ned's possession of a famously beautiful younger second wife, rather than an ancestral seat, that will carry the day for him.

Then Ned, astonishingly, goes on to lecture us—as if no one present has ever even once heard anyone mention climate change—on the importance of renewable energy and the depletion of finite fossil fuels. And how we all have to do our bit. And how he has been deeply influenced by Jesse Marlon's low-impact lifestyle—fervent glance in Jesse Marlon's direction—in this decision. And how he wants Godminster Hall to become carbon-neutral within five years.

He also points out that there always used to be a windmill on Hamble Hill, and claims you can see the foundations there still, which is annoying, as it implies he thinks sticking a white whirring triffid the size of Nelson's Column on a well-loved local landmark is merely a welcome return to the status quo ante.

So then Granville hits back, pointing out that the energy cost of erecting the turbine will probably be greater than the combined output of the turbine over its entire lifetime, and while it might generate enough energy to light some of the fourteen bedrooms in Godminster Hall for a year, maybe, what is absolutely clear beyond a shadow of doubt is that the turbine—

"I refuse to use the word 'windmill' "—would spoil the vista of Hamble Hill, not to mention the ancient tree circle of Pen's Clump—forever.

During all this ding-dong—I remember Jesse Marlon saying something like, "Green is now. Green is getting it on with the sun. Green is making energy from the tides and sweet music with the wind," which makes me wonder whether he was chanting a poem or actually saying something sensible—all I can think is . . . Bummer. I've just moved to one of the most beautiful spots, probably, on the entire planet, and now the local laird, this Dorset nob, is using his eco-credentials to ruin the views and shore up his annual income in one and the same fell swoop.

It has one immediate impact, though: I desist from trying to impress Lulu Bryanston, the gorgeous second wife, over the shirtfront of the Reverend Wyldbore-Smith. I have been over-egging my literary credentials with a view to being invited to the GodLitFest (just one of the many annual literary festivals held in all mini stately homes, market towns, and county capitals, not to mention Hay-on-Wye, Oxford, etc., etc.). But, strangely enough, Lulu does not seem impressed at my glorious previous career as national newspaper columnist.

She just said, "Should I have heard of you?" just like that old bat in the shop.

And when I said that I wrote about home life and so on, she just shuddered and said, "Oh, I can't be doing with any of that. That's GENRE. I'm only interested in LITERARY fiction, like Zadie Smith, or that marvelous writer who writes about how awful being a mother is, and how MARRIAGE is a form of MURDER—you know, that one . . . YOUNGER than you . . ."

I said, bleakly, "Rachel Cusk."

And she squealed, grabbing my arm with her tiny white paw in excitement, "Yes! Rachel Cusk! I think *she's* brilliant!"

Lulu then turned away from me to boast to Granville, who

it turns out reads everything, to discuss the latest Philip Roth they'd both read. "When I'm reading, I always know when something is really good," I heard her saying to a rapt Granville, "because my nipples get hard!"

I'm still trying to work out Ned and Lulu—although the Reverend Wyldbore-Smith was surprisingly forthcoming on the subject. He let slip that the old Bryanston money is running out, the GodLitFest is eating up capital, and there is no new money. Lulu wants to send the twins to Marlborough, because of the polo, of course, but also because the right sort of children go there, i.e., Otis Ferry (the Countryside Alliance's pinup and Burberry house model) and Kate Middleton (Prince William's squeeze), and he went there, not to mention one of the princesses Eugenie and Beatrice, he couldn't remember which. And, apparently, in his palmier years, Ned (who I have to admit is annoyingly attractive, with lazily amused eyes and thick rumpled brown hair and broad shoulders) was as prodigal with his forebear's resources as he is now frugal with the planet's.

As for Lulu (I didn't get this from the Reverend, but from Rose), she hasn't eaten anything for years, does yoga with a guru, and once confessed (again I had this from Rose) that she was "a secret nondrinker," which was a pretty brave thing to admit—I mean, not in New York or L.A. but in Honeyborne, where public displays of sobriety are greeted with about the same level of enthusiasm as an outbreak of Ebola virus.

"With Celia in residence, I think life's been a bit difficult for Lulu," the Reverend said, as he drank from his water glass, as if in solidarity with Lulu. "We must make allowances for her and not judge her too harshly." I wanted to ask him on what we would be judging her, but Ned's windmill intervention prevented me.

At the start of the evening, I would have said that if I had to go to bed with one of the men in the room who was not my husband—of course, not that I would—the order would have been (1) Ned Bryanston, forty-four, (2) Jesse Marlon Bryan-ston, twenty-two (or in reverse order—not fussy), and (3) the master, even if he is terribly seedy and speaks about women only in veterinary terms, and roars to Biddy, "Have you got Frisky, Bids? I'm just getting Jiggy in the Land Rover," and so on.

But I have to confess that, after the evening, Granville—who I had previously thought had all the charm of an Albanian people-trafficker—was moving up the inside lane like Jensen Button.

I liked the way he told me he was pleased we'd moved to Honeyborne because we brought some "Notting Hill edge" to the village, even though it wasn't true, and Notting Hill now is about as edgy as treacle sponge, but still. I liked the way he stood up to Ned.

But I also liked the way that Jesse Marlon threw his weight behind the plan, said how brave his father was and how right (even though, from what I gather from Rose, Jesse Marlon ap-parently prefers to live in a willow bender in the eco-village rather than stay with his father and stepmother at Godminster Hall). "Climate change is upon us, and we are responsible for it," he said, looking very noble, while all except Ned and Lulu stared down at their plates.

It may be the start of the dawning of a new Enlightenment, when the upper middle classes finally realize they are in the midst of a moment, a *climacteric*, in which they have to lead from the front, but that's not to say it doesn't make for a sticky evening.

"The wind turbine on Hamble Hill will reduce the con-sumption of fossil-fuel-generated electricity at Godminster Hall by seventy percent, but, even more important, it will serve as a visual reminder, as a positive environmental statement, that we each can do something," said Jesse Marlon. "Wind power is pure and free and causes no carbon-dioxide emissions, or nu-clear waste—"

At this point Granville interrupted and said, "But I thought they didn't work—isn't that one of the few things the Danes and the Krauts have ever managed to agree on?"—but Jesse Marlon had the bit between his teeth.

"I know that Dad feels, as a local landowner and local employer, he feels particularly responsible. Turbines are, you know, a symbol of our age, and we are going to see a lot more of them." He concluded, "I just want you all to know I'm four hundred percent behind Dad's plan."

"Thank you, Jesse," said Ned. "And I am pleased to add that the environmental-impact assessment we have commissioned from consultants is looking highly positive," Ned said, as if we would be pleased, too. "It's going to planning by the end of March. I know it's going to be an uphill struggle, but we are as a family"—at this point he looked at Jesse Marlon rather than his wife Lulu—"absolutely passionate about generating the energy of tomorrow."

Ned raised his glass, as if to himself.

We all sit and digest this, with the risotto and beef. I feel another wave of sleep wash over me, suddenly realize I need to go to bed *now* and stifle a yawn.

"Hold on there, Ned, Jesse Marlon, would you, a minute?" Granville says, quicker off the mark than anyone else, and I can just see why he's made a fortune in the City. For the first time, I sense the mind like a rat trap behind the bonhomous front, and I feel a little bristle of anticipation. "Wind is a nice way of raking in a few thousand in revenue every year without lifting a finger, thanks to the subsidy provided by the taxpayer, eh, Ned? We're told they're cheap, free, etc., but, in fact, they cost a fortune to erect and are subsidized to the tune of millions of pounds by the electricity companies, who are legally obliged to supply a chunk of their energy from renewable sources, i.e., wind. You're not harnessing the power of wind, Ned. You're skimming off profit—what will you get, ooh, let's see—my guess is something in the region of £15,000 a year? Mmm? Which will cover the cost of two terms out of the three for one of the twins at Marlborough, no?"

And then Granville reaches into the inside pocket of his jacket.

Across the table, Ralph's eyes meet mine, with that look that says, "Christ, Mimi. I know how much you love a good drama, but I'm perfectly happy with beans on toast at home. Why on earth do you insist on dragging me to these things?"

At Granville's words, Ned sloshes more Château Talbot into his glass. The wine has been chosen by Cath. She told Ralph earlier that she had discovered "her inner grape" after they bought a château in Bordeaux, and he had replied that it was jolly nice for them all that she had.

Maddocks wrings his hands impotently behind his elegant shoulder. Lulu takes another sip of Perrier. Henry and Biddy gaze into space, wearing that detached look you see on dog owners' faces as their pets void their bowels onto the green-sward of London's Royal Parks. Cath toys with her napkin, not looking at any of her guests, and I notice a red flush creeping up her slender neck, blotches on her embonpoint. The young Golden Couple are smiling, too wrapped up in their own fairy-tale narrative to see the plot twisting ahead. The Reverend Wyldbore-Smith is making a soothing humming noise, as if the sound will preclude anyone else from voicing anything more provocative.

Lastly, I glance at Virginie Lacoste, who, with her color-less and conventional husband Mathieu, has been in residence since Friday, leaving the children, twins Capucine and Cle-mentine, and Guy, back in Lonsdale Gardens with the uni-formed nanny, NouNou. Her silken blond hair hangs straight to her narrow shoulders, and she is wearing a puffy but narrow-wristed Chloé blouse tucked into a Nanette Lepore sailor skirt, a skirt that accentuates her tiny waist with a triple row of six gold, anchor-studded nautical buttons. I can't see her legs under the table, but when I inspected them earlier, they were clad in gossamer white stockings, and shoes with square buckles on them, which was annoying because, as every woman knows, only those with sensational legs can get away with anything but black opaques.

Jesse Marlon tried not to stare at her when she threw her head back and laughed, showing a pearly horseshoe of perfect teeth. But it was clear that he has not seen anything quite so blatantly, expensively sexy since Lulu went to London and came back with a pair of thigh-high Christian Louboutin red-soled boots that she pranced around Godminster Hall in, naked except for a pair of cami knickers and a lacy teddy, in front of me and Ned and Jesse Marlon and a pargeter who was carving a peregrine falcon on an architrave.

As my eyes meet hers, she gives me a tiny shrug and a pout, as if to say, " 'Ere we go again!"

Virginie finds the English love of a strain-making planning dispute, the intensity of their feelings for their pets, their love of comfortable clothes and nursery food, and their dogged but often doomed efforts to remain true to their spouses wildly incomprehensible.

The only silver lining in all this as far as I'm concerned is that the gathering storm might give Virginie second thoughts about her declared yearning to buy a property in what she calls the "countryside." More specifically, it might deter her from homing in on my patch.

I thought I'd cleverly dissuaded her from viewing any properties in Godminster. But, in fact, I've only managed to bring her even closer to home. As she told me over what she called the *zakouski* in the drawing room, she and Mathieu are staying over Sunday night so they can be the first viewers and prospective owners of the gatehouse at Hutton, a mini-estate between Honeyborne and Larcombe Ducis, owned by Sir Michael Hutton.

This hardly bears thinking about.

Granville finishes scribbling. "Here," says Granville, ripping off a check and handing it to Ned with a wolfish smile. "I think that should just about cover it, mmm?"

I see Cath crane over and decipher the amount.

"Don't worry," she tells me later. "Granville did cut Ned a big check, but it's okay. To Gran, it's still cab fare. Now, who wants tea? We've got 'erbal," (Cath dropped the h) "PG Tips . . . lapsang . . ."

"So it's a choice of gay, builder's, or posh?" I confirm.

"I'll have ze gay tea, pleeze," says Virginie, winking at me. "Limon and geenger eez my favorite."

"Builder's for me," I say.

"Well, as we all seem to be staying in character when it comes to our choice of tea," Ralph pipes up, "I'll have posh."

Rose

Of course, it's packed out. People are queuing as if they're trying to penetrate the Harrods china department at the beginning of the January sale, and standing two deep down the sides.

There's always an enjoyably municipal sense of occasion about the memorial hall in the village, with its curtained stage for am dram productions, its little bar off to the side, and the antlers sprouting off the walls at intervals with important wooden plaques underneath saying, KILLED CLOUTSHAM BALL 1927 or KILLED SPODDEN'S HATCH 1949. There are big wooden ceiling-height doors at the back, lofty enough to admit a hay wain, which can be flung open to admit views of hills and dale and gusts of our fine Dorset air. Today the doors are shut, as it is a raw February day, and windy, the sort of weather that makes the eyes water, the lips thin, and the nostrils pinch.

I sit next to Mimi, so we can together monitor the door to see who else is filing in, and where they'll sit. Mimi is looking pale, and wan, poor lamb, even though she is the curly ruddy type. "I hope they keep the door open," she whispers, sucking on a mint, which again is unlike her, as she usually complains about being too cold, not too hot.

Henry Pike and Biddy, plus Martin Thomas, the second whip, are in the front row already, as you would expect. With the hunting arrests, they are sharing equal star billing with Dick

Turbine, which is Ned Bryanston's new name in the village. Behind them sit the Hitchens, who have closed the Stores for this occasion, Dr. Ashburton, Garry and Debbie from the pub, and Scary Gwenda from the stables. I nudge Mimi to alert her to Gwenda's upright presence.

Her bearing reflects her ranking status as a horsewoman and active member of the foxhounds and staghounds at this occasion, which has been called partly to reflect outrage that the natural order of things has been reversed, and huntsmen rather than their quarry are being held at bay.

Behind them, in other rows, are the men in uniform: flat caps and tattersall shirts, maroon or green V-neck sweaters, and Hunt ties showing a gold pattern of gundogs or antlers against dark-green backgrounds. I spot Sir Michael Hutton. He has that look on his face that you often see on older members of the landed gentry, the one that says, "What on earth are we coming to?"

When Sir Michael refers to the war, he doesn't mean the Great War or the Second World War, he means the Civil War. I once made the mistake of asking how many acres he owned. "Acres of roof, dear girl, or land?" he had boomed. "Roof, or land?" And then he went on to explain to me that if I ever looked at Hutton, I would notice that from the said roofs sprouted a forest of chimneys—"But not all of them draw, y'know"—and when I asked why, were they blocked? he said no, it was because chimneys were a status symbol in the seventeenth century, because if a house had lots of chimneys, it suggested that the house had lots of fireplaces, and therefore lots of housemaids and child slaves to tend the fires and go up and down chimneys, as if that were all perfectly obvious. Sir Michael doffs his cap to Gwenda, who gives him a level stare as if to say, "There's no time for civilities now—my entire livelihood, as the proud owner of Honeyborne's livery yard, is at stake."

The wooden chairs creak under shifting, tweedy buttocks. A few sit nonchalantly in neck braces, following headlong plunges from horses. The older men have lumpy, crooked fingers, squished together like Wall's sausages in paper packs from long nights of lambing on windswept hillsides during raw March nights. At least two are wearing, without any irony, deerstalkers, and many of the men in their eighties are fiddling with their hearing aids, as if worried they aren't going to hear a word above the hubbub.

The women are the houses of Barbour and Puffa or the Edinburgh Woollen Mill, all except Mimi, who is in her Husky, and Cath Cobb and Lulu Bryanston, who are, as usual, looking stunning in their very different ways.

Cath is smooth in caramel cashmere with a little jaunty scarf knotted at her throat, a tweed skirt, and a pair of Ferragamo flat boots. Her blond hair shines like a beacon among the hairy sea of sage-green tweed and caps and head scarves. She is sans Granville, as Granville, one supposes, is in New York, or London, or Dubai, or Frankfurt, this week.

Lulu's rock-chick in extremely tight Seven jeans, a pair of those baby-girl-pink, suede furry boots with pom-poms, and a cardigan open to reveal one of her vintage seventies T-shirts. This one is an old Clash one, and dolly-sized. The section of flat, tanned belly (the Bryanstons always manage to go to St. Kitts at Christmas, despite professing to have no money) seems to deny the existence of the twins and completely rule out the consumption of one too many mince pies over Christmas.

And on the wooden, raised stage: Ned is at a long desk on the podium with Harvey Jones, chairman of the Parish Council, looking through paperwork. Ned is trying to look concerned and responsive to opinion—but he still conveys the arrogance of aristocracy, the superiority of the upper-class Englishman who feels he has nothing to prove, as his family already did that, to the monarch's satisfaction, over four hundred years ago.

"While he may talk about the human family and the environment, this whole windmill thing has only served to confirm what we already knew," I whisper to Mimi. "Ned Bryanston only cares about his family."

"Like, duh, Rose," says Mimi. "Of course he does."

Ned is sitting next to a man with white hair and a trimmed beard. There is a flipchart to the side, which we are all eyeing warily, in case we are forced to ingest data or understand diagrams.

"Hey, clock Lulu's T-shirt," whispers Mimi. "The Clash one. Saying 'White Riot.' I used to have one just like it about twenty years ago, and now the very same one appears on Lulu as retro or vintage. God, it makes me feel old! As if Lulu knows anything about the Clash! I saw them live loads of times," she continues, sulkily. "Well, okay, I saw them once. But she probably got it from Rellik on Golborne Road, for about £60."

As she speaks, I become aware that Colin Watts is framed in the doorway to the left, ahead of where we are ensconced.

For a nanosecond, when my gaze rests on the tall frame and dark hair and thick brows, I think of Jesse Marlon, so am disappointed when the leather jacket, the fag, and the jeans as worn without fail by Watts hove into view.

"Don't look now, but it's him, again," I say, nudging Mimi, who immediately swivels her head to the left, to see who's in the doorway.

"Oh God, so it is," she says, staring at him. "It's funny, I barely ever noticed him before. Now we all need a kind of human pop-up blocker to get rid of him. We have blocked a pop-up from Colin Watts! Click! We have blocked a pop-up from Colin Watts! Click!" She mimes clicking a mouse with her right hand. "Rose? Are you okay?"

"Very funny. Yes," I whisper.

I'd already treated Mimi to a highly colored but strictly edited account of Colin Watts's "break-in," which stopped just short of hinting that Ceci, I, and even Jesse Marlon and Pierre had all narrowly escaped sexual predation by the village rapist, and certainly did not extend to my lingering clinch with Jesse Marlon by the Aga.

I am distracted when Mimi asks me if I'm all right because

Ruth Wingfield is surging towards us, smiling brightly. She has put on lipstick, powder, scent, and a Hermès head scarf, I note, for her public appearance. "Room for a little one?" she says.

Mimi gets chatting to Ruth. "Have you been in this part of the world long?" Ruth inquires. She is being superfriendly to Mimi, but Mimi is not to know that the reason for Ruth's warmth is that Ruth is a relative newcomer, too (she has been a resident of Honeyborne for only five years, which counts as having just arrived). She is in her early fifties, and rather good-looking, sparkling blue eyes, high color, glossy dark mane, etc., the sort of woman described in her prime as handsome.

"So, do you ride?" I hear her ask, in a pause.

I see Mimi flinch at the question, which is going to force her into a shocking admission if she answers truthfully.

"No," says Mimi. "Well, not for ages. Not properly." But it is too late to row back—Mimi has already seen the look of horror cross Ruth's face, as if registering that the earth had slightly wobbled on its axis.

"What?" Ruth can't help but blurt out. She looks over to me for help. A woman with all her faculties apparently intact has left town—left London—and moved with her three able-bodied children to Honeyborne, Dorset . . . and she doesn't ride!

Mimi looks agonized. Luckily for everyone (I don't think I could face another excursion to the stables right now), Ruth relents, as Mimi explains that she is keen for the children to ride, and she is in the process of sorting it out now.

"Truth be told, even I can't ride at the moment. I've got this blasted horse," I hear her saying to Mimi, her mouth pulled down into a grimace, so we can admire a corn-yellow collection of niblets in her lower jaw.

Of course, I've lived in Honeyborne for years, so I know that when someone horsey like Ruth says, "I've got this blasted horse," it means they have a horse that's lame and no use to man nor beast, just as when a war hero says, "I've got this silly leg," what he really means is that he's had a leg amputated.

"Bodger's got pus," Ruth confirms, in a loud voice. "Bloody bore, excuse my French. Vet's been in not once but twice—that will be two hundred pounds, thank you very much—first thought it was a tendon, even though any fool could see it was the fetlock hot and throbbing. Didn't believe me till we took Bodger's shoe off and . . . well, I don't want to go into it, it is almost lunchtime," she goes on.

I tune out for a while, as Mimi gets on with outlining her fantasy riding plans for the children, and starts working on Ruth, clearly with a view to dumping her children on Ruth for long periods of time during the holidays. Still, Ruth seems inexplicably quite keen on the idea, and is responding to the heavy hints by describing the "daily drill" at Sweetoaks Farm, Ruth Wingfield's place on the Larcombe Ducis road, with enthusiasm.

"You can drop them off at eight A.M., wet or dry, I'm up with the lark, just make sure they have wellies and sou'westers, and do remember vests. I'll keep them busy!" Ruth says. "Take them straight out to the stables . . . grooming . . . I can soon tell who's made for it, who are the joiner-inners, and who won't want to do it again, I can tell you . . . I get them to clean tack and polish the bits, then I give them some lemon squash and a nice Club biscuit, for elevenses . . ."

I nudge Mimi to make her shut up. The chairman of the vale of Larcombe Staghounds, Harvey Jones, MSH, who also happens to be chairman of Honeyborne Parish Council, is at last calling the meeting to order.

Harvey Jones. I have a soft spot for him, and I think he knows it.

He's a tall, imposing man in his late fifties, a circuit judge, with dark, General Sir Mike Jackson–type eyes, and brilliantined, Max Hastings military-type dark hair combed over to one side.

He begins to explain things in his unashamedly plummy voice.

"Gled to see you all have the briefin' notes," he says, glancing at the sheets we are all holding on our laps concerning the planning application and a summary of the wind turbine proposals that we picked up from a pile on the table on the way in. "But orn the arrests first," he says. "The master and Martin Thomas have been released on bail, as we can all see from their presence here this morning. But the case is now, I remind you all, and all members of the press, sub judice."

He uses the stern phrase as if he could have addressed the meeting entirely in Latin, if he so chose, and gives a stern look to the reporter from the *West Dorset Free Press.*

"Anyway, I don't want to chunter on for longer than is necessary," Harvey continues, as I gaze at him, thinking, He's a real man, and mentally comparing him to Pierre, which I know is unfair, "because we all have jorbs to get orf to, animals to get back to, and there's another important item to consider, and Ned Bryanston and Ian Smith from South-West Wind, the energy consultants, are both giving up time to be here to explain it all to us, which makes this—I presume I am right in saying— an open plenning meeting."

Then the door pushes open again, and a murmur ripples through the chairs and the crowd of people who can't find chairs who stand down the sides and at the back. A uniformed officer stands uncertainly in the doorway.

"Aha," says Harvey. "Thank you for coming"—he pauses for effect—"Superintendent." Then he addresses the sea of sage in field clothing again, now whispering on their rickety seats. The tension has gone up by several notches. "We have a representative from the West Dorset Constabulary." He nods to the policeman. "Thanks for coming, Jim. We don't want to, ah, *hold* you lornger than is strictly necessary." The room erupts into claps and stomps, and Harvey raises a warning hand. "We've gort to at least try to keep it calm, please," he says, in clipped tones.

"Before we do move orn, though, I have some information. Henry Pike, the master, and Martin Thomas were arrested in their homes in the early morning last week, as you know. The constabulary had been supplied with apparent evidence of breaches of the Hunting Act. This evidence came in the shape of a video."

A low susurrus starts as this news breaks over the room.

"Quiet, please. I'm almost finished, and then Superintendent Jim Moore will be happy to address your concerns for twenty minutes about rural security, poaching, car thefts, and so on, which I know many of you here are very anxious to air." He holds aloft a long arm, like Caesar quelling the crowd in the Circus Maximus, and the room falls silent again.

"The video had been filmed in the meadow above Spodden's Hatch at Larcombe Foot. It was possible to see the blue flash of a pheasant feeder in one frame. And that is all I am allowed to say at present." Then Harvey moves on to the subject of the windmill and outlines procedures for the remainder of the meeting, and tells us by what date we have to get our letters in to the district council, and to whom they should be addressed, and the reference number. He then introduces Ned, who needs no introduction. At which Ned rises to his feet.

"I'd like to thank you all for coming," he says, which I think strikes an odd note. After all, we aren't there to please him. We are there because we want to manifest our concern about his plans to put up a huge windmill on the hill. "As you are all aware, Godminster Hall, in consort with our charity, the GodLitFest, or the Godminster Literary Festival, has submitted a planning application to erect one—I repeat just one—wind turbine on Hamble Hill."

Around me, I can sense the adamantine opposition of the audience to every syllable, and I almost feel for Ned. I've come to the meeting with an open mind, but I sense I am in a minority of two.

"It comprises a tower forty-four meters high, a three-bladed rotor with a diameter of fifty-two meters, and an overall height of seventy meters," he says. "It is, by comparison with other turbines"—he coughs, as if he knows he is lying—"of only modest size—" He pauses, fatally allowing the audience to interpolate loud cries of "Rubbish!" and "Bollocks!" and "That's the height of Nelson's Column." "It is of a modest size," he repeats, "and will be, from a distance of four to five kilometers, only a small and incidental feature on the landscape." He is reading from a notebook.

"Blot on the landscape, more loike," I hear a voice roar out.

"The context to this application is this. Godminster Hall is a big place, we have an active literary festival every year, we are a local employer, and we, too, are conscious of our responsibilities. But we all have a responsibility to the planet. We have to think about the big picture, as well as the small picture. Godminster Hall is a net contributor both to the local economy and to climate change. And this one windmill—once we have offset the impact of installing it, of course—will reduce our carbon emissions annually by seventy percent. We have engaged independent local experts to assess the impact of the turbine, and to carry out a bird and bat survey, and the archaeological, ecological, visual impact; also, shadow flicker, noise, and traffic generation studies have all been completed."

"Get on with it!" shouts someone.

"Photomontages of the site, before and after installation, have been prepared and are available along with all the plans and the detailed EIA—environmental impact assessment—in the Town Hall at Godminster and online at www.godlitfest.org.uk."

Ned continues drilling into the stony silence. The man next to him, from South-West Wind, holds up a sample montage of the site, a colored-in landscape that shows the stirring contours of Hamble Hill and Pen's Clump, and the windmill merely as an insignificant speck on the proud rise.

There are loud scoffs of laughter as people mutter and strain to make out the faint wind turbine, which, it has already been established at a meeting in the Farmers' Bar in the pub earlier, would stand as high as a twenty-two-story skyscraper. Finally, in the end, there are so many shouts of "Where's the windmill?" that the South-West Wind chap has to point a finger to mark the spot of the turbine.

"Not to scale," Ruth Wingfield peals out from our row, shaking an upraised fist. "Not to scale!"

"As for the location," Ned presses on, "the turbine will present a simple image within a large-scale, hilly landscape—"

"What rubbish!" comes the deep growly voice of Henry Pike.

"And experts have identified Hamble Hill as the ideal location for this simple, elegant structure. I'd like to make a strong visual connection between the windmill and Godminster Hall, which lies only about a mile away, to the northwest. The windmill will capture the wind, and, finally"—he looks around as if this is the decider—"windmills have always been part of the Dorset landscape. Indeed, there are the remains of a windmill on the top of Hamble Hill, as I expect many of you may already know."

After that, the meeting went to the floor, and the fun really started. Ned had the shit kicked out of him by everyone, by the Council for the Protection of Rural England (who talked about topple distance from footpaths), by the RSPB (who talked about birds and flight paths), by the local Jurassic group (who talked about the integrity of the landscape), by the local archaeological society, and by Uncle Tom Cobleigh.

"Utter tripe, with all due respect," was Henry Pike's intervention, the one that met with the most rapturous approval. "The developers are holding us to ransom while offering you, the landowner, the pot of gold at the end of the rainbow."

But the most persuasive case against was mounted by a little bearded man in the audience whom no one had ever seen before, which means that he probably lives at least two miles away. He admitted to being an electrical engineer, and furthermore confessed that he had investigated the specification and performance of the intended windmill, and that, basically, the wind turbine couldn't pull the skin off a rice pudding, let alone power Godminster Hall's many mansions.

During all this, I dart a look across at Lulu Bryanston. Her back is straight but rigid, and her rosebud mouth has set into a little mulish moue. There is no sign of the mother-in-law, Celia Bryanston, so there is a mutton-dressed-as-lamb-to-the-slaughter feeling about her as she sits there in her Clash T-shirt.

Then Harvey repeats the information about whom parishioners can write in to with their views, the deadline for submissions, and says that the council is due to take a decision by the end of next month.

Which is all terribly confusing.

I was ready for this windmill thing to be about new green versus old blue. But it doesn't appear to be so black and white after all.

Nothing ever is.

Mimi

"Mum, purlease!" Mirabel orders. "Stop scraping! I keep telling you!" making me think—and not for the first time—if I had *ever* spoken to *my* mother like that, she would have given me very short shrift, but now my life seemed to consist of *my* daughter telling *me* off, and not the other way round.

Is this normal? I wonder.

Casimir continues placidly reading the biography of Freddie Flintoff (while other people's children always seem to have their noses in a Penguin Classic, my beloved only son's limited thirst for literature is quenched only by sporting biographies and the literary output of Jeremy Clarkson).

Posy, another one of my children who has also, strangely, never exhibited the "rage to learn" that other mothers are always discovering, to their apparent consternation, in their severely gifted children, has finally put away as childish her collection of moist cleansing wipes, which was her pride and joy until her eighth year, and is now sorting by size and shape her extensive collection of travel-size toiletries—mainly shampoo, body lotion, and bubble bath, but with a few prized sewing kits and shower caps—a collection that has spread to three shoe boxes.

Ralph is in the sitting room, occasionally poking the fire. I am going round the playroom, collecting empty cups and yogurt pots, banana skins and apple cores, and muttering. Mirabel is sitting at the PC in the playroom, which I have removed from her bedroom and placed with the screen facing out, according to the diktats from the government about "keeping safe online," a transfer of only a few meters that Mirabel announced has ruined her entire life. Ana has gone to the pub. Garry and Debbie have taken her under their wing, a development that makes me wonder whether they are intending to poach her from under my nose, and whether I would mind very much if they did.

And I am planning to give Ralph a lovely home-cooked special supper à deux, and break the news that, in due course, we will be a family not of five (well, seven, if you're Posy and include Trumpet and Calypso), but six.

"What do you mean, 'scraping'?" I say, coming up behind Mirabel's left shoulder.

She clicks at the corner of the screen and then says something into her headset. "It's only my mum, Spike," she says, and then glowers at me, while hammering out a message in an open-chat area of the screen, Photoshopping a picture of herself that she is adding to her Bebo page, while at the same time googling something about Hadrian's Wall for her history homework. She is clearly online to Spike, who must be at a friend's house because, as we all know, there is no running water or electricity, let alone Internet café with coffee bar, at Spodden's Hatch. "Mum, do you have to embarrass me all the time? Why did you, like, deliberately walk into shot? You know I've got the webcam on! It's, like, so embarrassing if Spike thinks you're around when I'm talking to him."

While we are talking, my eye runs over a snatch of the chat exchange that was taking place, with someone called seximonki14, in a little box in the corner.

Mirabel: OMG, wt 2 do want to cry coz sooo bored!!! So boring where I live really miss London.

Seximonki14: gawjuz grrl, don't b down, K? I no loads who want 2b m8ts witu, and if u reli like them, then I mite let them. OMG PIR!! Watch out PIR

Seximonki14: I warned u POS POS!

So I say to Mirabel, as a responsible parent should, "Er, darling, I hope you don't think I'm out of line here"—bright smile, reassuring pat—"and your personal life is your own, I know, but, er, do you *know* this seximonki person?" At this point Casimir lets out a scornful laugh, as if it's really sad that I might think that Mirabel would know anyone she was communicating with online, as if I were missing the point. "And what on earth is that language you are talking in?"

Mirabel explains in a long-suffering voice that seximonki14 is Char, a friend she "met" online, as if all this is perfectly normal, they are talking in English, and would I please go now.

I go into the kitchen to call Rose.

"Not content with plastering her Web page with come-hither self-portraits she has somehow managed to upload herself, including one of her clad only in pants and bunny ears, Mirabel is now live to the nation on webcam," I whinge, as I lay the table. "I said, 'Why isn't there one of me, or Dad, on your Web page, or Calypso even?' and she said, 'You're so not important in my Facebook life.' I mean, is this normal? I told her that if she wanted to attract every perv and pederast on the planet, she was going the right way about it, but she just sighed and carried on chatting to someone online whose screen name was 'Seximonki14' and told me I didn't know anything and she was, like, totally fine and would I chillax."

"I know," says Rose sympathetically, and I hear her taking a sip of her drink. I can hear the *Archers* theme tune—*rum ti tum ti tum ti tum!*—start up in the background. "But what can we do?"

"I don't know, Rose. And by the way, did you know that

there's a link to Ceci on Mirabel's page, and the link says 'Ceci mybestfriend' and underneath that it says, 'We've had lesbian sex eight times?' What about that? Should we be worried? All I know is that at her age I was dressed by my mother in Laura Ashley smock dresses, and spent all my spare time lying on my bed reading *Ballet Shoes* and longing for a Labrador puppy. And, oh yes, what do the acronyms PIR and POS stand for?"

"Parent in room and parent over shoulder, I think," Rose replies, distracted because she is an *Archers* addict and is longing for her fix.

I return to the playroom and announce that the children can watch half a DVD and no more than half while Mum and Dad have supper, and that Ana would be babysitting the next night, as we were going to the opera. Which we are, even if it is only Godminster Opera's production of *Don Pasquale* by Donizetti in Godminster Hall, a privilege that Ralph would shell out serious money to avoid but is—not that he knows this yet—forking out £100 to attend in black tie.

Mirabel actually looks at me as if she might, for once, be impressed.

"Mum, no shit!" she says. "Really? Wow!" and she starts hammering the news to seximonki14.

"But I didn't think you were interested in opera or ballet, darling," I say, so pleased I don't tick her off for "no shit." Then I move in to peek over her shoulder.

"Hey, get this," she is writing. "You know my mum? You know I said she was, like, sad, and really old, and never goes out? And my dad thinks that Bart Simpson is, like, a baronet or a duke or something? Well, get this! They're going on *Oprah*!!!"

I have made a really nice supper, fish pie and spinach, and we are now on to the Somerset Camembert. I only have a glass—maybe a glass and a half, tops—but as usual now the red wine tastes bitter in my mouth, of course. Metallic, and vinegary. Ralph looks well, bronzed and weatherbeaten and blue-eyed after our long walk on Hamble Hill on Sunday, and I am thinking how good-looking he is and how lucky I am when he starts sneaking a hand towards a copy of this month's *Angler*, which he's brought with him from his study, in case there is a lull in proceedings.

So I think, Come on, Mimi. Better strike before husband loses himself in some blurry brown photographs of underwater carp or becomes too engrossed in a long piece about the joys of light tackle. I don't want to have this talk in bed, when we are too zonked by our daily overdose of pure unpolluted Dorset air—it's like Xanax—and, in my case, raging hormones, actually to speak to each other.

"Darling, you know I've been feeling even more tired than usual . . ." I begin, in a pleasant, conversational voice, as I clear, but leaving the Camembert and the wine.

"For someone who doesn't work, you're always tired, you must be ill," he jumps in immediately. "You know, I think you should see the doctor."

So I say, hurt and surprised, "That's funny, because I did. Did see the doctor."

Then Ralph looks at me, and I see alarm flare behind his eyes. He is on red alert, tense, a hair trigger. He starts looking around the room, as if men with nets and stun guns are going to leap out and bundle him into a waiting vehicle.

"I saw Ashburton, um, a couple of days ago."

"And?" says Ralph, something flickering across his face, like a cloud crossing over the sun's reflection in a puddle. My stomach is twisting with worry. Ralph isn't usually as grim and inhumane as this.

He is still staring at me as if he has never seen me before, as if I have not borne him three healthy children or cooked him supper or washed his socks once in my entire life. As if I am a stranger to him, and an illegal alien in my own kitchen.

"Well." I pause. It is hard getting the words out. Harder than I thought it would be. I am beginning to dread the reaction.

This isn't going to plan.

"I'm pregnant. Ashburton did a test."

There is a silence.

I turn my back on him and crouch down, below his sight-line, and pretend to do something with the warming oven of the Aga. I slam the door back shut as if we are in the middle of a dinner during a perfectly normal evening, having a perfectly normal marital exchange about a perfectly normal marital sub-ject, and turn to face Ralph. For a second I toy with adopting a faraway, I-am-with-child expression, but abandon this plan as soon as I see my husband's face.

Ralph sits at the table in our kitchen, with the dresser hung with Cornishware and random blue and white china behind him, Calypso is snoozing in her Cath Kidston basket next to the Aga, the clock is ticking, the wind is throwing itself against the windows, the fire is crackling next door in the sitting room, where all our furniture from Colville Crescent—Ralph's beloved tapestries, along with George Smith sofas and a footstool em-broidered with the Fleming family motto, *Dominus Providebit* (translation: the Lord will provide)—have all found a cozy new home.

His face is dark, and his blue eyes bore into mine.

"Is it mine, Imogen?" he asks.

I stand there, frozen in time and space. How could he say that?

Ralph never calls me Imogen. Unless he thinks I've done something wrong. He called me Imogen on that Guy Fawkes night, of course, when he revealed that he knew all about my fling with Si, who—just to complete the humiliation—was two-timing me with Posy's teacher. Then he said he had sold our house to Clare, i.e., the pluperfect tense, *had sold*. There was no going back, the action had been completed and achieved in the past. And then he said that Posy's teacher was pregnant. By the man I had slept with outside my marriage. It was all very complicated.

And then he said we were moving to Dorset, which we did, eighteen months ago.

So, yes, you could say that Ralph picks his moments to deploy the word "Imogen," my Christian name, which no one ever calls me unless they are really, really angry, like a lethal weapon.

"Oh God. I'm sorry, darling. I don't know why I said that . . ." Ralph mutters. But it is too late.

"And whose, exactly, do you think it is?" I hear myself yelling, enraged. In fact, I must be yelling my head off, because I hear Posy and Cas shout, "Shut up, Mummy," in rare unison, at the same time as Ralph is hissing, "Quiet! Do you want our children to hear?" I just can't believe Ralph dredged up Si and my moment of madness to throw at me now. "Is it mine?" he dares to inquire!

Well, I can't exactly get into the fact there isn't anyone bedable for miles around. Apart from Henry Pike, but he shags anything that moves—he once told me that he'd "covered the waterfront" in West Dorset of everyone between the ages of "sixteen and sixty" and then, proudly, in the next breath, that he had "serviced so many old boilers" that he was thinking of "applying for a Corgi registration." And apart from Jesse Marlon Bryanston, and Ned, and, actually, now I come to think of it, the chairman of the West Dorset Staghounds, Harvey Jones, also chairman of the Parish Council (any sort of power is terribly attractive) is handsome in a basset-houndy way. But I am obviously not going to go there. For Ralph is staring at me levelly, as if facing a firing squad.

He darts a glance towards the kitchen door, checks the playroom is still quiet, and takes a deep breath. "Listen, darling," he says, and heaves a deep sigh, as if what he is going to say is going to hurt him even more than it's going to hurt me. "I would like to make my position entirely clear," he goes on to announce, as if he's someone else, not Ralph, addressing not his wife, but a court of law. "You know my line on this. It's never altered one iota since Posy. I don't *want* a fourth child. We've got three children, and that seems to be more than enough for you to cope with already. Aren't three children enough? What's wrong with the three children we already have?"

He looks at me imploringly, but my heart is too full of sadness to answer. "I never wanted more, and, my love, I'm sorry, but I never will. I thought you were on the Pill. How on earth did it happen? Did you stop taking it? Whatever the case, it now appears that you're pregnant. I've no idea how this happened," he continues (like Dr. Ashburton, Ralph seems personally, even deeply let down by the tiresome propensity of women of child-bearing age to conceive after enjoying marital relations with their husbands, whose role in the conception is at this point conveniently forgotten). "But I can only assume that you allowed yourself to forget the Pill, and then you present me with a fait accompli," he continues, holding up a hand when I start protesting that I did, actually, remember to take the Pill, actually, only just not at the same time every day, to convey that he has no time or inclination to hear my pathetic excuses.

I know it was stupid of me to slip up, but I still idiotically thought that Ralph would take it on the chin after the initial blow had worn off, that he would square his shoulders, give me a manly hug, and say, "You silly old goose. Stop crying. Whatever you decide to do, I'll support you. I want you to know that despite my repeated refusals to give in to your wish to have yet another baby after Posy was born eight years ago, for all the reasons I have always spelled out, I would be truly honored if you would consider having my child."

But he didn't. It was all dismayingly clear. He wanted to have nothing to do with it. If this was the dawn of time rather than Dorset 2008, he'd have left me in the cave to whelp on my own on a pile of furs while he went off into the distance, an upright figure carrying a spear, running fast in search of bison . . . I know that we're middle-aged and that Posy would be coming up for nine when the baby's born and that newborns and teenagers are a hideous combo to manage; I know that money's tighter since I stopped working, but still. We are a pretty solid couple—well, I'm not saying we have the strongest marriage in showbiz, but we're as solid as any other married heterosexual couple, at any rate—and we live in a five-bedroom farmhouse in God's Own Country, and—

"Thing is, I really don't want this to drag on," Ralph says, interrupting my private ravings. "It won't get any easier. How many weeks are you?"

"Around six, I suppose," I said.

"Darling, for your sake, the sooner you . . . deal with it, the better it will be and we can . . ." Ralph pauses as he struggles to find acceptable English alternatives to phrases like "move on" and "reach closure." Then he starts saying he will pay for me to have it done privately, and, for some reason, this makes it all much worse because I know how Ralph hates parting with money, and the offer makes me realize that he's being deadly serious. He doesn't want me to have our baby. I didn't think he was going to dance a jig at the news, but I never expected this total brick wall.

During this speech I stand up and blindly make my way out of the kitchen, feeling sick to the stomach, and go into the playroom. And my three children are all sitting on the sofa in a row. They are watching *March of the Penguins*. They are glued to it.

It is getting to the bit where the daddy penguins stand in a freezing circle in minus 80 degrees for two months, cradling the precious egg on their feet, waiting for the mummy penguins to return from the vast, icy wastes, and then, when the mummies come back they practice passing the egg back to Mummy again, and if it rolls onto the ice for even one second the egg/chick cracks open, frozen solid in a second. I make them budge up so Posy and Cas and Mirabel and I sit together on the sofa in a row. Calypso comes to lie across our feet. Soon, tears are running down all our cheeks. Especially mine, and even Cas's.

Now, Cas has, I know, seen on the Internet hard-core stuff, things I never even knew were physically possible. And I have it on authority from Rose that all the children have watched something totally unmentionable on YouTube before it was removed. "It wasn't anything like . . . fisting, or something, was it?" I said to Rose. "Oh, I should think it was," she answered glumly. "Nothing seems to bother them."

But it does. They can't take the penguins at all. They just can't hack it.

"Turn it off, Mum," Cas begged, when we first watched it. "It's just . . . too . . . upsetting."

We sit there in a row, crying.

In my head, while I lie sleepless in bed next to a slumbering Ralph later, I consider all the minuses and the pluses of the road ahead.

On the minus side I can come up with a list as long as my arm: if I stand up to him and refuse to "deal with it," Ralph will be utterly furious and make my life miserable for the next nine months, in fact, make that forever, and the children will be repulsed at the evidence that we have had sex even once since Posy was conceived.

I'll be a scraggy, spent-looking, haggard older mother with a pram-face; people will doubtless inquire if I am the baby's "nan" at the pannier market; we will be straight back to nappies and sandpit and fingerpainting hell; I will have to stand glumly pushing a baby in a swing all weekend while three older children want to go to raves and take E. I'll be compared to Sophie Wessex (and not in a good way).

We'll never be able to go away again; we will be continuously exhausted from lack of sleep; we'll have to buy a Renault Espace, probably a cheap one on eBay; in fact, we will have to buy all that KIT, all over again; we would have a huge, two-week-long fight about what to call the baby (I love romantic, folksy English names like Tansy and Violet; Ralph likes Mitfordesque names like Pamela and Daphne). As for the child itself, we would be pushing sixty before it was at university and Ralph would never be able to retire if he were to keep the child in the plush, velvet-lined style to which all children these days are accustomed . . . and then, what if there was something WRONG with the child?

On the credit side, I can come up with only two reasons. (1) If I had the baby, I could go through life with the faraway look of procreative superiority I have witnessed on so many multiparous women before, as if stashed away in some drawer at home I have a Mother Heroine medal or have been inducted into the Soviet Order of Maternal Glory. Oh yes, whatever little else I have not managed to achieve in my undistinguished life, I would still have managed the feat of bringing four souls into this depleted, overheating, overpopulated world, and would no longer be reduced to writing love from Mimi, Ralph, Mirabel, Casimir, Posy, and Calypso at the bottom of the annual family Christmas card, as if I had four children rather than just three— i.e., half as many as most Notting Hill mothers—and a dog.

But that's not a good reason, I recognize, so on to reason (2), which is a good one. We would all—especially Ralph, of course, who dotes deeply on all the children in his understated English way—love the child.

Bringing the baby into the family would, on balance, increase the net amount of love in the world. And love—it's the best reason of all. The only reason. Love is the one that blows all the others out of the water. Love, as that ad for Sandals on London cabs and at the bottom of my *Daily Telegraph* always reminds us, is all you need.

But still, this is clearly not good enough for Ralph. Ralph is taking a very pragmatic, very Martian line on all this, whereas I am all too clearly from Venus. I reach over to touch him, and his shoulder. He's not asleep after all. His hand closes over mine. "Darling," he says, "please don't try to make me change my mind. I've got to be very tough, otherwise I will succumb to sentiment. Try to forgive me. Try to understand. But I'm not going to change my mind."

Then he turns over to face the wall.

So, obviously, I can't sleep a wink, and Ralph's not talking to me (being fast asleep), so I creep downstairs, to sit by the fire and seek comfort in the Lakeland Plastics catalogue. The rain lashes the windows and I am leafing through, realizing I need not just one or two things, but everything. I need Antibacterial Freshcling in a cutter box. Anti-Moth Natural Wardrobe Freshener. Asparagus kettle.

The fire has died down to the embers, which are popping companionably. I grip the catalogue tightly, as it already seems to promise me a safer future, more organized and mumsy, in a better-equipped and tidier kitchen. I can see me now, making gravy in the insulated jug, possibly wearing the annoying apron saying DANGER, MEN COOKING or wearing my freezer mitt to reorganize the fish fingers while Posy works quietly on her Binky Bunny knitting kit.

I seem to be gazing into a neat and safe world where everything has its place, and where nothing messy between man and wife could ever happen. For this reason I stare at the catalogue for ages, as if it holds the answer to my dilemma.

Meanwhile, Calypso occasionally emits a tiny yelp or snore, and I imagine she is chasing bunny rabbits in her sleep. The children are asleep in their beds upstairs, Mirabel way upstairs in the attic, where I can't stop her from texting Ceci and Aspen and Spike and listening to her iPod.

I look at Calypso, and something twists in my gut. I put down the catalogue, open on the page featuring the Krups Waffle Maker finished in smart brushed stainless steel with insulated stay-cool handles. When I had her spayed, I took Calypso to the vet in Addison Avenue. She whined piteously and refused to leave the waiting room, as if she knew. Carmichael had to drag her bodily by her lead into his room, and injected her before we could get her on that sacrificial surgical plinth in order to remove from her, as he put it so horribly later, "quite a lot of dog."

I remember how I felt like a murderer. How the children cried, after, about never having a puppy. And how Ralph cried, too—and blamed me.

Ralph comes from a background where the children are sent to kennels almost as soon as they are off the breast, but family dogs must be allowed to snooze on sofas and marital beds. I remember how even Calypso cried and shuddered for hours, and howled and strained on her leash if we even so much as passed the vet's thereafter.

"But we wouldn't be getting a puppy," I kept saying, in order to justify the spaying, "we'd be getting another dog. For *me* to look after."

And now I'm having to tell myself exactly the same thing, to stop myself from losing it completely.

I'm not having a baby, I lecture myself, in my Ann-Widdecombe-doing-*Question-Time* inner voice, which I reserve for moments of crisis. I'm having an adult, a human being to love and cherish, to feed, clothe, nurture, ferry about, educate, and doubtless house, because, as we all know, it's impossible for children to climb onto the first rung of the ladder these days. And even when this unutterably dear person is twenty, thirty, forty, even fifty, it won't make any difference, I will still continue to worry and care about him or her for the rest of my years (which means about another sixty-two years, as I have promised Posy faithfully that, whatever happens, I will make a hundred), so much more than I will ever worry and care about ME.

"Keep calm, and carry on," I say to myself and drag myself up to bed.

This morning, when I wake up, the bed next to me is empty.

Ralph has headed into Godminster, to take the 8:06 A.M. to Waterloo and to proceed with his life as if all hell hasn't broken loose. So around the time when the pub is filling up for the hallowed rural institution still known as "morning coffee," I rush round to the Dairy to tell Rose the awful news. Even though the thought of coffee makes me want to gag, I am looking forward to sitting in her warm, sunlit yellow kitchen, with its flagstoned floor and fresh flowers, the smell of Christmas chutney or Seville marmalade simmering on the Aga, and nibbling something home-baked and buttery.

"Rose?" I call out softly, as I am arriving unannounced.

I push open the glass back door, where her weathered, glossy Spanish tasseled riding boots are paired, like something out of a boot advertisement. The inner door to the hall is also closed, and today's post and *Guardian* are in a neat untouched pile on the wonky medieval oak settle that stands against the Germolene-pink plastered walls.

"Pierre?" I trill.

I am suddenly getting a strong feeling, like a loosening in my bowels, that I shouldn't be there. But I don't bother to pop my head around the door into the dining room, the study, or the drawing room, and march through the house to the kitchen. They live in the kitchen—well, Rose does.

As I approach the closed kitchen door, I hear Pierre scrimmaging about in the back entry hall.

"Rose?" he shouts in a plaintive voice. "What have you done with that special flint that I left on the ledge here, very carefully, which I said I was saving? Please don't tell me you chucked it out. I don't think I could stand it!" His plaintive voice rises to a wail. Then he glimpses me in the passage. I am standing in the kitchen doorway, watching Rose and Jesse Marlon.

Now, while I am not entirely spotless in the marital department myself (as everyone appeared to know within five minutes of my arriving in Honeyborne), I don't honestly think even I could ever have sex with someone I could have *given birth to*.

They don't see me for a few seconds, but then Rose opens

her eyes and focuses on me. For a second, I see relish flare in her eyes before lust disengages and conscience kicks in, and she pulls out of Jesse Marlon's arms and removes her hands from their resting place on his lean buttocks.

"Oh HALLO, PIERRE," I say in a loud, meaningful voice, flashing my eyes at Rose and raising my eyebrows at Jesse Marlon. "I'd love to have a look round your studio," I continue, as the lovebirds rearrange themselves and I back out of the kitchen, clicking the door shut behind me. "Could I have the guided tour of the east wing?"

"Not today, I'm afraid," replies Pierre, coming down the passage towards me. "We have a visitor. Rose in the kitchen? She has a visitor."

Behind Pierre comes a figure, a slim woman with brown, neat hair, tweed slouchy trousers from Toast, Cath Kidston Fair Isle tank over an immaculate, tailored white shirt. Weirdly, I suddenly realize that this is exactly what Rose would wear, if Rose ever wore trousers, that is.

I stand stock-still in the middle of Rose and Pierre's house, the lovingly restored Dairy of two of the closest (well, only) friends I have made so far after more than eighteen months in the depths of the West Country, and in walks the very woman who has put me here, and forced me away from my family home in Lonsdale Gardens, where the children were born, where I shopped and ate and moseyed around, and shopped, and gossiped, for fourteen almost entirely blissful years.

"Clare." I gulp, remembering to smile. "Goodness. Hey there! What are you doing here?"

Rose

Poor, poor Mimi.

What a *nightmare* for her. And for Ralph, too. It's been no picnic for him, either, the last couple of weeks, waiting for all this to be over, as I almost said to Mimi. But when I saw Ralph, I told him I knew about it and I said that I felt for them both, and then I hugged him, experiencing for a second a rush of compassion, as if I were Princess Diana with an AIDS patient.

He hugged me back briefly, but it was clear that he didn't want to get into it. "Rose, thank you. It's no one's fault," he said.

According to Mimi, the reason Ralph's been really freaked out by it all is basically work. While Mimi mooches around Home Farm, "a prisoner of her own endocrine system," according to her husband, alternately weeping and keeping a stiff upper lip, Ralph is at the end of his tether with the commuting, the never seeing the children, the "fucking awful" rail service, being driven totally bonkers by announcements about next station stops, by other passengers' iPods, staying overnight in London in people's spare rooms, living off Pret à Manger sandwiches (sandwiches that didn't even appear to have bread in them anymore—what was wrong with bread?), and then getting back to Home Farm and listening to Mimi whinge about Ana.

"It would be the straw that breaks the camel's back," he said, leaving me in no doubt what "it" was.

So I blurted out "I'll have it" as I dropped off some of Ceci's old clothes, even some Ralph Lauren ones it was a wrench to part with, but Ralph looked unconvinced. He must know we were quite happy with having just Ceci. Pierre couldn't wait for me to stop fussing and fiddling over Ceci so I could resume my wifely duties and attend to him. And I didn't mean it about having Mimi and Ralph's baby, and it was, I recognize, the wrong thing to say.

For this got Ralph going on the subject of the battle of the sexes, and he started talking about how men had such a "poor hand," and that they work and commute and work and commute until they die, but, at least in the old days, their wives would warm their slippers and attend to their every need, and they had *status*. In their own *households*. But now it was all about women finding themselves and something called self-actualization, whatever that is, and no one ever even *mentioned* men at all, let alone appreciated the daily sacrifice they made for their families.

I listened to all this with some surprise. I didn't think for a second that Ralph was a warrior in the gender wars. In fact, the last time the topic had come up, Ralph said that going out to work and bringing home the bacon till they dropped dead of heart attacks was "what chaps do." This time it was more as if he were trying to convince himself of something, that he had grounds for objection.

"If women are doing it all, at least they have their relationships with each other and their children, and we don't," he said glumly. "We men have lost whatever it was we were supposed to have once had."

And then I put my foot in it again. "Well, as the saying goes, there's never a good time to have a baby," I said, remembering with an almost physical rush how adorable Ceci was when she was a toddler and how she wore little matching knickerbockers underneath her dresses, hoping that this obvious truism might smooth things over, but it didn't.

"Look, Rose," he said patiently, as if talking to a small child, "I'm very grateful that you're taking Mimi into Godminster General. It's hugely appreciated. I wish I could do it, but unfortunately the Ukrainians have just switched off Europe's central heating again, and closed the pipeline, so there's a spot of bother in former Soviet satellites, and I've got to go into the DTI for an all-day crisis meeting. I hope you don't mind, but if I wanted to have The Debate, I'd have it with Mimi, and the thing is, I don't want to have The Debate, I can't have The Debate. I. Just. Don't. Want. To discuss it. And I don't want to discuss why I don't want to discuss it. I'm sorry. I do hope that doesn't sound too unfriendly."

"Ralph, look, look," I babbled. "It's okay, I'm sorry, it's really none of my business. If you really want to know, I have some sympathy with you both. It's just a miserable situation. Oh, by the way, you'll never guess who . . ."

I was going to change the subject and tell Ralph that Clare had been in Honeyborne, the same Clare who'd bought his house in London—a remarkable coincidence, and not a bad little nugget to drop into the conversation. But then I remembered that Mimi had seemed less than thrilled about the fact that Clare had appeared—I put that down to the moment. But I didn't get a chance.

"I just feel if we deal with it promptly, she'll get over it sooner," said Ralph, with tones of finality.

In the car, Mimi talks nonstop. Nerves, I suppose, poor lamb.

She holds on her lap a bag, which I presume contains dressing gown, slippers, and so on. I give her my copy of the *Guardian*, even though it has a long piece about *The Archers* in G2 that I was saving up as a treat.

"A small part of me's almost looking forward to it, Rose," she says, as we drive through the lanes with the dank hedges, dotted with bedraggled wildflowers, rearing up on either side, "but only because it'll be such a relief when all the churning in my head's stopped. The last two weeks . . . they've been the pits. I had no idea it took so long on the NHS. The absolute pits. So grim. I can't tell you." There is a long pause, then she resumes.

"One never thinks about it, of course, but there must be loads of married couples who've been in my shoes. Everyone imagines that the wife wins, gets her way, on the grounds that, when a couple has adored children already, it is, presumably, unthinkable to terminate the life of a future sibling. Well, you know what? It isn't. It happens. To thousands of married women every year. Tens of thousands, maybe. It just has to me, so I know."

I place my hand briefly on her leg, then back on the wheel, as if what she is saying is so profound that any reply of mine would only diminish it.

"If you think about it, one of them has to win, but then one of them has to lose, too. It's just that usually the woman wins, and the man is left in the position of saying, 'It's the best thing we ever did, of course I was terribly unkeen at the time, I know I was, darling' "—Mimi adopts the plummy, jovial tone of the English public-school father for this bit—" 'but once he arrived, how could I ever regret Archie, eh? He's the love of my life!' And then the wife looks smug, as if he should be thanking her for holding the line and overruling him during the bitter row over whether to have or not to have the baby. Rose, husbands and wives go head to head on this all the time, and I lost."

"You didn't lose as such, Mimi," I say. "I know it's horrible, but you have to think of Ralph, and the Whole Family Unit."

"I did lose," Mimi intones bleakly. "It was my turn to lose. Sometimes, you lose."

I knew what Mimi was talking about here, but I didn't pick up the thread. Her fling with some single sleazy billionaire who bought a house on her communal garden. Si someone. She had sex with him twice. Once in a hotel—the Grove, I think, that hotel for WAGS with a golf course, near the Watford Gap—and once on his stairs in Lonsdale Gardens, an episode that she described as "a stairfucking," which she described as "jolly bad for the back but a lot more fun than starfucking, which is all that most people do with any enthusiasm in Notting Hill."

"But that's the worst bit!" says Mimi. "The children. I was doing a good job of holding it together, but then Cas suddenly said, in the kitchen, when something came on the radio about the England cricket team, 'If only I had a little brother'—he's always longed to have someone to do nets with—'If only I had a little brother, I could teach him how to play cricket.' I thought I'd . . . black out! I had to rush to the larder."

"The larder?"

"That's where I cry," Mimi says, and gazes out through her rain-streaked window to the sodden fields.

I drop Mimi at the entrance, then park the car and go to the farmers' market and to have my hair done at Upper Cuts. Then I go to That New Place, for coffee, and to buy Mimi's cake.

"Anything piggy," she said, "and moist. One of their large slices of carrot cake with cream-cheese icing. Actually, no, make that two of their large slices of carrot cake with cream-cheese icing. Nothing will have passed my lips since midnight, so I think I can afford to be greedy. It's so important to have something to look forward to."

Then, an hour or so later, I go back to the hospital, repark, and thread my way through doors and passages, following signs, until I find Mimi sitting wanly in a chair, with her bag, surrounded by women in a similar state and, I assume, condition.

We get into the car. I am very carefully and tactfully not asking her to tell me anything about it. I look to see whether she is walking gingerly. But she is walking fine, I notice. It's only a minor procedure, I suppose. Then she starts talking, almost cheerfully.

"It was quite comforting actually," she says. "Most women were there with men. I couldn't decide whether they were showing moral support, or making sure that the women didn't bottle."

"I'm sorry I didn't come in, but you did say—" I venture.

"God, Rose, that's not what I meant," she says. "I didn't expect you to come into day surgery with me! You're doing enough as it is! As well as men, several of the couples had babies already, which didn't make it worse for me, but better, somehow, as if other women had known mother love and could still, you know, BE THERE." She gulps. I give her arm a pat, to show how brave I think she is, and that I *know*. "There was a bad moment at the beginning, though."

"Oh yes?" I say, still keeping it neutral, and let Mimi continue.

"We were called, one by one we were called. There was paperwork. In my case this took ages as I seemed to be registered at Colville Crescent still, not Home Farm, and then I remembered I had the letter from Dr. Ashburton, which luckily was addressed to me at Home Farm, and so I was then processed along with everyone else, which meant putting on one of those printed cotton gowns that do up the back and flap open with ties at the neck and hip and make you feel like a patient in Broadmoor."

She goes quiet for a while, as we inch out of the hospital car park and wait in line to put the ticket in the machine that will lift the barrier. She does not speak again until we are through.

"It was at this point that I began to feel as if my whole life was slipping from me, Rose. Here I was, a married mother of three, a former national newspaper journalist, standing in slippers and surgical gown, carrying my home clothes and some industrial-sized sanitary pads in a plastic sack saying 'NHS property' on it. Can you imagine?"

"So hard," I murmur. I know what Mimi is actually saying, which is that no married woman, who loves her children, ever expects to be where she was today.

I don't voice my thought, then we unfortunately get stuck behind a laundry van, and then I have to turn left by the Chinese place that sells filled hot dumplings and has a sign underneath the Chinese lettering that says HOT ASIAN BUNS, a translation we usually point out to each other and then laugh, because it sounds so ridiculous, like the title of a Richard Desmond magazine. But not today, obviously. "What happened next?" I ask. "Did you have to wait ages?"

"No, not really. I went upstairs to a ward, where there were big blue armchairs in rows, telly on, tuned to Fern Britton and Philip Schofield, all rather cozy, so we sat and watched daytime TV, we even watched the ads for distraction, even though watching them was a bit, you know"—she searches for the right word—"birdsongy."

"What do you mean, Mimi?" I ask carefully.

"You know, birdsong at the Somme, that Auden poem about the picture of Icarus, life going on, that sentiment."

I thought the Somme was a bit strong; the ward I had glimpsed when picking her up had seemed pleasant and clean enough to me, but I didn't say so.

"Then I had this odd sense that we women, we have the so-called show going on, which is school run, you know, work, looking after our houses and our children, but all the time, too, there's also this play within the play, which is the drama of female fertility."

"Go on."

". . . babies and childbirth and IVF and miscarriage and all of that, and that goes on, too, only in silence, and . . . we women seem tuned in to this show, so much more than men, and while we experience the drama, we live it, it's ours. They only witness it at one remove. It's as if our wombs are little screens—like the screens on the Teletubbies' tummies—on which a quite separate, quite private narrative can be played, to an audience of one. Does that make any sense?"

"Yes, I think it does," I say, in a cautious voice. I've heard of the Teletubbies, of course, but don't have a very clear idea what Mimi is talking about (I never allowed Ceci to watch children's television), and I am always very, very careful about contraception myself, in case we have another baby, but this isn't the moment.

We wait for an ambulance to overtake us. Godminster General, with its maternity unit, its A&E, its terrible on-site incinerator, is plonked right next door to the undertaker's, so this really is a one-stop shop for every stage of life and, as if on cue, we both watch without comment as two heavily pregnant young girls—children, they couldn't have been more than eighteen or nineteen—go past, pushing prams, on their way to antenatal clinic.

I wonder whether this is a good moment or a bad moment to point out that, these days, it's really weird, women are all either having babies before they're twenty or delaying it till they're forty, but Mimi goes on.

"Then we were shown our beds, in blue-curtained cubicles, with curtains that didn't quite shut, and told to place our plastic bags underneath them. Then a medic came and asked me lots of questions and wrote down my answers. She was very sweet. But one of them asked about my existing children, and why I was doing it. I tried not to cry. I just didn't know what to say. I felt so sad.

"Then she looked apologetic and asked me if I would consent to being examined by her, internally, under anesthetic, as part of her training. I looked at her. She looked at me, and blushed. As she was sweet and looked embarrassed, I said yes, though I have to say that I felt the hospital had singled out me, the lone middle-class mother, for this privilege."

"No, Mimi. I would have chosen you, too," I say stoutly.

"The anesthetists arrived in green scrubs, with their heads covered in white caps. I was quite pleased to see them, even though in a few minutes I would be dead to the world and exposed to them. It meant it would all be over. They were so gentle, Rose! One of them touched my arm and said, 'I'm John, darling. I'll be putting you to sleep.' It made a real difference. They all treated us sort of nonmothers with a tenderness I never expected. They were like human rights workers, on field trips to failed states."

Mimi gazes out the window. We are out of the town now, and winding uphill on the road that leads to Larcombe Ducis, and Honeyborne, a road I know so well I am not aware of taking it. "One of the nurses wheeled me to theater. I was really looking forward to the anesthetic—I love being sucked down into a brown treacly whirlpool, it's so delicious, makes you realize why everyone says crack and heroin are so blissful." Mimi stops talking.

"And was that it, till you came round in Recovery?" I ask.

"Pretty much," says Mimi, in a different voice. "I had a scan, and that was it." She puts her head back against the seat, and closes her eyes, as if she doesn't want to talk about it anymore. But I have to say something to her before she falls asleep and before I get her home.

"Mimi, love," I say.

"What?" she says sleepily, looking out the window at the green fields, the sheep, the houses, the lowering sky. It's been the most torrential winter, and spring doesn't seem to want to come at all. "I'm nodding off, Rose, sorry."

"I'm not surprised—the general anesthetic, you've had such a horrid time . . ." I say, changing gear as we go up a steep bit. "But I feel I have to tell you."

"What?" Mimi says again, leaning her head against the glass, not looking at me.

"Clare," I say.

"What about her?"

"Well, you remember, she showed up at the Dairy to talk to me about my business, and the commercial potential of small-holdings, and I thought she was coming the next week, and you were there?"

"Of course I remember," says Mimi, in a hard voice. "As if I could forget."

"Well, she's viewing Hutton, too, well, the gatehouse—you

know, owned by Sir Michael Hutton, it's that house with the iron gates and the walled garden between us and Larcombe? She's seeing it next week. She heard about it from some French-woman in Notting Hill, who was apparently here the other weekend and staying at Court Place."

"Oh, *fuck* Virginie," Mimi wails. "That little French dyke is nothing but trouble! I knew no good could come of it when she was at that dinner at the Cobbs'—the Parmesan risotto one I told you all about, when Ned told everyone about the windfarm!" There is a silence while she digests the information. "But the whole point about here is that it's too far to come for weekends—that's why it's so special, of course! Gideon would never put up with six, seven hours in the car every weekend; he's much too impatient. It would never work. And nothing around here is minimal or groovy enough for him. The ceilings are too low, and everything's at least three hundred years old."

And then there is a horrified pause as something else seems to occur to her. "They're not thinking of actually moving here, are they, and building something?"

"Look, I have no idea about their arrangements," I say, my heart breaking for her. "I've barely seen Clare since Cambridge. You know her much better than I do—you were practically her next-door neighbor and best friend in London." But I am lying. I have more than an idea why Clare wants to come to Honeyborne. And I wish, from the bottom of my heart, that she had never told me anything. That she'd never come near this place.

I put the car into fourth gear as we are on the Golden Mile between Godminster and Larcombe, with views stretching for miles both sides of the road, crops and hills and distant moorland a purple smudge on the far horizon, and race to get Mimi home to bed, to rest, to recover.

PART TWO

Mimi

"Oh goodie," I say, as the roar of an approaching vehicle takes the shape of a quad bike with a trailer. "What ho, Clive."

Maddocks is at the wheel of the top-of-the-line quad. Without looking at anyone, or answering my merry greeting, he leaps down and removes a folded-up trestle table from the trailer, sets it up, and then draws a folded linen tablecloth from one of his two matching, monogrammed L.L. Bean canvas bags, and then, within seconds, spreads the surface with Thermoses, sandwiches, fruitcake, a tea urn, napkins, glasses, tin mugs, and two ruby bottles of homemade sloe gin.

"Oooh—lunch!" I announce, rubbing my hands and moving towards the table. Even though it's been only an hour and a bit since our last meal, standing around in the fresh air always makes me hungry like the wolf.

The day started bright and early at Court Place.

Those who were staying were tucking into a large cooked breakfast in the main kitchen (as opposed to the staff kitchen and pantry). Homemade sausages, home-cured bacon, field mushrooms, toast, coffee, Cath's own mulberry and pistachio granola, freshly squeezed blood-orange juice in jugs, and newspapers were all being devoured amid plenty of bluff chat about high birds and bags.

Occasionally a gun and his wife make an entrance. As I haven't been staying, it's not clear at this stage who's a house-guest and who has come to shoot, although what is clear is that both categories are kitted out in the same plaid uniform: thick woolly stockings folded over just below the knee adorned with little woolly pennants and initials, trews, or breeks; a tanktop over a Tattersall shirt; a knitted tie; a flat cap; and, over the top, a shooting jacket with a big brass zip, multiple poppered pockets, all in a palette of pale greens and soft browns. And that's just the women.

It all makes me think that if Cordings or Holland & Holland made pants and bras of tweed, everyone would doubtless buy those, too.

At least two guns are wearing the Bamford shooting jacket, with a checked and patched inner lining, and plenty of soft, buttery suede trimming. This is like wearing a great big fluorescent flashing sign on your back saying NEW MONEY. I'd thought about getting Ralph one for Christmas. Until I discovered it cost £1,495, that is, and that even if I'd bought it, he'd never have worn it. Ralph wouldn't be seen dead in anything new, rather than handed down from father to son, and informed me that genuine nobs such as the Duke of Beaufort shoot in jeans and fleeces, partly in order to show those who turn up in the whole tweed kit and caboodle as noovs and try-hards.

But in the Court Place high-ceilinged kitchen, perfumed with frying bacon and Chanel No. 5, grinding coffee and moldy Barbours, only the tiniest variations on the tweed theme—i.e., Serena's Norfolk jacket, or Cath's silk scarf knotted at the throat—seem to be allowed, as if everyone is secretly taking part in a sartorial Spot the Difference contest.

When I'd asked Cath what to wear, she'd said, "Oh, we're very casual! Nothing fancy. You're not shooting, are you? Just Ralph, isn't it? Just make sure you're well wrapped, because the first drive is always chilly, especially when there's a wind up and the dew is still on the ground."

So I am clad in a purple cagoule over a navy fleece, and have pulled some waterproof teal overtrousers over my jeans, and some breathable hiking boots. It's not an elegant outfit, and I can barely hear myself speak I rustle so much when I walk, which I have to do with legs far apart. I may win no prizes for style, but I can be sure of one thing.

At least I won't be cold. I am so well wrapped that an elderly person would suffer a fit of packaging rage—and have to assail me with scissors, knives, and false teeth—in order to penetrate my outergarments to the epidermis.

In the kitchen Ralph had given me a doubtful look as he oiled his gun—his grandfather's, of course—with a rag. The kitchen filled with the smell of gun oil, but I was not to be deterred. He is still being extra nice to me at the moment, of course, and treats me with all the respect and distance a disposal officer does an unexploded bomb.

"There's no such thing as bad weather," I had said, finding an old gray bobble hat of Casimir's to complete my natty ensemble, "only bad clothes!"

As soon as I see Rose enter, though, I do feel I could have interpreted Cath's words slightly less literally.

"Pass the butter, will you?" one gun barked to another. "After you with the *Daily Mail*, old chap. I want to see if I'm in Richard Kay, and we haven't got all day till the first drive."

"Only if you'll stop hogging the marmalade, you utter swine," the other man had responded. "And you're not in Richard Kay, but you are in Ephraim Hardcastle, you media tart. As you're up, Granville, old chap, you couldn't pass me my cartridge belt over there on the dresser, could you?"

Ralph once told me that you could always tell which members of a house party had crept into each other's rooms the previous night, because they were always the two people who were rudest to each other at breakfast. He had also told me about a lecherous uncle of his—a very minor peer—who would go about the bedrooms, gently knocking on doors with his erection, until someone admitted him. As a result, I was monitoring the party at breakfast narrowly, and had pricked up my ears at this exchange.

Rose swishes in, wearing one of her long Ralph Lauren skirts, her Spanish riding boots, and a tight-fitted chestnut moleskin hacking jacket with a velvet collar and matching leather gauntlets. She holds a furry Cossack hat in her gloved hand. She is, I decide, definitely working the Lady Aline in *The Shooting Party* look. The wilder her personal life becomes, the more buttoned-up her attire.

"Hello, Rose," I cry out, giving her an especially warm welcome, given that Ralph has termed her "late-onset nymphomania" appears to be very public knowledge.

As for Lulu Bryanston . . . well, Lulu's wearing a Selina Blow frock coat and very tight jeans, and lace-up Ilse Jacobsen wellies in one of the new, hot colors, i.e., not pink or floral or patterned or even green, but putty-colored. I am ashamed I even know what the new hot colors in wellies are, but I do.

I don't greet her so warmly, as she must be at least a decade younger than me and does not need any encouragement whatsoever. Furthermore, Rose and I also suspect her of spreading the gossip about Jesse Marlon and Rose, though how Lulu knows remains a mystery. But then, as I've always wondered, how does anyone "know" who is going to bed with whom?

Pierre, as a gun, is kitted out appropriately—holey dark-green jersey, checked shirt, moleskin, the works—and is working his way steadily through a huge mound of hot protein. He and the other breakfasters are becoming flushed as the room fills with enough woven sheep to clothe Scott of the Antarctic and all his men, and their bodies fill with enough sausage, eggs, and bacon to keep them going till some time next year.

Looking at Rose and Pierre, my friends, together, contented and companionable, I realize how little anyone seems to mind about Rose's affair with Jesse Marlon. In London, the topic would have absorbed book groups and Pilates classes and cappuccinos at Ottolenghi up and down the Royal Borough for months on end, as people would have taken sides, recommended divorce lawyers, and generally had a wonderful time with it. But here, having an affair with someone half your age is clearly accorded the least-said, soonest-mended treatment.

"It's because, in the country, everyone has to muck in, they rely on each other, it's a small village," explained Ralph, whose mother, Selina, conducted a long, illicit affair with a belted earl for many years without anyone, least of all Ralph's father, complaining. "You can never afford to mount the *haut cheval,* you see, because it could always be you next." He gave me a meaningful look, which I ignored indignantly.

Last to arrive is a small but naughty-looking Frenchman, mid-fifties, who is wearing a green *forestière* hat with sprigs on it, a Loden hunting jacket replete with flaps, plus-fours disappearing into green socks with terra-cotta pennants, and fringed brogues on his rather tiny feet. Alongside is a woman of his age who unfortunately looks (1) cross and (2) old enough to be his mother.

"Esmond," cries Granville, warmly. "Jacqueline! You know everyone?"

When it comes to me, Esmond does that delicious, tummy-fluttering thing of raising my hand to his lips but not making contact while looking deeply into my eyes, as if he doesn't care a jot that I'm swathed from head to toe in waterproof Thinsulate, I am still one hell of a woman. Jacqueline does not even give me a glance, which is fair enough, as I am not well dressed, rich, or in the Almanach de Gotha.

As we leave the kitchen, I pull Granville over to one side. "As I'm going to be bored rigid and freezing for the next three hours, at least explain who those two are," I beg. "The baron's fascinating! But she seems, you know, less—"

"He's a mensch, and she's . . . oh, Jacqueline's perfectly all right really," says Granville, steering me into his study. "Shooting's just not her scene. She doesn't usually come, stays in Paris. And nor are the English her scene, to be perfectly frank." Then Granville closes the door behind us so we can continue chatting. Standing up by his desk, he clicks, and his screen makes a waking-up noise and fills with light.

I can't help seeing that on the screen is the draft of a letter he is writing. To the Tavistock Clinic. I quickly absorb its contents before he notices anything, and instantly see that it is a letter of application to start a training course, for counseling and psychotherapy. I can hardly believe this. Hunting, shooting, and shrinking!

While Granville fiddles on his computer, still standing up, and we hear the last breakfasters process down the passage towards the hall, I look around the walls. I've never been in Granville's study before, and, with the Tavistock news, I find myself trying to gauge his hinterland. There are photographs, big pictures of Granville with Branson at Necker, Granville with Murdoch in Hong Kong, etc., but nothing to denote that Granville is in touch with his ego or his id or whatever, so I begin to wonder whether it's for real, whether Granville can really afford to give up whatever it is he does to listen to other people's problems for hours.

Meanwhile, Granville carries on giving me the lowdown on the late arrivals. Obviously, I don't mention the letter that I couldn't help reading on his screen, but I do sort of look at him with fresh eyes. "Going back to the baron, I said to Esmond, a few weeks ago, I said, 'Who d' you want to bring to the shoot today, old chum, mmm?' " Granville is standing over the printer now, running off something I presume is the letter. "The baron takes the house and the shoot for a weekend every year, and I know, because the beaters tell me, that when he does, there's no shortage of young and beautiful women around, but no Jacqueline, if you get my drift."

"Yes, I do," I say, almost forgetting about the Tavistock, loving it.

"And he said, all hoity, 'When I pay, I invite whom I like, but when you invite me, as a guest, then, of course, I bring my wife.' "

Now, around two hours later, Maddocks is taking up a position behind the trestle table, ready to dispense tea and soup into tin cups, and the men have started ambling towards us, guns broken, some bringing dead birds by the neck to give to the beaters, others lighting up cigars.

I reach out for a sandwich.

"This is elevenses, Mimi," Rose says as she takes small sips from a mug of grouse soup laced with sherry, "go easy! There's still the Shooting Lunch." Her voice suggests this is a ritual on the same scale as Christmas Dinner. I notice Rose is looking at my bulk underneath the anorak with a slightly beady eye. "So leave room, I would."

So I hold back, and only have soup and a packet of crisps, but I notice that all the guns and the beaters fall on the provisions as if they haven't eaten for days, and neck long cans of ale, but still put plenty of distance between us and them.

After elevenses, there are two more drives. I know this only because I asked, feeling as if I still had double chemistry to go before my best subject at school, which was lunch, and wondering why it was that so much of English country life was arranged to suit the comfort and convenience of the Englishman; I mean, what are we women supposed to be *doing* while our menfolk blast innocent birds from the sky?

Well, it appears that what we do is clamber in and out of the backs of Land Rovers, which is easily the most energetic aspect of the entire day's activity.

Meanwhile the beaters, pickers-up, and loaders all pile onto a long trailer with haybales for seats, with their dogs and sticks and flags and muddy boots all mixed up together. No one, least of all them, seems particularly keen to bridge the class divide. I give a wave to Colin Watts, who is beating, earning some extra cash, and who seems to slot right in wherever he is, but otherwise I feel it's all upstairs downstairs.

In the back of the Land Rover, jolting down rutted tracks, I don't particularly mind sitting jammed together, pressed up against the other guns and their wet dogs (one very overenthusiastic Labrador definitely got to third base with me when we skidded across a verge), but so far as I can determine, the day involves an awful lot of fields but not much sport.

As we bounce about, cheek by jowl, with guns rearing priapically up between male legs and dead birds at our feet, I say, apropos nothing, "Er, in shooting, why doesn't one walk, between drives?"

"Because one never does," Ralph answers.

"Is that why it's called a drive, then," I ask, "because instead of walking a few hundred yards, you drive? Or have I missed something?"

Ralph does not answer this and contributes instead to a discussion about how many birds Granville laid down for the season (can't remember, but it seemed an awful lot of birds to breed, feed, and so on, in order to be shot by City bankers after a large lunch, in conditions of extreme personal safety).

I feel I am wasting my breath. Shooting, like fly-fishing, is one of the things Ralph never jokes about. He has just given Cas an air rifle. They are both taking it all very seriously.

Cas goes about saying, "Never, never should a gun pointed be at anyone." The air gun always goes into the locked gun cupboard, and I don't even know where Ralph keeps the key. He won't tell me as, according to him, I can't even be trusted with a penknife, let alone a loaded gun.

All this is, I think, because on Ralph's side of the family, several psychopathic or otherwise certifiable uncles and cousins (only referred to, with grim expressions, as "poor" Uncle Fergus/ Jonty/Kit by the few surviving members of the Fleming clan) have managed to shoot themselves in the head while either cleaning guns or climbing over stiles.

After hearing about several of these unfortunate male relations, I asked Ralph whether clumsiness ran in the Fleming family. He looked at me with surprise, and then with reluctance explained that they had all blown their brains out, but, in English or Scottish families, this act is only ever referred to, if at all, as a "tragic accident," with the strong implication that the poor soul was a silly whose main fault was not taking his own life but committing the much more inexcusable crime of not playing up and playing the game.

After the fourth drive, the beaters disappear into a barn for beef stew and beer, roll-ups suddenly appearing between their lips, and we bounce back to the house, with spirits aloft at what lies ahead.

As I remove my hiking boots in the boot room, surrounded by Barbours and wellies in orderly rows and fishes in mounted glass cases, house and team pictures of Granville at Harrow, young and fresh and limber in rugby kit and house colors and tails, I, too, am looking forward to a greedy lunch, but I also have that tugging, bittersweet feeling. There's something about being in a well-oiled, smooth-running English country house in the middle of the shooting season that always fleetingly fills me with, I now realize, a sort of lust: the lust to have the sort of money to live and to entertain on this grand scale. I'm not proud of it, but there we go.

It's not so much the huge drawing room, the bedrooms, the vast warm kitchen with four-oven Aga, the polished stone floor, the echoing hall, the billiard room, I envy: it's the game larder and dairy, the laundry room and the gun room and the boot room and the silver safe and the gents', the little rooms that provide the graceful flow and articulation to life, where everything is in its place, and always has been.

Whenever I voice this disgruntlement, Rose pulls me up sharply and says, "Cath may have a house, but you have a home," as if I have little samplers embroidered with pieties hung up above fireplaces, and gingham bonnets over my jam pots, and furniture gleaming with beeswax, which is, I regret to say, not accurate.

I know that we are always being told to be happy with what we have, and I am: Home Farm is dear and cozy, not to mention all we can afford. But after spending any time at Court Place, or any other vast pile, I always feel a slight shrinkage when I return home and step over a huge pile of muddy wellies and coats simply in order to gain access to my own kitchen, and it begins to feel as if we are living all jammed together in a hovel rather than in a highly desirable period farmhouse in one of the most beautiful places in the entire universe.

I feel like crying, "Hold on! Where's the greenhouse, the market garden, the walled garden, the rose garden? There's been a mistake! Where are the stables and the stable girls, the butler, the housekeeper, the keeper's cottage and the lodge, not to mention the loose box, the ornamental lake, and the ha-ha?"

The feeling, this Court Place-itis, soon passes, of course, but it does make me wonder whether anyone is free from these feelings, which do one no credit at all, whereby those who have a sweet-faced cottage envy those who have a spacious vicarage who envy those who have a Jacobean manor who envy those who have a Tudor hall who envy those who have an Elizabethan mini-stately who envy those who have a stately who envy those who have an Edwardian palace. It makes me wonder that the rich only think and worry about those who are even richer than them.

I do know that in the cutthroat world of gardens and gardeners, the turf wars are hotting up even faster than the upper atmosphere, especially since City traders—thanks to nurseries all over Europe—can buy an estate and have it turned into a landscaped woodland "park" within a matter of months, given enough money and the right designer. And while those who have a vegetable patch dream of a walled garden, those with walled gardens grind their teeth to discover that someone else's walled garden is designed by Tom Stuart-Smith, or Michael Balston, and so on and so on, ad infinitum.

The truth is, someone else has always got more and better than them, and this is what drives men on to acquire; it's the making of money, not the money itself, that becomes important and addictive. This is why billionaires like to carry on making money till they drop dead of heart attacks on their private jets, en route to inspect the submarine attached to the new super-yacht.

"Come through, please, everyone," cries Cath, her slim form twinkling ahead into the drawing room, "lunch in two shakes of a duck's tail! And do help yourselves to refreshments on the way"—I see Champagne, wine, spirits and mixers, ginger ale, lemon, and a bucket of ice set out on a round table in the hall—"then come and defrost by the fire."

Suffused with a sense of well-being, a sense that can be engendered only by several hours in the open air followed by the prospect of a copious, well-cooked meal, we fall into huge sofas with our drinks.

I begin talking to Andrew Lewis, the former editor of a national newspaper and well-known countryman and keen shot. Cath is sitting close to the vulpine Frenchman on a large sofa whose size only serves to emphasize her daintiness, while Esmond's wife, the defiantly hideous Jacqueline, is sipping a sherry and allowing herself to be amused—but only a very tiny bit—by Ralph.

"So tell me about shooting," I say in the direction of Andrew, who is sitting on the sofa next to me, his long legs ending in a pair of burgundy-colored stockings. I am glad to be sitting down, glad that normal social intercourse can resume. It's amazing how tiring simply standing by one's man in the cold can be. I think shooting might be a safe topic. "What is the real point?"

It's best not to talk about people, to mention names, let alone in any pejorative way, as it is a firm rule that, in the drawing rooms of England, the moment you refer to anyone disobligingly, a head will bob up and say, "Did you say Ed Blankety-Blank? That's so funny! He's married to a cousin of mine." When I asked Ralph why it was that this happened, as night followed day, he said, "Because in the aristocracy everyone is related to everyone else, you Irish peasant girl." I think he also told me—though I can hardly believe this—that when the Queen writes letters to the nobility, she opens correspondence with the words, "Dear Cousin."

"If you don't get it, I can't explain," Andrew Lewis answers, to my question about shooting. "Though I could give you chapter and verse about the rural economy and field sports, which contribute several billion a year, especially in depressed areas, but I won't, because the truth is, that's not the point at all." He sips his first drink of the day.

"Then what is?" I press. "Are grounds maintained, keepers and underkeepers retained, a hundred thousand pheasant put down, sixty thousand partridge put down, reared, then moved around two thousand acres of land, so that, twenty-one days a year, men can feel macho?"

"The only point is the fun of the actual shooting," replies Andrew, shortly.

The cheering sight of Maddocks appears in the doorway. The butler gives a minute nod to our chatelaine. "Lunch," announces Cath, rising in a swift movement from the sofa. "It's a *buffay*, I'm afraid."

Lunch is served in the paneled cuboid dining room, where the sun, which has come out now we are inside, sparkles on the polished crystal and carafes and silver and the sconces glowing with lit candles.

I am seated between a little financier called Max something and Andrew, sadly not next to the baron, but no sooner have I sat down than I have to get up again to help myself at the sideboard, where sliced *bœuf en croûte* stuffed with foie gras is squired by a julienne of seasonal vegetables, celeriac mash, buttered spinach, and carrots sprinkled with caraway seeds, i.e., enough to feed an army after a long march.

So then I flirt away with Andrew Lewis, while keeping an eye on Rose, who is flirting with the baron and Ralph.

Pierre is standing sturdily by with a plate, waiting to do full justice to the spread, and talking to Granville, who as host is bringing up the rear, and asking Pierre about Pierre's work . . . as if he's really interested, too.

Well, I say "flirt," but every time I try, the former editor seems more interested in the man on my left, a tiny little tycoon, a pocket plutocrat—Max somebody—with small, pudgy hands and curly hair, whose private equity company, Vobiscum, has apparently many billions "under management," whatever that means, and whose "carry," whatever that means, runs into hundreds of millions.

I gaze on with interest. While we can see all too clearly all that nurses and teachers do to earn their pittance, no one has yet adequately explained why men who work in finance get paid many millions a year simply for shunting other people's money around. And when you meet these men, it invariably becomes no clearer why they deserve to earn a thousand times more a year than nurses, either.

"If you don't mind my saying so, Max," says Andrew to this grubby little moneybags, "I think you paid at least a hundred too much for that newspaper group."

At this lèse-majesté, Max turns slightly purple and grabs the carafe of wine sitting on a snowy cloth in the middle of the table by its slender neck and pours himself a full glass, right up to the brim, as if only this action will prevent him from physically ripping Andrew's throat out with his bare hands. A purple stain spreads over the white cloth as he replaces it, and I feel horrified, but this little accident is beneath both men's notice, on the grounds that a linen tablecloth has been stained but someone will be paid to deal with it.

I begin to get my National Theatre feeling again, that something bad is going to happen and carry on happening, because one thing I know from my limited experience of being a journalist is that one thing City people hate, and will not tolerate from anyone, least of all a member of the loathed, financially illiterate press, is comment or criticism.

"Andrew, as you are a former editor of a national newspaper, I respect your views on many things," Max says tautly, "but business is not one of them."

Andrew tries to goad him further, describing how people laughed and chortled at the newspaper deal Max had just done, and then says something like, "Never has such a small fish been caught with such a big hook," which is clearly an insult. I think for a second that Max is going to ask Andrew to step outside, but then he laughs, and I'm finally able to get a word in.

"I can't think why on earth Granville asked you two," I say, batting my eyelids at Andrew, who was very powerful in his day, not to mention a soldier, and still carried that martial bearing about him. "All you do is talk about money, all the time. You're just lucky I'm not a business reporter from the *Sunday Times* and I can't understand a word you're saying." The two men start eating very quickly, taking advantage of the fact that I am talking to shovel food into their mouths. "But that doesn't mean I don't think you're both horrible. I can't understand why hunting wild animals is banned by law but factory farming and breeding birds to shoot them is positively encouraged. Just as I can't understand why the government allows cruelty to animals on an industrial scale and predatory pricing between producers and suppliers but simultaneously introduced an Act of Parliament to protect the fox."

"My darling girl," Andrew purrs, to my delight, as I love it when men, especially masterly ones like Andrew, call me girl, or darling, "shooting's a Klondike economy, it's the new Gold Rush. Tell me how many shoots opened around here last year."

"Four?" I say.

"Seventy!" corrects Andrew.

"Nooooo!" I breathe.

"Now tell me how Davey Wood in Godminster has managed to buy himself a new Jag and a villa on the Costa Brava."

"I can't," I whimper.

"Because he buys all the game from the shoots on the cheap, processes it, and sells it to France and Belgium to be made into terrine for the baron and Jacqueline over there. So many pheasants are being shot, the keepers can't bury 'em fast enough."

As an awful image of mass graves full of feathers and lifeless forms pumped with lead fills my mind, he goes on, "As for why I'm here, that's easy, isn't it, Max? A chap's only ever asked shooting for one of three reasons: (1) you are a very good shot, (2) you are very grand, (3) you have a shoot."

"You do talk a lot of rubbish, Andrew," says Max. "I am not grand, a good shot, nor have a shoot, as you very well know."

"Ah. But you're extremely rich," parries Andrew. "As everyone knows, shooting is all about debtor–creditor relationship. To pay back people who have invited you shooting, you have to buy a day, which can cost £10,000, which is a lot to me, but nothing to you. But then, I am an excellent shot, and you, as you have just admitted, are not." He swigs his claret as if he's won this round—though I'm not clear why—and then we all have homemade shortbread with homemade, salted caramel ice cream, and I almost faint it is so good.

And then all goes to plan—at least it does until the penultimate drive.

Pierre and Ralph are adjacent at pegs seven and eight. The baron stands on his own at peg six, his wife having taken up Cath's offer to look around the gardens and the farm shop and load up on cheeses and sausages and a Court Place Christmas pudding to take back to France. Rose and I are leaning against a fence watching the guns and talking about sex, and the elephant trap of sex, which is that it is very tricky to resist overwhelming sexual attraction but impossible to avoid paying a heavy price for years afterwards for thoroughly enjoying illicit sex. In other words, we are very carefully not talking about my recent excursion to Godminster Hospital, as if sex and the products of conception are two entirely different things.

"I think the point is, one feels lust so rarely at our age," Rose is saying, "and in a couple of years' time, no one will ever want to sleep with me again, because I will be old and invisible, and my breasts and everything else will have sagged. It just seems a total waste not to enjoy it while it lasts, and I can still get away with a bikini. So long as I'm discreet."

"Mmm," I answer. "Well, so long as Ceci's okay and Pierre doesn't mind too much, I suppose. But is he really okay about it? I mean, I know that you've been here before"—at this point I pause, delicately, wanting Rose to know that while I am not exactly a fallen woman (I had sex exactly twice with a man who was not my husband, so, in my book, I have been almost entirely faithful for fifteen years), I have some sympathy for her. I fleetingly lapsed myself.

"Well, I'm not clear how much he knows," says Rose. "Pierre isn't saying an awful lot and keeps to his studio—he seems to be there so much at the moment, maybe, for once, he's actually working. And Ceci doesn't know anything. Does she? Why? Do you think she does?" Rose then wails, "Ooh, this wind," and pulls up her collar. "It puts ten years onto the face." She has become much more appearance-conscious since the thing with Jesse Marlon, I've noticed.

We stop talking, because the birds are now coming thick and fast.

Serena comes over to join us, managing to look edgy in a belted Norfolk jacket over breeks, and a battered cowboy hat with a string of turquoise stones slung around the brim on her blond mane. Rose and I cover our ears as bangs echo over the valley, the pheasants thud to the ground, and the browny, downy feathers take their time to dawdle earthwards, insouciantly, as an afterthought, even as their owners lie twitching in their death throes.

All the while, the beaters are moving through the woods like a primitive tribe, making tom-tom noises, clacking, issuing high cries, knocking on trees with sticks, waving white flags as if in surrender, the primeval drumroll to the pointless slaying that will follow.

"Let's take the duck now," Granville cries. "For the last drive! Shall we all stagger down to the river, eh?" And so, for once, the guns walk on their own two feet down to the Lar, to where the numbered pegs have been stuck in the bank in readiness for their arrival.

I am paired with Andrew. Rose has gone to stand by Ned, who has been missing and scowling. One beater is counting each shot fired with a clicker. At the end of the day the ratio of birds to shots fired will be worked out. Max has noticed this and, being terribly competitive, wants the biggest bag.

"Look, Max, it's not a contest," says Andrew, noticing Max's blood is well and truly up after the claret, not to mention the sloe gin at elevenses, "so let's not play silly buggers, eh? It's not about who shoots more birds, it's about Granville's ability to show us high, testing pheasant and our ability to shoot them. A man's a fool if he's in some sort of damn competition, especially with me."

Granville, who never misses anything, notes all this, and I see him have a word in the ear of the second keeper. The keeper then moves quietly over and takes up a stance at Max's side, presumably on the pretext of helping by being Max's loader but basically to keep an eye on him, as Max has only shot in City syndicates before—i.e., much less than the other guns.

At our arrival, the ducks take off lazily and fly low, following the river.

"Where are they going?" I ask, wondering why none of the guns are shooting.

The guns stand at their pegs. It is suddenly quiet. All you

can hear is the wind in the trees, the whirring of wings, and the high whining of the dogs, panting to go and pick up dead birds.

"The birds will be better when they come back," replies Andrew with certainty. The weak winter sun goes behind a cloud. I zip Cas's anorak up and toy with the idea of pulling up the hood but vainly decide against it. "When they come back, they'll be higher, and faster," Andrew says, a cigar clamped between his teeth, "but still, there'll be a heck of a lot of sky around each bird, there always is after lunch, as I fear our friend Max will discover." He raises his gun to his shoulder. It is a beautifully tooled Holland & Holland, with silver etching on the oiled gunmetal barrel. Earlier, he told me it was a pheasant shooting gun from 1918 that used to belong to his grandfather, and I tried to look suitably moved.

"Holland & Holland make the best. It used to be Purdey. Now a lot of people are buying Berettas," he had gone on. "If you're going to reward yourself, the Silver Pigeon is a sound investment," and he continued to talk so knowledgeably about box locks and forged barrels that I began to regret asking anything about it in the first place, but I tried to look keenly interested nonetheless.

And then the ducks return, higher, as promised, and in formation. Andrew cocks his head, switches the cigar to the other side of his mouth, and squeezes the trigger.

Bang! Bang! Bang! Bang! Bang! Bang! Bang!
Bang! Bang! Bang! Bang! Bang! Bang! Bang!

And on, and on, as the guns keep a watchful eye on one another to see how many birds fall from the sky in relation to how many cartridges are spent at each peg, with cries of "over" and "shot," until no more duck. Duck all gone. Or so we think.

And so at last, after a whole day of this shooting and drinking and driving and standing, the head keeper peeps his whistle, long and loud. The guns fall silent. But just as everyone's mind is switching gear, from slaughter to tea, there comes a jam in the transmission. For one lone shot rings out—followed by a distant cry from the edge of the copse on the other side of the Lar River. "Oh fuckety fuckety fuck," Max screams, dragging his army-style ear defenders off his head. "I didn't hear the bloody fucking whistle. Didn't know it was the end of the drive. For fuck's sake!"

Max the pocket plutocrat sounds very cross indeed that he has shot someone. And not, it has to be said, in the least bit sorry. At his performance and outburst, the underkeeper, who has been standing by his shoulder, and loading for him, and telling him in theory which birds to aim at and which to leave well alone, pulls his cap off his head and throws it to the ground in disgust.

Serena canters gracefully down to the Lar, races over the Chinese bridge, and darts over to the stricken shape of the beater, who is lying on the muddy ground, clutching at his shoulder. All the other beaters move towards him, their business of emerging from woods and issuing nonverbal orders to retrievers and spaniels to fetch the dead so that the birds might be hung by their necks with red twine, alongside the braces of pheasant and other wildfowl in the trailer, interrupted by the lone gunman.

Serena rushes up and cradles him in her arms. After his Barbour has been removed, the couple make a touching pietà, especially when the blood starts to bloom redly on the white check of his shirt.

I stride up, fast. I've never looked at Colin Watts properly before. There's a streak of mud down one cheek, and his cap has fallen off his tousled head.

There's something terribly attractive about men who become dirtied and soiled in the act of committing masculinity (I refer the court to the muddied thighs of the rugby player, the sweating dirtiness of the hod carrier, and rest my case), and now I gaze down at Colin Watts with new eyes. He just lies there, blinking, enabling Serena and me to notice that it was terribly unfair. Just as men invariably have better legs than us, so do they always get the longer, curlier lashes.

"It's all right, miss," he says, casting upwards to Serena a look of bravery of which Saint Sebastian himself would have been proud. "I'll be fine. I've only been peppered. It's just a bit of shot." Colin struggles to his feet, trying not to cry out as he moves his shoulder. "Long as I can still open the bowling for Honeyborne this summer, that's all I care."

A beater slowly hands him a dense chunk of fruitcake wrapped up in tinfoil from a capacious pocket, where it has been warmed by a newly dead pigeon. His knotty hands are stained with blood. Colin nods, and slots it into a pocket.

A minute later, Granville trots up, looking stricken. "The ambulance is on its way—it's coming to Court Place—could you make it to the Land Rover, Colin?" he asks. Then his face sort of collapses, crumples. "I can't tell you. How sorry. I am," he says, and I see that his eyes are brimming with tears. "On the last drive, too." He stares at the ground. I see his lips move. He's saying something to himself, and shaking his head.

I didn't know where to look, to be honest. I hate it when men cry. Even the sort of man who is in touch with his feminine side, as I now know Granville most definitely is.

Andrew pulls up in a Land Rover, his army training very much in evidence. He jerks on the handbrake, leaves the diesel engine belching, leaps out, and steers Colin into the front, a maneuver that causes the wounded beater to cry out in pain. Andrew then marches up to Max. "You," he says to Max, in a blood-chilling deep voice, "should take some shooting lessons before picking up a gun again." He delivers this as if it were possibly the worst insult that one man could pay another, looking Max straight in the eye.

At this, a sort of strangled gurgle of rage emerges from Max's throat. He looks, for a second, as if he's going to hit Andrew. "It was only a peppering, Andrew," he whines. "I had my defenders on, didn't hear the bloody whistle. It really wasn't my fault," he goes on, as everyone looks at the ground and not at him. Then he draws himself up to his full height of five feet five inches, puffs out his chest, and stomps off.

"Bleats, shoots, and leaves," says Andrew, looking satisfied with this result. He doffs his cap to me, Rose, Granville, and Serena, and opens the door of the green Land Rover.

"I'm going with him," Serena says, her jaw jutting. Rose and I look at each other.

For a moment a different anxiety flickers across Granville's face, and I wonder if he is going to object, and on what possible grounds he can.

Serena seemingly dives headfirst into the open back, her pupils dilated, a high color flaring in her porcelain cheeks, her blond hair flying. Then the jeep, driven by Andrew, carrying Colin Watts and Serena and a few dead pheasant, guns across the meadow, following skidmarks of previous traffic, to the farm track that leads to the back of Court Place.

"Do you think he's going to eat the cake?" Rose asks me.

"No," I reply slowly, lost in thought. As soon as Colin Watts opened his mouth, after being shot, he sounded—well, middle class. He didn't say "foine" or "loike." He was like one of those women who wake up after a general anesthetic . . . speaking German. "I think he'll probably give it to Serena," I say.

Granville is now sitting like a bump on a log, staring into the moving currents of the peaty river, as they stream away from the bubbling headwaters of the hills and widen their way south to the level sea.

"Why do you say that?" asks Rose. "I don't think Serena does cake. Have you ever seen her eat carbs?"

"No, but she definitely wants something of his inside her, don't you think?" I answer, and Rose and I have to hide our cackles.

When we get back into the Land Rovers to return to Court Place, it is in time for, no less, the fourth meal in six hours. No one exactly *starves*, I can say that much, during a day's shooting.

After tea, I field a call from Home Farm on my mobile, which was trilling inside my pocket for ages before I noticed. I've almost given up on mobiles as there's never any signal. ("No, Mirabel," I say, answering the call. "I am sorry to report that your father and I have not, strangely enough, been at a shoot as in fashion shoot.")

Ralph is very glum. When I prod him to tell me why he looks so gloomy, he just says, "One doesn't talk about these things, Mimi. No point. Especially when it's a beater. It's—just—so much worse to shoot a beater than another gun."

The head keeper comes up as we are massing to depart in front of the house, braced to issue effusive thanks to the Cobbs. He looks grave. We all gather round, in case it's news of Colin, whose welfare is suddenly very dear to our hearts. He takes out a scrap from a pocket, and he looks to Granville with a bright look on his face, a look that speaks of earlier worries banished as the day unfolded: Would the guns pop vainly at the cracking high birds his beaters were driving over them? Would the birds all disappear without warning or explanation? Would there be enough lead in the air when the birds were coming thick and fast? "That makes two hundred and forty pheasant, sir, sixteen duck, and eight partridge. And one beater," he then adds, hanging his head.

"It's not your fault, Mike." Granville claps the head keeper on the shoulder.

"Pardon me, sir, it was, sir. It was on my watch, on my shoot," the head keeper says. "I thought if Jeff stood with Mr. Max, then . . ."

"It's okay, he'll be fine," says Granville, his hand still clasping the head keeper's shoulder. "He's in A&E now, and he's fine. I just spoke to Serena. It's really not your fault. It couldn't be helped. No, no, it's mine." And then Granville gives a sweeping glance, which takes in the valley tumbling down to the Lar, the woods, the landscaped gardens, the rough woodland, all his thousand acres, until his gaze rises to Hamble Hill, where it rests a few moments before returning to the convoy of Land Rovers and other off-roaders strewn untidily over his scrunchy gravel (so many jeeps and off-roaders, it could have been the Green Zone of Baghdad), waiting to bear his guests away from this almost entirely successful social and sporting event. "This is a teaching moment," he says, "a sign." Then he murmurs, "It will never happen again."

As we leave, something nice happens (as well as Cath presenting us with two brace of plucked pheasant in shrink-wrap, already covered in streaky bacon, which should do several meals). The baron comes up to me, and bows. Then he takes my hand, and, despite its being enclosed in my Thinsulate parcel, he bends swiftly to kiss it, and then, as he's returning to the upright position, he freezes and says, holding my gaze, "Madame, I hope we do not meet again, for if we do, I cannot promise to behave as well as I have today."

I went all gooey, of course.

I don't care if that's what he says to all the girls. It's what all the girls want to hear.

Rose

I'm in the squelchy cleft of the Lar Valley that encloses the collective, eco-village, commune, call it what you will, of Spodden's Hatch.

As I tracked my way through the trees to Jesse Marlon's house earlier, the residents were going about their business. They moved around slowly outside, glum-wellied, as if the mud were treacle. None of them ever seems in a hurry.

Between the woods and the water, I thought to myself. They nodded as I went by, and we said "Morning" to one another as I passed the roundhouse and The List. There's also an extra new notice asking all residents to attend the additional meeting that night, to discuss whether or not the eco-village should break its no internal combustion rule in order to buy a device to turn the coppice into wood chips for a biomass boiler, a discussion that so far only the decision to invade and occupy Iraq has matched in terms of fiery passion and bullheaded position taking.

Anyway, The List never changes much. Or hasn't since I've been around, which is only a few weeks.

The List
Bramley tree renewal
Clearing compost heap by bathhouse
Pointing up fencing and fenceposts
Taking back brambles by regeneration area

Scything nettles in orchard
Scything bracken and thistles
Collecting brashings from Douglas firs
Foraging for fungi, chestnuts, walnuts (children must
have passed both mushroom and penknife tests)
Taking ash and scattering in the woods
Knocking back laurel sprouts' regrowth
Greasing tack
WEEDING!!
WOODING!!!!

Today's something called a "communal day," where all work
is for the common good. So there are no jobs to go to today.
When I bumped into Sedge, one of Jesse Marlon's mates, by the
roundhouse, I didn't obviously mention that we're going skiing
tomorrow, Pierre and I.

It sounds so self-indulgent, un-ecofriendly, and almost crim-
inally *Condé Nast Traveller*ish. Frankly, just being here is harder
work than I've ever done—the business of staying alive, not
to mention dry and clean, when you have no electricity, no
water, no loos, no floors or ceilings, no dishwashers, no washing
machines, no Tesco Extra . . . it's more than a full-time commitment, it's almost as bad as camping, something I hate more than
anything in the world. Here, in this valley, I'm surrounded by
environmental fundamentalists, greenorexics, and eco-worriers
wedded to the principle that if one robin redbreast in a cage
puts all heaven in a rage, then one tumble dryer in a basement
will upset the balance of the whole firmament. This lot are so
green, they're almost capable of photosynthesis.

But they are also, frankly, thin, slightly underfed, and
exhausted-looking, despite their layers of woolly jumpers and
scarves and mittens and leg warmers and bobble hats, which
they remove completely only once a week, to use the communal bathhouse, which is a two-hour ordeal involving an ancient
wood burner, a back boiler, and a damp towel that is not quite

big enough and has trailed in the mud, and certainly one I've never been desperate or, indeed, dirty enough to undertake.

Here, there is earth to be tilled, vegetables—Swiss chard, Brussels sprouts, sprout tops, cabbage, broccoli (all brassicas at this time of year)—to be tended, a barn to be built from fallen or windblown wood, a cider press to clean, and the steam engine to maintain. There is always wood to be chopped to be burned in the individual dwellings or in the bathhouse or in the communal open kitchen, where apples are stewed or porridge stirred over the fire. There are two cows, Lazy and Daisy, a pig, Jade, and an evil-tempered albino horse, George, and the goat. There are always dishes to wash in the copper sink made from the top of an old boiler hammered into a pine work top, and with a plug in the middle that empties the dishwater into a trap made of a sieve—rather clever.

There are dishes to be dried and put away tidily in the outdoor kitchen, where blackened baking trays are piled in order of size on open shelves.

There are meat-free sloppy meals heavy on cheap grains and pulses, like quinoa and mung beans, to be prepared.

This morning, over dandelion tea, I asked Jesse Marlon what was on the agenda, apart from the biomass boiler. I asked as if I really cared, and he recited it—whether the vegan members should be required to milk the cows, whether they should inseminate the sow, how to massacre slugs. I rather regretted asking—after all, Jesse Marlon should by rights be there, with Sophy and Co., rather than with me.

As he spoke I couldn't help dwelling on my agenda and packing for the ski trip tomorrow. Skiing is a tough one, and I can't pack until I've decided my look for the slopes at Gstaad: Will it be snowboarder/baggy/technical, or English alpinist circa 1939 in Murren, with a chunky knit and stirrup pants and thick, black hairband?

As I worry about my ski outfits, and après-ski wear, I realize how differently I live from the Spodders. They spend much of the day moving about on their forty acres of Bryanston land, pulling at it, poking it, picking at it, as if it were a scab on the face of the planet. They eat communally, at around six-thirty, although the parents feed their children earlier if they like. Jesse Marlon says they're always ravenous after long days in the open air, not to mention long, long nights in the pitchy gloom of their smoky, homemade habitations of wood and canvas and straw.

During hours of darkness, the dwellings are dimly lit, if at all, by the orange glow of one low-energy lightbulb each, an electricity supply that depends on there being wind and sun, two elements that cannot be continuously guaranteed in a deep cleeve of the Lar River Valley in the middle of West Dorset many months before the summer solstice.

This rainy winter, the single spindly wind generator set on the steep hill next to the old gibbet stopped hissing and spinning. As the solar panels' black faces could absorb no rays of light at all, the Spodders had no electricity for days on end.

I know that, across the damp earth, a few booted paces away, Sophy is in her little yurt, or will be soon. It is one she has built by hand. She'll be tending Noah the baby, with Spike at school, and preparing those vegan salves and hand creams and lip balms made from herbs, groundsel, and cowslips and yellow dock that she gathers and dries and sorts and packages herself, writing out the labels on each little pot in her scratchy copper-plate pen, and then flogging them in Cath's farm shop.

Poor Sophy. No money, and always busy, especially since the unexpected arrival of baby Noah eight months ago, twelve years after the planned arrival of Spike, who's in the same year at Acland's as Ceci and Mirabel. "A happy accident," is all she said to me, by the communal kitchen. (It's her turn to cook tonight, so I asked what was on the menu. Nettle soup, mung bean stew—yum!)

I peeped in on her again, about twenty minutes ago, to give her the groundnut oil she'd asked for.

Baby Noah was placidly sitting in a grubby ski suit on the floor, occasionally finding something small enough to push testingly up his nose, or scooting across to the table to gnaw a leg (teething, according to his mum).

Sophy was at the table, potting gunk. She really does believe her tinctures and salves work and, even more scary, she believes that *her faith* in her pastes and potions is what does the trick.

"The people who come from this land, whose sickness comes from this land, should be treated by herbs from this land," I've heard her explain to visiting journalists who come to write articles about Spodden's Hatch. Loads come, to view those who walk the walk on the low-impact lifestyle and subsistence living. It's inevitable, I suppose, the press interest. As global warming threatens the importing of food and a future in which we will all have to dig for Britain again and never see a Kenyan green bean or a Spanish strawberry looms, glossy spreads about Spodden's Hatch have become a crunchy regular staple (like toasted rye flakes in muesli) of the weekend supplements.

Sophy believes her creams and potions work better because "the right sort of energy has been used in the making of them, the pure energy of healing, untainted by oil or machinery." When asked, she will reveal that her cottage industry brings in about £20 a week, which makes me feel guiltily well off. Twenty pounds! It sounds like nothing. It would be a small piece of Cheddar, some gardening gloves, and a latte and some granola in Court Place farm shop, but, in fact, it is enough to pay her sub to the community, a pot that stretches to buying food and shoeing the horse, and keeps her and the two boys for a week.

Thank God Jesse Marlon's house is at the edge of the settlement, on higher ground, farthest away from the Lar (the higher up the house, the drier the ground). It is made of straw bales, with frames of larch, and sits on a bed of tires. Jesse Marlon built it all by himself, he tells me. He calls it his greatest achievement to date.

Inside, it is warm and cozy. The walls have been covered in cob and painted white. There is a pine floor, a double bunk, and Indian rugs on the floor. Some chipped china mugs and plates sit in a pine rack. A lazy Susan encircles some organic Whole Earth ketchup, Grey Poupon mustard, an earthenware pot with sugar, a bowl of Maldon salt, a pepper mill, and other slightly sticky condiment containers, all of which attest to the very human need to have not a room of one's own, but a kitchen.

An iPod sits on the worktop next to it, a lead running to a three-point plug that links the house's wiring to the solar panels and the wind generator on the hill.

Although midmorning light seeps through the picture window above the kitchen sink, I am sprawled—that's the only word—on a fake fur throw by the open fire. Not a stitch on. I could be in my Egyptian cotton superking-size bed with its patchwork quilt, underneath my grouped collection of Dutch eighteenth-century still lifes of fruit and flowers in gilt frames on the wall, alongside chintzy bedside tables covered with really good knickknacks, the chaise longue I've just re-covered in striped linen farmer's sacks at the foot of the bed. But I'm not. I have abandoned all of that good taste and hot water and comfort for the altogether more dazzling richness of this.

I can feel my long hair sweep over my shoulders and caress my small breasts, and I know that my body gleams rosy in the firelight, like the inside of a cowrie shell.

Jesse Marlon has come in and, instead of making straight for me, is boiling water for tea. This takes ages, as he is having to feed small logs that were hewn by hand into the open mouth of the wood-burning stove. But then, everything in Spodden's Hatch takes ages. A meal can take up to three hours, just the prepping. The stove squats fatly on the wooden planked floor of the dwelling; it has a flat round iron top, on which the kettle sits.

I wondered about the kettle but decided that it doesn't matter having the occasional cup of tea made with water boiled in an ancient aluminium kettle, possibly risking early Alzheimer's. I'm having too much fun rediscovering sex and remembering with surprise how much I once actually liked it. Especially if this rediscovery is assisted by a young, ardent, and, above all, bewilderingly "considerate" lover (this is the euphemism I have decided I will use when I reveal to Mimi the young Jesse Marlon's delightful enthusiasm for orally returning the compliment).

Jesse Marlon is wearing a turquoise-and-white-striped kikoi around his narrow hips and some leather-soled Afghan knitted slipper socks that still smell slightly of sick, as all leather-soled knitted Afghan slipper socks do.

He puts the kettle on, then removes the kikoi from his waist and goes to the window. He stands there brazenly. Outside the house, the eco-village's goat, Cumberbatch (which means someone who lives in a valley divided by a stream, chosen collectively after several nights of heated debate), gives a high bleat and, inside, I stare at Jesse Marlon's impressive physique, noting that his buttocks are pitched at exactly the same jutting angle as those of Michaelangelo's *David.*

Then he gathers up the material and uses his kikoi to cover the window. For one brief moment, before the room is darkened, Jesse Marlon stands framed in the picture window, proud in his nakedness.

As I admire him, something flits uncomfortably across my mind. Mimi was right. Ceci and Pierre do know about Jesse Marlon and me. Not to mention Mirabel and all Ceci's friends. God knows how. Indeed, it is the talk of the village, if not three counties.

At Acland's, yesterday, I happen to know that Ceci and Mirabel were texting each other, their silenced mobiles presumably set to vibrate, while sitting next to each other during the TLN (total living nightmare) of double maths. I hacked into Ceci's in-box, and there it all was.

To: Miri (who is Mirabel Fleming, of course)
Can't tell u wot its like @ home. Mum's with that butters
Spodden's nark. Jeez

To: Ceci
Is she shagging him? He's well fit. Wotabt your Dad?? xxx

To: Miri
He's cool. Don't think he's noticed em copping off xx

To: Cec
Eh??!!! Y yr Dad dont care?

To: Miri
Really bizy 24/7. Hate them both so much right now! l8trzz,
LOL xxx

At this point, though, I don't care. I make a low sound in my throat. I am lying down, but have my head up on one arm. Jesse Marlon turns round.

I am able to give myself up because I have flipped that switch in my head from Pierre to Jesse Marlon, I have enabled the switching action that is necessary in the female to persuade herself that the imminent betrayal of her partner is not succumbing lustfully to temptation, but is, in fact, the only safe and sensible option available.

JM comes over and pushes me gently back down on the fake fur. I try to rise up to kiss him—it's so lovely, the kissing—but he pushes me down, again. He likes to kiss me all over before he does anything else. He starts with my eyes, and plants a tender kiss on each lid.

The house is completely quiet. There are no boilers or pipes clanking, no fridges humming, no radios playing, no telephones ringing, no doorbell ringing. It all feels calm in Jesse Marlon's house. That's because it is calm, marooned in mud and hills, and utterly removed from the modern world of getting and spending.

He moves on to my ears, a kiss that makes my nipples stand erect and me emit little moans that drown out to my own ears the loud, distracting sound of Cumberbatch swiping dock leaves and tearing nettles and long grasses very close to the rickety stoop.

JM's hands are caressing my breasts, now, and I am allowed to kiss him back, but not for very long, for he breaks off, to give each breast in turn the attention it deserves. As he nibbles and pulls with his mouth, his hands find my bush, and with light fingers he flutters about there, as if he is a moth caught inside a lampshade.

Almost screaming after five agonizingly pleasurable minutes, I make a grab, to put him, now angrily slapping against both our bellies, inside, but he holds both my arms down and puts his tongue to my core, like a cat lapping up a dish of cream so as not to miss a single drop. I find myself gripping his ears and tugging at the locks curling over them, beside myself, and a strange animal noise escapes from me as the mounting, Wagnerian crescendo overtakes me. I really do hope at this point that all the Spodders are, as requested, attending the meeting about slug clearance or whatever it is.

Jesse Marlon covers my body with his. "You should be available on the NHS," I say, laughing, and playing with his hair, lying there all soft and open.

His eyes flicker, and I glimpse that look of remote determination flit across his flushed, darkened face. I realize he has plans for me, plans he has carried out to a juddering conclusion on several occasions previously. He turns me over so that I lie facedown on the rug. I giggle, but a little nervously, as he pulls me up from the waist so I'm on my knees, ass in his face, at his mercy, before him, braced for what I know will follow. "It's the best form of contraception I know," says Jesse Marlon, "and easily the most enjoyable."

"Please. Be gentle," I say, head now buried submissively in the rug.

Outside the straw and cob dwelling, Cumberbatch starts up a sort of strangled bleating, as if in sympathy. I can hear the Spodders trudge past carrying armfuls of brashings cut from the Douglas firs, and hope they cannot hear the rhythmic cries audible from the straw house built by Jesse Marlon. Paces away, homeschooled children are sitting making mud pies, or playing with the camp kitty, known as Camp Kitty, and darting in and out of one another's shelters like swifts.

Jesse Marlon's kettle steams weakly from its spout, and a drip that has been trembling on the spout for ages finally falls, and hisses on the hot plate.

Mimi

Mirabel is poring over something on the computer with Ceci, and intermittently saying, "That totally sucks," and "Like, no way," as if she lived in Orange County.

Cas, who has been punting a football around outside, comes in, and I start counting the seconds until the words, "I'm bored," drop from his lips.

Posy is in the garden, feeding Trumpet carrots, while Trumpet takes the carrots in his mouth and paws at the gate to remind her that he is a pony, and thus reasonably keen to do pony things, rather than remain penned in the paddock.

Ralph is reading the papers, the default occupation of so many husbands during so-called "family time," a task that he can easily make stretch through till Sunday night, unless, that is, he feels a sudden, urgent need to cast his fly over untroubled waters.

And I am—well, I've cleared up the kitchen to the extent that I can put my laptop down on the table, and I don't have to think about preparing a wholesome family meal for at least two hours, so I am actually doing two things, reading through the answers to the ad I posted online for a new au pair boy and trying to work out the seating plan for Ralph's birthday lunch, which has, as these things have an ominous tendency to do, become bigger than springtime.

I send Rose, who is off skiing with the Cobbs, a text.

Ana's not here. She left last week, claiming that a grand-mother was gravely ill, a story that both of us knew was 100 per-cent falsehood. Still, I felt almost fond of her as we hugged and I felt her ribs through her thin sweater and anorak at Godminster station but, mainly, it has to be admitted, because she was leaving and I didn't have to sack her. I could have sacked her for any number of things—the fact that she never went outside, even though I took the trouble to show her the three counties walk, so she could do it by herself, and the fact that she once tried to ask me, in a rare communicative moment, what the "life of the bed" was like with Ralph. For her part, she could have walked out for any number of reasons, among them boredom, loneli-ness, an allergy to our house, and an aversion to mud.

I never really trained her to perform my bidding. It's my fault, I suppose, and the one time I asked her to walk Calypso she managed to be chased by cows and stung by a horsefly, plus there are so many bats in her bedroom that she had to sleep with her head covered by one of those domed mesh contrap-tions adorned with butterflies that I use to cover the cheese and summer pudding, etc., in the larder. So, in fact, fair play to her.

No, the real issue was the fact that she was not Polish after all . . . but Moldovan. And therefore illegal. "Did you not check?" Ralph demanded when I confessed that I had sneaked a look at her bag in her room to see if there were illegal drugs in it, or anything that could explain Ana's total disconnect with the real world, and found a Moldovan passport.

When I told the children, Mirabel was fairly beady, too, es-pecially after I confessed that I had hired Ana after reading her profile on a Web site. "I can't believe, Mum, after, like, how you totally go on and on at me about chatting to people I don't know online, that you actually bring a complete stranger you met on the Internet to come and actually live with us, in our house," she chided me. "I mean, get real, Mum."

So now that Ana was leaving, I embraced her warmly. "I hope you get a great job in London," I said. "There are more

Poles in London." (We were still going with the pretense that Ana was Polish—it was much too late to stop now.) "In fact, there are almost more Poles than Londoners; they should put the street signs in Polish, like they do in Chinatown."

"Yes," she replied, watching the notice board announcing the usual raft of delays and cancellations, as though if her eyes left it for a second, she would fail to make her break for the border.

Then the train arrived, and I thought it was pretty nice of me, in the circs, to have gone along with the whole Ana thing to the extent I did. It was now definitely time for me to hire a jolly, tanned, cheerful, muscle-bound Aussie who would play . . . football with Cas, of course! And teach him how to surf, and say, "No worries, mate," when I asked him to do things like scour the glory hole, or clean the boot room floor for the first time in, oh, probably only about four centuries.

So I composed an ad.

Sporty manny required for three children including cricket-mad 12-year-old boy. Must speak English as first language and love the countryside. Light household duties. Own room and bathroom and weekends free. Pay negotiable. Driver necessary.

I sat back, smugly, and waited for the tanned beach-blond dudes, all of whom came from huge families and fab gene pools, had experience with "kids," lifesaving, summer camps, and emergency first aid, and arrived with their own camper vans, surfboards, guitars, and the Jack Johnson songbook, to reply in their thousands.

The telephone rings in the kitchen.

No one stirs. "It's never for me," says Ralph. "I'm not answering it. It's always some member of your family, Mimi. Con or your mother or someone." It's true, when the telephone rings, it is always for me, but then I come from a large gabby Irish family, and he comes from the English upper classes, who think that communication (except with animals) is vulgar and prefer only to ring if there's some bad news to impart.

At this provocation I decide I'm not answering it, either. So we let it ring.

I'm looking at an e-mail from Cath, which she has sent me in reply to my call last week, before she went off to yet another of her houses in superprime locations, this one a château in Switzerland, taking Rose and Pierre. I'd called her to fillet her unashamedly for (1) contacts and addresses and so on, (2) ideas re: the menu and drinks, and (3) help, if not necessarily financial assistance, for Ralph's garden-lunch thing. For his fortieth.

"I'm loving the *déjeuner sur l'herbe* concept!" she wrote, after I roughed out verbally my plan for a picnic in the garden, possibly with people sitting on rugs spread around the orchard—in other words, a completely low-key, low-budget event.

"I'm a bit busy with the wedding at the moment, and May is only a hop, skip, and a jump away," she had written merrily, "but I'd run with a Venetian theme, that always works well"—I loved the "always" there—"with waiters dressed like gondoliers, and I can lend you the Court Place farm shop chef! Giancarlo! He's from Bologna—he did my Parmesan risotto. Do you remember?"

Indeed, I did.

I have already told Cath how wonderful it is that Serena and Colin are getting married, although, as Ralph dryly puts it, one can quite see why he might want to marry her, but not why she might want to marry him.

"They're in love!" I cried. "It's a beautiful, beautiful thing."

"They're children," he answered, "and she must be in pig."

I haven't dared ask Cath why her oldest daughter is getting married in such a rush, because I heard it was something to do with Cath wanting to have the wedding in the garden at its Chelsea Flower Show apogee of perfection, at the silkiest time of year.

"He can do you antipasti. And Giancarlo can also do a main course, he's excellent with fish, I'm thinking line-caught wild Cornish sea bass baked with herbs and rock salt, something simple—as a dry run for the wedding, when we have to seat two hundred fifty."

I am just about to reply to her e-mail, saying that I am now actually thinking more along the lines of pasta salad, cold ham and stuff, green salad, and birthday cake, and that my budget can't stretch to more than about £10 a head, but I never do, because there is a commotion, and I never send the e-mail.

"Who are those women?" Ralph is bellowing. "And what on earth are they doing in our garden?"

I rush to the window, to see who is out there. Ralph has not made it his mission—unlike me, who knows that my life literally depends on it—to know all the Village People by name. We all lean over my scarred enamel butler's sink and peer past my dusty jumble of pots of herbs and jugs on the windowsill.

Gwenda Melplash and Ruth Wingfield have got a sort of rope halter and are putting it over Trumpet's head.

"We called, but no one answered," Ruth yodels in our direction. "We've come for Trumpet; sorry we've taken so long to get round to it!"

"Have I got noose for you," says Ralph.

"Quick, Mirabel, Ceci, run!" I order. "Go and stop them!" I do not let on that I must have somehow given permission for this, during one of my baffling conversations with Ruth/Gwenda about cubbing or hacking, as I don't want any of my family to blame me.

"No way, Mum," Mirabel says, as if I have finally lost my last remaining marble. "(One) those women are well frightening, and (two) like, I'm wearing new Uggs and the grass is wet, yeah?"

Then I see them patting Posy, as if she is a pet, and then they start jogging with Trumpet very fast over the wet grass towards the five-bar gate, a slightly ungainly action that recalls the reliably awful bit during Crufts when owners have to canter on two legs around the show ring alongside their dogs. One of them—Gwenda—opens it with a flick, as if she's practiced it before, and they clatter off down the lane, all three at a rising trot, without even a backwards glance at the stricken Posy.

I let out a cry. I now remember, much too late, that there was a message about a week ago from Ruth Wingfield, saying they would pop up on Saturday, calling first to check we were in, but I don't recall Ruth spelling out what for.

I sigh. I know I can't fight it.

Since the arrests of Henry Pike and Martin Thomas, everyone in the village has been keen to rally round and support the hunt. And this, in my case, clearly means yielding up our darling shaggy family pet to the iron will of the "trot on" brigade, and watching impotently as they "borrow," i.e., "steal," our much-loved Shetland/Exmoor pony in order to have her ready for the cubbing season.

"It doesn't matter, children," I say, sliding the kettle on to the hot plate of the Aga. "We'll have him back soon."

Posy has come into the kitchen, a lone tear glistening like glycerine on her peaches-and-cream cheek. I feel awful. I thought Posy wouldn't mind that much—to be honest, she has always been much more interested in unicorns than ponies.

"I know—as it's ages before lunch, I'm going to take you on an adventure."

Three pairs of eyes switch over to regard me with the greatest of suspicion. Ralph is now plowing doggedly through the Family section of the *Guardian*, which this Saturday carries a harrowing account of a couple's decision to circumcise their baby son. He is the only man I know who reads every section of every newspaper, including the Style section of the *Sunday Times*, i.e., including all the girly bits that are literally designed to shake him to his masculine core.

"Not the dentist!" Cas cries.

"No, not the dentist," I say. "It's an adventure. A nice surprise."

"But that's what you said when we did, like, a massive twenty-mile walk to Godminster and back. And all we got was an ice cream. I don't trust you," says Mirabel. "Forget it. I'm not coming."

I refuse to be drawn, and chivvy them into the car.

And so it is that, in order to cheer the children up for the loss of Trumpet, I find myself, a few minutes later, parking in the soggy patch of ground at Larcombe's Foot, which serves as the car park and postal delivery center for Spodden's Hatch. We park by a box mounted on stilts for deliveries, don't bother to lock (we are learning country ways), and are soon tramping through brushy undergrowth to the eco-village, where Sophy is holding one of her master classes to "raise awareness of all of our herbal heritage."

Obviously, I haven't told the children. I just said in the car that we were going on an adventure that would involve magic potions and homemade biscuits—no doubt sweetened with carob treacle and made with spelt and with the mouthfeel of pebble dash—but there we go. They are still—just—children, and, to them, a biscuit is still a biscuit.

Rose

I sit on the chairlift with Granville, drinking in the wonderful 360-degree diorama of jagged peaks, the crisp air, the sheer delight of being somewhere else, and not being responsible for meals.

Oh, it was such a relief when we got the call-up, when Cath rang back in October and said they wanted to "pack the place out" for this Easter week, this March in other words, and were Pierre and I free? Us, free? To go skiing? To the Cobb Château? It was all I could do not to scream out loud before I said, as one must, that I would "check the diary," but I was pretty sure that "skiing would work."

The Cobbs have a spare castle in Switzerland, which they occasionally lend to friends and let out to those rich enough to afford it, because it comes with a chef, chambermaids, a driver, etc., attached. This category definitely does not include us, because, as I remind him, Pierre has not sold a sculpture now for three whole years.

To be quite honest, when Cath called, I wasn't sure we *could* do it. Even though the actual week itself is gratis, we could still barely afford to go, what with the train tickets to London and then Heathrow, the flight, the train, then taxi from Geneva to Gstaad to Rougemont, the tips to staff—but the Cobbs do have an account at the ski shop and guests can hire equipment as they please, try out snowboarding, and put little accessories like gloves and high-altitude lip salve on the tab; their guests ski in a red cloud of Swiss ski school instructors, like corpuscles, and the Cobbs always kindly refuse Pierre's offer, made through clenched teeth, of "taking everyone out for a meal."

As for the other guests: the cast is the Lacostes, Virginie and Mathieu—she's a very foxy Frenchwoman who skies like an Olympic champion, with much hip swaying. They came to dinner at Court Place, but Cath couldn't have Pierre and me, obviously, because of my form with Henry Pike—it would have been hard for Biddy (though not that hard in my view). Then there's the bonking baron and his wife—Esmond and Jacqueline—the four Cobblets, of course, including a slightly *piano* Serena, who is for some reason not so keen to ski this year.

A big topic of conversation over fondue and pflumli last night was neighboring Hutton, the gatehouse of which everyone thought was on the market but about which now no one seems very clear. It's obviously owned by Sir Michael Hutton, but that is all that is obvious. It's not necessarily on the market, but the Lacostes have viewed it, the same weekend they were staying chez Cobb. And so has, I know, Clare Sturgis.

I suppose the reason for the gray area is this: houses like the gatehouse, which have remained in the same hands for generations, unaltered and unimproved, are as rare as hen's teeth in Dorset, and landowners hate to part with anything before they die unless they really have to, as the most important thing to them is handing down the estate intact to their male heirs, but the snag here is . . . Sir Michael doesn't have one. A male heir, that is. So everyone's been tiptoeing around him. Sir Michael Hutton (address, Hutton Manor, Hutton, nr Godminster, Dorset—isn't that perfect?) is dealing with his solicitor only very intermittently, and nothing seems to be happening. No one, not even the land agent now, dares approach Sir Michael directly, in case he shouts and flings them into outer darkness, in perpetuity. Sir Michael is famously difficult, to the extent that no one would dream of asking him a direct question about his intentions regarding a house that has been in the family for centuries, plus a parcel of five hundred acres of prime farmland —it would be insolent even to suggest he might be selling. I do happen to know, though . . .

Clare Sturgis has rented a weekend cottage on the Bryanston estate (Ned and Lulu are asking her for £700 a month; I know because I asked) to see whether she likes the area. I found this out the same time Clare told me she had put in an offer for the gatehouse, via the agent. "For how much?" I asked. I thought I could. "Several million," is all Clare would answer.

My mobile beeps.

Even in the Bernese Oberland, I can receive a signal. Bound to be another text from Ceci, who's staying with the Flemings, saying, "I don't want you to be away! Come back. It's freezing and it's not fair!" and asking about her biology revision.

I dig my mobile out of my anorak pocket, which involves removing gloves, stuffing gloves between my legs, and asking Granville if he would mind holding my poles. "I'll hold your pole anytime," I say, making a poor joke at my own expense.

"I know you will, Rose," he answers. "Why else did I invite you?"

It is from Mimi, saying Ceci is fine, but there is text missing. Something about Ralph's party, I expect. Mimi has been very down, of course, recently. It's taken her a while to regain her bounce. But she's a cork. She doesn't sink, she bobs, and after all she went through in January, only a few weeks ago, really, I really think this party plan is a positive sign. She and Ralph are getting back on track. It shows she's getting herself together, and moving on, but also that she's making an effort, after the recent trauma, to be a couple, which is what entertaining is mostly about.

Also, the fact that she is actually being allowed to give a party to celebrate Ralph's fortieth shows that Ralph must be being extranice to her. He'd never agree to a party of any sort in normal circumstances, let alone one in which he was center stage.

I haven't said anything to her yet, but all this is for the best, because divorce—well, it's out of the question, in the country. Marriage is perfectly bearable, so long as one has distractions and can handle those long silent bits in between rows. One wouldn't wish the experience of being a country divorcée on anyone, let alone someone as nice as Mimi. All social life is organized by married women for the benefit of other married women, single divorcées are treated as vermin—and all because horsey matrons think you might try to steal their singularly ill-favored, stumpy, balding husbands, who like to express their fun-loving, zany personalities by wearing bright orange, red, or yellow elephant cords, or novelty ties.

Which is intolerable in every way.

I shove the mobile back, as I don't want to reply to the text and by mistake drop it down a crevasse, although doubtless Virginie would retrieve it in a trice. I settle back in the chair, feeling grateful that I am not freezing to death, and that we're in late March and I can still feel my extremities.

"How is Mimi?" Granville asks. "Is everything okay?"

"Oh, yes," I say. "She's fine. Well, actually . . ."

The long chair swings on its way to the top of the mountain (we were a bit early for lunch when we reached the lift, so Granville asked the operator to slow it down). We sit side by side and watch the snowboarders carve up the pistes, and the older couples gliding down in a more considered way. It seems the right moment to tell Granville, somehow.

As I speak, I enjoy the sight of the pine trees laden with smooth caps of snow, the sun gilding the peaks across the whole panorama, and we giggle at the English skiing very badly and laughing when they crash, and gaze in wonderment at the fearless little helmeted French children bombing straight down mountains.

Maybe it is the delicious freezing air, like breathing in chilled Krug, the prospect of a bubbling cheesy dish of *tartiflette* a few hundred yards up the mountain ahead, that nudges me into it.

Of course, I immediately have a pang of regret, as one does after revealing any confidence. Granville listens with concentration, concern, and sympathy. When I get to the bit about the hospital, at Godminster, Gran is horrified. He shakes his head sadly. I say, Please don't tell anyone I told you. He says, "What happens on the Wasserngrat, stays on the Wasserngrat," and checks how far we have to go till we glide off.

"This isn't the sort of merry chat we should be having, on a private ski lift taking us up a private mountain to a private club," I say. In a minute, we will ski off the chair together to have our £35,000 lunch.

Granville calls it this because he eats there once a year and this is the cost of joining the all-inclusive Eagle Club, a club that turns away princes and film stars and allows members to visit only a maximum of three times a year. Granville, I noticed earlier, had specially put on his Eagle Club jersey with its badge over his heart, which was designed by Valentino—one of the designer's conditions of membership.

"Look, Rose," he says, suddenly. "This is incredibly important. This Clare woman. Someone has to stop her moving to Godminster, don't you think? Will it be you, or will it be me?"

"Oh, come on, Gran," I say, patting pockets to check presence of lip salve, Vuarnet ski goggles, purse, and ski pass, items all provided by Granville—except my purse. "I'm sure Clare has no intention of destroying the Fleming family. She's only renting. It's all fine. She's not going to freak out. What would she gain? She has as much to lose as they do."

"Lord knows what she's really up to," says Granville, pulling on his gloves and checking to see whether I'm ready for him to lift the bar so we can glide off the lift in the direction of the £35,000 lunch. "Sounds like a bloody dangerous game, though."

Anyway, Cath and Granville are very merry at lunch, as we all are—it's always such a relief on a skiing holiday when everyone meets in the right place at roughly the right time, as so much of the holiday is spent waiting at the top of ski lifts and mountains for people who never appear.

Granville kicks off by ordering a magnum of rosé and some crostini with dark morel mushrooms in a savory cream sauce, scattered with parsley.

During the meal, I see something. Granville has changed.

He starts telling me all about some course he's signed on to in London. Psychotherapy. I don't let on that Mimi has already given me advance warning of this. Mimi had said that in her part of London, it was routine: women stopped working because their husbands were making so much money, then they had low self-esteem, and then they saw therapists to address the low self-esteem, and then they became hooked on the talking drug and trained as therapists themselves. Mimi knows about Granville's change of course because she saw some letter or something.

"Yup, he's shrink-rapping," says Cath, without letting on whether she's for or against.

"But what about the hedge fund?" asks the baron. "*La famille* Cobb still has to eat, *non?*"

Then everyone laughs, as Granville doesn't *need* to make any more money, he has just reached a plateau where he doesn't really *want* to make any more money anymore. He wants to do something else, a change of direction.

And there I was, thinking that it was invariably those who are most in need of psychotherapy who are most attracted to it. When I consider Granville, who is the sanest and most sensible man I know, I can admit it. I was wrong.

So I listen with respect when Gran tells me that he is doing a course at the Tavistock. He does, admittedly, use the word "journey," and the awful word "learnings," without batting an eyelid. But most of all he talks about acceptance, and not trying to change the things that are beyond his control, which I take to mean, reading between the lines, that he doesn't mind the fact that his daughter, the lovely, twenty-two-year-old Serena, is in a relationship with the rumored village rapist and recipient of Max Simon's bullet, Colin Watts. My hunch is confirmed when, apropos nothing, Granville suddenly comes out with, "He's okay, you know, Colin Watts. He's okay."

He is refilling my glass with San Pellegrino, while Virginie Lacoste, in a boatneck sweater from which crisply emerges a white collar, gives me a cool glance. I feel faintly unsettled under her gaze.

Cath is struggling manfully with Mathieu, who may be a Nureyev when it comes to marketing L'Oréal hair products but with whom chitchat rarely achieves liftoff.

"I spoke to the police," Granville murmurs, for my ears only, "and it's not at all clear that Watts was the culprit, mmm? It's complicated. I can't say any more, actually. It's all a bit close to the knuckle, and we're a small village. And Serena . . . well, she adores him. They always have adored each other, since they were kiddies."

"But who was supposed to have been raped by whom, then?" I ask, slightly ruining the moment, and tell Granville, doing a fair impression of the Darrrset accent of the publican, all about the time Garry from the pub told me with glee about how he didn't mind a "spot of malarkey" himself but that Colin had "had her both ways," if I knew what he meant. Granville shudders at this, then describes Watts's alleged victim, says she was an alternative type, lived in the eco-village, single mother, and herbalist.

All this is fascinating, but I have to do my duty as a guest, and Cath's being encouraged by Virginie—by this stage she is flirting with everybody, even the waiters and the wine bottles, with a naughty look on her face—to tell everyone about her plans for the farm shop.

"You must tell everaybody about ze sausage, Catherine," Virginie begs. "Rarely, you 'ave been, 'ow you say, busteeng your bootay zees past few weeks."

"Sorry, darling?" says Granville. "You've been what?"

"Busting my booty," says Cath. "It's American for working hard."

"Ze sausage at ze farm shop eez so good," Virginie continues, "I am sending 'eem to *Maman* in Soissons, and I say, zees sausage, you do not 'ave to see heem made, because in Honeyborne, Catherine Cobb is God, and so, I 'ave met my maker already."

Everyone laughs at this tribute to our hostess, who takes up the thread.

"We are introducing some new lines," Cath says. "For the relaunch in the Tithe Barn. I'm very, very excited by them. I'm doing a Court Place paint, the special gray-green color on all our woodwork, because—you'll never believe this—but when guys come to the shop, they flake bits off to match it at Homebase. So we're launching Court Place Gray-Green. And then, yes, Virginie, there's our new fennel and venison, thank you. It's a team effort, as these things always are, and, well, I work hard to make sure I have a great team." I am wondering why she is talking to us as if we are investors or shareholders, but not for long, because she raises her glass. "When I'm finished," she announces, "Carole Bamford and Debo Devonshire will be looking to their laurels."

"Wow, Cath," I say. "Really? Because Daylesford Organics . . . well, it does seem to set a new standard. I haven't been to Chatsworth—always longed to—but I've been to the one in Gloucestershire and the one in Pimlico, the flagship one, and I have to say, I did think, How can you exceed this? Everything is so smart, and perfect in every way. Even the milk in degradable packaging made of, what is it, chalk? They wrap the aged Cheddar in organic linen that has been dipped in organic lard. The sleek stores, the hand-roasted coffee, the hand-kneaded breads, Viscount Linley always popping in for a latte, all those Tamara Mellon types in there, and those cheeses . . ." We all pause reverentially as we each recall magical moments, thanks to Lady Bamford's many emporia of exquisiteness. "It's just . . . well, hard to compete with that, isn't it?"

"I agree, you can't," says Cath instantly, "and I wouldn't want to. It's all credit to Carole that she's made such a success of the enterprise. And I just lo-o-ve the product," she gushes, with the fervent sincerity of the cup-always-full American. She loves the success of others, she is never happier than when giving credit where credit is due, and always looks on the bright side. "But here's the USP, the wild new idea. I'm ditching plans to get the fully organic certification—"

"Except for *vos seins,* your breasts, Catherine," Virginie interrupts with a wicked look, and her hands flutter above her own pert chest. Virginie is complimenting Cath on the fact that her breasts are all her own! I decide she is a little drunk. "It eez such a plaizhair to see an American woman, from ze West Coast, who does not 'ave all ze work. *Vraiment,* ze women in L.A.—I nevair saw one gray 'air. And zair faces, zay look"—Virginie pauses, shakes her head, as if lost for words—"as if zay 'ave been in a terreeble 'ouse fire."

"I'm glad you think I'm aging gracefully, Virginie," says Cath. "From you, that is praise indeed. I just can't be bothered with plastic surgery. To me, it's like all the folks who jump off the Golden Gate Bridge—a permanent solution to a temporary problem. But back to the shop. Organic certification, as I was saying. It's way too complicated, if you want a café and a shop combined. So I'm going local. The Court Place Farm Shop is going off the reservation here. We're going to provide organic produce and so on, but everyone's hip to that now, so here's the kicker. I'm going to serve it up at prices even locals can afford. I know our prices have been a little . . . punchy" (I almost say "exorbitant" but manage to bite my tongue), "so the new deal is, no markups, no food miles. Everybody will be able to buy my sausages now, not just Virginie."

Everyone claps as if all we worry about, too, is the ethics of a farm shop at which a steel magnate, or Russian oligarch, arrives by helicopter, spends £8 on some carrots and £1,500 on a cashmere dressing gown, and choppers back to London, squirting kerosene straight into the ozone layer.

The baron raises his glass. "To Madame Cobb," he announces, "the Queen Bee of Honeyborne. Long may she reign over us."

Everyone laughs as if the baron has executed a dazzling wordplay, and toasts Cath energetically. After all, it has been a long hard morning of at least three red runs. And then we had a fairly liquid lunch and penne à la Geoffrey, as in Geoffrey Moore, the son of Roger Moore, and raclette at a private club where the pecking order of tables was more complex than the parking precedence of horse boxes at a Pony Club polo match.

At this moment, our table is approached by a bronzed Taki, the Greek playboy, wearing the sweater with the round Eagle Club badge, same as Granville. With his eyes on Virginie, the Greek invites us all to a party the following night at his chalet in Gstaad. "It's at the Palataki," he says, his eyes never leaving Virginie. "My chalet. It means small palace. It's a sort of pun combining 'palace," and 'Taki,' " he needlessly adds, as if only silver-tongued wordsmiths would understand without explanation. "Just ask any taxi driver."

Virginie and I exchange a look. That sounds fun, and Taki is exuding an unmistakable, up-for-it whiff. But though we all look visibly thrilled, as is only polite, and thank Taki for his invitation, when he has moved on, the baron—egged on by a boot-faced Jacqueline—and Granville and Cath all say that they don't want to go and why do old Eurotrash goats frolic with girls who could be their own granddaughters and things like that, which seems most unsporting of them.

And the party is ruled out.

Later, though, some of us had . . . a party of our own.

I was in the sauna, out in the grounds. I'd picked up the wrong towel, the sort of midsized one between the hand towel and the bath towel, and was trying to get it to cover my breasts and bottom, when the door pushed open.

There was still an hour or so until our sit-down four-course dinner.

Virginie entered, with the towel draped around her hips, revealing high round breasts with small round pink nipples perfectly positioned in the center of each, like bosses on a shield.

"Hello," I said.

" 'Ello," she drawled in reply. She dropped the towel and lay down on the bench opposite me, proud and naked. In the orange light, her golden bush looked as if it were on fire. She raised a knee. Then her hands went to her chest, and she started playing with the moisture that had beaded between her gleaming, pointy breasts.

I began to feel very hot. I couldn't take my eyes off her. I was still a bit merry from lunch, I suppose.

She turned her head on one side and regarded me speculatively. "Take off ze towel," she said. "I want to see you."

It had been so long since anyone had ordered me around, let alone a very bad Frenchwoman with a reputation for seducing both sexes with carnal abandon, that I felt a thrill of submission.

I smoothed the towel out on the hot wooden slats, then sat on it, to reduce the contact of buttocks with sizzling wood. Then she sat up on her bench, so we were facing each other.

I looked at Virginie, and she looked at me. Since the thing with Jesse Marlon, I've lost weight, and I did not feel conscious of my stomach, or my breasts, but simply enjoyed displaying myself to someone who—for whatever reason—wanted to look at me. And Virginie—she'd pinned her blonde hair up, but some tendrils were sticking to her slender neck. I could barely keep my eyes from her breasts, but when I lifted my eyes, I saw that her lips were pink and swollen, a tongue was playing around pearly teeth, and her breathing was coming fast.

"I sort so," said Virginie, after we had been staring at each other for a time.

"What?" I asked, and suddenly I found that I was squirming my thighs together, and the towel had dampened underneath me.

"Some women, zey 'ave a animal drive, and ozzers, zey 'ave zee drive *maternelle*," she said, as her eyes held mine. I am thinking, Oh my God . . . Virginie . . . she isn't making a pass at me, is she? Then her hand moved down to between her legs, which had unashamedly parted, and I think, Oh my God, she is, she's trying to *turn* me, as one leg had risen to rest on the slatted bed rather than the floor, and it was as if a cloud of butterflies took off in my stomach.

Mimi

And we are all now packed into the yurt.

Admittedly, this time last year, Casimir would be at a Chelsea match at Stamford Bridge. Mirabel would be in Top Shop. Posy would be playing hide and seek in the communal garden, while Ralph and I "assembled" a delicious lunch of imported ingredients bought from local Notting Hill delis for the price of a small car.

But we are, with Ceci, in Spodden's Hatch, in Sophy's yurt, where the entry cost is 50p, materials are free, a paper cup of Spodden's Hatch own-label apple juice is 50p, honey-sweetened oatmeal cookies made by Sophy 20p each, gluten-free soya milk, spelt, and blueberry muffins, made by Sophy's friend Rain, 70p apiece.

The children have been issued with thin gardening gloves and pots and are shooting me murderous looks.

Baby Noah is sitting close to the central open fireplace, pushing a crayon up his nose. Spike is sitting looking desperate on a sort of bunk covered with rags, scraps of patchwork, knitted blanket, and so on, which have an awful unwashed look. He is clearly mortified that Mirabel, in his class at school, can inspect him in his habitat, as if he is a panda in a zoo.

Sophy is sitting in front with an assortment of herbs and jars on a table.

"Is she the witch?" Posy asks audibly, staring at Sophy's purple, hand-knitted long cardigan, black hair shot through with gray, and sheepskin boots. This is annoying, as I have never said there was a witch.

Sophy does not wear a bra, but she has one of those figures that still looks pretty good, regardless of how effectively she shrouds it in widow's weeds.

"No, of course she's not, darling," I say. "She's a sort of magician."

We spend half an hour or so pulping leaves and sniffing essences and learning about the properties of various herbs, while Spike reads, on his bed, a Just William book from the mobile library, occasionally laughing out loud, which makes me think what a nice boy he must be.

At 12:50 the session ends, after the "work party," during which bladder campion, catnip, lavender, borage, dill, hyssop, lemon balm, thyme, lovage, and rue have all been identified and rubbed between thumb and forefinger to release what Sophy, sniffing deeply, her eyes closed in ecstasy, describes as their "individual signature scents."

Even though the children, after an hour, are all sighing, rolling their eyes, and begging to go, even my usually biddable Posy, I, for one, feel tremendous. As if I have, definitely, connected with nature. I feel in my waters how right I am to have taken the children away from the materialist society of West London. I have removed my children from the society of other children who announce at circle time that they have been bought flats in Lansdowne Road/inherited huge lump sums/just returned from eco-safari or the Maldives (a part of the Notting Hill curriculum which Ralph used to call "show off and tell"). I have removed them from the posse of pushy mothers who ferry their overstimulated, force-fed, privately educated, and additionally tutored children from violin to philosophy group to chess tournament simply so their offspring, bristling with extracurricular add-ons like Grade 8 lute, catch the eye of the admissions tutor at Eton.

And I have elevated them to a community where children

learn about herbs, read Just William, and eat gluten-free honey-sweetened cookies in yurts.

I exhale with satisfaction, thinking that I am giving my children a chance, a once-in-a-lifetime chance not to be serial consumers of the digital age, a chance to be bored, a chance to invent games, breathe the fresh air of West Dorset, and whatnot. Indeed, I almost feel able to attend Sophy's next workshop on biodynamic composting. But not quite. Not yet. You can take the girl away from Notting Hill . . . "I wish I could come to it, Sophy, but I think I have . . . another commitment that day," I say, as if I am meeting Gordon Brown to discuss the state of the union. "But is there anything you'd like, Sophy? Anything you need? I'd love to be able to give you something, you know, back . . ." I swell with deep self-love, and am filled with a rush of emotion that I normally get only when I take all my empties and cardboard and newspapers to the household waste place in Larcombe Ducis, to recycle them ethically.

Sophy follows my eyes around her yurt, with its clothes and cotton nappies hanging like bunting from the inside walls, the wood burner, the packed-mud floor covered with rugs of indeterminate hues, its plate rack full of drying baby dishes, the low bookshelf full of cast-off paperbacks (impossible to read without full daylight), the one lightbulb hanging down. "But I don't need anything," she protests. She takes another sip of her herb tea. She says she is drinking it because she is used to bitter tastes, and sage discourages milk production, and that she knows that now Noah is almost one, she must make an effort to get to that scary place called "out there" again.

I look at Spike, wondering how much longer he is going to put up with living in a bender with a lactating single mother who can afford only pulses and legumes, a screaming baby, and no TV, when all his friends from school live in lovely new boxy houses with rectangular white walls, hard flat floors, and something called "plasmas," or in lovingly restored three-hundred-year-old vicarages, mills, or farmhouses.

According to Mirabel, when Spike comes home from school, ravenous at four-fifteen, to ask what's for tea, Sophy always answers, "Lentil surprise," and Spike apparently always says, "My favorite," even though there's nothing remotely surprising about her garlic and onion lentil bake and he has it every day.

I am being extranice to Sophy, asking her if she needs anything, because we are about to leave, even though the herbal heritage session goes on for another hour. I give the signal to the children, who muster with alacrity by the entrance, which beckons to us like a triangle of light in the pitchy gloom of the yurt. And then Sophy's eyes fall on the wood burner, to where smoke is seeping out of a crack in the iron gullet that feeds outside. Then her eyes flash. "Well, a new chimney, perhaps."

Sophy zips up the snowsuit and replaces Noah on the floor. He sits motionless for a couple of seconds, and then sets off in a fast crawl over the packed earth of the bender towards the aperture and the world beyond, to get even dirtier and muddier, and to discover yet more new and pleasant objects to pop into his gummy mouth.

Sophy watches his progress as she might a wind-up toy: with detachment, and a curiosity about where it might fetch up. She wonders, as she must do, oh, only about every ten minutes or so, how she is going to do this, every day, for the next eighteen years, on her own, and hopes this desperation doesn't show in her eyes, but it does. I really feel for her.

"I know what I need," Spike mutters, eyeing Mirabel. "Flat walls. A floor. And then, perhaps, a PS3."

"So Mum. Is that what passes for fun in West Dorset?" asks Cas, who, like Mirabel, has zero tolerance for the hey-nonny-no aspects of rural life. We are trudging back to the car, occasionally passing a yonder peasant gathering fu-uuu-el or picking berries. "If we were back in London, I could be doing nets at Lords with my friends from school, or in the Portobello." He echoes my thoughts. "Instead, we're paying to see a bunch of hippies and join in something called a herb walk, followed by a herb work party, in which we get to 'meet' "—Cas's fingers waggle the inverted commas around the verb—"wild weeds and medicinal plants. The only upside is that none of my old friends can see me now. Thanks a bunch, Mum."

When we get back, and after lunch, I remember. The au pair job! After Ana left, the children had solemnly made representations to me and explained that they would prefer not to have anyone at all. Even if that meant that I was in a bad mood all the time. I had hugged my secret—that I was going to find them a godlike Aussie—close to my chest. There should be scads of replies by now.

Eagerly, I open my in-box, leaving the lunch things piled by the sink, as if in anticipation of an extra pair of willing hands to tackle them.

I have forty-six new messages. Yippee!

> Hello!
> My name's Slawek Im 24 and I am graduated the university last year—English—that is why my english is fluent yes! I love children, animals, I am very active a non-smoking person loving going to cinemas strolling around and working on computers. My English is also fluent in computers and Internet—I use it at home I come from Poland and Im looking for some job like helping peoples, childrens like taking care, as for man Im good with all house duties: loundry, ironing, and so on apart from cooking ;) I have also clear Drive license. Looking for some Job.
>
> Best regards
> Slawek

I click open the next one.

> i am monica from spain and i am very interesting to travel london the soon as posible, my first language is spanish but

i want to make better my english . . . i am very spotty, honest
and lovely girl!!

Monica

Wondering whether they're replying to the wrong ad, I go back
to the Gumtree Web site and check what I have written. In
bold capitals, my ad does say what I thought it did about English as first language and that I wanted a boy.

I return to my in-box with a sense of doom.

As I open the next one, I of course realize the following
catch-22 of my own, carefully worded ad: if the applicant, Drag-
olbug, Bogdan, or whoever, doesn't speak English, then my stip-
ulation for a sporty—or even a spotty—Anglophone male will,
necessarily, pass him or her by.

I feel for these girls, these women, these young men, and
their lives, and almost understand their transparent yearning to find paid work in the West, their eagerness to spend
twenty-four hours on a bus to Victoria coach station, spinning out a small bottle of water and one ham sandwich, in
order to wash my family's underwear. But still. I am determined not to repeat my Ana mistake. I open about thirty
more e-mails, my eyes are beginning to hurt, and the children
are asking, "When's tea?" and then I click one with the address ry@campervan.com.

Hi my name is Ry, I am a 25 yr old Australian male, I have
recently arrived in London and am currently living in Notting
Hill.

I have 1 year experience with an active little boy 8, and
a girl 6.

I hold a UK drivers license, Valid First Aid Certificate,
and CRB check. I am a non smoker, very active in sports
and hobbies. I play football, tennis, cricket, and surf regu-
larly in Australia, and I write and play my own songs (I

enclose a download of three sample tracks from my first album).

Hope to hear from you soon.

Life is finally looking up. I send Ry an e-mail back by return and, despite Mirabel's dark warnings about people on the Web, tell him we have a deal.

Rose

Ned is standing in a headmasterly way by his desk in his study, looking grayer and thinner than I remembered, as if he, too, is in need of a good holiday. Whenever there is footfall outside, in the passageways that lead off to the billiard room or the green baize door, his eyes flicker. In case Lulu comes in. There's only one person that Ned Bryanston has ever been frightened of, even more than his mother, and he's married to her. It's often the way. Husbands and wives, even attractive ones, are often yoked together not by love or lust, but by fear and loathing.

His stance confirms me in my suspicion that I have been summoned, rather too late, for my formal dressing-down. I am braced for the worst. A few days after we got back from skiing, Ceci found another note from Jesse Marlon.

It was in my dressing-table drawer. The girl is going slightly Goth or punk—though Ceci's term is "emo"—and she says she was looking for an eyeliner sharpener, to sharpen her black eyeliner.

I'm not sure I believe her, but, be that as it may, she was clearly hunting high and low, because the note was right at the back, underneath a flat leather box from Phillips in New Bond Street that contained my diamond necklace. Ceci laid it carefully on Pierre's desk in the studio, just by the *Dictionary of Medical Symptoms*, where he would be bound to see it.

Well, in this letter, Jesse Marlon was begging me to recon-
sider my decision, and to come back and resume my morning
activities at Spodden's Hatch. Such bad luck that Pierre is provided with actual documentary evidence of my adultery after
the event.

So Pierre finds this note, which my own daughter has con-
siderately passed on for his perusal, and the rest . . . well, the
rest is history repeating itself. I have to say that it was extremely
unfortunate that Jesse Marlon in this missive referred to at least
one practice that is banned—so Ceci tells me; the young are so
judgmental—in several U.S. states.

So it's all been a complete nightmare. Ceci is lying in bed
sobbing and texting Mirabel, and even Spike, their friendboy—we're not allowed to use the word "boyfriend," unlike
all my sad single friends, who use it willy-nilly of their creaky
pensioner consorts—has rushed round to sympathize. As I
tiptoed past her bedroom I heard Ceci saying to Mirabel, loud
and clear even though they were playing Lily Allen on the
iPod speakers, that it was "way gross," and that I was "well
ancient," and then I heard Mirabel say, yeah, I was almost as
old as *Liz Hurley*, and I heard them all sigh. Then Spike said,
"I've pretty much given up on grown-ups. Every single one
I've ever met has either screwed my mum or someone else's
mother."

"They're, like, totally skanky and sad," Ceci agreed.

When Ned called and asked whether it was convenient to
come to Godminster this morning, I took particular care with
my appearance, obviously so as not to underscore the two-
decade age gap between me and their son (Lulu's stepson—
Lulu is much too young to be Jesse Marlon's mother, as her Ugg
boots and miniskirts signal very loudly). So I channeled Demi
'n' Ashton, rather than mother and son, and wore an Agnès
B vest underneath a denim playsuit (I wore the vest tight, the
dungarees loose) with the legs cuffed up to midcalf, and Havai-
anas flip-flops.

When I parked on the gravel by the statue of Pan in the forecourt, the huge mahogany doors of the hall were open, so I wandered in. "Ned?" I called.

Silence. I looked around at the family portraits, and a Beechey and a Gainsborough and a Ramsay all stared back at me, in a quizzical, seen-it-all way I found comforting. There was that smell of library and woodsmoke, overlaid by the sweet scent coming from a huge vase of lilies on the round table in the hall.

"Rose?" came Ned's voice. "In the study."

I was braced for a thrashing, for having corrupted Ned's hunky and horny oldest son. And now, as I learned, this thrashing was going to be administered in the study, which was more than fitting. The study is, after all, where, according to ancient Tudor lore, some forebear of Ned's murdered the Godminster priest, having discovered him "chockinge his wife under ye chinne," and where an indelible bloodstain in front of the fireplace is supposed to stand as proof of his crime, and proof that though years may pass nothing ever, really, changes between the sexes.

I saunter in, all innocence, and take a seat opposite Ned, who remains standing, in a low armchair with velvet upholstery the color of damson jam, worn threadbare in places. And then . . . so weird.

Ned doesn't mention my liaison at all. He just starts talking about how complicated it all is, and raving about *Little Ned*.

Which is too bizarre—his son Little Ned is only eleven, and I can't think where I could come into any discussion of the child, as I immediately make clear.

"What has Little Ned got to do with me?" I ask sharply. I don't add "and Jesse Marlon" out of deference. After all, I am still married to Pierre, and it would be highly disrespectful to bracket myself in a breeding pair with Jesse Marlon. And I also don't say "and Jesse Marlon" because, to be frank, all this has come out too late. I could have killed Ceci for finding the letter from Jesse Marlon, days after I had already finished with him and found someone else, someone gentler, someone kitten-softer.

"Oh gawd," groans Ned. "The cat's among the pigeons. Errr. Agggh." He runs his hands through his hair, so it sticks up in spikes off his forehead. "Rose, you're my only hope."

"Ned, what are you talking about? You're talking like Obi-Wan Kenobi." I allow myself to sound more assertive.

"Listen, Rose, I've always liked you, and I don't honestly give a monkey's what you get up to, never have, each to her own, it's your funeral, but, er—it's like this." He ruffles his hair again. "It's about Godminster. The estate." I mentally exhale. "I just thought we were all sorted, done and dusted, you know, and that Jesse Marlon would never want to take it *on*, and Lulu was naturally very keen to see the old place pass to Little Ned and all that. But then, it turns out that Jesse Marlon—"

"Sorry, Ned, to interrupt again," I say, "but you haven't ex-plained where I fit in." I may have enjoyed—more than I can say—my hours with Jesse Marlon, but the last thing I need is to be roped into some estate-planning quagmire of the Bryan-ston family. Frankly, with a husband, a hormonal daughter, a hot ex-lover, and an even hotter new lover, I am feeling pretty overextended already, like the British army when it opened up a new front in Iraq as well as Afghanistan.

"Look, what you get up to in your own marriage, even if it involves my own son, is thankfully none of my business. But it would help me out of a terrible hole if you would help to per-suade him to maintain the status quo," Ned groans.

"What is the status quo, though?"

"Lulu thinks that Little Ned stands to inherit, because he is called Little Ned and I'm called Big Ned. It's too long and bor-ing to explain, but the first Bryanston son and heir, so to speak, is always called Ned, it's a family custom, so she assumed as I did, frankly, that that would be all right."

"But Ned isn't the first Bryanston son," I point out. "Jesse

Marlon is. And he's called Jesse Marlon, not Ned," I add un-necessarily.

"I know, I know, but Jude, my first wife, Jesse Marlon's mother, didn't believe in primogeniture, so she wouldn't go along with it," he says, "the Little-Ned-Big-Ned custom. It just didn't seem like . . . an issue twenty years ago or whatever it was, when we were young and groovy and counterculture."

"But why is it an issue now, then?" I give Ned my intelligent look.

"I've, ah, never dared tell her, as in Lulu, of course, that the whole Godminster estate is entailed. Every time I was going to broach the subject, I bottled. It's all my fault. And now the lawyers have just confirmed that I can't hand it to Little Ned even if I wanted to. And I've tried the National Trust, believe me—I mean, the place has been in our family for hundreds of years, it's got all the furniture, and tapestries, and pictures, and china, the pastry larder, the game larder, it's got the lot—but the Trust said, 'Only if it would be a,' quote unquote, *'catastrophe for the nation'* if it were snapped up by a ring-tone king who wanted to tear it down and put in an underground car park, or ozone pool, or something equally frightful. The Trust couldn't have been less interested. So it's Jesse Marlon's to bloody give away."

He sinks to a chair. I note that it is a mahogany armchair with a carved top rail and cross bar and reeded scroll arms. And like everything else in Godminster Hall, it is fine and inherited, with a history as long as your arm.

"Please help me, Rose; you're the only one he listens to. My life won't be worth living. It's jolly difficult, what with two sets of children out of two different mothers and just the one estate to hand round." He says this without any apparent irony.

"I'm sure it is," I say, in a slightly pointed way, designed to remind Ned that many people would wish they had his problems and that Ned had made his own bed. My voice also carries the whiff of my plight: I am—as I often complain to people—

the main breadwinner, as Pierre is not good at bringing home the bacon, and we are living off the capital of the sale of our London house in Barnes, not income, and the capital in question is running out fast. "So, let me get this straight," I say, wondering if Ned is ever going to offer me tea. Or better, a drink. "You want me to persuade your eldest son to waive his rights to the estate and sign them over to Lulu's son, Ned. Despite the fact that the place is entailed."

"Well, it's a thought," Ned says. "Even if it's not strictly doing things by the Bryanston book."

"You are clearly worried that your heir, Jesse Marlon, whom Lulu doesn't know stands to inherit rather than her own son, might, despite being deeply unmaterialistic at the moment, at some point in the future change his mind, as all lefties do in the end, and decide he does want all this after all." My wave encompasses the haunted study, with its stain on the floor, its paneled windowseats and walls, the molded overmantle on the heraldic chimney, the Reynoldses on the walls, the terrace and walled garden and landscaped grounds, the woods and the lake and even the smudge on the horizon that is the Lar Valley containing Jesse Marlon's abode of Spodden's Hatch. "And if he does decide that, after all, he can squeeze Godminster Hall into his life after you die, Lulu will never sleep with you ever again? Right?"

Ned nods dumbly. "If Ned's not going to inherit the house eventually, and I don't have any money, there's nothing in it for her. She'll divorce me," he says, "and go back to London, where she's always wanted to be. You don't know what she's like."

"Oh nonsense!" I retort crisply, deciding not to tell Ned that I have kicked his son into the long grass. I don't mind Ned thinking that I am the best Jesse Marlon whisperer around. I am thinking that Ned is probably right. If anyone can be relied on to follow the money, Lulu can.

But then, I mull a little further, Lulu now considers herself to be a literary personage, and spends all dinner parties dropping the names of famous writers she's invited to Godminster for debates and lectures and round-table discussions so that slow countryfolk can pick them up in wondering admiration. Also, divorce is invariably fatal for women. Even women as pretty and lissom as Lulu. So it's not a done deal, either way.

"She can't divorce you, even though I don't doubt it's hard for her sharing the Hall with Celia, who isn't"—I pause delicately—"the easiest of mother-in-laws." (Celia Bryanston's loathing of her daughter-in-law has, if anything, increased as the older woman sinks further in Lulu's debt, as is predictable.) "The thing is, babes like Lulu can't survive as single round here. Unattached women are treated by other women with as much compassion as farmers treat stray dogs, as if all they're interested in is worrying other women's husbands; they're liable to be shot."

At this Ned snorts, his shoulders relax, and he hands me a couple of sheets of A4 that are on his desk.

It's an e-mail, printed off.

"And that's not the only problem I have at the moment," he says.

To: lulu@godlitfest.org
From: ccobb@courtplacefarm.com
Cc: gcobb@thegreenfund.co.uk,
     nedbryanston@btinernet.com
Dear Ned and Lulu,
I hesitated to write, but I really feel I must. As an American, I do think that the shortest distance between two points is a straight line, so let's get it over, without, I hope, putting any kind of crimp in our long friendship!

I'm sure that you're acting with the best of good intentions and that you would never set out to hurt either Granville or me, or anyone else in Honeyborne. But this will, honest to goodness, be the inevitable result of the plan you outlined around my dining table.

I have thought plenty about this and I hope that you take a moment or two to consider this letter.

• We cannot accept your plan to put a windmill, with all the visual disruption that will necessarily result, onto Hamble Hill.

• We do not find the environmental case you have presented logical or compelling, especially given the output record of the windmill you are proposing to erect.

• We do not think that the loss of the whole sense of peace and harmony that brought us to this unspoiled green valley will, in any sense, be compensated for by the knowledge that Godminster Hall is being fueled by alternative energy sources and renewables thus conveniently helping to meet target EU figures to which Britain has signed up.

Hearing you and Jesse Marlon on the subject does, I'm afraid, raise the worrying thought that you have sacrificed good sense to some sort of misguided symbolism. Look, I want my grandchildren's grandchildren to see polar bears as much as you do—as you well know, everything I do at the Court Place farm is driven by ecological concerns that actually exceed organic standards.

But a windmill on Hamble Hill gives us both reason to pause. In fact, I can't understand how you and Ned can even contemplate it. I trust that the rumor that you are also accommodating a mobile mast on the windmill is just that: a rumor!

Though we are friends, when it comes to the application, you cannot count on our friendship. You can count on us to be concerned members of the public, anxious residents.

I know you are busy planning this year's GodLitFest, which I particularly look forward to—the cast list sounds terrific! The debate with Jilly Cooper, Lady Bamford, and Joanna Trollope sounds like a total slam dunk. Reserve me a front-row seat!

But please bear in mind that—

I stop reading. I have read enough.

If the Cobbs are anti the windmill, it will never happen. And if Lulu's pulling names like Trollope and Cooper, she'll never leave. She's got her own little Port Eliot, here in Dorset—a hobby festival to play with till the cows come home.

"Look, Ned, never mind Little Ned and Fred and the estate," I say, trying to cheer him up. "Never mind the cottages, the income from the cottages, the walled garden, the big house, and the land, you and Lulu can't get divorced." I lay the e-mail back on his desk. "Unlike Countess Spencer, who started the literary festival at Althorp and then had to walk away, Lulu would never give up her LitFest and schmoozing all those big-name writers. She'd sooner see Little Ned and Fred eaten by wolves."

"You're right," says Ned. "I'm being silly. And, when I think about it, it sort of makes sense, sticking to plan. Say what you like about primogeniture"—Ned looks at me pleadingly, as if he wants me to confirm that handing everything to one's firstborn and excluding the others, especially if they're female, is the best system available—"but it does work."

Mimi

At last, the longed-for day (longed for by all but the birthday boy, I should say) of Ralph's party arrives, a week after Ry, my new au pair boy.

I am hot-desking at the kitchen table, working out the placement for guests, who will all be seated at round tables in the marquee, which I can see now out of the kitchen window, its rigging flapping gently in the breeze.

Ralph is looking white. Bad timing, I'm afraid. He's had a call from Number 10 asking him to write a piece for Monday's *Guardian*—well, not under his name but, as it were, signed by Gordon Brown, which is apparently what happens: all those pieces by Cameron and Blair and so on are written either by speechwriters or by random experts, but never by Brown or Cameron or Blair.

"What's the piece about?" I ask. I feel I am the journalist of the family, even though my writing career is now confined to 150-word articles on spelt therapies at spas, i.e., not exactly Pulitzer-level.

"Implications of oil and gas becoming a security issue not a resource issue," he says, as I try to stifle a yawn (it's a reflex whenever Ralph talks about his work; it's rude, but I can't help it). "No, not one for you, my love. Can I use *your* laptop, darling? I left mine in London."

"Can't you use Mirabel's?" I say. "I *am* trying to do the placement for eighty."

"I suppose I could," Ralph says. "I'll try telling her that I am writing the article for the prime minister, and see if that carries any weight with her, which I rather doubt."

Dear Ralph is trying to put a brave face on today's ordeal. He's wearing the blue shirt we bought in Venice that exactly matches the color of his eyes, a pair of Cordings moleskins, and the Lobb brogues we stole off the Guy back in Lonsdale Gardens before it went on to the November 5 bonfire and, when I remember to look at him, I mean really look at him, I think he's the best-looking man anywhere.

But he still needs hours of tenderizing, like a tough steak before a barbie, before he sees any of his old friends (and to qualify as an old friend in Ralph's circles, you have to have known someone at least since the age of eight, so his old friends are Crusty, Harry, and Fucker from prep school—Sunningdale, of course). So he is exuding dread at the arrival later today of several dozen new friends as well as old muckers he tolerates not because he likes them—but because he's known them all his life.

Luckily, Ry, the new au pair boy, is so far perfect in every way, but he is no less than six feet five inches tall, a fact I failed to elicit during our communications by e-mail. This means he can move about in Home Farm only at a crouch, bent double, which daily reminds me and Ralph that our new abode is a former peasant hovel where Dorset yeoman farmers lived cheek by jowl with their own cows and sheep. In fact, Biddy Pike showed me an ancient black-and-white picture of the kitchen of Home Farm in the 1930s, and there were orphan lambs nestling on burlap sacks all over the kitchen floor, in a part of the house she called the shippon. The picture made me cry (again—hormones are all over the shop) and Posy almost expire with excitement and make me promise to provide her with a baby lamb to replace Trumpet, who is as I speak happily thundering about the indoor school at Honeyborne Stables on his tiny hooves.

Ry's been here only a week but he has already achieved god-like status, as he has promised to teach Cas how to surf and Posy how to skateboard and Mirabel how to download iTunes on her mobile, so the children and I, at least, are thrilled.

I am trying to work out how to mix up my guests, who all fall into separate socioeconomic categories. There're the second homers. There's the Notting Hill crowd. I can't for the life of me work out how to mingle old money, new money, and no money, and, above all, I have no idea how to distribute the locals.

"It's horrid when people have to seat themselves," I say out loud, "buffet-style. There's nothing worse. Panic sets in when it comes to sitting, and it all becomes like a game of musical chairs as everyone rushes to find the people they already know before the table fills up and they're stuck at the children's table or next to someone's deaf great-aunt."

"Don't be ridiculous, Mimi," says Ralph. "If you try to work out where everyone sits, you'll only get it wrong, and the village will regard you as a terrible snob and climber. Just let everyone get on with it."

But I am sitting here, worrying. Though I love them more than life itself and depend on my neighbors for fuel, whiskey, gossip, tire pumps, baby lambs, lifts to Godminster, important information such as which Saturday in August is the fête, and which weekend the entire village gathers together to chase an eight-pound wheel of Godminster Cheddar down Hamble Hill, or makes rafts to race one another at Larmouth, there is no question that the village does need some . . . mixing up.

For a start, where do I put Mr. and Mrs. Hitchens, from the Stores and Post Office, who know where all the bodies are buried, and who are up in arms because (1) not only is the windmill likely to receive approval and (2) Pike and Thomas will probably go to jail over the hunting thing that I still don't understand but (3) the Honeyborne Post Office and Stores has been placed on the deathlist of rural sub-post offices to be felled by the government axe?

"It puts it all into perspective, doesn't it?" all the villagers are going about saying gloomily, as one does when one receives news that a great friend has breast cancer, or a little old lady has been mugged in her own home, or a dog run over.

And where do I put Scary Gwenda Melplash and Ruth Wingfield, who are coming on very strong with me now, offering me round-the-clock lessons for the children, begging me virtually to demand long hacks across the hills at the drop of a hat, and all because I gave them Trumpet (now I think about it, the actual owners of Trumpet remain Johnnie and Sophie Boden, who were kind enough to lend him to us when we moved—but I don't think that Gwenda and Ruth need to know this, nor indeed do Johnnie and Sophie, who I am praying won't ask fondly after Trumpet during lunch).

I keep showing possible placements to Ralph, who keeps rejecting them, on the grounds that I have put him next to someone he can't stand.

"No, darling, you can't sit next to Posy," I've already told him once. "You have to sit next to Cath, because she's lent us the Raj tent, and Giancarlo."

"Giancarlo?" Ralph cried, as if he had been stabbed. "Who on earth is Giancarlo? I thought this was supposed to be a party for my friends!"

"Don't be silly, one never gives parties for one's friends," I answered. "Giancarlo's not a guest, Giancarlo's the chef—you know Giancarlo, at Court Place. He's bringing the caponata. It's so sweet of Cath, don't you think? He's from Bologna."

"The what?" cried Ralph.

"The antipasti," I answered patiently. "It's all going to be delicious. We're having homemade gnocchi, and risotto. You always say you like gnocchi."

"I know what antipasti are, Mimi," Ralph said. "But why

you thought I deserved the punishment of a full-dress Venetian gala picnic with waiters dressed as gondoliers, as if we are on the Grand Canal rather than in a muddy field, I will never fathom. As far as I'm concerned, a hunk of bread and a small piece of cheese, perhaps, is more than enough, especially at lunchtime."

But Ralph did agree to establish a "top table," which was something. "No way am I sitting next to Biddy Pike, she reminds me of Princess Anne; definitely not Gwenda, thanks, she only talks about horses. And please, please not the gloomy witch woman you go on about who lives in the yurt."

"But Biddy's got a lovely seat," I say, and Ralph looks at me with an odd expression, as if I've gone either mad or native, "and Sophy's not coming because she has to look after Noah or she has a composting workshop or something, but Spike is, her son, who is a very good friend of Mirabel's at Acland's, so please be civil."

"And as it's my birthday I would really be grateful," he continues, "if there was a buffer zone between me and Gloria Saville. I had her on the train for two hours, talking about her polytunnels. Sorry, darling. But she's a founder member of Densa."

"What about Suki Rous?" I try, naming the pregnant heiress, one half of the Golden Couple, married to the Tory law partner, who is trying to secure a local safe seat. Ralph looks stricken even at the prospect of prolonged interaction with Suki, who I thought was about as perfect a specimen of womanhood as I or anyone else could bring to the party.

Mirabel is looking at us during all this with curled lip. "I don't understand," she says. "All these people are your friends, and you've invited them to Daddy's party, so why are you saying horrible things about them like you don't want to sit next to them, like, behind their backs? You're both so mean."

"I promise you'll understand when you're older," I say to Mirabel. "And you've got to sit next to Cath Cobb," I say to Ralph. "They've had us three times and we've only had them once." (At a riotous dinner where the table collapsed after the first course, and, worse, there weren't enough plates to go around, and so I told everyone that they had to eat their fish pie off the same plates they'd eaten Parma ham and melon. The next day, I had an express delivery from the Conran Shop in London of twelve large white porcelain dinner plates, accompanied by a note from Granville, saying, "Next time, darling Mimi, remember that I don't eat pig or shellfish, let alone off the same plate, but never mind, you domestic goddess, you—it was the best dinner party I've been to in ages.")

"That's fine," says Ralph, looking more cheerful as he heads off to write his piece under Gordon Brown's byline. "As I think Cyril Connolly once said of someone or other, the Cobbs are definitely more dined against than dining."

The guests arrive, and are given Bellinis by the children ("Venice in a glass!" Cath bubbles when she takes hers from Ry). They mingle, and stroll, and the hubbub rises. Luckily, it is a balmy spring day, the little white clouds pass the sun quickly and the garden is bathed in a buttery radiance, and daisies and daffodils are showing their little white and yellow faces in the lush green grass. We've put the marquee between the orchard and the paddock, but drinks are on the lawn (well, the shaggy bit of grass between the paddock and the farmhouse, where we sometimes lie on rugs when it's not raining, and Cas plays football).

It is all going swimmingly. Even Ralph is circulating or, at any rate, Ralph has found the one guest who is also a fellow member of the Piscatorial Society, and is chatting to him animatedly in order to repel any other approaches, any advance from someone who retired from the City aged forty-five and has started his own fund and who seeks out Ralph to tell him, without Ralph asking (my husband is unmoved by money), that "It's really doing *rather well*, actually."

Then Posy bangs the gong, and everyone tries to find their

names on the seating plan tacked to a child's wooden easel that I have established at the entrance of the marquee. This takes ages, as no one has their glasses, and there is much wandering around with cries of "Is this table six? Am I at table six, darling? Can't read a thing! I haven't got my glasses! Darling, where are my glasses? Where's table six?"

Finally, everyone takes their seats, and the gondoliers—i.e., Court Place staff borrowed for the occasion—wheel through the tables with plates laden with antipasti and uncork Chianti with popping sounds and pour it into Cath Cobb's unparalleled and extensive collection of Murano glasses in jewel colors. The players from Godminster Opera, supplied by Ned and Lulu, sing hair-lifting arias from Puccini and Verdi.

I am hugging myself with the triumph of it all.

"You've done a marvelous job on the tent," people keep saying to me, as they eat their marinated peppers and baby mozzarella and salami starters, on platters, and drizzle olive oil from baby bottles placed at each table. I nod modestly. In fact, Cath has done a marvelous job on the tent.

There are swags of pink roses tied around the struts . . . brightly colored cotton shirts and striped tea towels are strung from washing lines, as if we are in the alleys of the Dorsoduro . . . table decorations in the shape of papier-mâché gondolas . . . ironic outsized pepper mills . . . it is warm under canvas, and the sun has come out, making it warmer. I close my eyes, take a long sip of my second Bellini, and feel the bonhomie rise in me like the *acqua alta* lapping the pavements of Venice.

Admittedly, there are several acres of wrinkled flesh, but this is enlivened by the frequent glimpse of pert taut skin, glossy tumbling hair, and peachy buttocks . . . and that's just the waiting staff! I've invited friends of the children, like Spike, as well as various fitties, like Colin Watts plus fiancée Serena Cobb, and Jesse Marlon, and as for Virginie Lacoste . . . as even Ralph admits, she is a sight for sore eyes. I feel awfully grateful to her for being so pretty and well dressed. As anyone knows, but few are prepared to acknowledge, there's nothing like prolonged exposure to countryfolk to make one feel the first guilty twinge of gerontophobia.

After the antipasti and then the risotto and even all the olives and focaccia have been devoured and plates cleared, I leave the table to supervise in the kitchen, where the final touches are being put to the pudding. I hover anxiously as the ridiculous rococo tiered birthday cake piled with bouncy early English strawberries and curlicues of whipped cream (the work of the pastry chef at Court Place) is borne to the table by a trio of waiters dressed as gondoliers. On the very top a putto reclines pudgily, with a harp.

The sponge is that deep yellow that suggests to drooling observers that the legendary eggs of the legendary Court Place farm hens have been richly incorporated into the confection. The cake has drawn an admiring crowd of children and teenagers, including Posy, Cas, Ned 'n' Fred Bryanston, and Mirabel, who is guarding it with Cerberus-like ferocity.

Waiters rush around with bottles, filling glasses, and the roar in the tent reaches a crescendo, as everyone is now either very drunk or getting on famously and the ice has been decisively broken.

I gaze around.

Serena Cobb, at my table, is sitting on Colin Watts's lap, and he is whispering in her ear something about going "up the paddocks"—I think Dorset code for a quick shag—and Serena is shaking her head.

Virginie (channeling Tadzio in *Death in Venice* in tailored city shorts and a Celine sailor suit with an organza collar, designed to appeal to admirers of both sexes) and Hugh Fearnley-Whittingstall (whom she calls "Eugh") are getting on like a house on fire, while Rose, I notice, is looking grumpy and is ignoring Pierre, as she has done for many years.

Mathieu Lacoste is failing to talk to Suki, the pregnant and glowing heiress married to the Tory lawyer, and watching his wife waltz through the tables and exit the marquee, in what could be hot pursuit of a celebrity chef.

Ralph rises like a flick knife to his feet. He tings his spoon on a bottle. "Can you all pipe down," he says. "You're making an awful racket.

"I won't go on for long," he starts. "My golden rule in life is never say anything to anyone, but there are very special occasions when I am moved to break it, and this is one. First, I would like to thank Catherine Cobb and the team at Court Place for helping to decorate the tent and for inspiring the Venetian theme, and so on, all of which are so terribly well done." Cath beams at his side. Everyone claps. "And I must also thank Ned and Lulu for supplying the Godminster Singers as live entertainment. The Singers are donating their fee to the Venice in Peril fund, and I might take this opportunity to remind you that any of you who feel moved to making a similar gesture in support will find details in the leaflet on your tables.

"Secondly, I would like to thank all of you for coming, some from as far away as Chesilborne"—he nods to the Golden Couple—"and Hutton"—a nod to Sir Michael, who raises his glass back in a courtly way. "Believe me, I know what a strain it is dragging oneself across the county, especially on a Saturday, when sensible people are riding or gardening, so well turned up!" He raises his empty glass to the assembled company.

"And thirdly, I would like to thank Mimi." Ralph pauses, and looks at me with palpable fondness. I feel tears prickle behind my eyes, and my throat congests. We are a team, I think. A couple. We've had our ups and downs, Lord knows we have, but we've got through them, and here we still are. "My wife," he announces, as if correcting a universally held misunderstanding.

He gazes at me again, as if at a loss for words to express what I mean to him. "If it weren't for her, I would never be having this party," he says, in a heartfelt voice, "and, er, anyway, I'll pull up stumps very soon, so I just want to say, well, actually, just that I'm very proud of how she's taken various things on the chin, thrown herself into country life, and so on. You've done awfully well, darling." Ralph raises his glass to me, and in his eyes I can read the ineffable gratitude the husband feels when a wife, despite very good grounds for doing so, declines to make a fuss.

I feel my eyes fill with tears. It's not every day that one hears an Englishman, let alone an Etonian, pay such tribute to a woman, let alone his wife. "She's shown tremendous bottle in bullying me into having this party, for my fortieth birthday. I'm so glad she did, I honestly am—I think the clincher was when she pointed out that I hadn't had a party since my twenty-first, and we hadn't had a party since we married. So now let us kill the fatted calf or, failing that, cut the candled cake, and, without further ado, I would like you all to raise your glasses, please, and join me in a toast."

And then Ralph freezes. He goes white, and his shoulders suddenly stiffen, as if he is bracing himself for a volley of shots from the firing line. Not everyone seems to notice, as they are all grabbing their glasses and laughing. I follow the line of his gaze to the rose-swagged entrance of the tent.

Framed in the door of the tent is Clare Sturgis. In her arms is a small boy. He has brown hair, and a blue hand-knitted jersey with a collar, and brown corduroy shorts, and some short Paddington Bear blue and red wellies that already branded themselves on my memory a decade earlier.

Everyone turns briefly to look, following his gaze, and just as obediently rises to their feet as one when Ralph's arm involuntarily rises, his glass with it, the knife to cut the cake in the other hand.

Holding their glasses aloft, all look to Ralph for his cue. But none is forthcoming. His eyes are fixed not on the woman in the door, but on the little boy in her arms, as if he's seen a ghost.

"Don't I know that woman?" I hear Sir Michael roar, as if I'm under water. "Didn't she look around Hutton? Kept going on about food security, and whatnot? Unhinged, if you ask me," he informs his neighbor.

"To Mimi," everyone choruses, to cover the confusion. "Tight lines!" roars Ralph's fellow member of the Piscatorial Society, which is, I think, what fishermen say to wish each other luck.

"To Mimi!"

And that is the last thing I hear.

One Week Later

"Well, I suppose there are some upsides," I say as I sip my Planter's Punch, "to discovering that your husband has had a love child by your old best friend and new worst frenemy in the middle of a party, especially one you have single-handedly organized for him yourself, down to the carnations in the Chianti bottles on the middle of the table. By the way, the Chianti bottles and pepper mills and carnations were supposed to be ironic—do you think everyone, you know, clocked that, Rose? Sooo embarrassing if people didn't."

I have already forgotten that I had roped in other willing and more competent hands to do much of the heavy lifting, i.e., provide and assemble the tent, order in chairs and tables (Cath), decorate the invitations and place cards (Rose), and make the food (Giancarlo). As far as the record went, it was all my own work, and I intended—despite the Grand Guignol finale to proceedings—to take full credit.

"I think all anyone was clocking was you, Mimi," Rose answers in a waspish voice. "It is quite *dramatic* for the hostess to faint just as the entire party has risen to its feet to toast her."

"Oh, come on, Rose, I didn't do it on purpose," I protest, squirting on more factor 40.

"Darling, I'm joking," Rose says. "I think you're being amazing. What a time you're having. With the . . . you know, and now this. I'm absolutely admiring of you, I really am."

I don't answer. I'm remembering. When Clare appeared framed in the tent, apparently I (and this is according to Mirabel, who accused me of "attention-seeking" because Daddy was making a speech "for the first time for, like, forever") fainted. Into Michael Hutton's lap.

The child in Clare's arms looked exactly like Cas at eighteen months, the child in Clare's arms looked exactly like the little brother Cas had begged for, and not only that, the child in Clare's arms was wearing exactly the same clothes that Cas himself had worn as a toddler, right down to the pair of red and blue Paddington Bear Wellington boots, and when I saw the child, I knew for sure something that I'd known, subconsciously, for a while.

Rose and I are lying on two teak loungers, dressed with cream cushions with navy ticking. There are white towels behind our heads. We are poolside at Sir Michael's Great House in Jamaica, called Perdition.

"Not bad, Sir Michael's little place in the Caribbean," I remark, to change the subject.

"Mmm . . . very Ralph Lauren," is Rose's observation. We do not know, at this point, that it was after a visit to Perdition, with its palette of navy and white against tropical hardwoods and aged crackly chestnut leather, its storm candles, break -fronted bookcases, polished wide-planked floors, hanging lanterns, four-posters, green sweeping lawns, tropical gardens, including a tree that produced a strange, sexual fruit that none of us, despite our advanced combined ages, had ever tasted before, that at least one of Mr. Lauren's Home Collections had been inspired.

I squint over my fruity drink to the pool. It's not an infinity pool—nothing so vulgar—but the old-fashioned blue rectangle, because it was put in in the fifties, so the Huttons could keep up with Noel Coward, up on the green hill, at Firefly. I sniff deeply, as if trying to imbibe the warm air laden with sweet musty scents, just as intoxicating as any rum.

Outside the back door, a lovingly maintained Ford Falcon with weathered leather red seats and chrome trimmings is not there. The "boys"—as we have taken to calling our husbands—are off on a jaunt. When he first saw it, Ralph said it made him long for the days when cars had wings and sanitary pads didn't, or if pads did have wings, it wasn't something that the manufacturers felt obliged to point out on television to the viewing public every five minutes.

"I can't believe I'm here," I say, still luxuriating after three days of indolence so profound that it can take me all morning to stir from my lounger to fetch my reading matter—the new Jilly Cooper—from my bedroom, with its four-poster, and tiled bathroom, and heart-catching view of azure sea. "I have to say, it does make up for things a bit." I think warm thoughts towards mine host.

After I fainted into his lap, Sir Michael definitely rose to the occasion. He turned out to be one of those men who was simply impossible when tiny things went wrong, such as when the keeper brought the Range Rover instead of the Land Rover to the meet, or the butler laid out the wrong tie, or someone spilled their claret—but second to none in a major crisis.

Basically, what happened was this, I think.

Sir Michael bearded Granville. Granville filled him in on the salient details. Rose confessed that she had shared with Granville "almost everything" on the ski holiday, though I did not have the energy to see how many issues they covered: the origins of our exit from Notting Hill, the causes of Clare's mysterious presentations in Honeyborne, my day trip to Godminster . . . I mean, my life recently has been more complicated than the Peloponnesian War, to the extent that even I can hardly keep up with what's been going on, let alone understand it.

I wasn't given any options because Granville and Sir Michael insisted, without brooking opposition, that I should be medevacked out to the Caribbean, at Ralph's expense, to stay at Perdition. I had been privately pondering whether to ring Fenella, to see whether I could go after all to Somerset and review the spelt spa, have some time solo, and feel sorry for myself while being dermabrased with grains in the Mendips. "There's nothing I like more than a lovely decadent holiday somewhere hot that I'm not paying for, trust me," I said. I've already decided that the title of my autobiography, if I ever write it, will be *Born Freebie*. "But . . . what about Ralph?"

But Ralph, it turned out, was already on board, as were Rose and Pierre. Rose would not dream of not coming, too, and said that she had put some money by for a rainy day, and Clare Sturgis turning up like that and my fainting at Ralph's fortieth definitely counted as a rainy day.

"Much as I loathe holidays, strange beds, and air travel, sunny weather and lying around reading novels, I recognized it would be entirely disobliging of me to refuse their embarrassingly generous offer of Michael's gracious colonial home," Ralph had apparently said, to Granville, in Rose's hearing. "So I am, this once, prepared to make an exception."

That was Ralph's way of acknowledging publicly, I suppose, that he had hurt me.

Anyway, as Rose and I lounge poolside, Ralph and Pierre are on the links, enjoying displacement activities and a holiday from The Topic.

The Topic. The whole debacle at the Venetian picnic.

Which was not Colin being caught in flagrante with Serena by the Reverend Wyldbore-Smith, who tripped over the couple coupling in the gents' at Home Farm. Which must, I thought, be a first for our downstairs loo, into which Colin and Serena had ducked, thinking they would be safe because there were smart Portaloos, with real ceramic sinks and everything—they were unbelievably smart, much smarter than our own facilities in the house, to be quite frank.

No, the real debacle concerned Ralph and me. And Clare. And, of course, Joe.

When I came round from my faint, I found the children's faces peering down at me anxiously.

"Mum, now you've finally woken up, can we have some of Dad's birthday cake?" asked Posy.

Ralph was nowhere to be seen.

He had gone to "deal" with the "Clare situation," and returned grim-faced just as the guests were finally leaving. Ralph and I did not stay to say good-bye to our guests, but fled in the Subaru.

The Court Place SWAT team, led by the Cobbs and the Huttons, had swung into action, and the children were swept off by Ry, the towering Australian manny, to build a tree house. We drove in silence for about eight miles until Ralph turned off the A30 or the B339 or whatever it was and said, after we had driven on an unmade road a couple of miles, through a sun-soaked wood, "I think . . . I'll park . . . here." He was being very deliberate. Very quiet. As though if he moved or spoke too loudly, it might provoke violence.

Then we walked a bit through the wood, following a path, until we came to a hut by a river, where Ralph keyed in a code and pushed open a wooden door. We entered a dark space, with trophies and plaques with gold writing and fishing rods hung on the tongue-and-groove walls. Bookshelves full of books about carp and grayling and gold-tooled volumes of the *Fishing Gazette*—i.e., an eclectic library—lined the walls. There was the head of a pike lying on a salver offering a silver beaker in its open, sharp-toothed jaws, reels scattered across a polished mahogany dining table, and polished gavels backed with the commemorative heads of five-pound trout. Piles of waders snaked together in a little room on the right, with a couple of ancient waterproofs, and some stray wellies.

In other words, it was exactly the sort of place where Ralph would feel safe and happy. "Here we are," he said, and sighed almost, as if now we were there, in this holiest of holies, we could talk.

"Ralph," I said, in a choking voice, going to the window. "Please don't tell me it's true. I just don't think I can handle it. Not after—" then I stopped, too choked to speak. The tears, never far from my eyes, welled and spilled down my face. I didn't think they would ever stop. A stabbing pain started up in my chest. I sank into a chair, in case I was having a heart attack, which would conveniently delay the moment that Ralph would have to explain to me exactly why Clare, my former best friend, had turned up at our house with a boy who looked exactly like our son Cas.

Despite being blinded by tears and emotion, I found myself reading a little hand-typed sign that listed ten rules. The list had been taped to the tabletop in the bay of the window. Number six was, I noted, "When members are fishing, they may wish not to be disturbed. The aim is to do all that is conducive to the peaceable fishing by being slow-moving, quiet of foot, and, as far as possible, hidden from the fish."

This only made me realize how uncharacteristic Ralph's behavior had been. Like all keen fishermen, Ralph's main, if not only, aim in life—not just on the riverbank—was the achievement, and then the extension, of a period of peace and quiet.

None of it made sense. And I didn't see how anything he could say would ever make it better.

"I know," Ralph said brokenly. "I know. Believe me, I know how bad this looks, my actions must appear utterly indefensible. I will endeavor to explain, and I implore you to listen, if not to forgive." He brought two dark, carved chairs and set them on either side of an oak table, where members could sit and watch the dusk gathering over the liquid dark of the Lar, if they ever tired, that is, of admiring the stuffed fish in glass cases with little yellowing notes attesting to the location, weight, and author of the catch. Then he went to a cupboard and took out a bottle of whiskey and two glasses.

I sat still, too harrowed even to look up, or notice that on Ralph's chair, a head of the pike was carved in bas-relief in the mahogany back, set against biblical bulrushes. He took my hand and wrapped my fingers around the tumbler. He had never done that before.

"Whiskey," he said, unnecessarily. And then he explained.

What he said was that Clare was willing to add a "huge supplement" to the price of the sale of Lonsdale Gardens if he agreed to help her get pregnant, although that offer was never spelled out in forensic detail. "The market wasn't white-hot like it is now," he said. "I thought the house was so shabby, we wouldn't get what we wanted for it on the open market, so Clare's offer . . . it just seemed like the right thing to do." Then he paused. "At the time."

I flinched.

At the time, of course, I was besottedly running after Si Kasparian. I was breaking my marriage vows. I was cuckolding Ralph. Not that Ralph would ever say so. He was too proud, and, after all, I may have erred and strayed like a lost sheep but I was, for good or ill, still his wife, as he had so proudly confirmed at the disastrous birthday lunch.

He sort of implied that they had not had sex in the accepted sense, but he had supplied the needful. I wasn't sure whether to believe him. I couldn't work out what was more improbable, Ralph having actual intercourse with Clare, or doing the laboratory thing with a receptacle. He said that he had done this on the very strictest of conditions, that Clare had sworn to adhere to: (1) that no one would ever know, and (2) that the child would never know that he was the father, and not Gideon. Ralph paused, as if he had almost squared the circle.

I took a deep breath.

"Ralph," I said, shaking my head, looking him in the eye. "It doesn't add up. It doesn't make sense. You know there is never, ever, any such thing as no strings attached. There are always strings. No free lunch. You must have realized. Even the law has changed, so children can find their own birth fathers, even if they were student sperm donors doing it for beer money or whatever. There's traceability, and all this stuff about people being entitled to their genetic inheritance. Why did you think these rules wouldn't apply to you? Because you're so bloody marvelous?"

Ralph blenches.

"I can't believe you took such a big risk with our whole family life, and your children's happiness, just for a few hundred thousand pounds."

"I made a mistake," he said. "I thought I could trust her to keep it between us, as she promised, and swore, and only ever between us. And I felt sorry for her. There's stuff about Clare, I don't know if you know . . ."

Ralph swallowed. He looked stricken. As I well know, Ralph's first rule in life is Never say anything to anybody, and his second rule is Never trust a woman, because they can never deliver on the first.

"You must believe me, darling. I did it for the financial reason; there was absolutely nothing—*nothing*—between me and Clare, but it was terribly hard to refuse her, after what she said about Gideon. I just felt that I wanted to show her that men weren't all complete shits, and I've ended up being one myself."

Then he repeated miserably, as if he couldn't believe he had fallen for them at the time, some of the other specious and manipulative arguments Clare had used to persuade him to part with his DNA. As he spoke, I realized it was a stroke of luck for Clare that Ralph had somehow managed to avoid the endless discussions about the sperm shortage on *Woman's Hour*. It just wasn't his thing. Trade row between Russia's Transneft and the nation of Belarus, hell yes. Earnest debate about the identification of donors' body fluids, not in a million trillion years.

"And what about the baby, the boy?" I went on. "What on earth can Gideon think? Suddenly, his wife insists on buying your house. Suddenly, his wife gets pregnant after ten years of trying, and you disappear to Dorset with two million pounds of her money—well, one million, not that it went very far in the end—and then, oops! there's a baby who looks exactly like you and Casimir. He looks so like Cas did at that age. Those ringlets! It's all a bit, well, iffy, isn't it?" I felt a terrible sadness. "If he was very short and covered with a thick black pelt, like a caveman, it wouldn't really matter so much, but how on earth is Clare going to pass him off as Gideon's? And if you were so okay about having another child"—I went on, coldly, my dry eyes boring into his—"why did you want me to get rid of ours?"

Ralph stared at me, levelly, which was brave. Lesser men than Ralph would have quailed before my gaze.

There was a long pause. Ralph looked out at the peaty river, at the pools and eddies, the wet backs of round stones on the bank, the dappling evening light, at the trees moving in the evening breeze, as if at old friends. He unfolded himself from the chair and went to the window, as if to spy a pike in a pool or to ascertain the location of a wild trout from a bubble on the river's surface or a special stone in a dark place.

He stared at me.

I was sitting very still, wearing my Venetian picnic outfit of a smocky peasant top and a tiered skirt, with bare legs and espadrilles, over which I had flung Cas's anorak. My face felt dirty and smeared with tears and cake.

Ralph came and stood behind my chair, and started kissing my neck, and whispering to me.

I tried to resist. After a time, I yielded.

We repaired to a sofa with the stuffing coming out, which was in a dark corner, underneath a watercolor of Queen Victoria foul-hooking a trout.

"Lie down," Ralph ordered, pulling off his jersey and Harvie & Hudson blue double-cuffed shirt, and covered my round, protuberant body with his lean flat one. I wriggled out of my clothes, but left my skirt on just in case a gillie chose to replenish his fly box at the moment of crisis and I needed to flip it down fast.

"Ralph," I panted as the sofa juddered and I felt I must tell him before I lost the power of speech and was carried away like a leaf on the rills and eddies of the Lar, burbling and chattering away outside. "Ralph, there's something you need to know," I whispered urgently, even though telling him would have interrupted this rare spontaneous moment of unbridled passion between man and wife.

"Don't tell me now," groaned Ralph, and he quieted me by finding my mouth and covering it, until we both broke off to cry out and clutch at each other.

"I'm not quite finished with you yet," I said, restoring my clothing, my cheeks all pink. I unpeeled a brown kiss curl that had plastered itself to my forehead. I was now feeling relieved that I hadn't told him what I was going to, but I was wondering, When am I going to tell him? If not now, when?

"What did you say this place was again?"

"The rod room," answered Ralph.

I raised an eyebrow. "Of course it is," I said. "Is there a loo?" Ralph gestured to the door.

"There's a khazi round the back," he said. "Although none of us usually bother, to be honest. Go in the rushes." Ralph's face looked younger, clearer, as if the storm had passed, leaving blue, rinsed skies once more.

"It's okay," I said. "You still haven't answered my questions." I sucked in damp evening river air through the window Ralph had opened, as if to cool things down.

"I'll try," Ralph answered. "Okay."

Another long pause.

"First, I never slept with Clare," he repeated.

I raised an eyebrow again. "I should hope not," I said, still unsure. I couldn't imagine my husband, in a million years, performing anything other than plain vanilla sex with my ex-friend in order to ensure conception. But now, it appeared, he had . . . diddied about with . . . eww!

I didn't want to think about it. Life was full of surprises.

"And she's not pretending the baby's Gideon's. She's already told him . . . Joe's not his. Her psychotherapist told her to. You know that Clare's, um, training to be a psychotherapist herself, I take it?"

"Oh my Lord," I said wildly, reaching for my whiskey. "Is there some law that dictates that all psychotherapists have to be total nut bags before they start training? So this is why she's seeing a shrink?"

"No, it's the usual drill, so far as I can tell; this really isn't my area of expertise," Ralph answered, in a more relaxed voice.

"Not another!" I wailed, and then decided not to comment on the fact that yet another friend is taking that particular path on life's journey—it was beginning to make me feel *left out*. In the States, educated women approaching forty with time on their hands become estate agents; I don't know why Englishwomen in same boat are impelled to become therapists; it must be something to do with the property shortage. "So how did Giddy take it?" I asked.

"Well, here's the thing," said Ralph, adding to his glass. The whiskey made a reassuringly expensive gurgling sound. "He already knew. The main bit, which was that Joe wasn't his. He'd known. Since before Joe was born."

"But how?" I said, fascinated. Even though I felt like shit, and was considering hurling myself into the Lar, like a Labrador whose very blood calls for repeated immersion in freezing waters, Ralph's rare piece of actual news about people I actually knew had prodded me back to my usual self. And the fact that Giddy knew about Joe's paternity all along definitely qualified as a choice nugget.

"Gideon can't have children," said Ralph. "He just never told Clare, let Clare think she was infertile, for years, let her think that his seed was, as it were, falling on stony ground. So when Clare got pregnant, the first time, in around October, but lost it a few weeks later—"

"I remember," I said.

"Well, Gideon, of course, knew then that someone else must have made Clare pregnant, because it wasn't him."

"Okay," I interrupted. "I see. What a shit. Did he have a vasectomy, or something?"

Ralph made a distressed noise. This was his signal to me that this was simply not the sort of question one chap would ever ask another, let alone a chap's wife. It was like asking another chap whether he'd ever slept with someone. Not done. If you asked, and you were answered, then you knew. And then, someone else might ask you, and instead of answering, honestly, that you didn't have the faintest idea, you might have to say something. You might even have to *lie*. So that was why chaps, on the whole, sensibly didn't talk about these things. It was a form of self-defense.

"So Gideon knows that Joe's not his, fine. But does he know Joe is yours? Is that why Clare is in Honeyborne all the time?" I asked in a low, controlled voice. "What does she want from us?"

"Erm," said Ralph, looking out the window, as if hoping that rescue might come in the shape of a passing fisherman in search of a woolly bugger, or any other sort of fly. "Well, here's the bad news . . ." He gazed intently at a spot on the Lar, as if that spot was the lair of a large and evasive trout. "She was quite keen for me to, er . . ." he looked at his feet. Ashamed, as well he might be. After what he put me through. My husband has impregnated my former best friend seemingly in return for my having sex twice with a completely irresistible (to me, anyway) single billionaire who'd made a pass at me just when I'd got my figure back (seven years after having Posy, which may sound like a lot but is actually my land speed record on regaining prepregnancy body weight).

I'd say that creating a second family is a lot bigger betrayal than a quickie, or two. I feel as if I have been swept, by a current stronger than both of us, onto the moral high ground, where I intend to remain for as long as I can. I am determined not to lose the advantage of height in the difficult months that I know will follow this particular crisis, as I happen to know that the next crisis is coming fast on its heels.

And, so far as I'm aware, there is no moral equivalence between adultery (my crime) and turning my friend into my husband's impregnee behind my back (my husband's). So I am inspecting Ralph fiercely as the words, "What does she want from us?" drop from my lips. Things can't—so far as I can see, unless she wants Ralph to acknowledge paternity—get any worse.

But they do.

Ralph sputters to a halt.

"What. Does. She. Want?" I repeat, fuming at Ralph's god-given ability to appear morally superior to me when he isn't.

"Well, darling, it's not going to happen, of course, but she, erm, wanted me to"—I stare him down—"provide the child, Joe . . . with a sibling."

The water dazzles my eyes. A bird sings loudly in the tree that is hung with clusters of the strange sexual fruit. I realize that I have been silent for a long time, motionless.

"I'll never forgive myself for not telling you about Clare," says Rose. In a graceful movement, she sits up and looks across at me. "I just didn't know what to do."

She is very cute in her gingham bikini, so cute that I can quite see why Jesse Marlon fell for the famed Rose Musgrove charms, the talk of three counties, and why Virginie, I now learn, wanted a slice, too. She has a slender waist, hair cascading Bardot-like onto slim brown shoulders, lush breasts that lie like wholesome brown farm eggs in a tray in her balconette bikini top, and the most wonderful, finely etched ankles and feet.

"I should bloody hope not," I reply, punishing her, and feeling slightly lumpen in my one-piece boy-cut costume, lying on my back so at least my hips are—if I suck in my strangely large tummy (about which, tactfully, no one has commented)— faintly prominent. "I can't think why you let her confide in you. Did I tell you that she not only stole my house," I continue (glossing over the fact that it was the Fleming family London residence), "but my housekeeper, Fatima—Fatty—too?" (glossing over the fact that Fatty, my cleaner, came reluctantly, and by bus, no more than three times a week).

"Many times. It's part of the pattern, isn't it? As you say," Rose says, glancing up as a car with a throaty exhaust pulls up on the graveled forecourt, "she has to have what *you* have."

"God knows why," I say, watching Ralph unfurl himself from the Ford Falcon, clad in linen trousers and a long-sleeved cornflower-blue cotton shirt and looking brown, like something out of a Hollywood comedy with Peter Lawford or Cary Grant. The door makes a satisfying noise as it slams shut.

"So, presumably, as soon as she found out you were pregnant, she had to be pregnant, too. You were having another baby. So she had to have another baby. It's very logical. Even though you're no longer neighbors, she still has to keep up with you. There's only one thing I don't understand. How did she know you were pregnant?"

"I told her," I say, feeling silly, remembering the long e-mail I sent her back in January, which I'd regretted as soon as I'd pressed send. "Actually, hold on, Rose. That's a very good point. I just told her I thought I *might be*. I never actually told her I *was*. Did you tell her?"

"No way," protests Rose. "I didn't know her that well at Cambridge, and that was twenty years ago. She got in touch with me, remember, and when she came to the Dairy, I didn't even know you used to know her, too, and were on the same communal garden till you turned up that day, and she was there. I'm not exactly going to share the most intimate details of your private life with Ralph with an acquaintance, am I? The cow," says Rose cozily.

We watch Pierre and Ralph—neither of whom ever lies in the sun, or dips a toe even into the pool, exposes their limbs, or removes his shoes and socks—go into the house with the English newspapers tucked under their arms. In an hour, it will be time for a late lunch on the terrace.

"Well, I don't know how she found out, but she picked the wrong couple to mess with," I say stoutly. "I don't see how she thought she could swing it. You don't repay a, um, *happily married man* who has helped you out of your fertility black hole out of the, ah, *goodness of his heart*" (I gloss over the financial incentives, which were not inconsiderable) "by threatening him that you will tell his, er, *innocent wife* all about the paternity of your son unless he provides you with a *second baby*, do you? It doesn't work like that. Ralph is impervious to any sort of emotional blackmail—believe me, I've tried. He just welcomes it. As a test of his moral fiber." I sink back.

"Mimi, are you sure that Clare was blackmailing Ralph? It seems—just—rather strong a word to use. Clare's so . . . drippy. And I know this isn't what you want to hear, but . . . she seems quite nice."

"No, I don't know for sure that she is blackmailing him," I say. "But why did she show up at my party, then, like that? That's not wet behavior. You don't just show up if you're not invited. What was all that about, then?"

"I don't know, Mimi. She was stuck in the gamekeeper's cottage, on her own, with Joe. Gideon is fairly semidetached these days, I gather, from the family unit. Everyone was coming to your *Death in Venice* extravaganza, she doesn't hunt, she can't even go for walks because Joe's in a pushchair, so maybe she lost the plot and thought, 'I'll just turn up, Ralph will take pity, and Mimi will be my friend again, and it'll all be all right.' "

"I've never not been her friend," I correct Rose, "it's just been *tricky*. And it's not exactly going to make it a whole lot *less tricky* now I've found out she has persuaded my husband to give her a baby." Luckily, Rose doesn't bring up the abortion. It makes me realize, though, that my situation vis à vis my own husband right now is humiliating enough already without needing to bring that up.

"Er, Mimi. You don't have to answer this." Rose twiddles an elegant ankle. "Are you going to tell the children?"

"Tell them what?" I arrange my forearms on either side of my body so they tan evenly, and spread my fingers on the toweling coverlet.

Tropical birds are singing a fraction too loudly in the canopy above our heads, but, otherwise, it is all perfect. We are in a deeply comfortable, highly tasteful pad in Jamaica with congenial company. (I can't understand why Rose repeatedly cheats on Pierre, who is funny, artistic, good-looking, and, best of all, nice to me, but then—I'm not married to him, Rose is. That explains everything.) It isn't even unbearably hot, despite Ralph's gloomy predictions and, so far, the only whining sound is coming not from mosquitoes but from me, when meals I haven't had to lift a finger to prepare are late in appearing.

"About their little half brother. Joe. The baby. He's very sweet . . . Even if he is Clare's, he's Ralph's, too, as if anyone could miss that."

"Isn't he?" I agree, and close my eyes. "Especially when Clare tricks him out in the very baby clothes of Casimir's I gave her and brings him to his father's party for his first public outing." A silence falls between us, as I recall the shock of seeing Cas/Joe aged eighteen months in Clare's arms, wearing Cas's old brown cords and the navy jersey that my own mother had knitted, and what I felt was a look of secret triumph on the other woman's face. And the Paddington Bear wellies.

"Of course I'll tell the children about Joe," I say. Though I haven't yet convinced myself. I can't think how I would break the news. "Darlings, er, Daddy and I have something to tell you! It's a lovely surprise! Do you remember Clare, from Lonsdale Gardens? Well, isn't it lovely! Clare couldn't have a baby with Gideon, so she asked Daddy very nicely, and . . ."

I can't go on, even rehearsing the conversation. It is too gruesome. On so many levels. Not even Posy would buy it. Not for a second. And as for Mirabel . . .

I'm feeling very tired. When Ralph and Rose ask me why I'm so tired, I tell them it is the heat, the jet lag, the stress. We are always being told how tiring stress is. And how stressful.

"I'll tell them when I feel up to it." I lever myself up off the lounger and slide into the tepid oblivion of the pool.

Rose

Cath Cobb is natty in a khaki suit and Tod's loafers, the
ones where the studded rubber sole lips over the back of
the shoe, drinking what she calls a seltzer and lime. Mimi is in
wellies and jeans and her Husky over a baggy checked man's
shirt (vodka and tonic), still looking brown and streaky-haired
from Jamaica. And much happier, thank God. Her cheeks are
rosy, and she is wolfing a packet of cheese and onion crisps. I
never feel hungry, particularly, so I find myself rather envious
not only of Mimi's lusher figure but also her appetite.

Sir Michael Hutton (Scotch, no ice) is with Lady Elizabeth
(sherry). Granville is supposed to be arriving by helicopter, according to Cath, with Kasmin, the famous art collector, and his
wife, Pernilla, the telly cook, who are coming for the weekend.
Sophy (spicy tomato juice) is here from Spodden's Hatch, wearing an assortment of darned clothes, like a Cabbage Patch doll,
which, worryingly, look as if she might have made them. And
there are loads of others.

We are all crammed into the snug Farmers' Bar, sitting behind the important notice that has been pinned to the door
saying PRIVATE MEETING. I have ordered a glass of Goody-Two-
shoes mineral water, and am sitting next to Cath, trying to look
like a respectable mother, jam maker, and hamper purveyor
(rather than scarlet woman, village hussy, or stealer of other
women's husbands) and am smiling defiantly at a couple of tut-

ting county matrons, their hair curled into the permanent waves of Hokusai paintings. I have learned from experience that the more ashamed one appears, the more one says sorry, the horrider people are, whereas if I do my walk of shame with head held high, this penitential part passes much more quickly.

As it's 6 P.M., Cath glances at a watch on her slim wrist. In one and a half hours, according to the note that was circulated earlier alerting us to this meeting, there will be a show of hands on the following, in the Village Hall: (1) the future of the Post Office and Stores, (2) the windfarm, and (3) the hunting arrests. I note that both the Hitchenses appear incandescently happy, despite—or is it because of—the shock announcement from London that Honeyborne PO and Stores, their livelihood, and their life, was earmarked for closure, along with hundreds or even thousands of other rural sub-post offices.

There is nothing the Hitchenses love more than a good disaster, especially one of which they are fortunate enough to be the epicenter. At one point, I heard Mrs. Hitchens remark with great satisfaction that in the middle of difficulty lay opportunity, and that someone clever had said that so it must be true. Einstein, or someone.

"Cath, I can't believe you're here," I say, laying my hand on her arm. "I know what you have on your plate. The farm shop. The wedding . . ." I trail off.

According to Mimi, the affianced Serena has morphed, as so many young women do at this point in their lives, into a female preternaturally interested in her own appearance, shopping, white goods, high-thread-count linens, and cutlery—in other words, Serena has blossomed into a raging Bridezilla and is demanding a full-scale white wedding for 250 guests, and is even playing *OK* and *Hello!* off against each other in a manner that suggests she might have retained Max Clifford as her own personal bridal PR. "Apparently she spends a lot of time in her wedding dress, standing in front of three-way mirrors, with her veil on and then her veil off, and twirling, asking everyone if her bump is showing, and gazing at her own perfection," Mimi had said, back at Perdition.

"Her bump!" I had shrieked, amazed at my lack of observational powers, before realizing that in Rougemont Castle, during the week I'd actually been skiing with the newly pregnant Serena, I'd had eyes for only one woman, and it wasn't La Serenissima. "How did you know she was pregnant?"

"Ralph told me," Mimi had replied.

"But how did he know?" I had asked.

"He worked it out. I asked Granville and he ummed and ahed and admitted it."

"That explains why she didn't ski in Gstaad, then!" I had cried. "Is that why they're getting married?"

"Rose, don't ask me. Why does anyone get married?" Mimi replied, slightly testily, I thought.

After the shock had worn off about the Post Office, everyone was doing a fine job of mourning openly with the Hitchenses, and saying that they couldn't imagine anyone else in the shop, and they simply couldn't believe it, knowing full well that in a few months' time, the Hitchenses would be gone and nobody would be giving the Stores a moment's thought. Because life moves on.

We are all secretly feeling guilty that this wouldn't have happened if we had all done more shopping there, rather than whizzing off to Waitrose in Godminster, when Cath pipes up, having given her Breguet another meaningful look, accompanied by a tiny, decisive tap. "Guys, can we get going?" she says, in her sunny-side-up way. "Have you all got drinks, somewhere to sit? Fabulous. Why don't you two"—she gestures to the gray-curled matrons—"sit here. Now, here's where I'm at with this. We don't need to accept the decision from on high that the Post Office has got to close. This is nothing to do with government. This is about community. What I say is, we can do it for ourselves." She then produces a color-coded folder from an L.L.

Bean canvas holdall with her initials on it, as I reflect that, true to form, the woman in the village who already runs three large houses, four children, a husband, a farm and a farm shop, and is planning a strictly bridal wedding in May is the one to volunteer for yet more selfless civic duty. "I've spoken to the CEO of the, er, Village Retail Services Association," she continues. "This is how it would work."

Cath then explains, with admirable and blessed concision, how the Honeyborne Post Office and Stores could be converted into a community-owned village shop and retain all the Post Office functions, and indeed its counter and hatch, for at least two hours a day most weekdays.

We are all stunned. What Cath outlines is so simple, and so obvious. Why did none of us think of it before? There are a few questions, such as how many shifts will be needed, whether shiftwork will be paid out of profit or a community sub, questions about local suppliers, organic suppliers, food miles, accounting, and so on, but otherwise, nothing seems to stand in the way of the shop remaining open other than traditional, good old-fashioned English apathy.

"Let's have a show of hands," Cath says, after a good while of all this, "as we are all due in the Village Hall in less than ten minutes. I'm in," she announces in a louder voice, an elegant arm arching towards a beam. I can't help checking whether there are any darker marks on her cream silk shirt from Anne Fontaine, but no. She hasn't even broken a sweat. "I hereby swear I will bust my booty for the Honeyborne Collective," says Cath, placing her hand on her heart in an affecting, one-nation-under-God gesture of allegiance to the country of her residence, but not her birth. "Who else is in?"

A forest of hands. Cath pinks with pride.

"Terrific," she says. "Good job, you guys! I am so proud to be part of this community." She looks around. "Oh yes," she adds, as if in afterthought. "I've persuaded Granville to do the books."

A ragged cheer arises, as Granville—who hates personal publicity and was furious to appear on the *Sunday Times* Rich List—is, according to the *Daily Telegraph*'s business section, Britain's third most successful hedge fund manager. To my mind, this rather answers the question about whether he could afford to be a psychotherapist or not, although when I asked him, he just laughed in a newly knowing way and said, "The question is, could I afford not to be a psychotherapist, mmm, Rose?"

Everyone leaves the pub for the Village Hall charged with optimism and alcohol. Sir Michael is singing, There'll always be a Post Office, while there's a country lane, wherever there's a cottage small, beside a field of grain, and only the Hitchenses are—to my mind—looking a tiny bit glum.

Later on, same evening.

Granville Cobb, Sir Michael Hutton, and Ned Bryanston are back in the Farmers' Bar sitting round a small table that has one leg shorter than the others and threatens to spill drinks into laps at the slightest touch. I am waiting at the bar for Pierre to join me (he couldn't come to any of the meetings, he was too busy in his studio, but he said he could have a drink with me and take me home in time for me to make supper). I am pretending to read the *Mail* but am watching the three men closely—after all, Ned came in for a terrific beating, and I am in shock, too.

Ned has already knocked back one large whiskey.

"Another?" says Sir Michael.

"Yes please," Ned answers, in a chastened voice. "Thanks awfully, Michael."

Sir Michael notices me at the bar. "Rose—why don't you come and join us?" he suggests, dragging a fourth chair to the rickety table. Ned puts his head in his hands.

I don't know where to look, either, and sit down as bidden.

Then Ned looks up, and a light of amusement flickers behind his dark eyes. "You know, my great-great-grandfather once had a Jack Russell. Called him Mud," he says, conversationally. "Why? So he could say, to anyone who asked, 'His name is Mud.' "

Sir Michael lays a consoling arm on his shoulder. "Ned, old cock," he says. "All families go through bad patches. Just weather the storm. Keep buggering on, eh, old chap."

Then Granville and Sir Michael exchange a glance. Granville then moves the conversation on to safer, and higher, ground. He reinforces what many said at the meeting, after the plan to convert the Post Office into a community store had received the unanimous thumbs-up, that is. In fact, at the Town Hall, the entire village had become wildly overexcited, especially after Cath had fleshed out her plans a little more to make an "entrepôt" for "Dorset produce" and a "destination food store," and dollar signs clearly started dancing in front of little old ladies' eyes. I have to admit, Cath really was magnificent. Of all the stars in the Honeyborne firmament, she is definitely the twinkliest.

"I'd like the children in the school to eat healthier, too," she'd announced. "I'd like everyone to provide vegetables for school lunches and the collective, I'd like us all to have what in the States were called victory gardens, where folks grew their own food and sent it over for the boys. You'll all notice the difference," she said. "At least eighty-five percent of an ingredient's flavor happens before it reaches the kitchen, and I'd love to convert the whole village, if I could, to the joys of seasonality—but I'm happy to start with the children. I'd like to fill their taste-bank memories with freshly picked berries and leaves. From the roadside. From the woods and fields. From your kitchen garden. From Court Place Farm. I'd like to open up everyone"—Cath looked around the Village Hall—"to all the wonderful flavors of *my* home."

Even though Cath sounded like the love child of a Californian hippie and Jamie Oliver, at the time we all simply lapped it up, especially when she announced her plan to fund an "edible school garden" at Honeyborne First School, on the grounds that if kids had close contact with what they ate, they would always choose spinach over junk food. A future filled with slim, nut-brown children scampering around wildflower meadows and foraging for dandelion leaves seemed to loom tantalizingly ahead.

But where Ned came to grief was item two. The windmill. And another item, which wasn't on the agenda.

First, though, the dreaded windmill. After a retired electrical engineer had made a compelling case against the windmill and spoken knowledgeably and, it has to be said, at some length about load factors and topple lengths, the village had basically voted to a man against it. Furthermore, under encouragement from a hardcore of Spodders, among them Sophy, it was suggested that Ned should coppice his woods, convert to woodchip, and use a biomass boiler instead (as had already been agreed by the eco-village in an earlier meeting), as biomass boilers are more energy efficient and less visually intrusive than the windmill. And that wasn't all. The village also decided that *Ned* should pay the *Spodders* to do it rather than the other way round, in true the-peasants-are-revolting fashion.

Ned had stormed out to the pub. Jesse Marlon wasn't even there at the meeting. After his support for Ned at the dinner party and at the Village Hall, I thought that was a little odd. At least I did think it was odd until Mrs. Hitchens leaned over and told me, in a stage whisper, that Jesse Marlon Bryanston was in Godminster Police Station, being interviewed.

"What for?" I whispered back.

"Rape," Mrs. Hitchens hissed. I turned to look at Garry from the pub indignantly—why on earth had he told me it was Colin Watts, the creep?—but he would not look at me. Jesse Marlon and rape? My heart somersaulted. I knew it wasn't possible and, although I had, of course, moved on, I knew I had to be there for him.

So I went to the pub after the meeting, which I thought was very brave of me.

When Sir Michael returns with Ned's double scotch, and places it carefully on the wobbly table, Ned takes it to his lips and sips bleakly. I am not saying much. Granville is trying to comfort him over how things have turned out, while conveying nonverbally his disbelief that my (ex-) boyfriend Jesse Marlon may or may not be the village rapist, and not his (future) son-in-law, Colin. It's a complicated message to get over, I allow, but I have to say that Granville manages it with grace and humanity.

"Listen, Ned, a deal's only a good deal if both sides feel a little bit screwed," he says, referring to the new arrangements with the Spodders and energy supply. We are grimly keeping away from the ghastly news about the police and the alleged sexual assault. "That's how it works."

"But Granville, you great goose, I've been totally screwed!" Ned protests. "With this new deal, they win hands down, and I lose! In all honesty, I wasn't berserk about the windmill plan to start with," he continues in a quieter voice. "But I thought if I could be seen graciously to bow to pressure, it would build up enough goodwill . . ."

"For what?" I ask.

"Well, my thinking was—I don't mind telling you now this is clearly not going to happen—my thinking was, I'd bow to pressure and not erect the windmill, which I didn't want to see on Hamble Hill anyway, but in the afterglow of warm feeling to me, the compassionate landowner, I would sneak by plans to sell off some land by the Lar, very near Spodden's Hatch," he said.

"How near Spodden's Hatch, and what for?" I demand to know.

"A small, er, carbon-neutral, um, solar-powered . . ."

"Yes?" asks Sir Michael. "Get on with it, old bean, stop blinding us with all this ghastly green science, I can't tell you how bored we all are with it."

"A housing development," Ned admitted. "A small one, very sympathetic to the landscape, and completely sustainable, not that it matters now, though," he says, with heat. "I'll never get it now! Will I? Now I'm actually paying the Spodders market rates to live on my own land. Bloody hell! Sodding little . . . *tinkers*! Since when did land ownership come to mean stewardship? What the fuck is coppicing, anyway, and why is it suddenly so important? Jesus, Mary, and Joseph! Why have I ended up supporting a whole bunch of hairy rancids, instead of exploiting them? It's against nature."

"Oh, I wouldn't worry about that," says Sir Michael. "We all do that. It's called the price of privilege, old chum. Property is theft and all that."

"Privilege? And what do I know about privilege, I'd like to know?" Ned expostulates. "I've spent my entire life unblocking my tenants' chimneys, clearing their drains, and going to their endless children's endless christenings. All I ever wanted to be was a documentary filmmaker. But I'm a sort of general factotum instead. I've had to live in a crumbling ruin with my mother round my neck all my life, worrying about the roof. I can't even sell off a little bit of land to pay for the rewiring. I can't have any life of my own, and I can't even pass on the estate to the son who might make something of it, Little Ned, who has just the combination of nastiness and greed necessary to get rid of the tenant farmers and make something of the estate. I've got to hand over the whole shebang to the son who's on no-speaks with my wife and wants to turn the place that's been in my family for four hundred years into a vegan commune run on dung. It's a total harry balls-up." After his long wail he puts his head in his hands.

"Don't worry, old chap," says Sir Michael. "These things tend to come out in the wash. And as for Jesse Marlon . . ." he pauses delicately. "Well, all I'd say is that there's everything still to play for. Let's see how things pan out, eh?" Sir Michael coughs, and avoids looking at me or Ned.

At the mention of Jesse Marlon, Granville leaps to his feet and says that if he doesn't get back to Court Place to join Cath and his guests and the Michael Greens for dinner, he'll be in very hot water with the wife.

As he's leaving the bar, he pops his head back round the door. "Oh yes, Rose . . ." he queries, "are you and Pierre free tomorrow around teatime? I thought I might bring Kasmin, who's staying with us with Pernilla, over, to look at Pierre's etchings."

Sir Michael stays on manfully. It's a dirty job, but someone has to do it.

"All right. So what's he done now?" Ned says. He is talking about Jesse Marlon. He throws me a sharp glance, as if I have corrupted his precious baby, which is very annoying, especially now it turns out that Jesse Marlon might be the village rapist though, frankly, if Jesse Marlon is a sexual predator, I'm Myra Hindley. "It wasn't him who sent the video of Henry Pike and Martin Thomas hunting with a full pack of hounds, was it?"

"To be quite fair, not exactly," says Sir Michael. "I had a word with Henry afterwards. We don't know who sent the video of the hunt. At first we thought it might be that Sophy girl, who has all those fatherless children, the one who made that splendid green ointment I was telling you about that worked wonders on the terriers' impetigo." He glows at the memory. "Absolutely marvelous stuff. I think there's been some confusion because she did give a package to Jesse Marlon, with whom she seems to have one of these trendy, modern relationships—don't ask me—and told him to drop it into the Post Office and Stores on the way to his work at the Dairy. She doesn't leave Spodden's Hatch much; I think she has a young child. Well, Jesse Marlon—not the sharpest knife in the drawer, but there we go—didn't spot it said God-minster Police on the envelope, and Mrs. Hitchens did the rest. Total cock-up, basically. He gives it to the Hitchenses, who put two and two together and make five, i.e., it's the usual thing."

"But what was in the parcel, then, if it wasn't the hunting video?" I ask, although I have a jolly good idea.

"Don't ask me," Sir Michael Hutton replies instantly. "And anyway, it's water under the bridge, now, isn't it? Ned, I think you missed the shock announcement then, at the end of the meeting, about the hunting case? You shot off, didn't you? Case dismissed. So the video—whoever shot it, and whoever sent it—is history. The Crown's dropped the case. There's some technicality."

"Goodness," says Ned faintly. He looks confused. "But why did this woman Sophy want to . . ." It is clear that Ned has no idea about the rape story, and neither of us wants to enlighten him. He is interrupted by Sir Michael, who has risen to his feet and is looking down at us.

"So everyone should be very grateful to you, Ned. You've been a jolly good egg to abandon ship on that infernal plan for a windmill. And you're a jolly good egg, too, to let the hippies live on your land, and grant them a living on it, too, if you really do go ahead with this coppicing idea. Frankly, the Bryanston family is coming up smelling of roses all round, and I'm sure this nonsense about Jesse Marlon will be over in a jiffy. Jolly good! And now, I really MUST go."

Pierre arrives and picks me up. "What was all that about?" he asks when we're in the car.

"I'm still trying to work it out myself," I answer. I think I followed most of what went on in the Farmers' Bar, but I can't be sure.

I try to explain it to Pierre. "It seems that Sophy might or might not have been raped, and it wasn't by Colin Watts, it was more likely to have been Jesse Marlon"—I hurry past my mention of Jesse Marlon, and Pierre does not detain me for further questioning, which is decent of him—"and she has sent the police something in a parcel that proves something one way or the other, and, meanwhile, there's to be no windmill on Hamble Hill, no jail for Martin and Henry, and the Spodders are going to make some money by selling biofuels to Godminster Hall."

"Well, I can only be grateful that I at least wasn't involved," is my husband's response.

One Week Later

I go to the Haybarn (the spa at the Brambletye) with Lulu and Mimi.

As soon as we all received our invitations to the wedding, so stiff I could keep it in the car to scrape ice off my windscreen with, Mimi and I knew we had only a short time, a matter of days, to make up for years of neglect. So we have a whole day of female admin—legs, toes, fingers, hair, bikini, mustaches, and so on—ahead of us before the wedding in order that Mimi and I can come anywhere near Lulu's level of presentation and grooming.

We went in Mimi's defiantly unvaleted Subaru, having shoved everything on the backseats—Lakeland catalogues, cartons of juice, sweet wrappers—into the footwells at her request. "Why go in comfort in three cars," cries Mimi, as she hurtles round blind corners in narrow lanes, and we all shriek girlishly as we are thrown together, "when we can all cram into one filthy one?"

After we'd signed paperwork (I notice that the management now not only demand information about allergies and operations but plastic surgery, too) we all went into different cubicles. Mimi went off to be "deforested," which I think meant a leg wax, and for a lash tint, while Lulu was booked in for eyebrow shaping and a vitamin C facial. I had booked in for collagen eye treatment, a hydrating facial, and a fruit acid pedicure.

At lunchtime we meet by prearrangement in the relaxation room at the Haybarn, and we're sitting in brief towels, dimpled and hot like human dim sum, as we've been steaming. I am remembering with a sort of voluptuous shiver the last time, in the sauna, with Virginie, the time that I realized . . . who I really am. "It's such a relief, actually," I say, banishing this thought as I sink back onto the lovely white toweling cushions on the slatted loungers and arrange the pillow thing behind my neck so I can relax totally.

It's nice. I can look a whole day of pampering in the face. Especially now I have some money to splash around again, at last.

"I realize, now, that I love Pierre very deeply. It's a real challenge—it's been a real challenge, I mean—living in rural isolation with a man who's more interested in flints than his family, so I think I was reacting to that, a little. In the past."

It's true. I have accepted that Pierre's decision not to pitch in, not to help around the house, something I've complained about since our honeymoon, was a cry for help. What he was expressing was, I think, not an inherent laziness that went with his artistic temperament (and his high tolerance, it has to be admitted, for mess) but his own private rebellion against my domestic hegemony.

It is all clear to me now.

There is water with lemon and mint and black things in a jug on the table, together with all this month's magazines— *Vogue, Vanity Fair, Tatler, Harper's.* I pour myself a glass, and instruct the others to have lots of it, because the charcoal in the water is supposed to balance the pH, or something, in the system. The people who run the Brambletye started out in San Francisco, and it shows.

Both Lulu and I have taken the precaution of oiling our hair and slicking it back, so we both look like sleek seals. Mimi's hair is standing out around her head so she looks a bit like Phil Spector during the Wall of Sound years.

"Listen, Rose. I think it's bloody great. I didn't think that sort of thing ever happened in real life. Just remind us all again what did happen?" Mimi cues me up.

"Well," I say, trying to hide my pleasure, "last weekend, when he had Kasmin and Pernilla to stay, Gran asked Pierre and me to tea, on the Sunday—no, it was Saturday, because it was the day after the Village Hall meeting. Then he rang and said, actually, would it be all right if they came to us. I can't remember which way round it was. So I said, of course."

Lulu turns a page of her *Vogue*, as if the story that Pierre's entire collection had been snaffled up by Kasmin, the greatest modern art buyer of recent times, was of considerably less significance than a new moisturizer stroke filler with pearlescent microbes for the delicate under-eye region.

"So, what could be more natural, after we'd drunk our first-flush Oolong and eaten my homemade scones in the kitchen, than to wander out to the cutting garden, the kitchen garden, so Pernilla could pick some herbs to take back to Cottesmore Gardens? Taking in Pierre's studio en route?"

"Nothing," says Mimi, waggling her feet, as if that will dry her toenails faster.

When we pushed open the door to his studio, Pierre had been standing in the middle of the dusty floor, his face shining. At the sight of us—and the collector, Kasmin, of course—he looked animated and engaged in a way I hadn't seen for years.

Inside, there was a series of egg-shaped sculptures, more like pods, arrayed before us, each about five and a half feet high. Some had openings, clefts, and some had protuberances, like phalluses. They were astonishingly powerful. They must have taken *ages*.

"Darling! What are they made of?" I asked. I felt excited, but mainly because I was with Kasmin, who is famous, rich, and powerful.

Pierre didn't answer, and then, as we wandered around them, he explained that he wanted to explore deep-rooted metaphysical polarities: presence and absence, being and nonbeing, place and nonplace, the solid and the intangible. "I want to make body into sky," Pierre said, and Kasmin nodded, as if this made perfect sense. "Male into female."

"Yes," said Kasmin, caressing a pod. "Is it about whether the content is resident in the viewer, or whether it's resident in the work?"

"It's a subtle, yet very clear . . . *manipulation* of the act of looking," answered Pierre.

The only jarring note, apart from the two men talking blithering pretentious nonsense, that is, was that in another bit of floor space, there appeared to be a carefully constructed pile of logs.

Kasmin even started asking Pierre about them, while Pernilla and I wandered around them. I pretended I knew all about them. I think I pretended at one stage that I'd even helped. Suddenly, I wanted to be part of it, now that someone so famous and influential and loaded was willing to part with good money, to invest in Pierre.

"I do hope you'll all come to the private view," I say to the girls, pouring more water and drinking from the glass, to plump up my skin. "At the Kasmin Foundation. We hardly know anyone in London anymore, so we need all the support we can get. Mimi, you don't know any of the art critics? From your days as a journalist?"

"Um . . ." parries Mimi.

"Is it true he paid three million pounds for the lot?" asks Lulu sulkily.

"Uh-huh," I say, with nonchalance. "After all, Pierre did throw in the logs."

"So you may have to drop your complaint, then, Rose," Lulu observes.

"What's that, Lulu?"

"No longer can you legitimately whine that Pierre's annoying habit of working away in his studio round the clock, rather than doing a proper job, has cost the family hundreds of thousands of pounds in earnings foregone."

"Mm, it's a shame, that," I answer, "but I can live with it."

All this is clearly too, too irritating to Lulu. As we all know, she and Ned are living off capital and the rents from the cottages, and as for the GodLitFest—it costs them a fortune every year. And now the Bryanstons can't flog land to developers, either, without totally pissing off the whole village. They're even forking out to keep the Spodders on their own land, which is a deeply gratifying conclusion to the affair of the windmill to everyone in Honeyborne, apart from the Bryanstons themselves.

I gaze at Lulu smugly. When she sees me looking at her, I smile, which seems to provoke something in her, because she chooses this moment to lay down *Vogue*. "Rose, actually . . . there's something I've being meaning to tell you, too," Lulu says, in an odd, strained voice. Mimi and I look at each other in alarm. "I've been wondering whether I should, to be honest, but I saw a psychotherapist—well, actually a friend who's training to be one—and she said I should. In fact, she said I shouldn't keep things like this bottled up, it would be detrimental to my health and accelerate aging if I did."

"Oh yes?" I ask, my heart sinking. What is it going to be, the grisly revelation that I am about to hear? After all, there are numerous possibilities. Is Lulu going to "share" that Jesse Marlon had been cheating on me? That Jesse Marlon is the rapist? That Pierre has been cheating on me? That—aaagh—*Virginie* had been cheating on me?

Mimi and I both swivel eyeballs to look at Lulu. She pours herself some charcoal-filtrated spring water, and seems to extend her moment in the spotlight. But it is none of the above.

"I'm afraid Ceci has got a boyfriend," she says, choosing her words with care. I don't like the sound of this at all. Why would Lulu be afraid? What is it she is trying to say?

"What did you say?" I ask, even though I'd heard perfectly well. Ceci—my one, perfect daughter, who has never watched television, or eaten sugar, let alone processed flour, not at home at any rate, of whom I have high hopes of the art scholarship to Marlborough. Ceci, my perfect daughter, who's only thirteen!

"And it's Spike," adds Lulu.

"But we love Spike," protests Mimi.

"Yes, and so does Ceci, apparently."

"Exactly what do you mean by that, Lulu?" I ask, deciding that I've never liked Lulu and it was a terrible mistake to have included her in our girlie spa day.

"Well, I know. Ceci and Spike use Jesse Marlon's, while he's doing your garden, or whatever it is he does at the Dairy"—Lulu has a meaningful sneer on her face at this point—"and they do it by the fire. They just let themselves in. She—well, the person who told me—found condoms. I presume they were biodegradeable."

"That's not funny," I yelp. "Just how do you know this, Lulu? It's Sophy again, isn't it?" I had seen Sophy's face every time I trudged through the mud to Jesse Marlon's house. She used to watch us, from the opening of her yurt. I gave her a bottle of groundnut oil. I thought she didn't mind about Jesse Marlon and me. I mean, she's supposed to be a hippie, not a gold-plated bunny boiler.

I am in shock about Ceci. Just hearing the word "condoms" makes me feel sick. I want to throttle Lulu.

"You're right, it was Sophy. She called me, very upset," Lulu says smugly. "She seemed upset, as if Ceci was leading Spike on. You can't blame her, I suppose."

"What on earth do you mean by that, Lulu?" Mimi comes in to bat for me, cold as ice.

"You can't blame Sophy because it turns out, doesn't it, that Colin Watts didn't rape Sophy at all. Did he, Rose?" Lulu's not playing dumb anymore. Her little white teeth are almost bared in a snarl, like a fox. "He was just taking the rap for Jesse Marlon, wasn't he?"

Mimi turns to look at me. I shrug, and pick up *Tatler*, which I've just spotted has a cover line saying "Five Go Mad in Dorset, Camilla Long Makes Hay with Cath Cobb." I find the contents page, and then turn to it slowly. "Look, everyone, there's a piece about Cath," I say. "Lovely photos of the herb garden."

I read the piece in its entirety, not taking all of it in. Basically, it was one of those lavishly illustrated articles about someone richer and nicer and with better taste than everyone else designed to make the reader feel poor and diminished in her own life. There is a particularly fetching picture of Cath wearing a ballgown in the chicken coop and holding a bantam, underneath the headline, "Poultry in Motion."

I lay the magazine down and pick up my water glass. Mimi picks it up, chuckling with pleasure over a piece entitled, "Throaty, Sexy, and Utterly Husky—the return of the Puffa jacket."

"Lulu, I make a point of never listening to village gossip," I say. "So I honestly haven't a clue what you're talking about, I'm afraid. I think the whole rape story has become a little overblown, from what I gather. And anyway," I continue, putting in the boot, "you'd better be a tiny bit careful when it comes to your stepson. After all, in a few years, you'll be down on your knees asking him whether little Fred can have a barn and whether you can live in the stable cottage, so I'd tread carefully, if I were you."

PART THREE

Saturday 9 May, 10:30 a.m.

Mimi

So we walk, despite my high heels, to the gray-stone Norman church, set on a hill, the white and red Cross of St. George flying from the steeple. Parking anywhere near it today would have been impossible. I am a little out of breath, and my feet hurt.

On the way, though, I can't help loving how the land looks greener and plumper than ever. Catkins are jiggling on the branches, and in the mysterious, bushy cleeves, clenched buds are stickily unfurling. The sky is blue, with high white cotton-wool puffs of cloud; the blossom lies heavy on the bough; and the lambs frisking in the fields are unaware that after a few short but blissful months of hopping and butting and nibbling, they will appear on Sunday-lunch tables throughout the county, slathered with mint sauce and red currant jelly. Honeyborne has truly excelled itself, to the extent that even the combined efforts of Hollywood image makers and Richard Curtis could not have presented a West Country village and its inhabitants in a peachier light.

Spring came late this year—I thought it would never come— but is now in full fig.

The mellow-toned church bells are pealing, rocking out the

nuptials all over the valley. And now, as I sit gratefully in the polished pews of the small seventeenth-century church of St. Mary of All Angels, I can almost hear the tearstained troths between bachelor and spinster of the parish being pledged up and down the land.

The six ringleted bridesmaids, scudding about in puff-sleeved taffeta empire-line gowns the rich thick color of Cornish clotted cream, trimmed with dark-green velvet ribbons and bows and furbelows, were being marshaled into position as we drew near, to totter solemnly into the church in adorably matching pairs behind the ivory-sheathed loveliness of the bride. In the lanes, black vintage Bentleys lay like sharks basking in the shallows.

So here we are, tucked in our ringside seats in a tight row to see Granville give away Serena at this traditional English country wedding. Outside, the scent of wild garlic and honeysuckle is heavy on the air, but inside, the ancient nave and rafters are festooned with lavish swags of blooms arranged by Cath.

A different sort of rich wife, in a different climate, might have had the floral arrangements taken care of by a celebrity Knightsbridge florist and a plant doctor. But not Cath. She wanted her daughter's wedding to reflect not just her own taste and personality, but also her concerns. So Cath has done all the flowers herself, with her own hands, out of love and pride. "True simplicity is the greatest luxury of all," as she says, as if no one but a brute could ever think, for one second, that money— and not love or family or community—was the sixth sense that makes the other five come most fully alive.

It is time. Cath Cobb slips into her first-row pew, and is sitting as erect and slim as a birch tree.

Next to Ned Bryanston is a shrunken figure with powdery wrinkles and a black spidery hat atop her white hair, which has been spun into a special helmet for the occasion, and piercing blue eyes. Celia is, I notice, looking ancient, but then people one doesn't see for a year or two, or even just a few months, so often do. Especially at parties. In the pew behind Lulu and Ned and Celia, Jesse Marlon, and Judith and her civil partner, Kit, and their daughter, Jeremy, who have made the trip over from the Catskills, are sitting in a marvelous display of the limitless possibilities for lasting emotional trauma posed by the blended or recomposed family, a flawed but modern institution whose obvious, inherent limitations such occasions can test to the hilt.

Sir Michael and Lady Hutton, who are devoted to Celia, are in front of them, occasionally turning to see if Celia is all right and to frown at Lulu, who is texting into her mobile.

So all of us are seated in the cramped mahogany pews, inhaling the heady scent of the flowers, the dust of old hymnbooks, and the stale must of embroidered prayer cushions, ever more eagerly awaiting the moment when the organist will strike up the chords of "Here Comes the Bride" and we'll finally clap eyes on the radiant vision of Serena.

Five minutes of hush pass. Ten minutes. Twenty. It is now twenty minutes past the anticipated hour. Ralph keeps telling me how long we've been sitting here, as if he is doing the time checks on the *Today* program.

"We must have been here forty-five minutes now," he says without expression.

Colin Watts is beginning to look abject and young, even from the back, and the altar is beginning to take on the air of an Aztec Chac-Mool, as if ready to receive the blood offerings culled from the youngest and strongest of the tribe to appease the great sun god.

I am staring straight ahead, annoyed that I have already cried once (I made the terrible mistake of reading the honor roll of names and ages of the young men of this church and parish, beautifully inscribed in gothic gold on dark wood, who gave their lives in the Great War), and the service hasn't even started yet. Any occasion perfumed with emotion—be it a special assembly at school, a father–son cricket match, anything to do with the Queen, veterans in uniform, children's hospices, causes me to well up. I seem to be crying constantly these days.

I am wondering what could possibly have happened to make Serena so late on the biggest day of her life so far.

By now even Cath, who does everything with such admirable, snapping zip-de-doo, is looking anxious.

"Has Serena put the bouquet down somewhere? Has she run off with another (frankly more suitable) man?" I whisper out loud, brain racing, and, as the long moments pass, I find I am crying again. I wipe my eyes and nose on my sleeve, and am glad—for lots of reasons—when Ralph takes my warm, damp hand in his dry one.

"You okay?" he whispers.

"Mmm," I whisper back. "Bit hot, though."

"It's global warming," Ralph mutters, for the first time that day. He's taken to saying this after anyone makes any remark about the temperature (either hot or cold), or the weather (wet or dry, or in any way unseasonal "for the time of year").

"Mum," Posy whispers, clawing at my arm in a sudden fit of anxiety, as if she's suddenly remembered something.

"Yes, darling?" I answer.

"What happens to dogs in global warming? Do dogs die?"

I don't respond to this awful question. Ralph is looking at the straight back of Colin Watts, the groom, a sight that conveys the hangdog, surrendered appearance of all men in his position. Occasionally, Ralph mutters "lamb to the slaughter" and "head in the noose." Posy pulls at his sleeve and tells him to shush because we're in church, at which point Ralph starts humming "Another One Bites the Dust" under his breath instead, which I decide, after a moment's thought, is not disloyal.

Pierre and Rose and Ceci are sitting a few rows in front of us. I feel a rush of affection for them. As I look at her, I find Rose perfect in every way—she's beautiful, boho, talented, creative, with astonishing taste and a wonderful eye, and she can make an Easter garden or a Christmas wreath or assemble a gourmet picnic complete with sweet potato and goat's cheese tortilla and marinated char-grilled fillet of beef in fresh herbs and home-made bread faster than it takes me to make a round of buttered toast and a shambles of my own kitchen. And Ceci, Ceci's glorious, too—a woodland creature with tumbling, copper curls—and spirited.

Pierre is deliberately dropping his order of service on the floor and picking it up again, and chewing Nicorette with a maddening clacking sound, which tells me that, though his ship may have come in, his main aim in life remains irritating his wife.

Rose

As the bells peal and the organist, Dotty Smallpiece, belts out "The Arrival of the Queen of Sheba," everyone is filling the seats in church amid excited chatter and elevated expectation.

I take an order of service from the usher and sit a couple of rows in front of Mimi, Ralph, Mirabel, Cas, and Posy, who take up a whole rickety pew. The Cobb family fills up the left-hand side of the church and much of the right-hand side of the church, too, as Colin Watts and family could fill only a couple of pews, vastly outnumbered by the opposition.

On his team are the butcher from Godminster, with veiny cheeks, a man who has grown in stature since several local abattoirs closed and the only one left is owned by him (you now have to book pigs in at least six weeks in advance). There are the cousins who run the Horse Supplies, the couple at the garage, and various aunties and uncles, all done up in their best like Tom Kitten before the fine company arrives, slightly bursting out of their finery.

The Watts contingent is dressed in rented morning suits or sensible twin sets from that shop in Godminster that does separates and wedding outfits, and low heels, whereas the rest are dressed to the nines. The church is a vision of English lovelies at their best, the girls and women in teetering heels, edgy couture, and bonkers millinery. The women on the Cobb side break up the morning suits on the dark wooden pews with splashes of color and feathery fascinators, like iced gems in fruity colors scattered on a chocolate cake.

Lulu is looking quite spectacular, next to Celia, in her Veronique Branquinho dress. Ned is in his great-grandfather's tails, on the other side of Celia. Mimi is wearing a skirt from Whistles, which she has revved up with some secret new shoes from Net-à-Porter.com (she told me she now bribes the postman to deliver only when Ralph's car isn't outside Home Farm) and a little shrug edged in velvet. I'm wearing the peasanty floral dress—red paisley on white background—from Gucci, with big shades pushed up, and high-heeled strappy sandals, all of which combine to make my legs look lean and brown. Ceci, whom I have on a very tight leash since Spike was packed off to boarding school (fees paid for, needless to say, by Granville and the newly minted Pierre), is in Top Shop, as is Mirabel.

Sophy is there, wearing a patchwork skirt and a velvet bustier, and looks rather luminous and beautiful. Her Titian hair tumbles over her milk-white shoulders, and Henry Pike occasionally throws her a stormy look, which Biddy ignores. When I see Sophy, I remember with a slight sinking feeling that someone had warned me that she was to declaim a long poem in celebration of the nuptials. "It's a census, a *sound map* of the Lar River, from the headwaters in the moors, to Larmouth," Sophy had said, as if she didn't want to give away too much of some very special surprise, a rare treat that would enchant us all. "An epithalamium." And then, as if adding the cherry onto the cake, she said, "Although I did read the poem about the Dart River, of course, I wrote 'Lar' myself."

And Biddy is in Boden, or more precisely, Biddy is in the Hotchpotch Printed Skirt teamed with the Ruffle Silk-Trim Cardigan.

I'd never wear Boden, but Biddy in Boden is absolutely right.

Mimi

As the minutes tick by, and everyone has checked out one another's outfits and hats quite enough already, we begin to wonder what on earth's going on.

"Mum, I'm hot," Posy whispers, as if I can turn down the temperature in the church if she complains. She is wearing a Young England tweed princess coat, a hand-me-down from Ceci's extensive archive of designer children's clothes but still the best thing my darling Posy has. I lay a comforting hand on Posy's arm, reaching across Ralph.

And then someone scuttles importantly down the aisle to whisper in the ear of the Reverend Wyldbore-Smith, whose beatific smile is becoming somewhat strained as the long minutes pass and the organist plays "The Arrival of the Queen of Sheba" from the beginning for the fourth time. He looks startled. Whispers and shuffling and craning of necks flutter through the congregation, which is feathered and primped and prinked as birds of paradise in Philip Treacy and Cozmo Jenks and Stephen Jones millinery.

At last Serena manifests at the back of the church. Everyone gasps, and turns.

And she does look, as all brides do on their wedding day, incandescently beautiful and supernaturally refulgent. Plus, there's something glittering and twiggy twinkling in her hair, which causes a professional murmur of appreciation, as might be emitted by the editors of *Vogue* from the front row at a mold-breaking catwalk moment during Paris fashion week.

Everyone exhales, the groom unclenches his fists, and the best man gives him a reassuring pat on the shoulder. Tears start to every eye as the bride floats down the aisle like a cherry blossom on a stream on the arm of her father, who is to give her away for the first and, we all fervently hope, the last time, and the six little bridesmaids stumble behind her like geishas styled by Kate Greenaway, in ivory slippers, clutching their wands trailing ivy and with wreaths of fragrant sweet pea sitting athwart their bobbing baby curls.

But the relief and the delight at the scene, designed to melt even the most hardened matron and confirmed bachelor's stony hearts, does not last long. Just as the couple are about to exchange their vows, a figure makes an entrance at the back of the church and gives everyone, as Mrs. Hitchens repeated ad nauseam in the village shop to whoever would listen, "the shock of their lives." Mrs. Hitchens repeated this with all the certainty of a Crown witness even though, as we all know, Mrs. Hitchens was at her usual perch in Honeyborne Post Office and Stores. (Cath Cobb worked off the village with vintage Champagne and sumptuous nibbles a few days ago, at what Ralph termed the "serf and turf " party, knowing that while the spoiled rich groan inwardly at the prospect of yet more foie gras and rivers of Krug, one must always be seen to push the boat out for staff.)

Proceedings have just reached that spine-chilling bit where the reverend gets to ask if there are any persons there present who know of any lawful impediment why the bride and groom should not be joined in holy matrimony. We're all enjoying the musical sound of that archaic trope, and then—something happens to remind us all that, despite the expensive timbre of the uptown occasion, there are still tumescent buds waving outside the stained-glass windows and that, despite the showboating second homes, the chalets in the Alps, the châteaux in France, the villas in Tuscany, and the bastides in Provence, this is Wessex, where maids will always give birth to love children in bothies, Wessex, where simple stable lads will always push each other grunting down wells.

". . . Speak now, or forever hold your peace," intones the vicar, the Reverend Wyldbore-Smith, his mobile red lips working in his prayerful singsong in a way that is somehow difficult to watch, and right on cue there's a commotion at the back of the church, and a ripple of shock and a crackle of electricity shudder through the pews as everyone turns to look.

And this time, for once—as if it were a special treat, laid on to amuse in case of boredom, like the addition of plasma screens to London buses—someone actually does.

"It's global warming," says Ralph, still looking straight ahead, clearly wishing he were standing thigh-high in the Lar in his waders, casting a fly over that clever trout who liked to lurk in the pool by the dam, rather than wasting precious weekend time at a splashy society wedding.

"Shhh!" say Posy and I, flanking him like firedogs and twisting our necks to see who or what it is.

My eyes search past the rows of waving orders of service, fuchsia feathers, and elaborate hairpieces in the shape of artists' palettes, Eiffel Towers, and bunches of grapes; past a fruity Gloucestershire filly wearing, in a direct homage to the late lamented Isabella Blow, a vertical unicorn's horn that thrusts like a twisting, pointy phallus from her white forehead and pomaded hairline. My eyes search past that blonde who looks as if two large, silvery-diamanté dragonflies have alighted on her Princess Leia–style up-do, complete with blond plaits clumped in muffs around her ears, and come to rest on a defiant figure, wearing an arresting outfit, standing framed in the doorway at the back of the church, where, only a few moments before, Serena Cobb in her Alexander McQueen wedding gown and her proud father in his bespoke Huntsman morning suit had been so picturesquely composed.

"Oh my God," I say, as I, along with the rest of the congregation (apart from Ralph, regally impervious to gossip and scandal), take in the astonishing details of the surprising personage, in her narrow tailored suit of dusty pink moiré and killer Emma Hope suede peep-toe heels in exactly the same shade.

"Wow," says Casimir, as he turns to look. "Everyone's right. The world is definitely getting hotter."

The apparition's outfit is topped off with a black mantilla that manages to combine perfectly a nod to the presence of so many high-net-worth guests with a respectfully somber attitude to the sacred estate of holy matrimony.

"What on earth," I hiss to my husband. "Is she! Doing *here?*"

Rose

With the sunlight streaming in, it is difficult to make out the identity of the speaker at the back of the church and, like a digital video camera, I have to adjust to the darkness within the church and the glare outside before I can make the person come into grainy focus. Ceci and I and even Pierre, the veterans of more boring church weddings than I care to remember, are agog with excitement at the interruption.

"I do!" comes the stentorian cry from the back of the church, as the entire congregation rivetedly looks on. "You didn't think you were going to start without *me*, did you?" the woman says in carrying tones that, on a clear day, can reach from the top of Hamble Hill all the way to the gibbet.

Then, oh my Lord, it's Gwenda Melplash stalking down the aisle with all the chutzpah of a Naomi Campbell returning to own the catwalk for Cavalli after a long stint of boiler-suited community service. It is a dramatic solo echo of the recent procession of Granville, Serena on his arm, and the six bridesmaids. And she looks fantastic. She's in proper tailoring. If not couture.

Scary Gwenda marches right up to the front pew, where Mr. and Mrs. Watts, the butcher, and sons are sitting with Colin's auntie Joan, who used to be married to a Jehovah's Witness whose name I forget.

"Not without the mother of the groom, I hope," Gwenda continues unabashedly. "Come on, budge up, Mike."

Everyone scoots along obediently, and Gwenda takes her place in the pew. Alongside Sir Michael Hutton. She folds her gloved hands in her lap and gives a quick glance from side to side, making sure everyone is looking at her, which they are.

Serena looks as if she is going to cry. Colin looks startled, but is holding it together. He has taken Serena's arm. The Reverend Wyldbore-Smith is frozen in midflow, while Sir Michael and Lady Elizabeth Hutton's faces are stony in their determination not to betray any emotion whatsoever.

The village of Honeyborne is enraptured. And so am I. Not so much by this public declaration that Scary Gwenda is Colin Watts's mother; no, we all knew that Colin was adopted and there had always been village gossip about the Watts family, and there was a bit of speculation, now we all remember, when he started helping out at the stables every weekend. No, it is Scary Gwenda's structured, tailored outfit with those cutouts at the clavicles—a jacket that I can easily identify as a Galliano piece—combined with her publicly calling Sir Michael "Mike," and the distinct hint that "Mike" was Colin's father, which showed almost kamikaze bravado.

Colin Watts seems to wink at his birth mother, then he gives a reassuring smile to his parents, Mr. and Mrs. Watts, and a shrug, then pivots on his heel to face the Reverend Wyldbore-Smith, whose look of pained acceptance of human foible is slowly turning—as this scene progresses—into a ghastly rictus that says, Please let this be over soon. Serena is managing not to storm out of the church but, mainly, I think, because the retinue of bridesmaids is still standing in the aisle, blocking her way.

I don't dare look at Mr. and Mrs. Watts, because it's too awful to contemplate how they are feeling. I peep quickly at the

Huttons who, like the Wattses, are about the only people in the church not staring at Gwenda with horrified fascination. Sir Michael, I notice, has gone a funny color.

Gwenda gives a short nod, and the Reverend Wyldbore-Smith continues to conduct the service. After all, this is merrie England—not California—where everything is still kept tucked in, not left to hang out, so the Reverend goes on as if nothing has happened. Indeed, as the ancient words roll from his red lips, the same words in the same order that have been voiced here for four hundred years, it is as if nothing has *ever* happened.

We all sigh, and smile with relief. The show goes on, as it should.

I'm sure Serena wouldn't, in an ideal world, discover that Gwenda is her new husband's birth mother on her wedding day, and also find out that there is now clearly some doubt over his father, who might or might not be Sir Michael Hutton. But there is always endless speculation about who belongs to whom. There always will be. The important thing, at this potentially embarrassing juncture, is not to make a pointless dull drama about it and ruin everything.

It's one of the many reasons why I love living in the country, rather than Barnes.

Mimi

We are in the receiving line by the ashlar stone main entrance to Court Place, known as the Little Hall.

Serena, having flung back her veil, has processed out of the church with her scrumptious gaggle of bridesmaids with as much dignity and composure as the poor lamb could muster, and we are now all pretending, in a very English way, that the little pantomime during the service had been laid on especially by the management, simply to jolly up proceedings a trifle.

Ralph and I are standing in silence, with our children behind us, fidgeting and thirsty. I'm not sure Ralph has taken it all in. The extraordinary business in the church, with Colin Watts. And Gwenda. And, even more bizarrely, *Sir Michael*.

Mirabel is clutching the bouquet, having announced earlier to Ceci, "I am so catching the bouquet," and her dearest wish, thanks to Serena's expensive forehand lob, has been granted.

"You may have lost a daughter . . ." Ned is saying to a proud Granville and Cath, with glad-handing bonhomie. As we stand outside I note that Lulu, in a new toga bought specially for the occasion, is standing immobile and expressionless, like a caryatid, at his shoulder, no doubt thinking, in the manner of all beautiful women, how she looks. Celia Bryanston, who is, curiously, wearing black, is sticking to Lulu like a limpet, and I notice has clamped a clawlike hand on Lulu's arm. ". . . but look at it this way, Granners," Ned is saying, "lucky Serena's gained not only an extra father-in-law, but also, possibly, the gatehouse at Hutton Hall, if you play your cards right."

I think to myself if anyone else makes any more brilliant remarks about losing daughters but gaining replacements, I might scream, but I beam politely instead.

Granville's face takes on an alert, concentrating look, and I can almost hear his brain whirring as he works out that Ned has made a very good point. If Sir Michael's going to let anyone else have the gatehouse, a lavish gentleman's residence—and goodness knows he has hummed and hawed about selling for years—it is now obvious to whom he was duty bound to let this plum, this prize, go. Not to the Lacostes, not to the Sturgises, praise the Lord. But to his only long-lost son, of course, Colin Watts, his heir, who, only a few minutes ago, conveniently fused with the daughter of new money, Serena Cobb.

Still, the small matter of the gatehouse, as both men must know, is not going to be settled in a hurry.

Outside, in the sunshine, the ambulance carrying Sir Michael to Godminster General makes a yelping noise, and its blue light twirls importantly in the broad daylight. At Sir Michael's insistence, it is dropping off Lady Elizabeth at Court Place first.

"Michael told me for goodness' sake to go to the reception," Lady E, who is rather deaf, is explaining in a loud voice to puzzled observers, including Ralph and me. "He said he intended to have plenty more grippers before *porping orf,* I couldn't do anything anyway, and he couldn't absolutely guarantee me another sumptuous do at Court Place laid *orn* by the *Corbs.*"

One could see Sir Michael's point. Magnum upon magnum of organic Californian Champagne is chilling in the Lar. The waiting staff—who number about fifty—the bridesmaids, the entire bridal entourage, even the Court Place dogs have all had their hair and makeup or coats professionally groomed at the expense of Cath Cobb, who has determined that as much produce as possible, from Champagne to olive oil to wedding cake, is sourced from the Cobb family estates.

It is a wedding not to be missed.

At first I was surprised that Lady E seemed unmoved by the revelation that Sir Michael had sired a son by Gwenda. Then Ralph pointed out it is because she knows nothing about it. As far as Lady E is concerned, Sir Michael had a minor heart attack during the service, and Gwenda sat down next to him a few moments before, but the two events are in no way related.

As soon as I saw Gwenda, though, and heard her say, "Mike," I realized along with the rest of the congregation that Sir Michael Hutton must have taken an "outside ride" with Gwenda at some point more than two decades ago, most likely when both their horses became separated from the field, a parting that the lusty pair must have consummated with a quick knee trembler against the sweat-stained, twitching flanks of Sir Michael's splendid stallion, Nelson. Sir Michael must have thought—as he clutched at his shoulder, racked with sudden pain—that Gwenda had come to signal, if not to announce, his paternity, on this occasion of their son's marriage.

I looked at the bridal couple, and it was hard not to smile inwardly. One only had to look at Colin Watts to see by whose noble, leaping loins he had sprung.

The white ambulance in the forecourt conveys a gritty touch of both inner and Holby city to the upper-crust society scene, a memento mori, a reminder of the funerals amid the weddings. It has already had to execute a sixteen-point turn in the narrow lane leading to the church, a lane blocked with the Bentleys and women clutching their hats to their expensively blow-dried locks and the order of service booklet bearing the words, "Serena" and "Colin" and "St. Mary of All Angels, Honeyborne," and the date, in expensive bumpy black writing, before disgorging Lady Elizabeth from its back doors. Then it drives off, siren blaring.

Ralph and I finally totter up to Cath, me almost fainting from the combination of tight skirt, a complete lack of Champagne, high heels . . . and so on. Cath has her welcome smile applied as carefully as maquillage to her face. I smile back, and stretch out my arms to give her an especially meaningful hug and a kiss in a this-is-simply-too-beautiful-for-mere-words way.

But then something weird happens, even weirder than Gwenda's showing up in church in a killer designer outfit, and even weirder than Sir Michael's having what his wife stoutly calls "a gripper" after just one of the many dark secrets of Honeyborne being exposed after decades of gravelike silence.

Cath Cobb appears to trip, and fall.

In alarm, I reach out an arm to steady her. "Help!" I cry. The awfulness of the mother of the bride collapsing on her daughter's wedding day, the stress, the whole Colin Watts debacle, I think to myself—not even Cath Cobb can cope, I can see that in a flash. But then, slightly too late, I realize that Cath has not collapsed like a pricked inflatable. Cath has dropped into a deep curtsy.

For a flitting millisecond I am puzzled, and my whole Dorset life seems to flash before my eyes. Why is Cath Cobb—i.e., not even an English subject but a citizen of the United States—curtsying to me?

After all, I am not rich, nor titled, nor famous. Nor even thin. Nor well dressed. I am not a pillar of the community. I've never got on the rota for church flowers or for bell ringing, never been asked, nor even thought about joining the Women's Institute. I've never entered my own home-grown sweet peas or gooseberry jam to the summer fête, and probably never will. I've never lingered proprietorially around the long trestle tables in the marquee, upon which are grouped strange Venn diagrams of items at the fête, ready for judging: my new potatoes, sliced along the midsection; my glossy green, bristly courgettes and bulgy-flanked marrows like speckled green Zeppelins; my carrots with their tops neatly trimmed, tied with raffia; and parchment-yellow onions similarly docked and arranged with much curly parsley.

I've never baked and entered my own sausage rolls, flaky with fat and golden-brown, never even made a Victoria sponge, or attempted a cheesecake, round glistening heavy discs of crushed biscuit and animal fat, violently garnished with maraschino cherries. I've never made my own yellow piccalilli, green runner bean chutney, lemon curd, because the children would never eat them if I made them, or preserved them in sterile jars with gingham bonnets and affixed carefully inscribed labels to the sterilized jars.

In fact, I haven't even bothered to have my hair done for the wedding.

It is only when an elegant shape sweeps past me in a blur of ivory duchesse satin and a whoosh of expensive scent and surges up to the bent and crouching figure of my hostess that it dawns on me, much too late, that Cath Cobb's salutation is not recognition that I am Honeyborne royalty.

For the curtsy is not for me.

The curtsy is for the Duchess of Cornwall. Camilla! Camilla, the Duchess of Cornwall, is here! And Princess Michael of Kent, in shalwar kameez, and her bearded husband the Prince!

And it all clicks into place.

Camilla is why, of course, Cath Cobb did not want the whole village coming to the wedding, and why she worked off the village people, such as the Ashburtons and the Melplashes, and Ruth Wingfield, and the Brindles, and so on at the "serf and turf" party. Which could have been her fatal—and perhaps only—mistake. Though she had no idea she was perpetrating the insult, this meant that Gwenda Melplash was not invited to her own son's wedding, and royalty was.

Ouch.

But much more woundingly, she wasn't invited to see Serena—whom Gwenda herself had taught to *ride*, and taken out on her *first hunt*—be given away in marriage.

Now, one could frankly accuse Gwenda Melplash of many things—abrasiveness, devotion to horses and other women's husbands, pony-napping—but one could never accuse her of (1) seeing a dumb animal suffer or (2) taking an insult lying down.

As the Princess now sails up, a galleon in full sail, Granville makes a bow, from the waist. As he straightens, his face is pink with exertion and pleasure. Ralph and I move away discreetly, lest our presence distracts in any way from their relish of their social interaction with the crowned heads of Europe.

The Cobbs look incandescently pleased, and it is hard not to imagine that their delight is not merely because their firstborn daughter Serena has just got married but because three ranking members of the Royal Family have come to her wedding.

And then, just as things could hardly get any more regal, or exciting, or thoroughly marvelous, we all simultaneously hear the distant *chugga-chugga* in the skies that portends the arrival of a helicopter. "Exactly on time," says Granville smoothly. "That should be Prince Harry, putting down on the helipad by the Tithe Barn."

"Prince Harry!" shriek Mirabel, Posy, and I in unison. Mirabel thrusts Serena's bouquet into Posy's arms, but I take it to dunk in a vase back at Home Farm later, when our feet are back on solid ground again.

Ralph and I grab flutes of Californian bubbly and duck away, without having to gush sincerely to the Cobbs about how happy we are for them, how perfect the service was, how imaginative the marquee is, how pretty the orchard looks with little round picnic tables encircling quince trees and decked with flowers for the lunch.

All our words would be redundant, because the whole brilliantly and poetically staged event speaks for itself.

"Fancy old Princess Pushy coming," I say, impressed. "And Camilla. Blimey."

I'm about to snaffle another glass from the tray of a passing waiter, realize I am still holding my first glass, so deposit my empty, and hesitate between a ginger and lime zinger and a glass of freshly squeezed mandarin juice, and sip the latter virtuously.

"Mimi, darling, you are so easily impressed," says Ralph. "Helipads are like swimming pools, gyms, and burglar alarms. Only for noovs. I thought even you knew that."

I look around for canapés, and see a waiter within reaching distance and beckon him over. I stand in the path of a rather delicious-looking waiter with unruly black curls and something wanton about the mouth and take two roundels of crispy polenta topped with baby mozzarella and pesto, and eat them quickly, one after the other. "I bet they drove all the way from Kensington Palace, too," I say out loud. "It's not as if it's round the corner. That's a bit of a coup for the Cobbs." I tell the waiter to hold on, and reach for a couple more. They are meltingly crisp and hot and cheesy. "Like all members of the Royal Family, and anyone who has to exist on inherited wealth, rather than millions a year of earned income, the Michaels must be always looking at new ways to save money," I muse.

"And just how much do you know about inherited wealth, eh, darling?" Ralph asks me dryly. "Which reminds me. We've been married for fourteen years, Mimi, and I keep checking my accounts, but I still don't think I've received any dowry yet."

"Ha-ha-ha," I say. "But isn't it quite a relief to discover that the Cobbs aren't entirely perfect after all? I'd never have pegged them as throne rangers."

"I don't think you're being fair," says Ralph. "The Michaels are probably old friends. And Camilla's a neighbor from when they lived in Gloucestershire. Anyway, it's always delightful, Royals turning up," he goes on, as he makes the mistake of declining the offer of a date wrapped in Parma ham, which is easily the best thing I've put in my mouth all year.

"Especially for me. Since Granville's given up his shoot to become a shrink, social climbing's about the only exercise I get these days."

Rose

I am sitting on Cath's bed, in Cath and Granville's bedroom, which is draped and sumptuous, with its de Gournay wallpaper. (I happen to know it was done by Nicky Haslam. When Nicky came to tea here a couple of years ago, bringing some table lamps from his South Ken shop, at the height of his spiked hair and tanned face and leather rocker phase, I didn't recognize him at first. When I'd last seen the famous interior-design queen, he was a correctly attired white-haired man in age-appropriate suiting, with a free bus pass. "Nicky!" I'd said. "It's Rose! Rose Musgrove. I used to know you . . . in London . . . when you were *old*.") While I am admiring the wallpaper, Serena is bleeding in the bathroom.

I found her up here. I'd repaired to the bedroom floor to call Virginie on my mobile. Just for reassurance, I suppose. And to tell her to forget about her plans to snap up the gatehouse at Hutton. That prime country residence, conveniently close to me, is no longer in play. Old Sir Michael's found his heir at last.

I'm not having a good wedding, in other words. All that palaver with Gwenda, the ambulance, Sir Michael being taken ill, and now poor Serena. It's rather threatening to sour my mood over Pierre's newfound success, especially as Virginie's cunning plan to turn the gatehouse into a Petit Trianon retreat, complete with lambs and doves and me, seems to have crumbled into dust.

And the other thing. The sight of Sophy, Noah clamped to her bosom, deep in conversation with Jesse Marlon, was a slightly disturbing one. I went up to them, and Jesse Marlon disengaged from her, and we went off into the walled garden, and he sort of explained the whole thing. He said that "Soph," as he called her, is very emotional and a very fragile person.

"I could have told you that," I said.

"Yes and, anyway, she's had a really rough time and . . ." He trailed off. "A while ago, over a year ago, she and me got together," he said, his grammar reminding me painfully how young he is. "And, anyway, I wasn't that into her, and stuff— well, I *was*, I just didn't want us to share a yurt. I wanted to be friends. It doesn't work having relationships with other eco-villagers, and I didn't want the others to know. But she went crazy, and apparently she reported the next day that she'd been assaulted, sexually assaulted, which was rubbish, but when the police came round to Spodden's Hatch, she'd completely changed her story and hinted to the police that it wasn't me, it was Colin Watts, and it wasn't assault, it was rape."

"That explains the line in her poem," I breathed, "about *men falling in love before, women after.*"

"Whatever," said Jesse Marlon.

A lightbulb popped in my head. "Noah," I said slowly.

"Yes," said Jesse Marlon.

"So Noah's your son, and one day he will . . ." Jesse Marlon gazed into the distance, as if into his future, looking noble, as I joined the dots. "One day, Noah will be the tenant of Godminster Hall," I finished. "In fact, the owner."

"Well, until Noah has a son of his own," said Jesse Marlon.

So, I thought as I made my way back towards the throng, leaving Jesse Marlon. The father of Noah is Jesse Marlon. And I didn't think for a moment that Jesse Marlon had raped Sophy. Not for a *moment*. Though Jesse Marlon is . . . adventurous, sexually, what he was guilty of was not falling in love with Sophy

Mills, the second she fell for him, and sleeping with her when he had no prior feelings for her.

Well. It has happened before, and it will certainly happen again. But why did she ring Lulu about it? And rat on Ceci and Spike? I sit on the bed, upstairs where it's quiet and peaceful, away from the madding wedding. Perhaps . . . when Sophy saw Jesse Marlon carrying on with me, in front of her and Noah's noses, she took her revenge by telling Lulu and pinning the rape on him, in the hope that Ned and Lulu would disown him and he would stay in Spodden's Hatch forever, and maybe, even, share in Noah's upbringing.

Not that I will ever find out.

"Darling Serena," I call out, getting up from the vast four-poster bed and going to examine the family photographs on the mantelpiece opposite. There is a very sweet one of Cath sitting on this bed, in a broderie anglaise nightie, clearly having given birth to her fourth baby, Florian, while all the other children cluster round her with shining faces in their crunchy pale blue PJs, or matching white nightie, in the case of Serena. Cath looks awfully good given she's just delivered, and her hair is in a shining updo. It is rather annoying. I still looked like the Wreck of the *Deutschland* six months after having Ceci.

"You mustn't worry too much, I promise! I had bleeding with Ceci. It's really common, darling. It doesn't necessarily mean anything. I know it's scary. But after the party we'll run you into Godminster, they'll scan you, and I'm sure you'll be fine." Poor Serena's bleeding started before the service, she told me. That's why she was late arriving at church, and why she gave us all panic attacks that she wasn't going to show up, and we all thought Colin was going to be stood up at the altar. But she did show, bless her. It was light bleeding then. But now, the bleeding is heavier. And she has cramps.

I hate to think of her, in there, on her own, in her white wedding dress. She hasn't told Colin, or her mother, because she doesn't want to spoil the reception after all Cath's work and all Serena's demands re: doves, Raj tents, ogee arches, Royal attendees, and all that. The whole thing is just so painful.

Then something awful happens. The door pushes open, there's not even a knock, and Lulu and Celia barge into Cath's bedroom. I feel like a lioness defending my cub. "What do you want?" I say to Lulu. "Hello, Mrs. Bryanston," I say more politely. "There's another bathroom down the corridor."

Serena comes out, looking drawn and composed, white enough under her makeup to audition as the corpse bride. "I think I'm going to go down," she says to me before spotting Lulu and Celia. She nods and says hello but passes the pair to rejoin her guests.

"What's wrong with Serena?" Lulu asks.

"The silly gel should never have got married," I hear Celia Bryanston say in Serena's mother's bedroom. Celia, who has seen a thing or two in her time, has nipped into the bathroom after Serena and must be taking the whole sanguinary situation in at a glance. A pad with a Rorschach blot of blood is, I bet, visible in the bamboo wastebin. "Let alone to *him*. Most unsuitable." She shudders, passing me. I decide that she is very unpleasant, that she and Lulu deserve each other, and that Celia must be the last person apart from Lady E to find out today's big story, which is that Colin is not quite so lowborn as the nasty snobs would believe. Not that birth has got anything to do with anything. Except it does.

"Honestly," Celia Bryanston tuts. "In my day, one waited for three months, after one had Started a Baby, just to make sure it *took*."

Hours later, we stagger home. Via the shop, to pick up a few things for supper. I'm going to do something simple, like a three-cheese soufflé and salad.

Pierre and I are relieved to have escaped Court Place. It's 4:30 P.M. Half an hour ago, Serena and Colin pretended to leave as if for their honeymoon, but actually slipped off to the antenatal unit at Godminster General. Both looked deathly. Lulu and Celia Bryanston have been driven back to Godminster Hall at speed after Cath Cobb and Serena, who were both in the gazebo, overheard Celia and Lulu speculating about the bridal pair from the depths of the grotto, and Celia bellowed something about whether Serena and Colin would ever have got married if she hadn't been "in pup," and Lulu answered something about the pair having got "weddinged" rather than "married," as if the whole point of their union was drawing attention to themselves, presents and so on, rather than making their lives together because they loved each other.

It was unfortunate. Celia has a very loud voice, being deaf, and, as for Lulu, I don't think she even realized that what she and her mother-in-law were debating was in the poorest taste. Granville had a quiet word with Ned, and that was that.

Mimi and Ralph and the children left at about the same time, Ralph audibly saying to Mimi as they got into the Subaru, "Well, that was very lavish, but I stick to my guns, give me a decent funeral every time," but everyone else was still pretending that nothing had gone wrong, that it had all been a simply perfect English country wedding.

In the Stores, Mrs. Hitchens is in full flow, standing behind the till, ringing up baskets containing clotted cream, Marigold gloves, Astonish cleaning products, bottles of Badgers ale, local milk, cheese, butter, eggs, chocolate. "I can't wait until this becomes a community shop," she's saying to the usual captive audience of people waiting to pay. (Mrs. Hitchens has staged a miracle recovery from the news that the Post Office will no longer receive a subsidy, and claims to be right behind Cath's plans to turn it into a collective.) "Can't happen soon enough for me," she asserts. "If I wasn't stood here on my two feet all day, I could have been up at Court Place, with all the posh guests."

She sniffs, and rings up some Astonish oven cream cleaner, in a tub, on the till. Mrs. Hitchens must have heard the helicopter, too, and had presumably done a brisk trade in hot pasties to dark-suited heavies talking into their necks.

Even though Mrs. Hitchens hasn't left the shop for a second, she is, of course, among the first to know the full import of Gwenda's epiphany. As we wait our turn, she is losing no time in imparting the salient details to Debbie from the pub, who has nipped in before the evening rush for sunflower oil for the pub's extensive repertoire of fried foods.

"So, the secret's finally out," she says to Debbie as she rings up the sunflower oil, and I wait patiently behind her in the queue, worrying about Serena. "A bit of a shock for Sir Michael, eh? Not surprising that he decided to have a heart attack rather than face the wedding on the arm of Lady E."

Debbie looks bemused, an expression Mrs. Hitchens reads with satisfaction, as it means she is the first to impart the news that will be round the village like brushfire by the time the last guests, Champagne-sozzled and weary, have left the parish.

"Funny to think that the son Sir Michael never had . . . turned out to be Colin Watts, isn't it?" says Mrs. Hitchens, placing the plastic bottle of oil into a crumpled plastic bag and withdrawing Debbie's few pence in change with a triumphant ting of the cash register. "Will that be all for now, Debbie?"

Mimi

"Sorry, Hogget, you're what?" asks Ralph.

Ralph has taken to calling me Hogget, as he says I have reached that "plump and juicy" stage of womanhood that is "no longer lamb but not yet mutton." His eye flickers from the open box of dry flies that is lying tantalizingly on the kitchen table, next to Mirabel's iPod, several sections of the Saturday *Telegraph*, the Bridgewater butter dish saying BUTTER in black capitals full of bright yellow butter, a fat block of sunshine, and a Cornishware jug filled with a posy of late snowdrops and tooting daffodils.

"What I said was, I'm in a good place," I say, lifting the Aga lid and sliding the kettle onto the hot plate. "It's that horrid phrase that people doing AA say. It's what Clare said, that time she came, when she told me that she'd decided not to move to Dorset after all but to Suffolk. To restore a huge Elizabethan or something walled garden, and become self-sufficient, and write a cookbook about English heirloom vegetables, whatever they are. Like curly kale and broad beans."

I do not say that if Joe does get into Ponsonby Prep after all, the whole kitchen-garden-cookbook plan will, of course, go on hold. Everyone, even back-to-the-land organic plantswomen like Clare, has their price.

I realize I didn't really eat very much at the wedding—eating canapés standing up doesn't count—and it's still a couple of long hours till I make my signature supper of pasta pesto with pine nuts and bacon, and even talking about Clare's cookbook is making me hungry, by association.

I cut two thick slices of Court Place granary bread to eat with thickly applied layers of butter and honey, which I will wash down with drafts of weak tea.

While I'm waiting for the kettle to boil, I pick up the linen scrim and start polishing the closed silver lid of the simmering plate. I can't resist leaning over briefly to admire my bright eyes and rosy cheeks in the mirrorlike reflection, and remember the last time I saw Clare.

Rose and Ralph were surprised that she came, but the thing is, I'm no good at feuds. I can't nurse them, and drop-feed them milk, like prize marrows, until they take up the entire vegetable patch. Life's too short. And marriage is too long, for that matter. And Clare, to be fair, behaved quite well in the end. So when she called up, I said, Well, why don't you come down? She came, minus Joe, under a fortnight ago. We sat here, in this kitchen. On my territory. She said that she was sorry, and that she could not expect me ever to forgive her, or ever to want to see the child, but she wanted as far as she could to put things straight between us. And, most important to me, that she would never ask anything of Ralph again. There were, she assured me, no strings.

And it was then that I surprised myself. When I saw Clare, it was terrible. She looked so drawn, so scared, so guilty, that I couldn't find it in my heart to hate her at all. Granville, it turns out, had told her about my . . . procedure. She was almost ill with the guilt, after the Venice picnic fainting thing, and had unreservedly apologized to Ralph for breaking their agreement and promised not to trouble him any further.

No, I couldn't find it in my heart to hate her, not even when she used a new, solemn voice—as if she were talking about someone else, someone more important than her—whenever she mentioned her psychotherapy training course, the one that she's doing at the same place as Granville. So I just had to put her out of her misery.

"Don't worry about it, Clare," I said. "Just don't do it again. Not with my husband, at any rate." I didn't raise her dastardly plan to score another baby off my husband, in order to keep her wondering whether I didn't know, or—better—was quite simply too dignified to mention it.

I have to say, I felt quite proud that I had acted like an upper-caste Fleming—as if messy relationships both sides of the blanket were below my consideration and best not mentioned—rather than true to my lowborn, violent, Irish peasant stock. The possibility of my behaving really well—i.e., offering to take Joe if both she and Giddy went under a bus—even lurked offstage as a thoroughly noble gesture that I might make, way beyond the call of duty, during our emotional exchange.

But I did tell Clare that, on the whole, I'd rather keep the fact that my children have a little half brother they don't know about quiet. After all, as I revealed to Clare, Posy (if not all the others) thinks that Ralph and I have only got "married" three times, in order to produce her and Cas and Mirabel, and it would totally gross out the others to hear any reproductive details in which their father played a part.

They're too young.

But what I didn't tell Clare was this. I was still pregnant. I didn't tell Clare that I didn't have the abortion, after all. That I couldn't. I was in the anteroom to theater. They scanned me and I saw the heart of the little scrap, shaped like a paisley bud, beating for all it was worth, and I couldn't. They were so kind.

But I did have to tell Ralph why I now weigh ten and a half stone. I bit the bullet after we got back from the Haybarn, where I noticed Lulu giving my new fuller shape narrow looks. Obviously, Ralph has been trained never to mention my weight, but I have to admit I was surprised that not even Rose, who always notices everything, has mentioned it outright. (Mirabel, of course, my harshest critic, commented sharply that I was getting "porky," but I just said that, because we still didn't have central heating,

I was merely taking the sensible precaution of "laying down fat for winter.")

So I gave it to him straight. I could have told him it was that time in the rod room, when it wasn't safe and he shushed me, but I didn't. No more lies. It was no messing about, this time, with no Dr. Ashburton droning on about viruses and contact with animals and completely failing to understand that I have only to leave my wellies next to Ralph's in the boot rack to miss a period.

"Ralph," I said, "I'm still having the baby."

After having staggered about grayly, clutching his head and groaning indistinctly, as if he had been asked to act as an infantryman taking a fatal bullet at Passchendaele in an after-dinner game of charades, he had rallied. He'd lifted his chin, and said, "Well done, darling. You always get your own way in the end." Since then, he's appeared almost pleased (i.e., glumly resigned). This time, after the whole Clare catastrophe, he owed me. It was my turn to get my way, although I don't think it's about winning or losing. It's about love and compromise. I honestly think—and here's the weird thing—that this time, Ralph would accept the baby even if it wasn't his. I admit, I thought about pretending it was someone else's, just to twist the knife, to get my own back, but I decided I was now too mature and grounded and dismissed the temptation as unworthy of me.

So things are looking rosy—well, fairly rosy, and much rosier than they were just a few weeks ago. As even Ralph—whose Scottish blood does manifest itself from time to time—acknowledged with a heavy sigh, when it came to the money side of things, an area of life in which I have always tried not to involve myself too much: "Never mind, darling. Let's hope that the *Dominus will Providebit*, in the sense that the Lord will provide, if only a bit."

Ralph disappears upstairs, to relegate his morning suit to the depths of his wardrobe until its next, infinitely dreaded outing.

When he reappears, he's wearing green cords, an old navy jersey, a tweed cap, and a pair of green thigh-high waders. I love functional uniforms—white medical coats, hunting pink, camouflage—anything that immediately discloses to the observer the exact activity or pursuit or service in hand.

"Are *you*, though?" I ask, taking a big bite of toast, buttering my chin, gazing at him.

"Am I what, my darling wife?" Ralph asks, distractedly sorting through the fly box and dropping it into the pocket of the Barbour he has disinterred from a pile of outdoor coats in the hall. He clearly has no idea what I'm talking about, but is prepared to humor me in my current state.

"In a good place," I repeat. What I am thinking is—if I hadn't been through all *that*, I wouldn't be *here* now. I am almost feeling grateful for all the misery and heartache of the last few months, simply because the contrast of the long dark winter of the soul with these sunlit uplands is so heavenly I can almost taste it, and I know what Clare meant when she said to me, as she left, holding my hand, "Today is a gift, Mimi. That's why it's called the present."

"Is that an expression of Granville's . . . or Clare's?" Ralph asks, with a slight but tender hesitancy.

I think it is very brave of Ralph to say her name, to show that we have *moved on* and that the Clare business is *behind us*. As far as it ever can be.

"I've just explained what it means," I say. "It means, you know. *In a good place*. It means, like, happy. Are you?"

But I decide not to say anything about Granville or Clare. Or psychotherapy. I decide to put all thoughts of Clare and Joe away, to be taken out and looked at later. When I have the strength, and when I am slim again, which may be many years hence, if my past record on postpartum digestive-biscuit intake is anything to go by.

I move over the flagstoned floor to the warmth of the recessed fireplace.

"Of course I'm happy," he says. Ralph could never use a phrase like "in a good place" without physical pain. I know now that he wanted me to have an abortion because he was terrified about having fathered Clare's child, a fourth child, that could never be ours, an act of madness he claims he committed when he was in a panic about money, and the legal and moral consequences of which he admits he did not weigh up with enough care, an omission for which he declares he will hold himself to account until his dying day.

He comes over, his waders making little squeaking noises on the stone floor. I have taken up my traditional position at the Aga, my hand holding the barre of the silver rail, in the first position. Then I go into second position, and do a grand plié.

In my head, for months, I have been plotting my future, where I will make myself a very rich woman, as a result of my own, Mimi Malone, patented "Agacise"™ exercise manual, "Agacise"™ DVD, "Agacise"™ cookbook—indeed, the whole "Agacise"™ way of life, and I now decide to add a whole chapter about Aga exercises and recipes for pregnancy and—yes! Aga baby food—to the bestsellering tome.

I know that "Agacise"™ will one day make me rich, so rich that I might even be able, one day, to buy Posy, if not another pony, and definitely not a unicorn, at least a pet lamb.

Something occurs to me, and as my husband stands alongside, it is suddenly important that I do something. I reach for the Birthday Book, which I keep by the Aga. I flip through the months, past Mirabel's and Cas's and Posy's and Ralph's birthdays, past Calypso's and my birthday, past Perry and Slinky Fleming's birthdays, and my brother Con and his four children's birthdays, and even past his saintly Austrian wife Gretchen's *Geburtstag,* and past Trumpet's birthday, and past the birthday of Caroline, the only nanny we ever had who stayed, until I come to October.

Then I place a cross in pencil on the due date of our forthcoming fourth child (and Ralph's fifth child, not that we want to dwell on that, not after Ralph wept when he said, "Darling, the reason I couldn't face your being pregnant, well, one of the reasons aside from sheer panic, and terror, was that thanks to my complete cock-up I already had four children, and I thought five children, including one I couldn't tell you about, was pushing it, slightly."). I close the book and slot it back next to Sarah Raven's *Garden Cookbook*.

I smile at Ralph, who has watched me mark the Birthday Book with a baffled look, thinking, Men are not all destroyers, just as women are not all nurturers. Men have a right to say no, too. They should have a vote, if not the veto. Just as it takes two to make a baby, ideally, it should take two, not one, in a marriage to keep it.

Ralph is still watching me in silence, so I tell myself to shut up, even though I'm not talking out loud. In my own head, I'm beginning to sound like Hillary Clinton—i.e., never a good sign. Then Ralph whispers something in my ear, words that make my heart melt, pats me lightly on the bottom, and then strides towards the open door. Then he pauses, as if he is going to say something else.

But he clearly thinks better of it and, after giving me a farewell wave, dives through the honeysuckled porch and hurries away across the green, sweet meadows strewn with buttercups and daisies and primroses, across the fields of asphodel, down to the river, as if succumbing to some masculine, primordial urge I will never understand, to catch the evening rise on the Lar.

Acknowledgments

Thank you to Sir Antony Acland, Claire and James Birch of Doddington Hall, to my "stalkees" Sophie and Johnnie Boden for submitting to this for a second time; Hector Christie, Gus Christie, Oliver Claridge for help with "agrivistes," wind farms, and other rural affairs; the residents of Tinkers' Bubble in Somerset and especially Mary and Joe for eco-village hospitality and actuality; Zara D'Abo for help with heritage cheddar; Nicky Marks of the Raj Tent Club; Johnnie Standing for "fucked a bloke"; Alan Cubitt for Celia Bryanston; and on the publishing and editing side, huge thanks for brilliant advice and tender counselling as ever to Juliet Annan of Fig Tree, Jenny Lord, her able assistant; my London agent, Peter Straus; my New York agent, Melanie Jackson; and Trish Todd of Touchstone Fireside and her crack team of Danielle Friedman and Martha Schwartz at Simon & Schuster; also thank you Katherine Stroud and Jessica Jackson, my publicists in London; editors Sarah Day and Sarah Hulbert at Penguin; and finally thanks Roger Field for the libel read. Phew!

Glossary

Aga—The Aga is a two- or four-oven cast-iron cooker but oh so much more than that. Draped with socks and Irish linen tea towels, and always containing something crumbly in the roasting oven, the Aga, like a lovable old Labrador, is the warm heart of the English country kitchen.

Almanach de Gotha—The Almanach is the hardback directory to the dodgy lineage and show titles of Europe's highest nobility and gracious royalty, otherwise known as "the Eurotrash."

Ambrosia creamed rice—As its name suggests, Ambrosia creamed rice is heavenly, comfort food of the first order, best eaten sweet and creamy-cold straight from the tin and fridge.

Argos—Low-rent, high-street shop (with catalogues) and Web site (with e-brochures) aimed at bargain hunters of foot spas and faux-leather chocolate sofas. Slogan: Don't Shop for It, Argos It.

The Art Newspaper—Weekly periodical that refreshingly and unpretentiously treats the art world as part of normal life.

Bamford—Bamford and Sons is the men's clothing emporium and part of Lady (Carole) Bamford's organic empire.

Barbour—The Barbour, preferably the Beaufort Classic in gooseshit green, is *the* jacket for the country dweller, made of stale-smelling waxed cotton that, like its owners, we hope, is supposed to improve with age.

Isabella Blow—Isabella Blow, the towering fashion-forward figure who committed suicide in 2007, is credited with discovering Alexander McQueen and models Sophie Dahl and Stella Tennant, the granddaughter of aforementioned Debo, Duchess of Devonshire (see below).

Selina Blow—Designer of directional tweed pieces.

BSE—Bovine spongiform encephalopathy, otherwise known as mad-cow disease, is a fatal neurodegenerative disease in cattle that can be transmitted to human beings who eat meat products from infected animals, which is a terrifying thought, given what we've all put in our mouths over the years.

Jensen Button—Jensen "Jense" Button is a British Formula 1 racing champion born in Frome, Somerset.

cagoule—A cagoule is a thin, supposedly wind- and waterproof-hooded jacket made of nylon that rustles cheaply when you move.

Center Parcs—Center Parcs, with its annoying Franco American spelling, is a chain of family-friendly holiday camps in forested areas with spas, tree trekking, and bike trails for the hearty and outdoorsy middle classes.

champ—champ is a pretentious way of describing potatoes mashed with milk and another item, such as chives or spring onions.

Max Clifford—Max Clifford is a publicity supremo who once represented the Beatles and Marlon Brando, who brokers lucrative kiss-and-tell stories and celebrity exposés for large sums to tabloid newspapers.

courgettes—Zucchini.

Crufts—Annual dog show run by the Kennel Club and acknowledged highlight of the frantic canine calendar.

Deborah, Duchess of Devonshire—Debo, the Duchess of Devonshire, one of the six Mitford sisters, was chatelaine of the magnificent Chatsworth, in Bakewell, Derbyshire. As Nigel Nicolson said, "Chatsworth; its situation; its garden;

its palatial appearance; its works of art; its ducal atmosphere. All these are incomparable."

Dorset Cereals—Dorset Cereals range of "honest, tasty, and real" mueslis and so on, made in the village designed by the Prince of Wales, Poundbury in Dorset, and packaged in expensive, we-saw-you-coming, muted shades.

Elle MacPherson—Elle MacPherson Intimates is the top-selling lingerie range featuring lacy thongs and satin bras, the success of which has made the life of the woman only known as "The Body" complete and utterly serene.

farrier—A farrier is a specialist in equine hoof care trained to trim and shoe horses's hooves, in other words, one of the most important men in rural life.

Hugh Fearnley-Whittingstall—Scraggle-haired food writer, celebrity chef, and owner of the compassionate "River Cottage" industry.

Freddie Flintoff—Andrew "Freddie" Flintoff is an all-round cricketer and good egg who plays for England and Lancashire.

Orlando Fraser—Orlando Fraser is cherubic barrister and aspirant Tory MP, married to Princess Diana's bridesmaid, the supernaturally glowing and highly bred Clementine Hambro.

Fray Bentos—Fray Bentos pies, with their gold pastry, meat fillings, and gravy contained in a tin that doubles as a dog dish, are worshipped as gods by many real men.

girls in pearls—The ironic title of the famous photographic frontispiece feature in *Country Life*, showcasing a well-bred filly invariably called the Hon Clarissa or Lady Venetia that has appeared in each week's edition of the shire's house mag since the dawn of time.

Sheherazade Goldsmith—Achingly slim and beautiful ex-model wife of Zac Goldsmith, who swapped high heels and catwalk for wellies, children, and an organic farm in Devon.

growbags—Growbags are sacks of fertilizer used for growing vegetables, tomatoes, etc.

gurning—Gurning is a pastoral sport once common in traveling fairs and freak shows in which contestants have to distort their facial features as much as possible.

Ephraim Hardcastle—Ephraim Hardcastle is the nom de plume of his spikier counterpart, Peter McKay, also in the *Mail*.

Nicky Haslam—Old Etonian interior designer to the rich and famous who is in his sixties (we think) but dresses like a Brazilian rent boy one day and master of foxhounds the next.

Heat and *Grazia*—*Heat* and *Grazia* are weekly mags devoted to the weight fluctuations, babies, and boyfriends of undistinguished identikit celebrities.

Horse and Hound—*Horse and Hound* is a monthly magazine for key developments in hunting, dressage, showjumping, racing, and so on and is invaluable if you're trying to offload a secondhand horse box.

hot-desking—Hot-desking means using any available surface when a dedicated workstation in the shape of a home office is unavailable to the mother of the house given the male's propensity to colonize all available reception areas for himself.

Ilse Jacobsen—Danish designer of covetable lace-up Wellington boots in fashionable colors like mocha, cream, and army green.

Richard Kay—Richard Kay is the boyish and kindly gossip columnist in the mighty *Daily Mail*.

Le Parfait—The smart French wide-bellied preserve jars nine out of ten domestic goddesses prefer, with rubber sealing rings and metal clip.

Nanette Lepore—Designer of tiny, exquisite clothes for stork-legged boy-women or the French.

Vicount Linley—Nephew to the Queen, via her sister the late Princess Margaret, and a high-class joiner.

M&S—M&S is short for Marks and Spencer, the purveyor of unfrightening clothing to the middle middle classes.

Tamara Mellon—Tamara Mellon is a slinky glamazon and former accessories editor of *British Vogue* who went on to found the high-heeled shoe empire called Jimmy Choo.

Andy Murray—Andy Murray is a top-seeded British tennis player and the next greatest whitest hope for Wimbledon since Tim Henman.

Ocado—Ocado is the online grocery shopping and delivery service attached to posh supermarket Waitrose.

Ottolenghi—Ottolenghi is a café-deli run by the eponymous Israeli Yotam Ottolenghi in Ledbury Road W11, much frequented by Hollywood celebrities, supermodels, and those who think nothing of dropping £13 on a minuscule tub of handcrafted organic chermoula.

Pannier Market—A covered area for a weekly market for local meat, produce, cheese, and gossip common in West Country market towns such as Barnstaple, Tavistock, Plymouth, Bideford, South Molton, etc.

Sarah Raven—Sarah Raven is a wife and mother, but she is also a Web site, a catalogue, a TV presenter, a cook, and a garden writer, as is the way of these things.

Rizlas—Rizlas are a brand of roll-up cigarette papers, i.e., skins for spliffs.

skunk—Skunk is a mind-bending Class C drug made from cannabis, available in select headshops in Amsterdam and, needless to add, every posh public school in the U.K.

Spar—Spar is a Dutch-owned cooperative foodstore of the sort that does not make the heart exactly leap upon entry.

spurtle—The onomatopoeically entitled "spurtle" is a primitive wooden implement used for stirring gloopy porridge, or oatmeal.

to swank—To swank means to brag or boast.

tattersall—The checked shirt in brushed twill cotton worn by countryfolk to denote a devotion to field sports.

Tipp-Ex—Tipp-Ex is a white correction fluid.

Waitrose—Posh supermarket with an immaculately sourced range of upmarket products and eco-credentials.

Whole Foods/Fresh & Wild—Before the arrival of the juggernaut Whole Foods owned by Big Organic on Kensington High Street, W8, Fresh & Wild on Westbourne Grove was the mecca for organic fundamentalists. Whole Foods bought Fresh & Wild, but only—it turned out—to close it down.

Wild Bean Café—So-called concept café (me neither), tied to BP Connect service stations, which attempts to assuage motorists' mounting rage at filling tank with an inflammable and finite liquid as expensive as Cristal, with free sippy cups.

Woman's Hour—*Woman's Hour* is a daily program on BBC Radio Four, sometimes referred to as the "Daily Cervix," that never shies away from subjects that most women and all men would prefer to forget, like mucus or—cough— "dryness." I did warn you.

The Women's Institute—The WI a is mainstay of rural life and power in the land, famous for its female-bonding properties, its annual fêtes, and its fearsomely competitive jam-making.

"The Wreck of the *Deutschland*"—Poem by Gerard Manley Hopkins that uses the German's steamship, which ran aground off the Kent coast, as a symbol for the fallen and shipwrecked in the stormy seas of life.

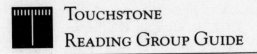

TOUCHSTONE
READING GROUP GUIDE

In a Good Place

For Discussion

1. "I shake my head, enjoying the fact that, with Mimi, everything is a drama and a crisis" (page 18). Is Rose's perception of Mimi accurate? If so, why does she like that about her? Could the same statement apply to Rose as well?

2. How do you perceive Mimi's "Ten Rules of Country Living" on pages 39 to 41? Is she truly happy living at Home Farm, or would she rather be in London?

3. For most of the novel, we see Ralph and Pierre as described by Mimi and Rose instead of hearing them actually speak. Why do you think Rachel Johnson wrote them this way?

4. Were you surprised by the revelation that Rose has had several extramarital affairs? Why did she decide to share this information with Mimi?

5. "I was ready for this windmill thing to be about new green versus old blue. But it doesn't appear to be so black and white after all" (page 122). What does Mimi mean by this statement? What are your thoughts about the town dynamic?

6. How would you describe the role of motherhood in the novel? Based on the way Mimi describes them, how do country mothers compare to those in London?

7. When Rose discovers that her daughter, Ceci, knows about her affair with Jesse Marlon, why doesn't she care? Does Pierre know as well? And if so, why doesn't he confront his wife?

8. "Like all keen fishermen, Ralph's main, if not only, aim in life—not just on the riverbank—was the achievement, and then the extension, of a period of peace and quiet" (page 234). Considering Ralph's demeanor, why did he consent to father Clare's baby? Do you believe him when he says they didn't have an affair? Does Mimi?

9. What role does tradition play in the novel? Who in Honeyborne is tradition important to and in which ways?

10. "Indeed, I almost feel able to attend Sophy's next workshop on biodynamic composting. But not quite. Not yet. You can take the girl away from Notting Hill . . ." (page 205). By the end of the book, to what degree has Mimi acclimated to country living?

11. After Pierre becomes a success in the art world, Rose says, "I realize, now, that I love Pierre very deeply" (page 258). Is she saying this only because Pierre is finally contributing financially? Do they truly love each other?

12. By the end of the novel, which characters do you believe are "in a good place"?

A Conversation with Rachel Johnson

You live in England, and the novel is set there. What challenges existed in making *In a Good Place* accessible to readers worldwide?

To be brutal, I didn't set out to try to make it "accessible." I just tried as best I could to render accurately the experience and pre-credit-crunchy concerns of a certain, high-toned middle-class milieu: people who had largely left town for the green fields and slower pace of the rural idyll, only to find that the canvas for competition had merely . . . got bigger. Think tweedy types hunting, shooting, and fishing colliding with Alice Waters on food and local produce and Martha Stewart on pickles and preserves and you have about the size of it. So, yes, the setting is very English and yet, as with *Notting Hell*, all societies have their elites, and this applies to the ritzy areas of the countryside too. (In the UK, the well-heeled counties, like Dorset, Devon, Wiltshire, Hampshire, and so on are called the Shires, and the book was published under the title *Shire Hell*. Just in case you thought, looking at Amazon, that I've managed three books in three years. Wish I had, but no.) I think everyone can recognize the one-upmanship and the competition that go on wherever you are, especially among groups where the women don't have to hold down office jobs and instead get in a total snit about who won the longest carrot contest or took first prize for summer chutney in the August fête.

Why did you decide to have two narrators, Mimi and Rose, share their perspectives in alternating chapters? Was it difficult to maintain a consistent flow with two such different women narrating?

I have a really short attention span, and this helped me along to vary the pace and the outlook. I used the same device in *Notting Hell*, and I hope it worked here. You have to be very careful using the first person and varying the narration, obviously, because you really don't want the reader thinking at any point, "Whose the hell head I am in here?" It should be obvious. Should be, I stress . . .

Do you relate the most to Mimi, Rose, or another character? Did some of your own friends or acquaintances inspire anyone in the novel?

I've said it before, and I don't mind admitting it again. My heroine, the curly-headed, scone-loving Mimi, is very much after my own heart (that's why her name sounds the same as *me-me*). As for the other characters, UK newspapers have had some fun trying to link my cast to real people. Some minor characters are based on folks I know, but not in any serious way. Not so serious as they would sue, anyway. When you start to write you realize how important it is that characters are strong and recognizable and themselves. Real people are too subtle. It's like you have to put pancake makeup on someone, otherwise she fades out under the bleaching glare of studio lights. They need to have real presence and stand out on the page.

Before becoming an acclaimed author, you were already a well-known journalist. What prompted you to write novels? Do you find one form of writing more enjoyable than the other?

Tough one. I love writing journalism because it's all over in two hours and comes straight off the top of the head. Writing novels is soooooo much harder. It's the hardest thing I've ever done. Even harder than delivering my first baby whose head size was in the ninety-ninth percentile and who was in posterior position (since you asked, a thirty-six-hour-labor followed by forceps followed by surgery). And another thing—unlike childbirth, it never gets any easier. You just know how hard it's going to be for the next two years of your life with ever more certainty each time.

Like several of your characters, you're a mother with a busy work schedule. How do you balance your time? What advice can you offer other working mothers?
There's only one thing I can say here. Don't worry about never having time to write. Just write what you can in the time you do have and give yourself a big clap on the back, followed by a double latte and a blueberry muffin. You've done well. P.S. I am writing this now amid the litter of takeout Thai food in pajamas while my daughter is Facebooking instead of completing her history project and the dog is licking out the containers. Today I wrote a thousand words of my new novel in the London Library, interviewed a source over a sandwich in Piccadilly at lunch, saw my disabled mother for tea, and then walked the dog and ordered the dinner and the week's groceries. It's 8:31 P.M., and I still have to write my column for the *Evening Standard*. And P.P.S. I've had two glasses of pinot grigio. I needed it. I really needed it.

Mimi has conflicted feelings about leaving London for life in the countryside. You yourself divide your time between Notting Hill, London, and Exmoor, Somerset. Where do you prefer to live?
My favorite question! I think about this all the time. I fantasize that I would be happy living in the depths of a river valley minus central heating and hundreds of miles from the nearest vodkatini, but the truth is, I am spoiled, and I love and need and relish both. Both town and country. I love the London life (see

Thai takeout in vignette, above) but I am most happy sitting by the fire in my Wellington boots, listening to my collection of Miles Davis LPs, with a big book in one hand and the other patting my dog, Coco. London is very stressful. But after six weeks in Exmoor, I pine for the pollution and noise and, above all, the easy availability of the strong skinny latte.

So many of your female characters are competitive with one another. Do they have true friendships?
Miaow! Course they do. English people are famous for never speaking out but only saying what they really feel about you behind your back. Americans believe the shortest distance between two points is a straight line. I like exploring those, er, differences in national snippiness.

Several of your characters have had extramarital affairs. Why did you make that decision?
Because it's true to life and stuff has to happen in fiction. It doesn't reflect any amorality or casual approach to the sanctity of the wedding vows on my part, in case you were wondering.

Based on the feedback you've received, do American audiences react differently to this topic than British ones?
American audiences tend to be a little bit more Puritan judgmental. Hope that doesn't offend anyone . . .

Have you ever spent time in an eco-village like Spodden's Hatch?
Yes. I spent a day or so in a place exactly like Spodden's Hatch. Called Tinker's Bubble in Somerset.

In the second and third parts of the book, there are several time shifts. Why did you employ this storytelling device?
Because I was trying to be clever and mix it up a little, I suppose. Showing off?

Besides your editor, whom do you first allow to read your work?
Only my editors at Touchstone Fireside and Penguin! I send the work to my agent, Peter Straus in London, and Melanie Jackson in New York, too, and value every word of their advice. My husband wants to be a reader, but I always tell him, Not until it's in hard (or soft) cover, babe.

Have you ever belonged to a book club? If so, did you enjoy the experience?
No!

Can readers expect to hear more from Mimi and Rose in the future?
Not immediately . . . I'm deep in another project. But I don't ever rule it out. I'd love to see how they're getting on. And Clare . . . and Si . . . and Ralph, too.

Enhance Your Book Club

1. Can't get enough of Rachel Johnson's witty and entertaining characters? Want to know about Mimi's life back in London? Then check out Johnson's first novel, *Notting Hell* http:// books.simonandschuster.comNotting-Hell.

2. After reading *In a Good Place*, are you now an expert on all things British? A very helpful (and humorous) glossary is included, so why not quiz one another about "M&S," "Waitrose," and other brand names and personalities you might not have known about before reading the novel.

3. The eco-village Spodden's Hatch plays an important role in the novel. To better understand this kind of community, do research on similar places and share photos with the group.

4. To read all about Rachel Johnson, find out what it's like to go on a book tour, or even send her a note, visit her official website: http://www.racheljohnson.co.uk/.

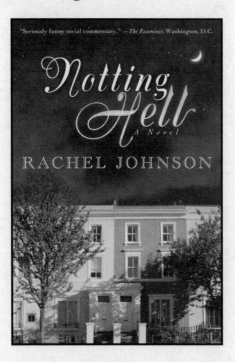